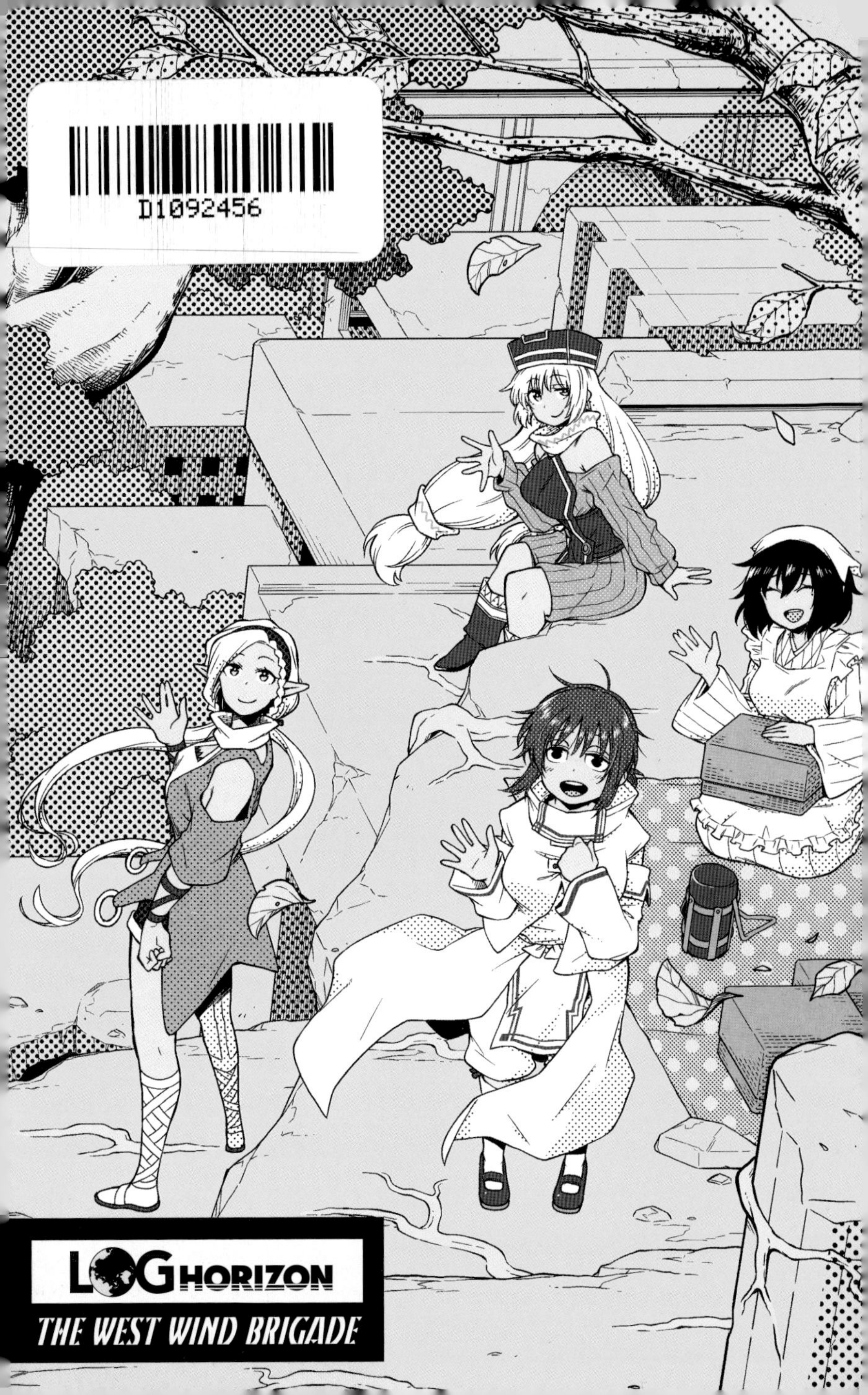
LOG HORIZON
THE WEST WIND BRIGADE

[CONTENTS]

LOG HORIZON **THE WEST WIND BRIGADE** 11

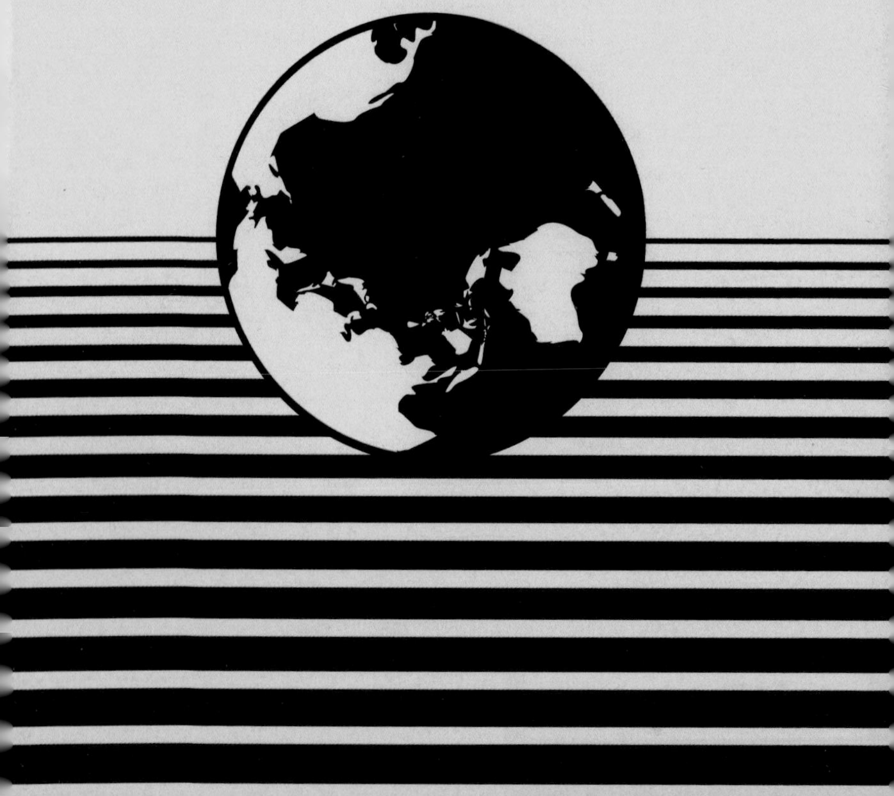

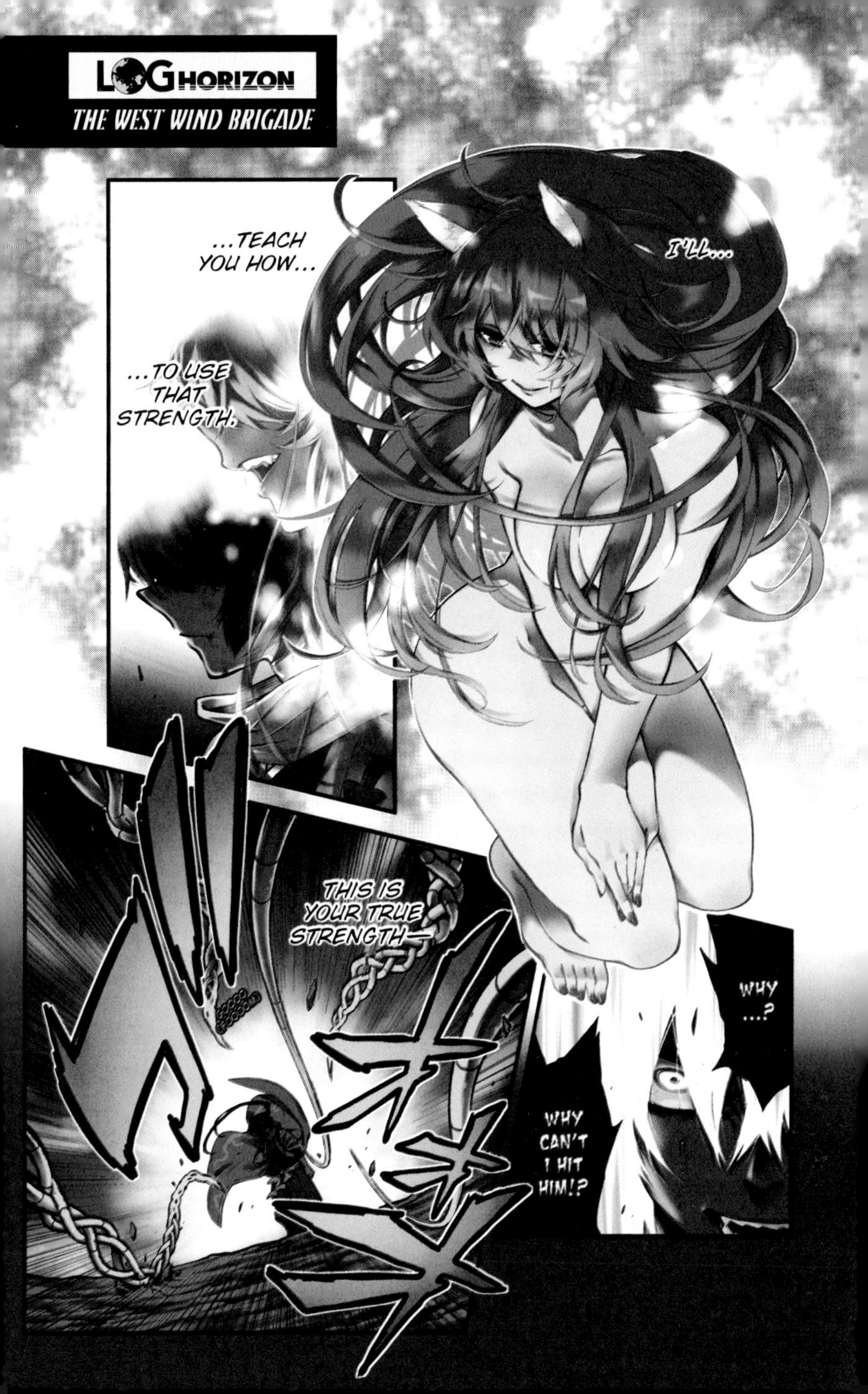
LOG HORIZON
THE WEST WIND BRIGADE
I'LL...
...TEACH YOU HOW...
...TO USE THAT STRENGTH.
WHY ...?
WHY CAN'T I HIT HIM!?
THIS IS YOUR TRUE STRENGTH—

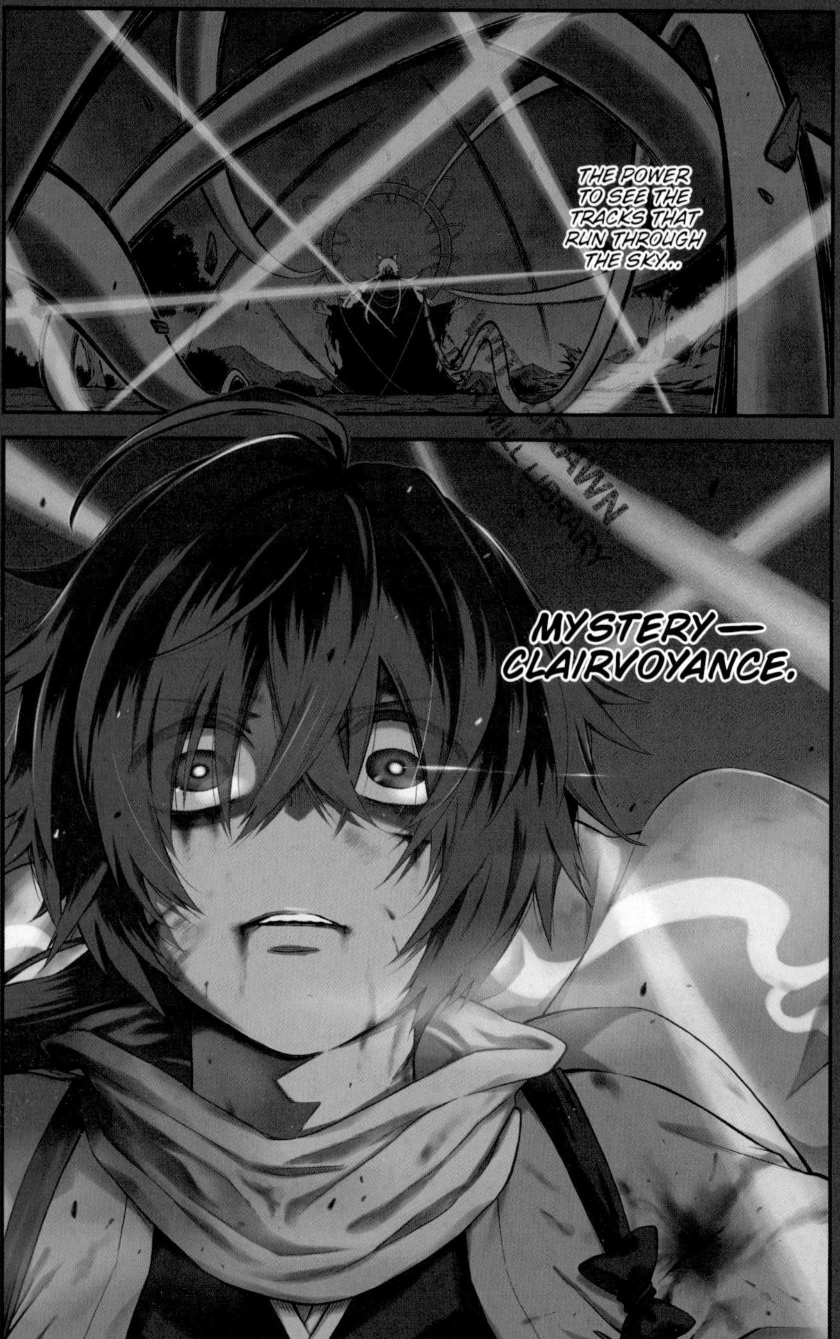
THE POWER TO SEE THE TRACKS THAT RUN THROUGH THE SKY...
MYSTERY— CLAIRVOYANCE.

[CHAPTER : 60] Believing

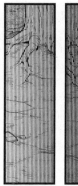

HFF...

HFF...

ZURU
ズ
ル
・・・

*ZURU
(DRAG)*
ズ
ル
・・・

ヨロ
*YORO
(STAGGER)*

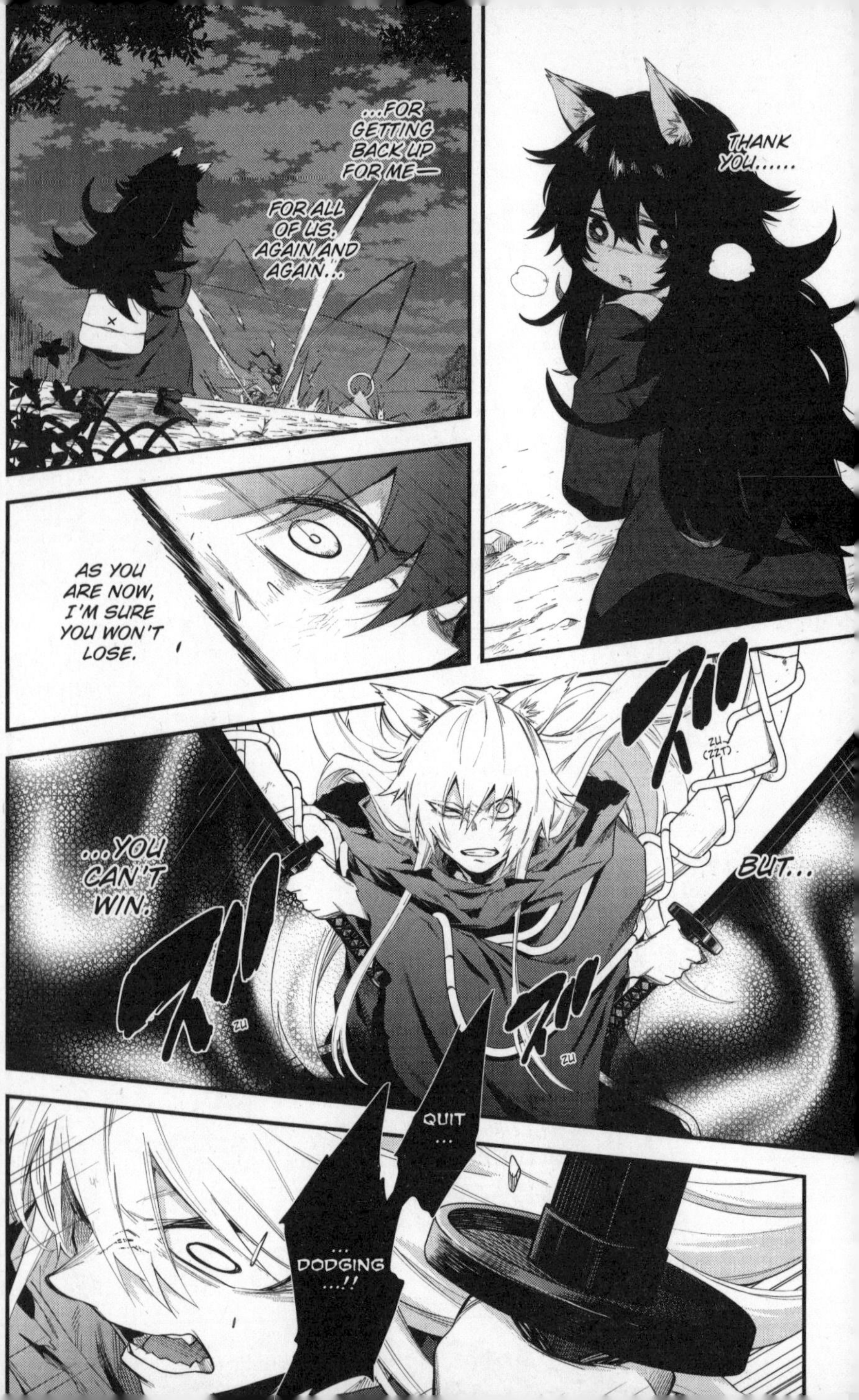
THANK YOU......
...FOR GETTING BACK UP FOR ME—
FOR ALL OF US. AGAIN AND AGAIN...
AS YOU ARE NOW, I'M SURE YOU WON'T LOSE.
BUT...
ZU (ZZT)
...YOU CAN'T WIN.
ZU
ZU
QUIT ...
... DODGING ...!!

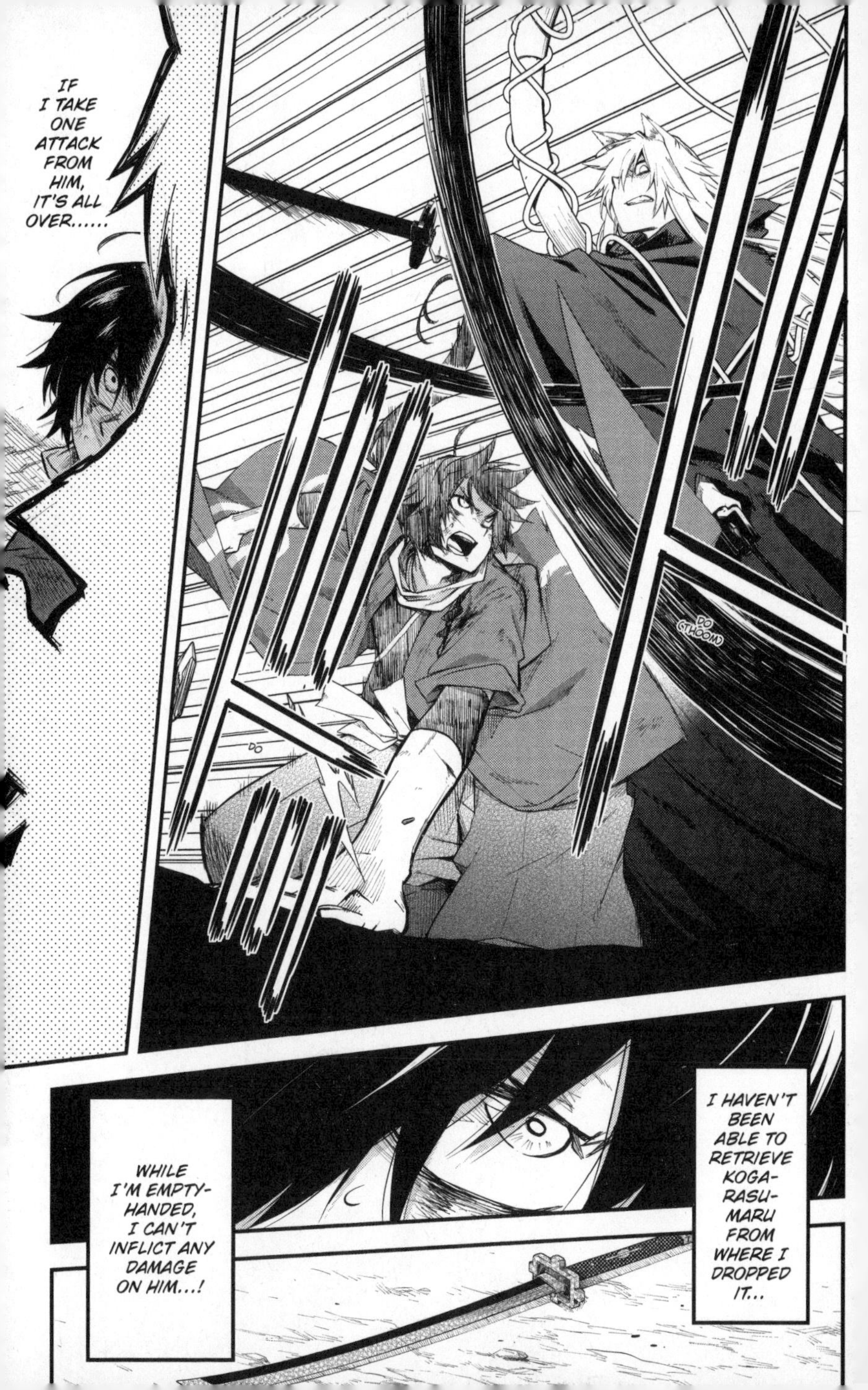
DO (THOOM)
DO
IF I TAKE ONE ATTACK FROM HIM, IT'S ALL OVER......
I HAVEN'T BEEN ABLE TO RETRIEVE KOGA-RASU-MARU FROM WHERE I DROPPED IT...
WHILE I'M EMPTY-HANDED, I CAN'T INFLICT ANY DAMAGE ON HIM...!

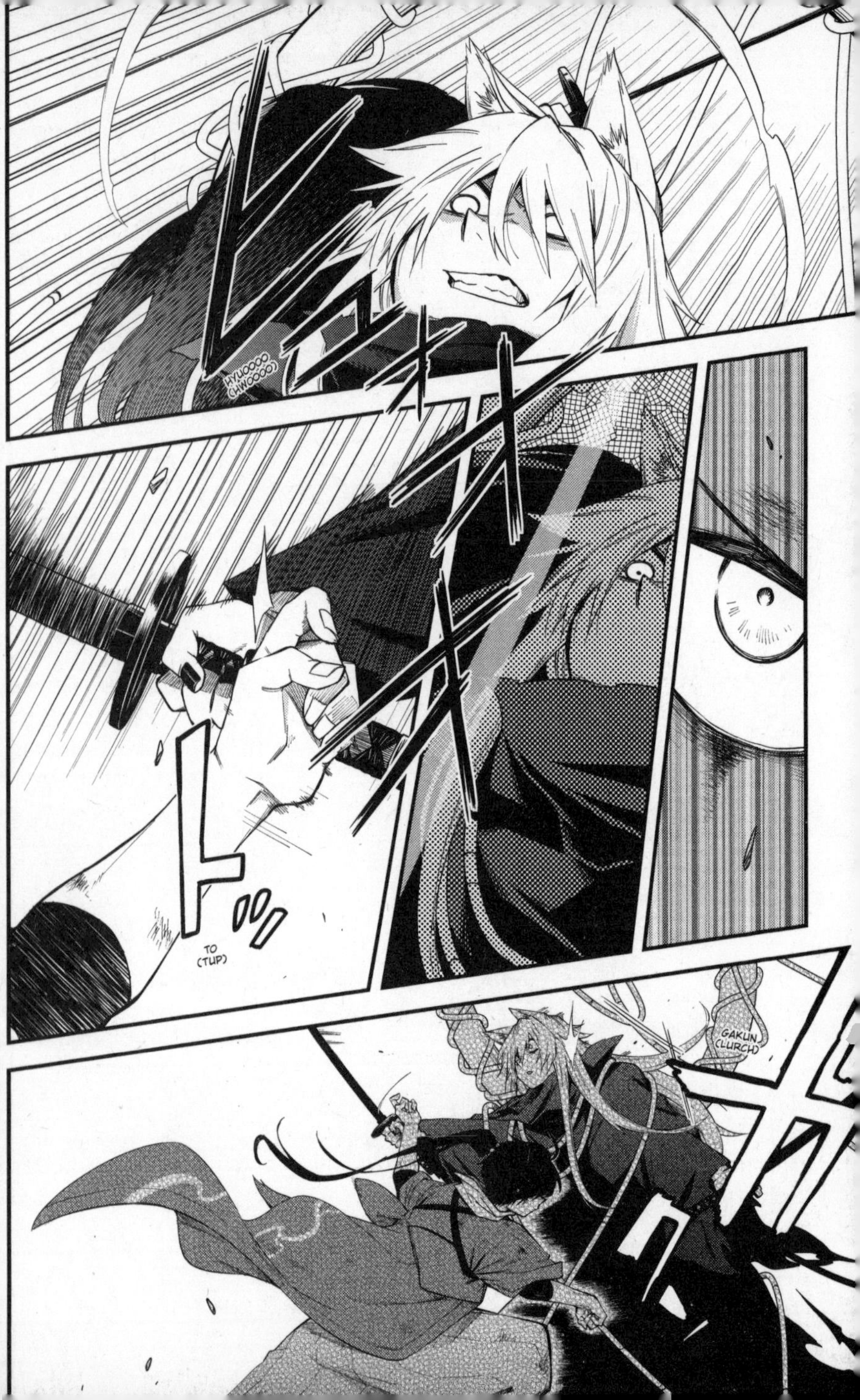
HYUOOOO (HWOOOO)
TO (TUP)
GAKUN (LURCH)

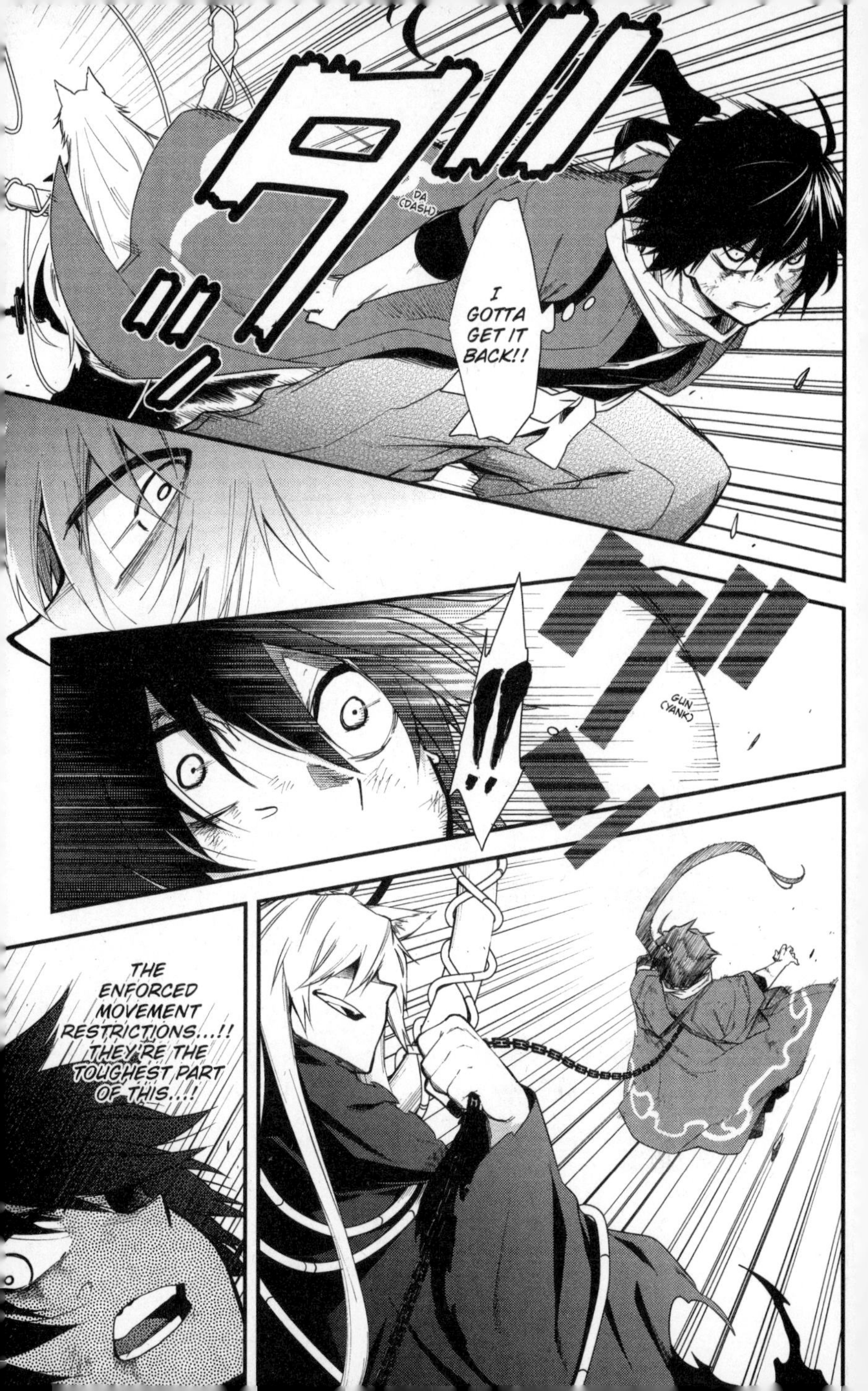
DA (DASH)
I GOTTA GET IT BACK!!
GUN (YANK)
THE ENFORCED MOVEMENT RESTRICTIONS...!! THEY'RE THE TOUGHEST PART OF THIS...!

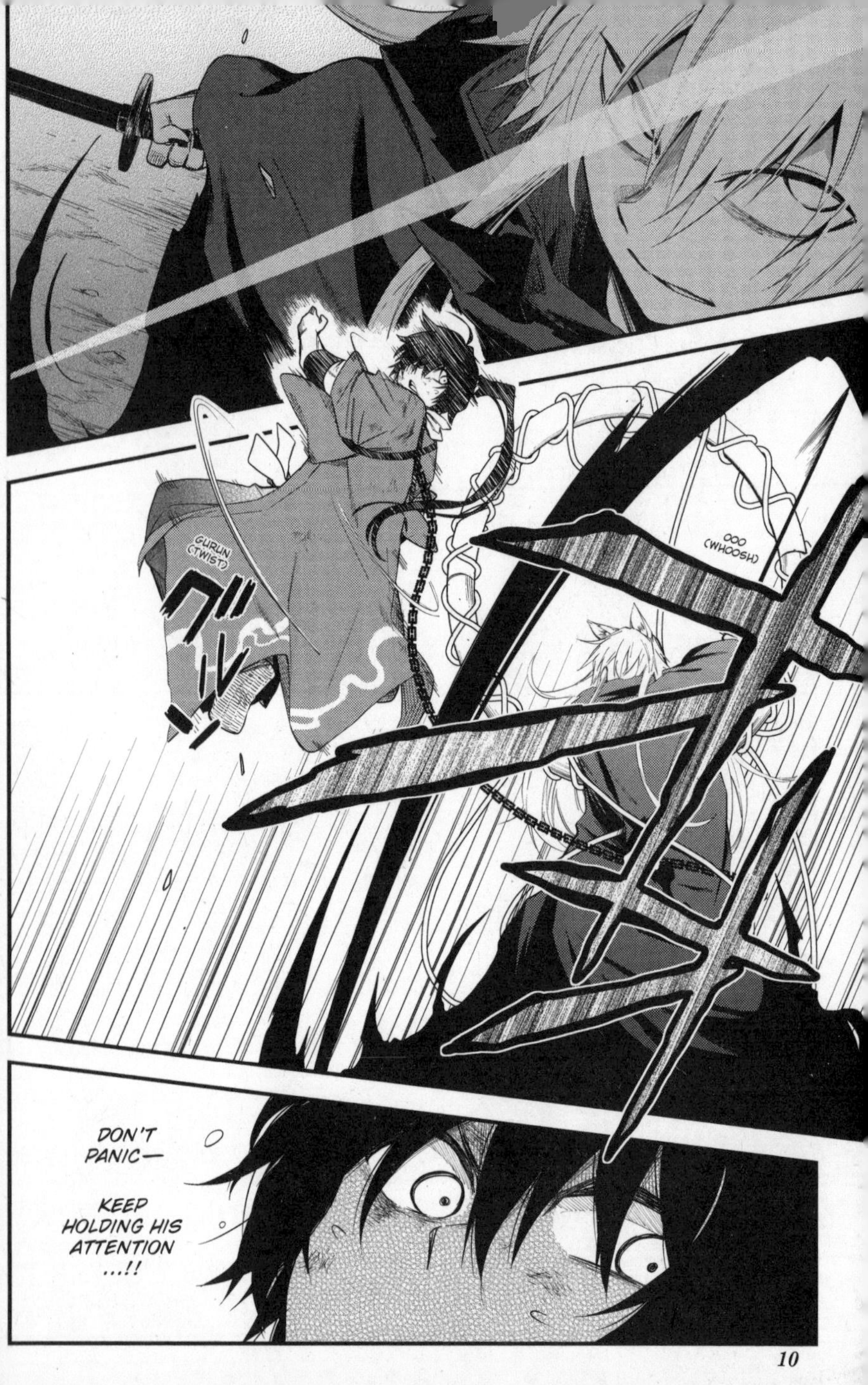
OOO (WHOOSH)
GURUN (TWIST)
DON'T PANIC—
KEEP HOLDING HIS ATTENTION ...!!

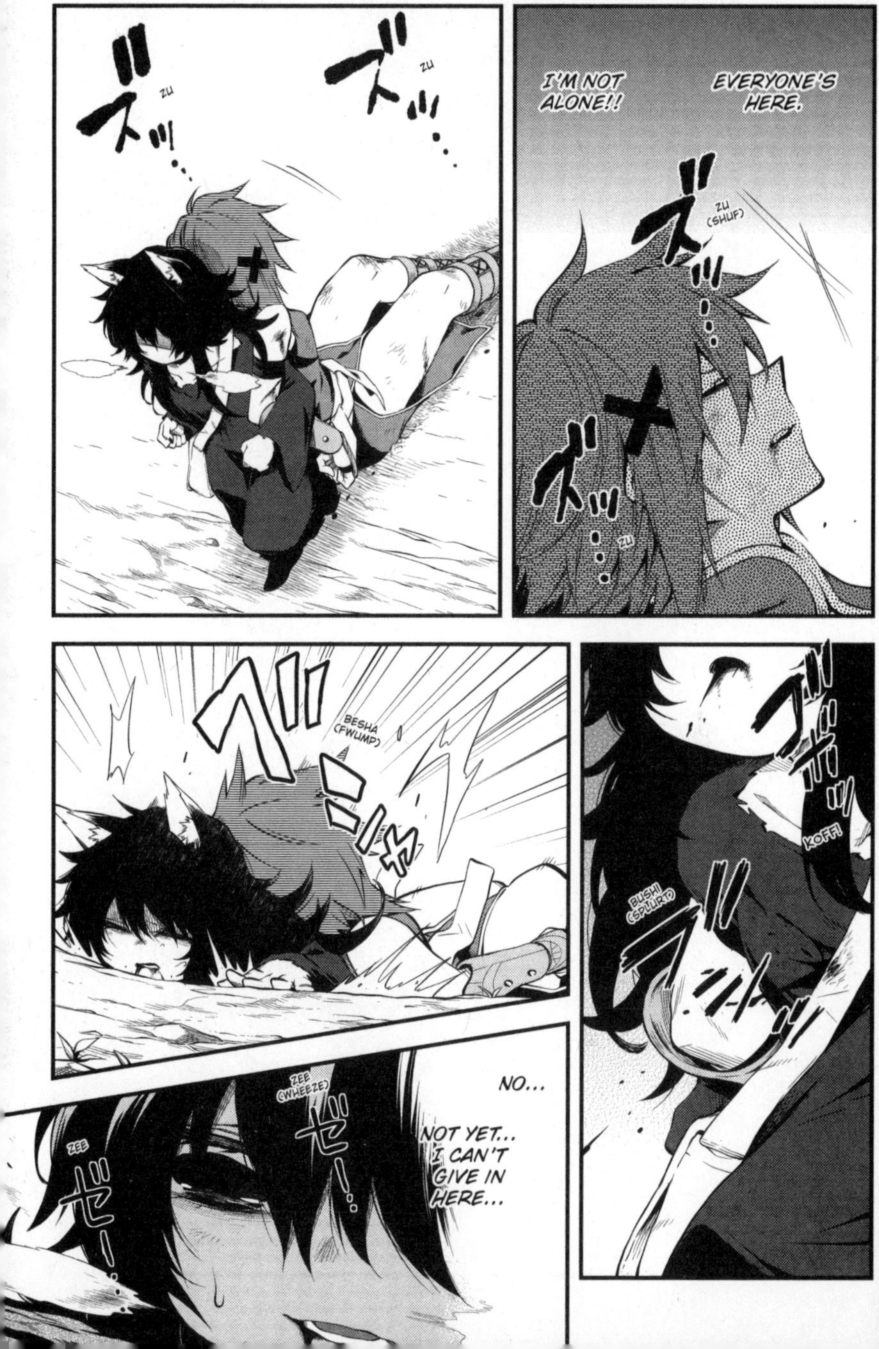
EVERYONE'S HERE.
I'M NOT ALONE!!
ZU (SHUF)
ZU
ZU
ZU
KOFF!
BUSHI (SPLURT)
BESHA (FWUMP)
NO...
NOT YET... I CAN'T GIVE IN HERE...
ZEE (WHEEZE)
ZEE

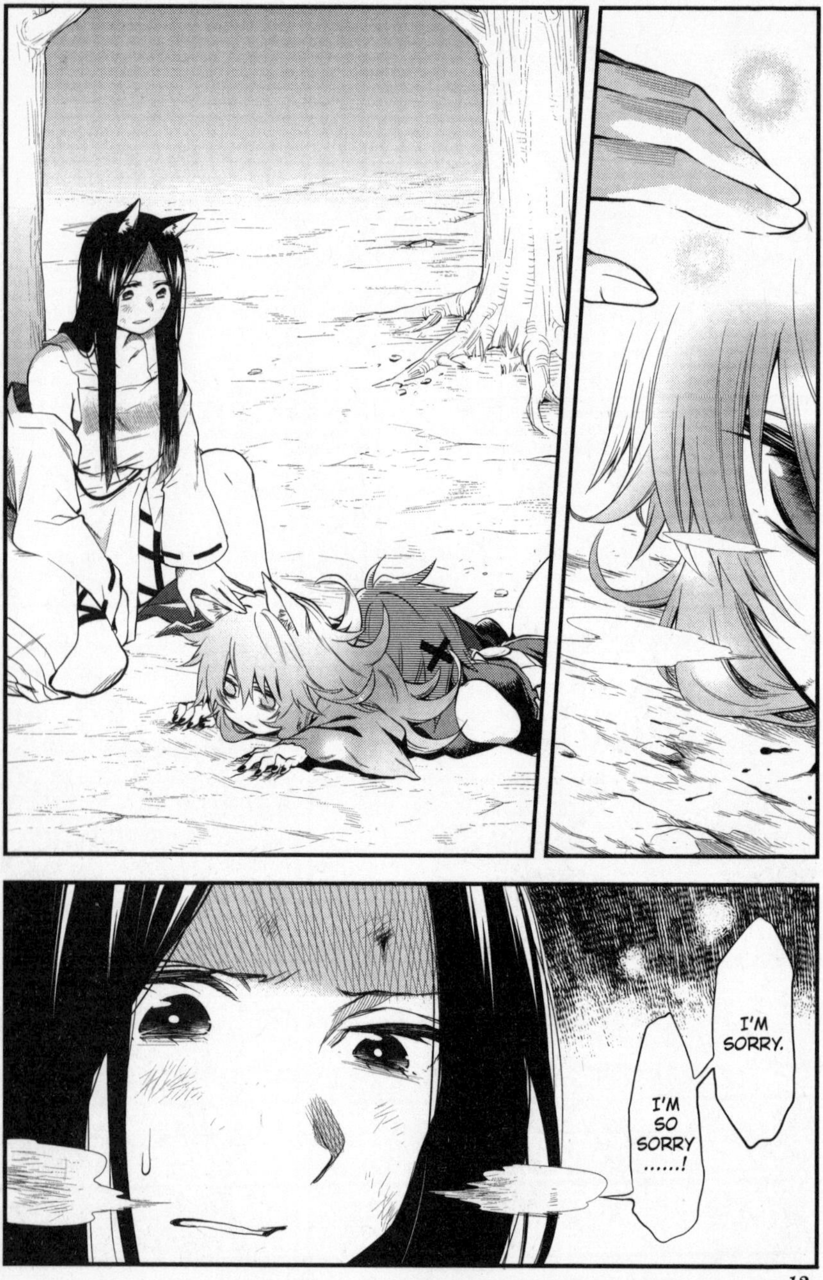
I'M SORRY.
I'M SO SORRY ......!

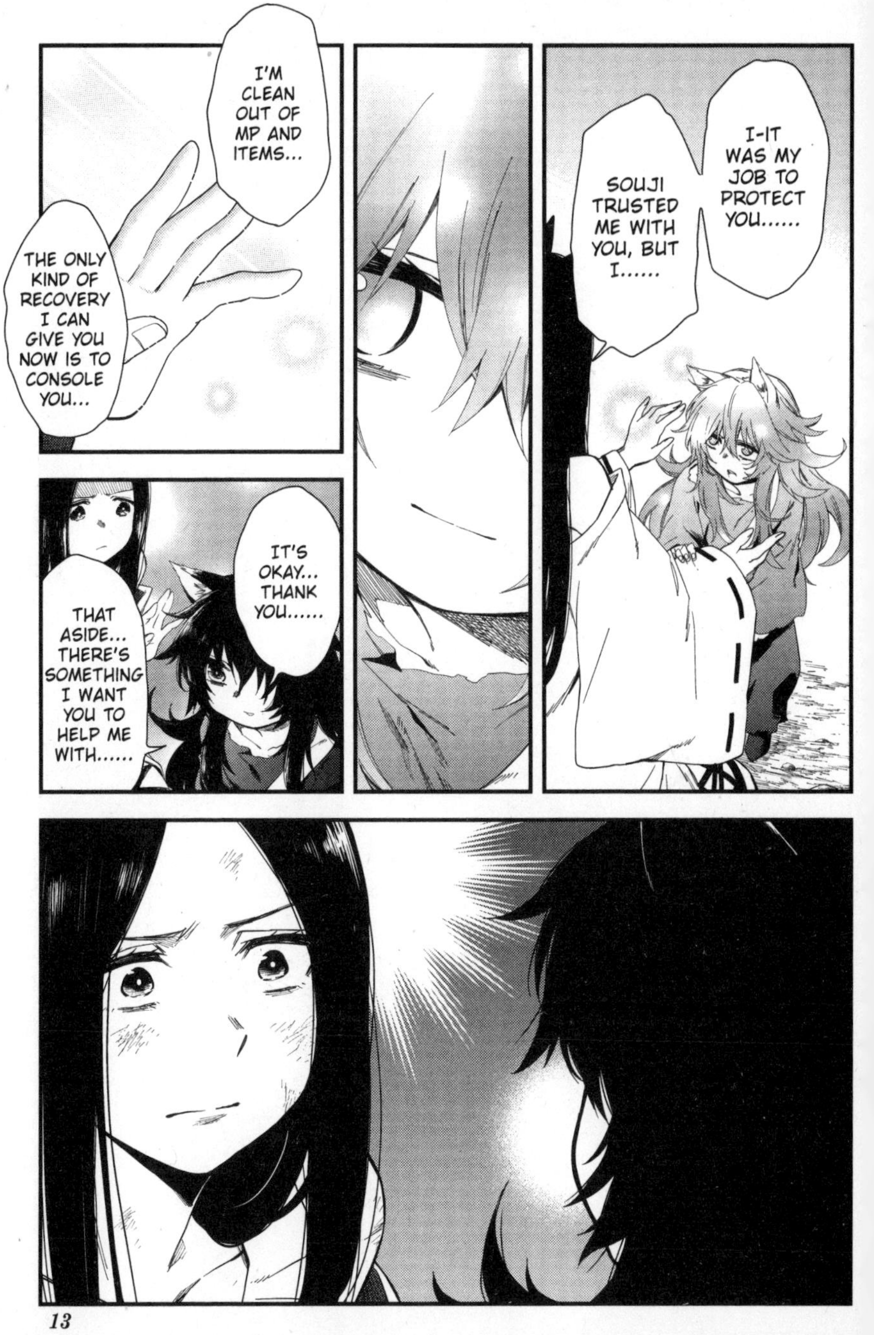
I-IT WAS MY JOB TO PROTECT YOU......
SOUJI TRUSTED ME WITH YOU, BUT I......
I'M CLEAN OUT OF MP AND ITEMS...
THE ONLY KIND OF RECOVERY I CAN GIVE YOU NOW IS TO CONSOLE YOU...
IT'S OKAY... THANK YOU......
THAT ASIDE... THERE'S SOMETHING I WANT YOU TO HELP ME WITH......

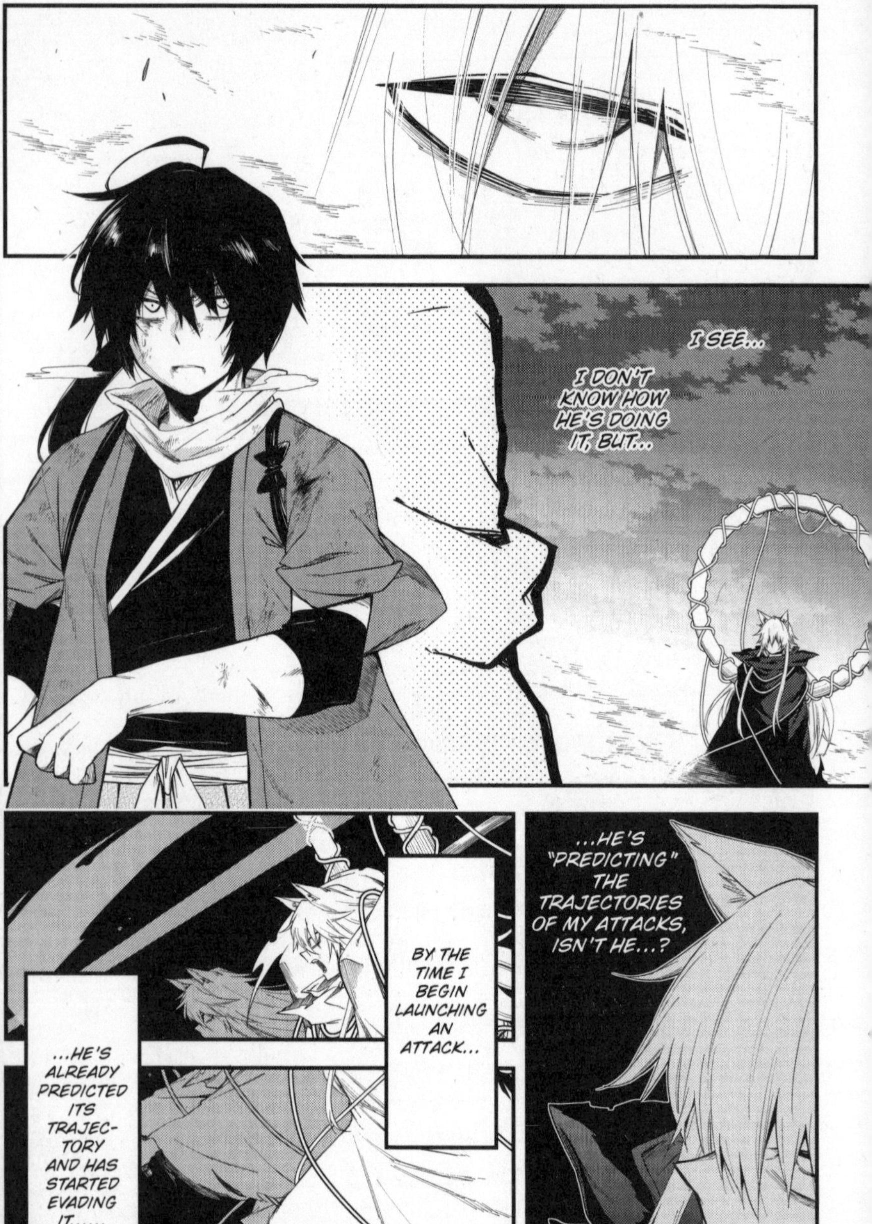
I SEE...
I DON'T KNOW HOW HE'S DOING IT, BUT...
...HE'S "PREDICTING" THE TRAJECTORIES OF MY ATTACKS, ISN'T HE...?
BY THE TIME I BEGIN LAUNCHING AN ATTACK...
...HE'S ALREADY PREDICTED ITS TRAJECTORY AND HAS STARTED EVADING IT......

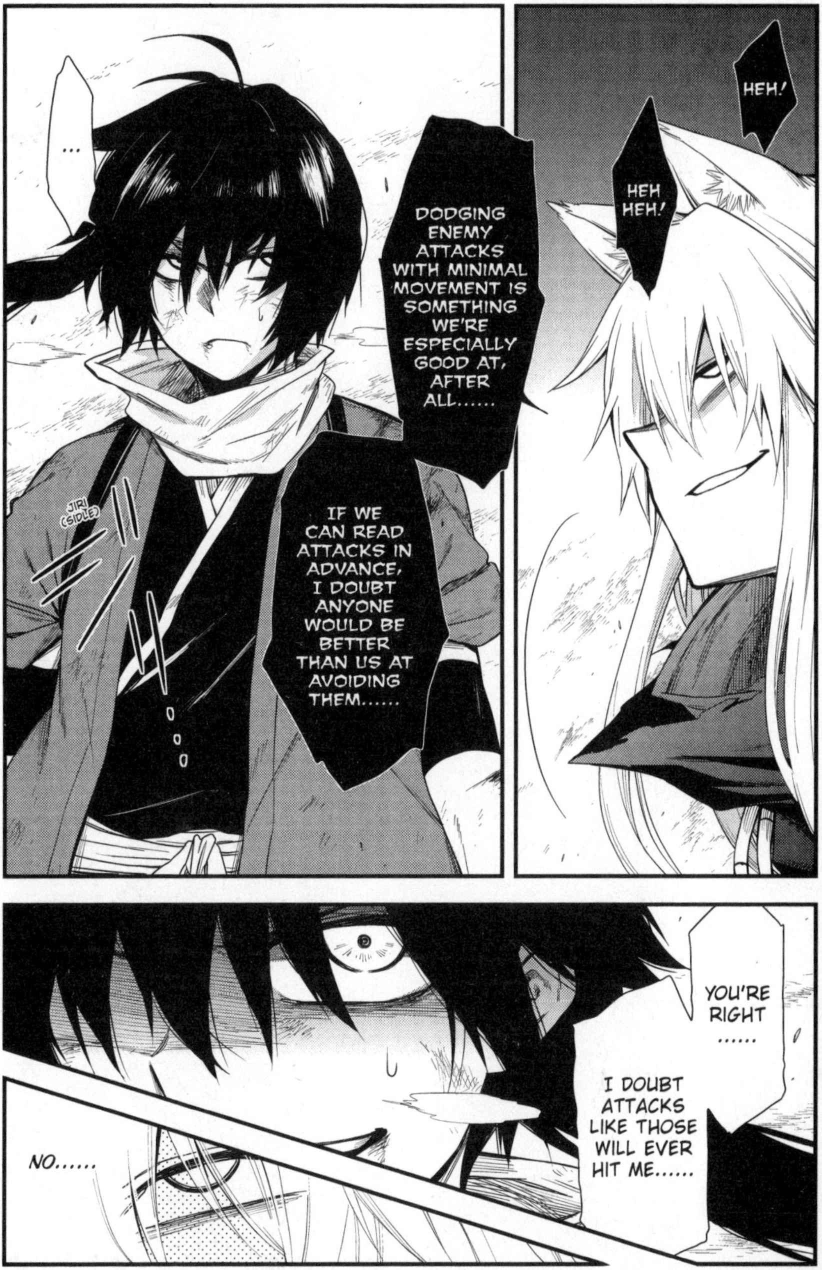
HEH!
HEH HEH!
DODGING ENEMY ATTACKS WITH MINIMAL MOVEMENT IS SOMETHING WE'RE ESPECIALLY GOOD AT, AFTER ALL......
...
IF WE CAN READ ATTACKS IN ADVANCE, I DOUBT ANYONE WOULD BE BETTER THAN US AT AVOIDING THEM......
JIRI (SIDLE)
YOU'RE RIGHT......
I DOUBT ATTACKS LIKE THOSE WILL EVER HIT ME......
NO......

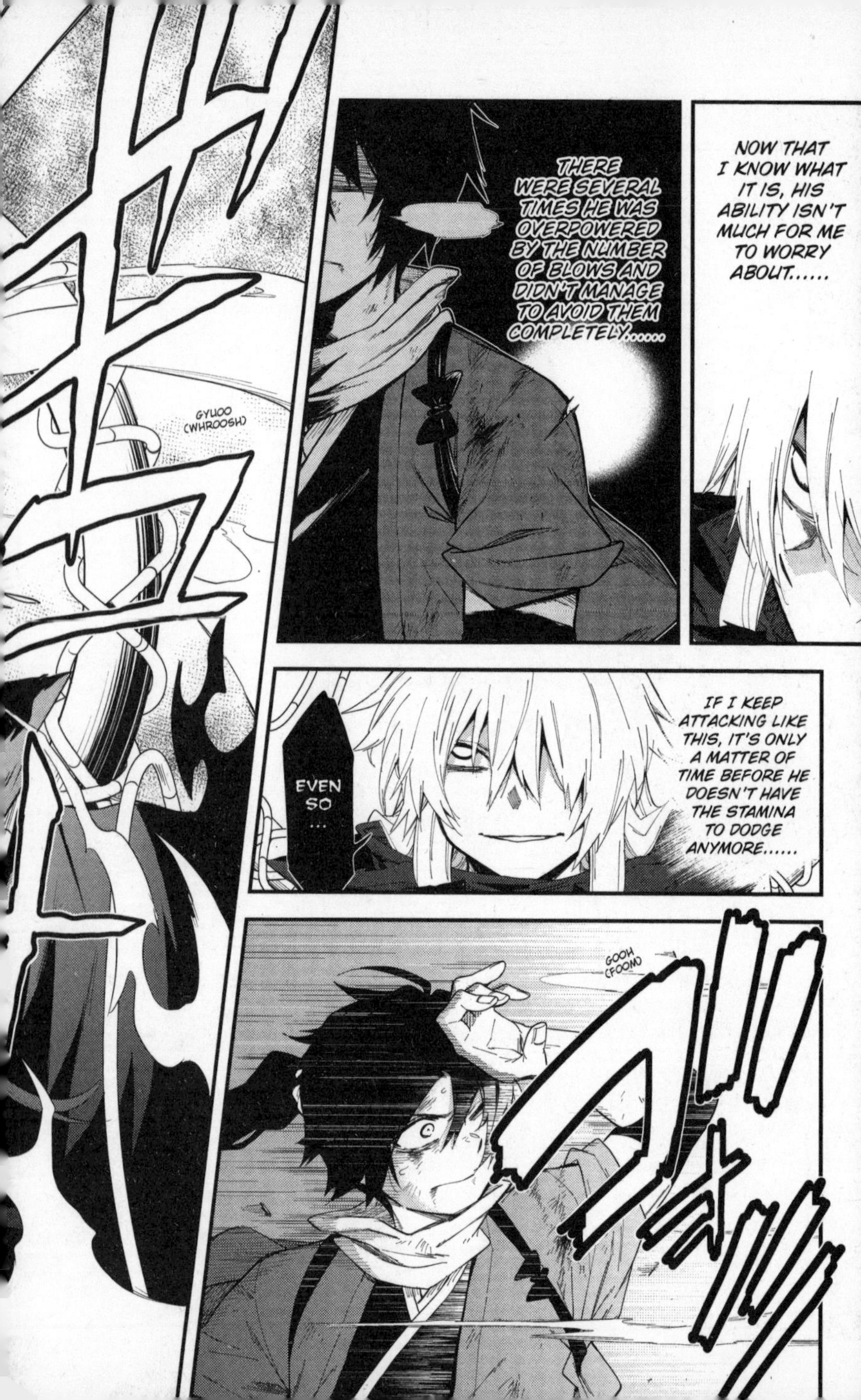
NOW THAT I KNOW WHAT IT IS, HIS ABILITY ISN'T MUCH FOR ME TO WORRY ABOUT......
THERE WERE SEVERAL TIMES HE WAS OVERPOWERED BY THE NUMBER OF BLOWS AND DIDN'T MANAGE TO AVOID THEM COMPLETELY......
IF I KEEP ATTACKING LIKE THIS, IT'S ONLY A MATTER OF TIME BEFORE HE DOESN'T HAVE THE STAMINA TO DODGE ANYMORE......
EVEN SO ...
GOOH (FOOM)
GYUOO (WHROOSH)

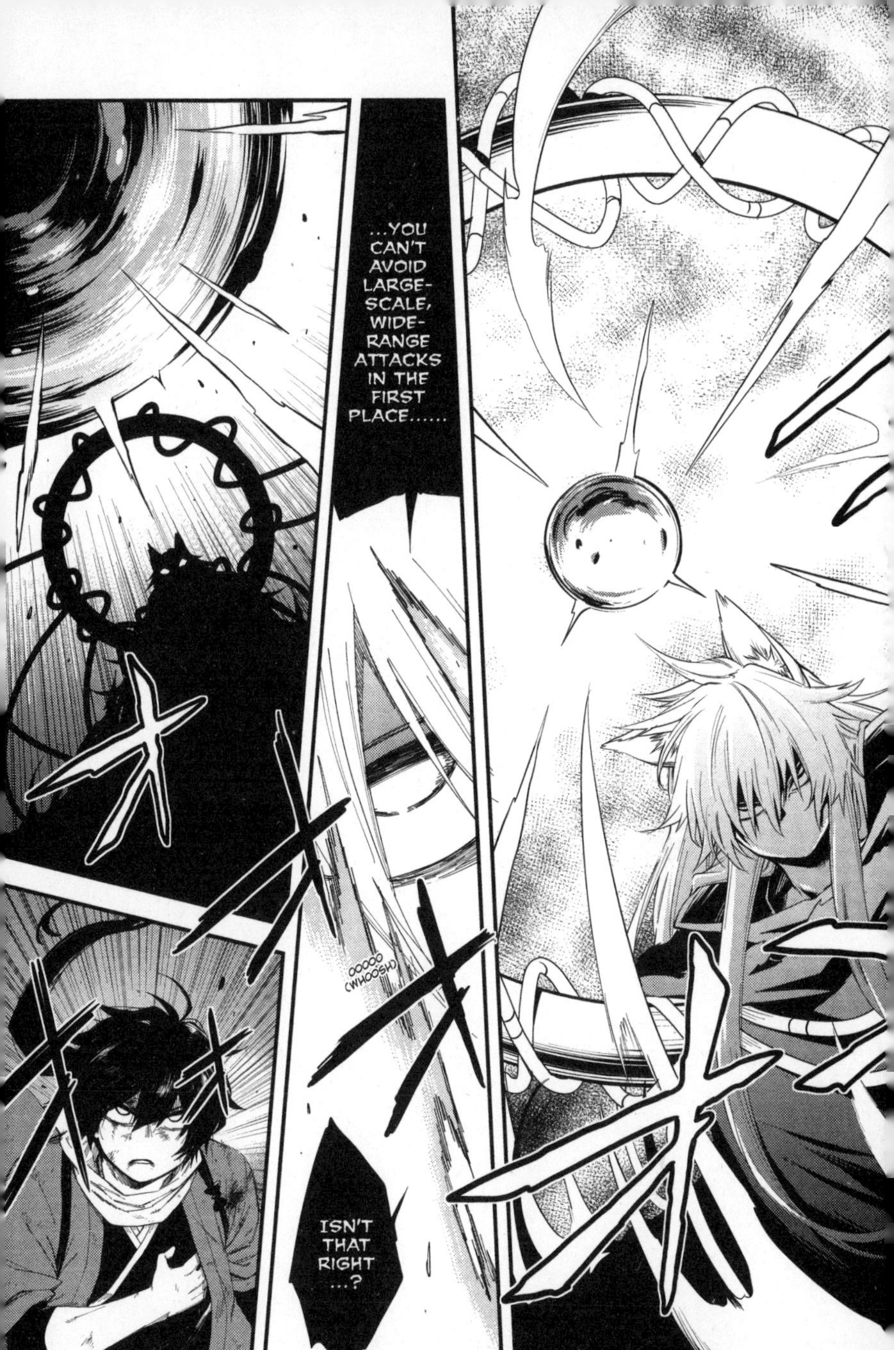
...YOU CAN'T AVOID LARGE-SCALE, WIDE-RANGE ATTACKS IN THE FIRST PLACE......
OOOOO (WHOOSH)
ISN'T THAT RIGHT ...?

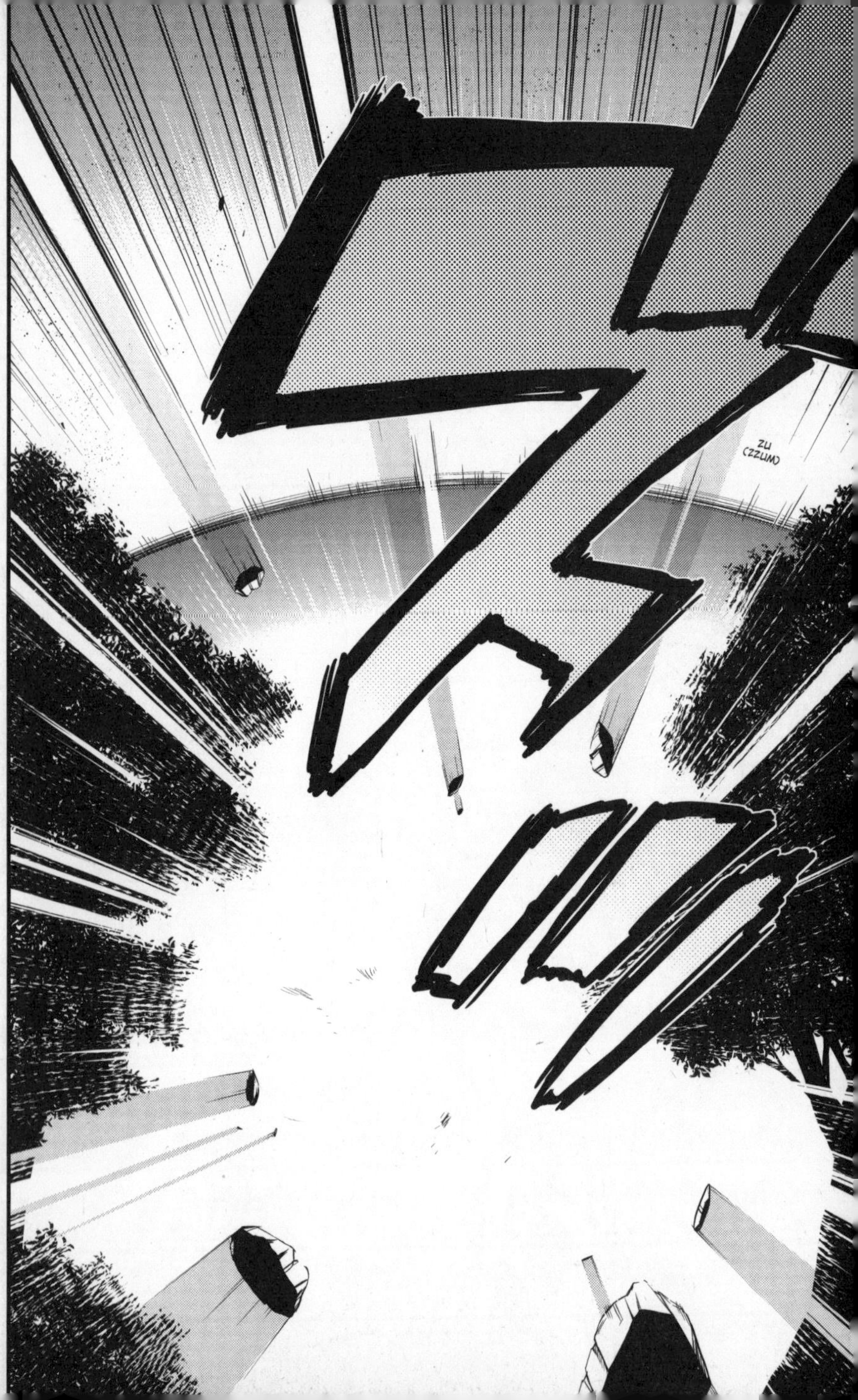
ZU
(ZZUM)

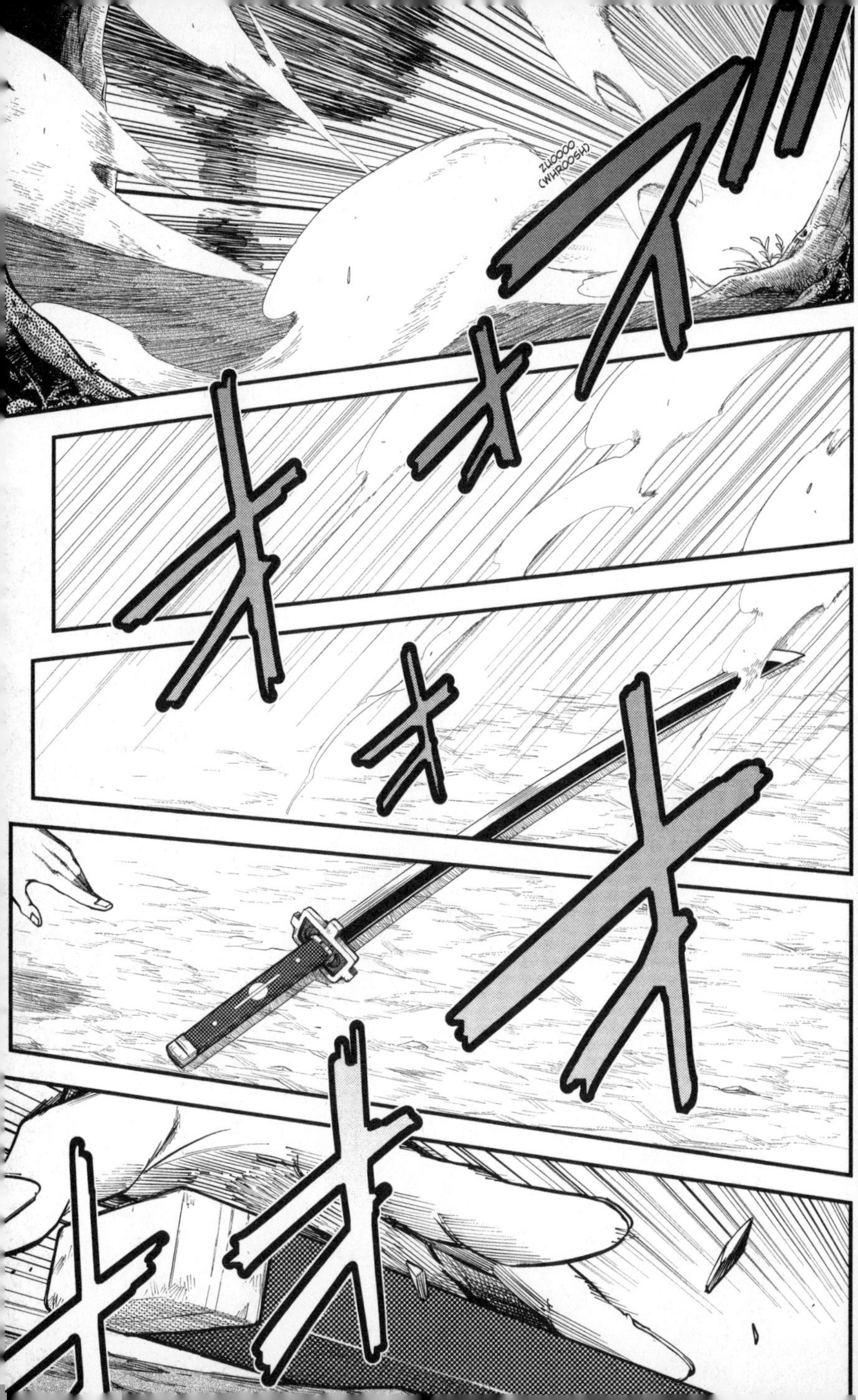
ZUOOOO
(WHROOSH)

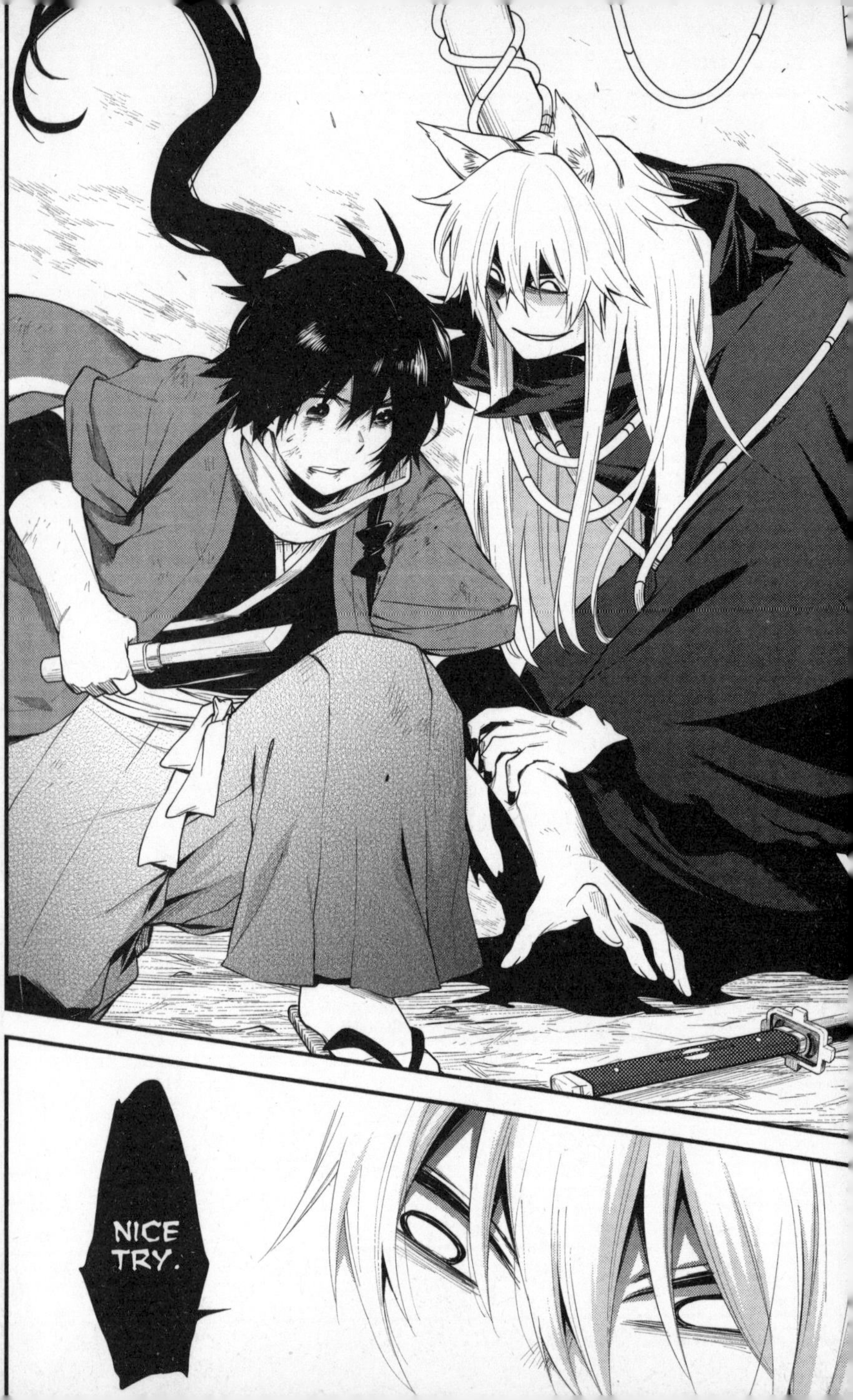
NICE TRY.

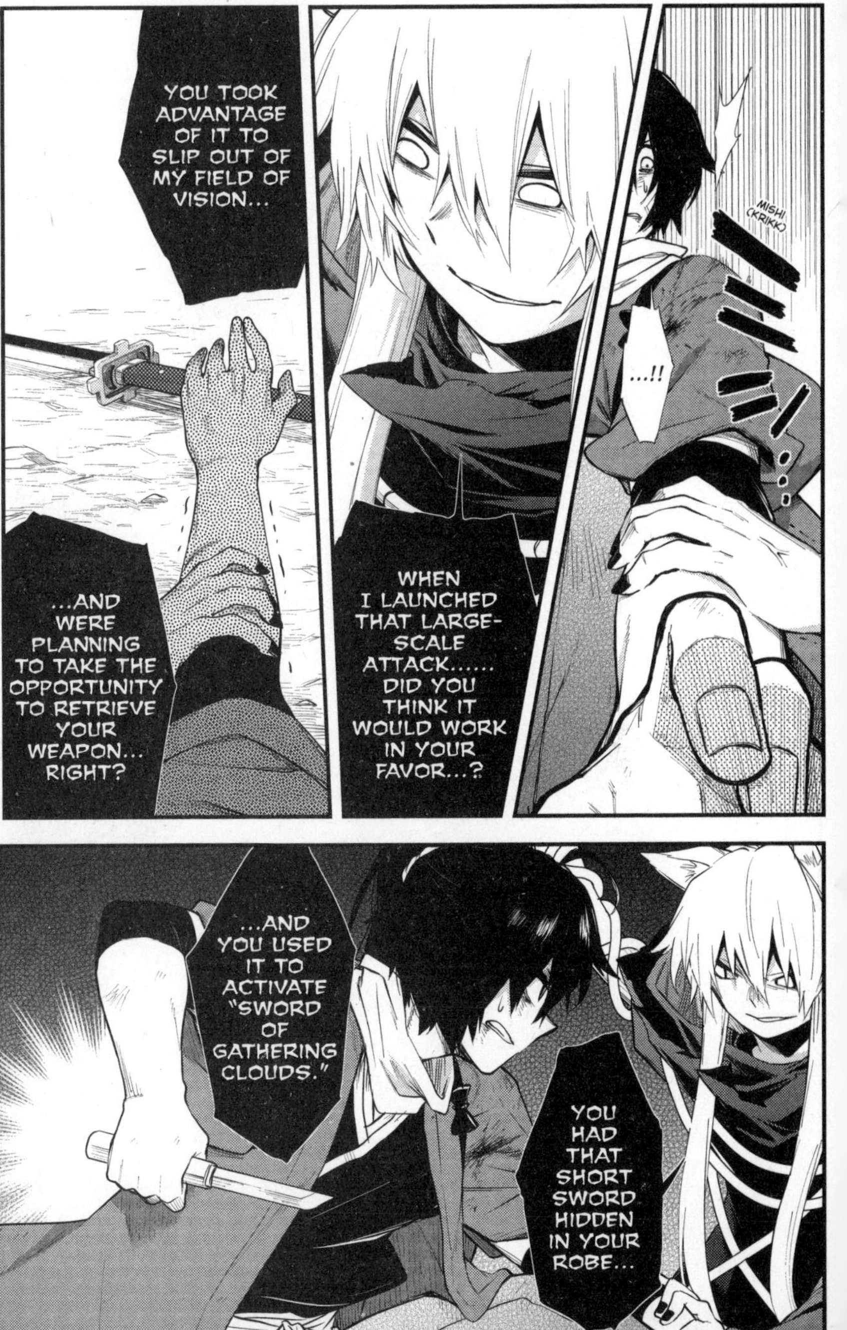
MISHI (KRIKK)
...!!
WHEN I LAUNCHED THAT LARGE-SCALE ATTACK...... DID YOU THINK IT WOULD WORK IN YOUR FAVOR...?
YOU TOOK ADVANTAGE OF IT TO SLIP OUT OF MY FIELD OF VISION...
...AND WERE PLANNING TO TAKE THE OPPORTUNITY TO RETRIEVE YOUR WEAPON... RIGHT?
YOU HAD THAT SHORT SWORD HIDDEN IN YOUR ROBE...
...AND YOU USED IT TO ACTIVATE "SWORD OF GATHERING CLOUDS."

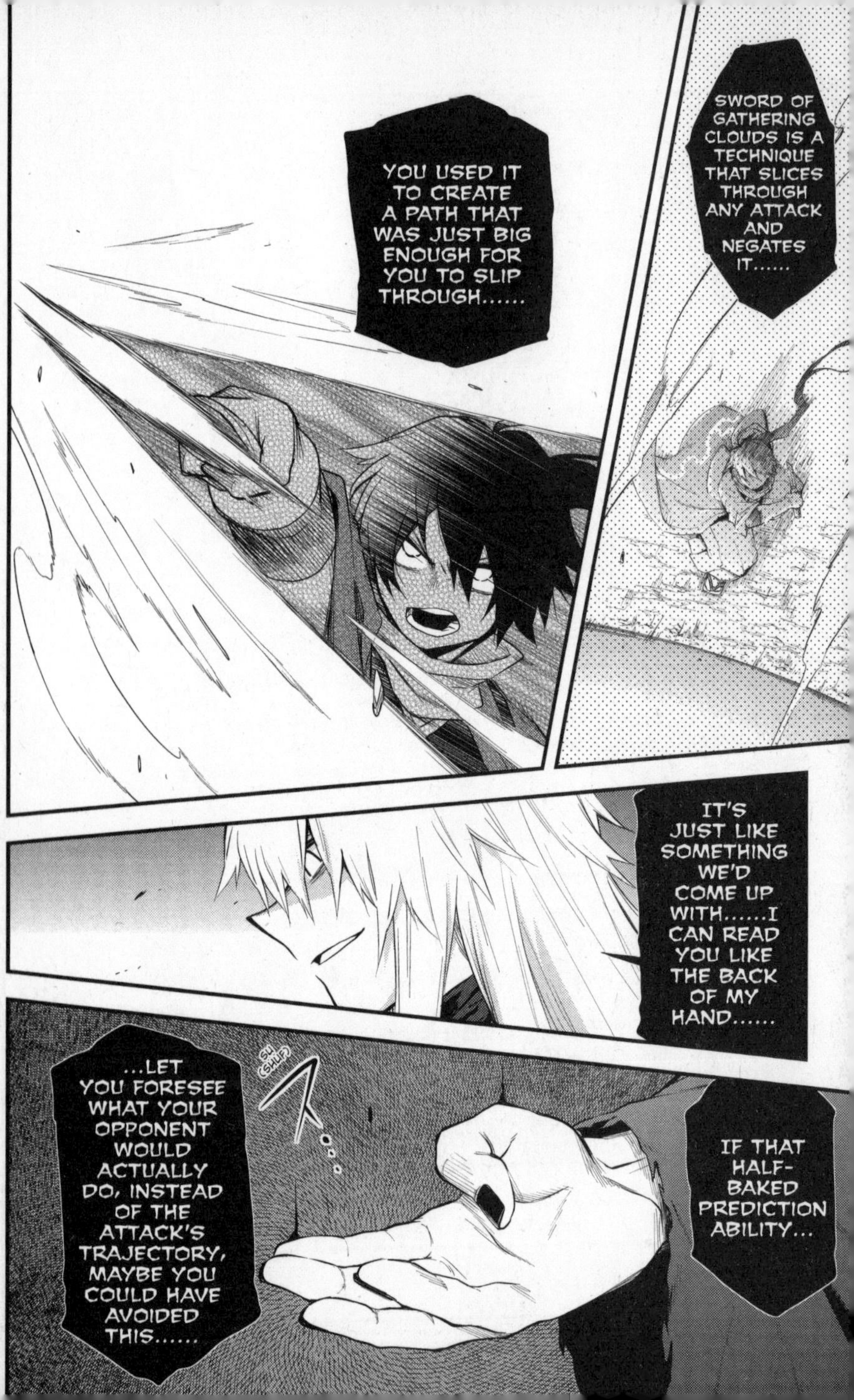
SWORD OF GATHERING CLOUDS IS A TECHNIQUE THAT SLICES THROUGH ANY ATTACK AND NEGATES IT......
YOU USED IT TO CREATE A PATH THAT WAS JUST BIG ENOUGH FOR YOU TO SLIP THROUGH......
IT'S JUST LIKE SOMETHING WE'D COME UP WITH......I CAN READ YOU LIKE THE BACK OF MY HAND......
IF THAT HALF-BAKED PREDICTION ABILITY...
SU (SHLIP)
...LET YOU FORESEE WHAT YOUR OPPONENT WOULD ACTUALLY DO, INSTEAD OF THE ATTACK'S TRAJECTORY, MAYBE YOU COULD HAVE AVOIDED THIS......

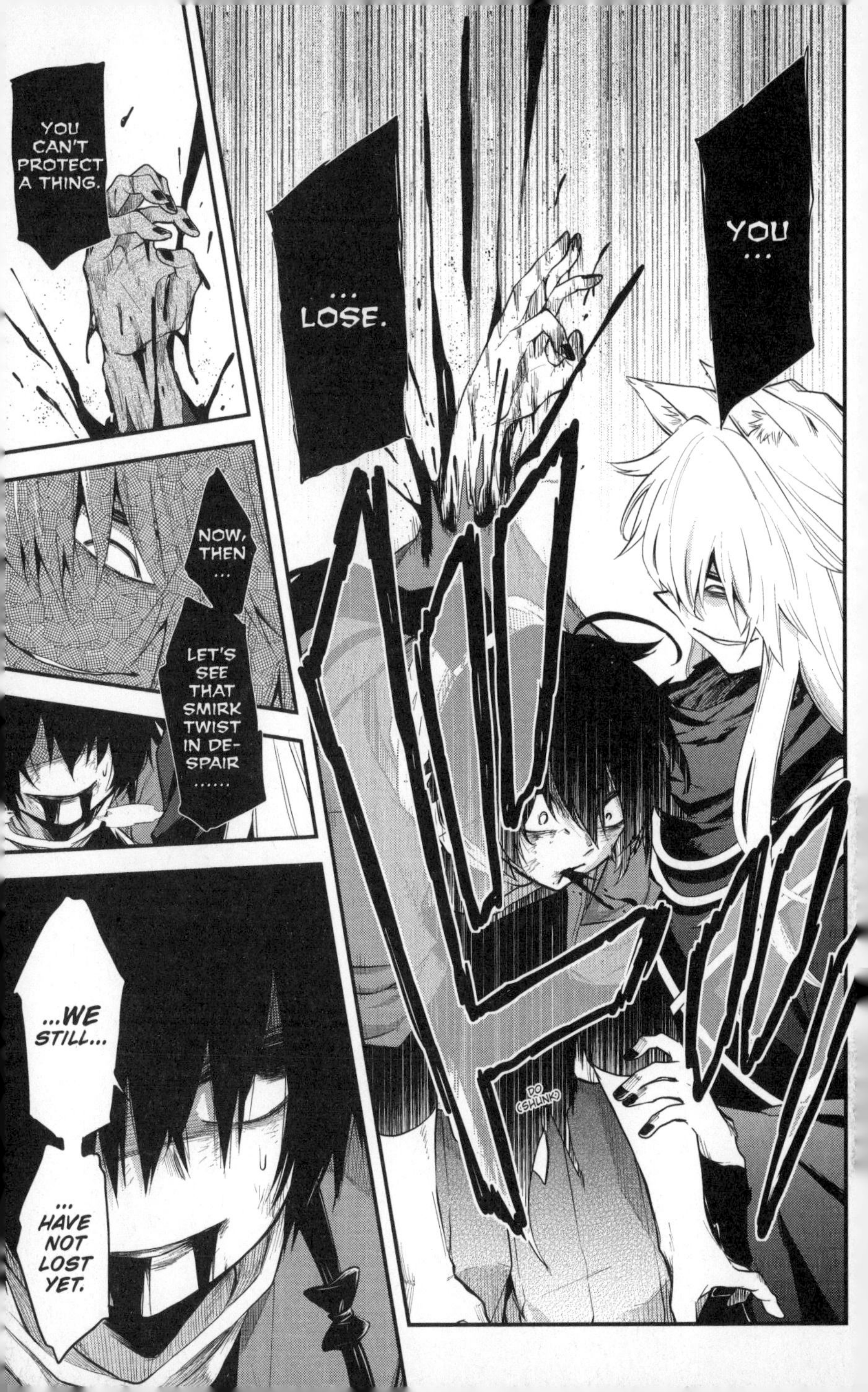
YOU ...
... LOSE.
DO (SHLINK)
YOU CAN'T PROTECT A THING.
NOW, THEN ...
LET'S SEE THAT SMIRK TWIST IN DE-SPAIR ......
...WE STILL...
... HAVE NOT LOST YET.

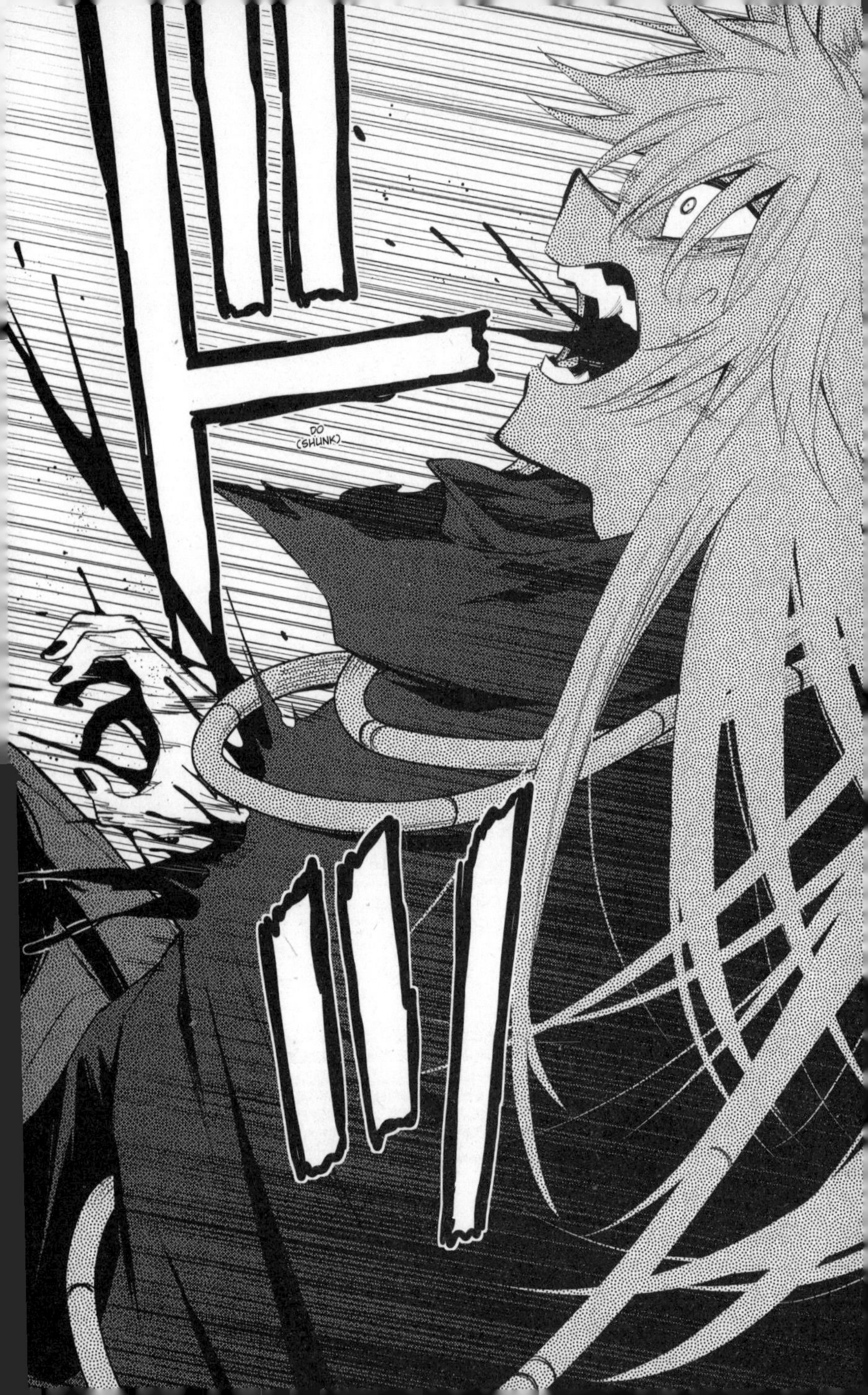
DO
(SHLINK)

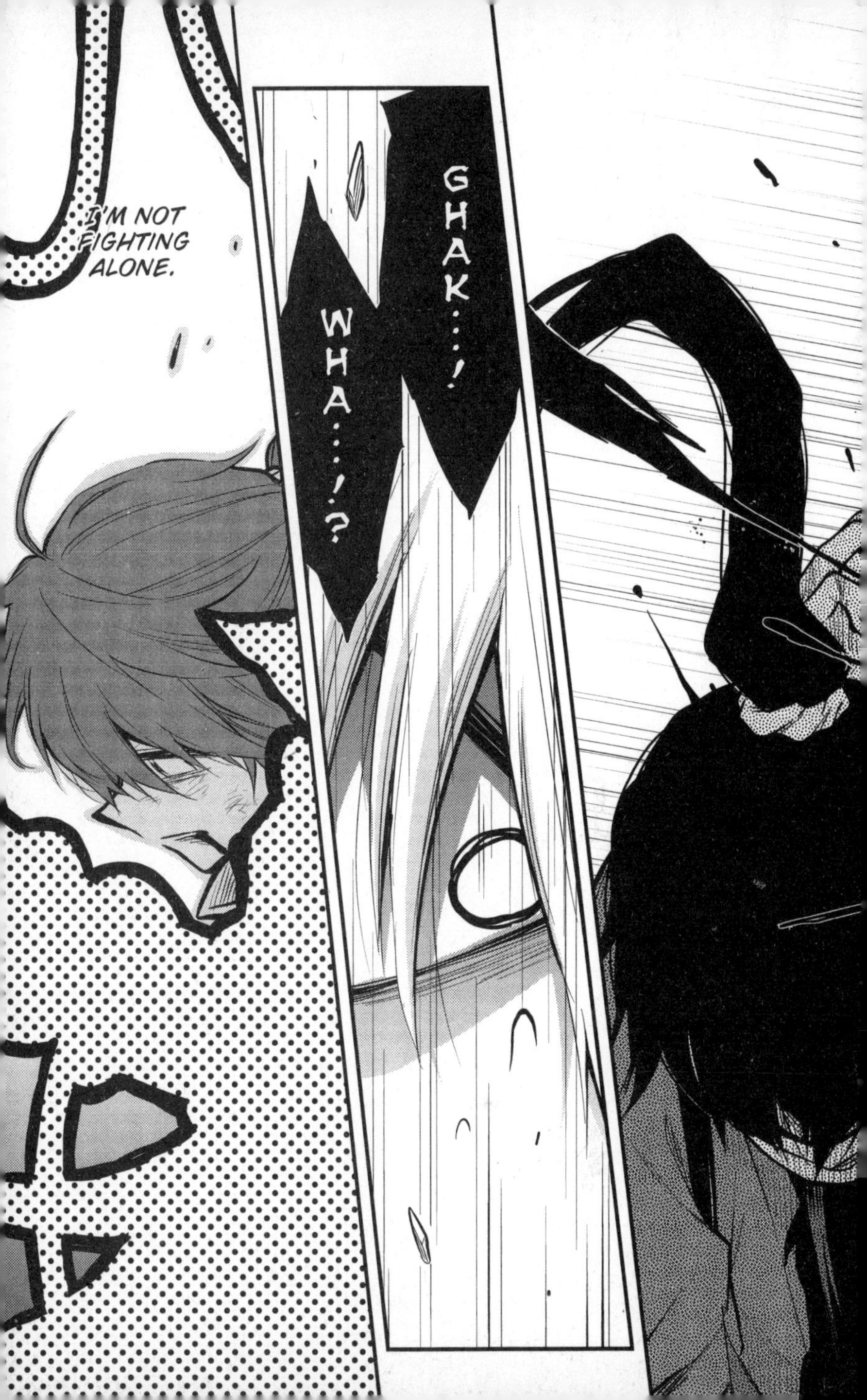
GHAK...!
WHA...!?
I'M NOT FIGHTING ALONE.

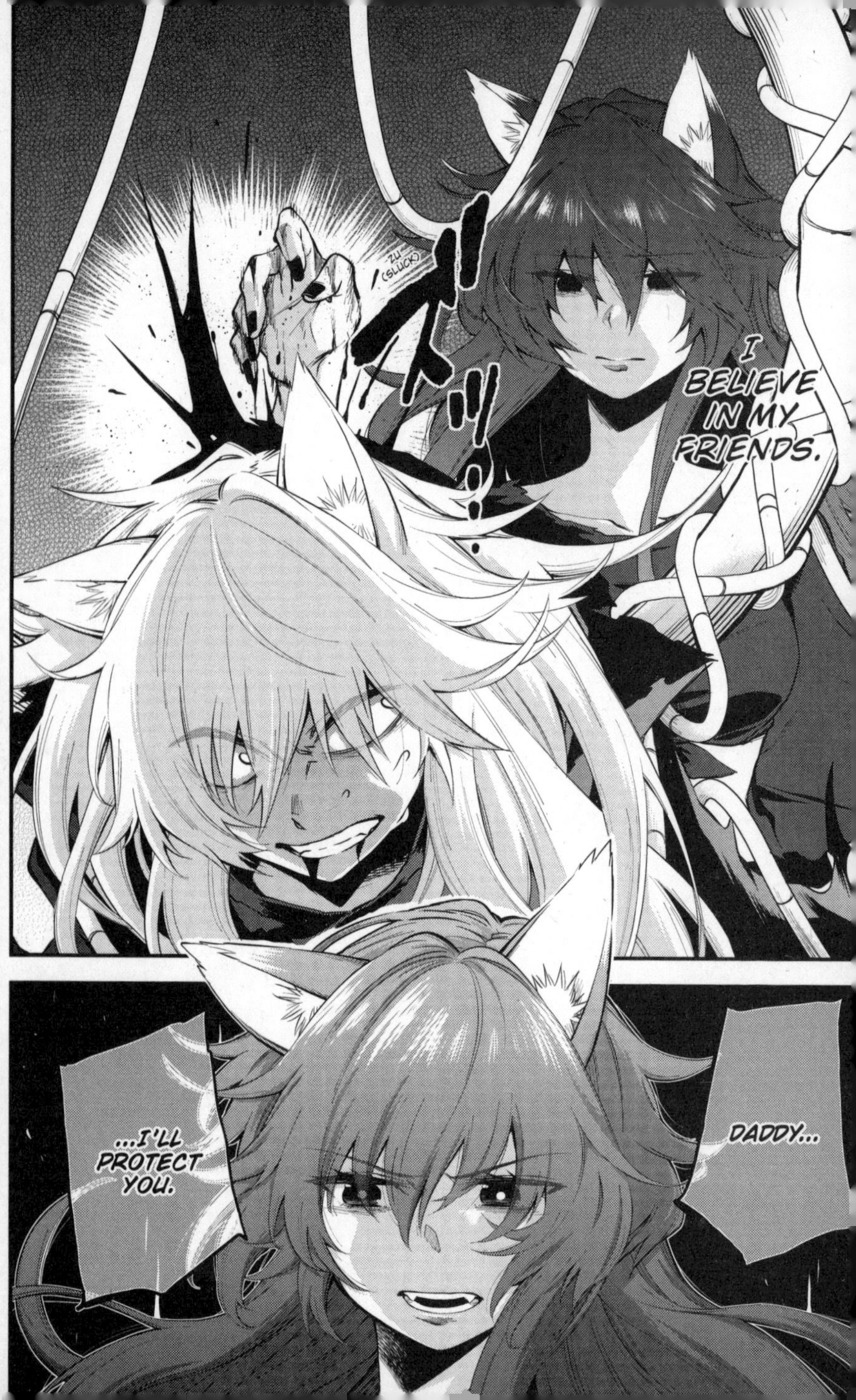

I BELIEVE IN MY FRIENDS.
ZU (SLUCK)
DADDY...
...I'LL PROTECT YOU.

LOG HORIZON

THE WEST WIND BRIGADE

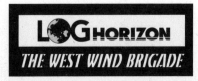

LOG HORIZON

THE WEST WIND BRIGADE

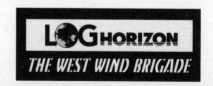

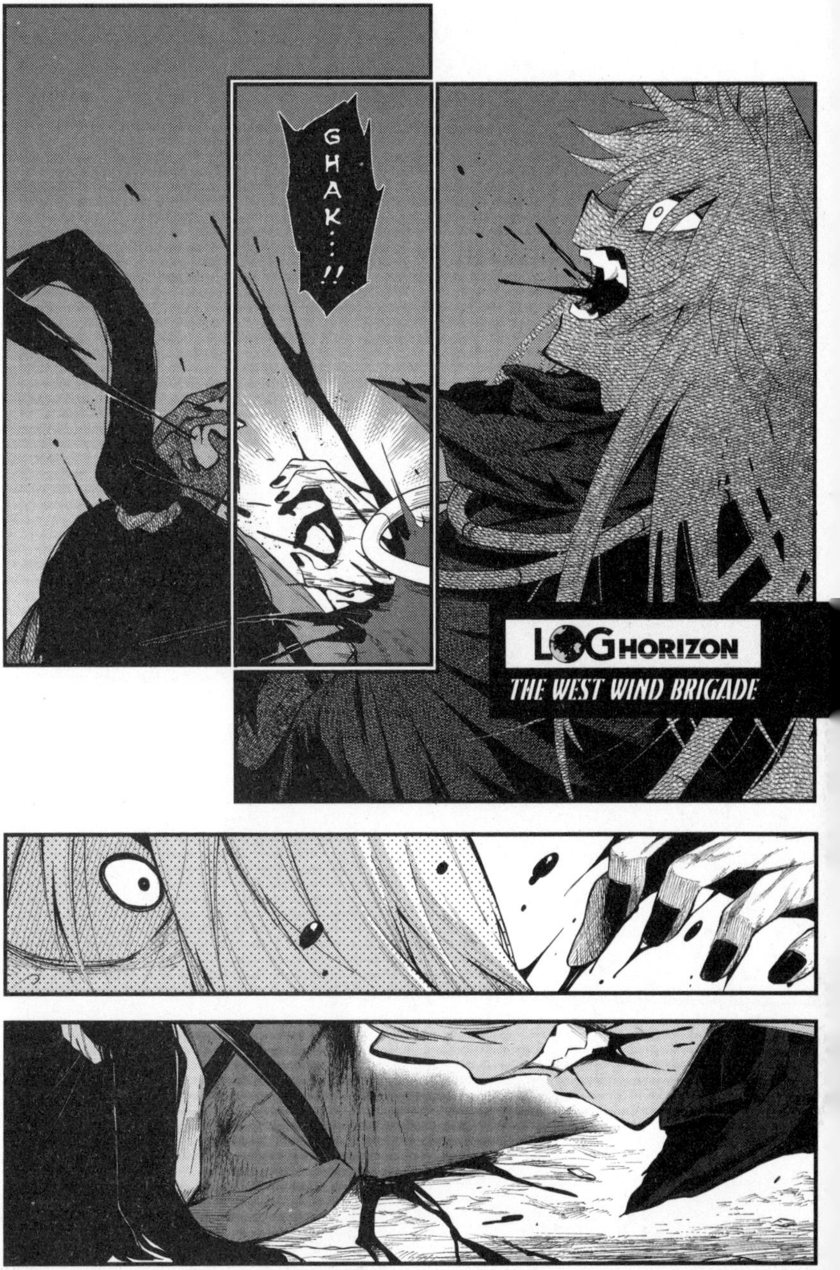
GHAK...!!
LOG HORIZON
THE WEST WIND BRIGADE

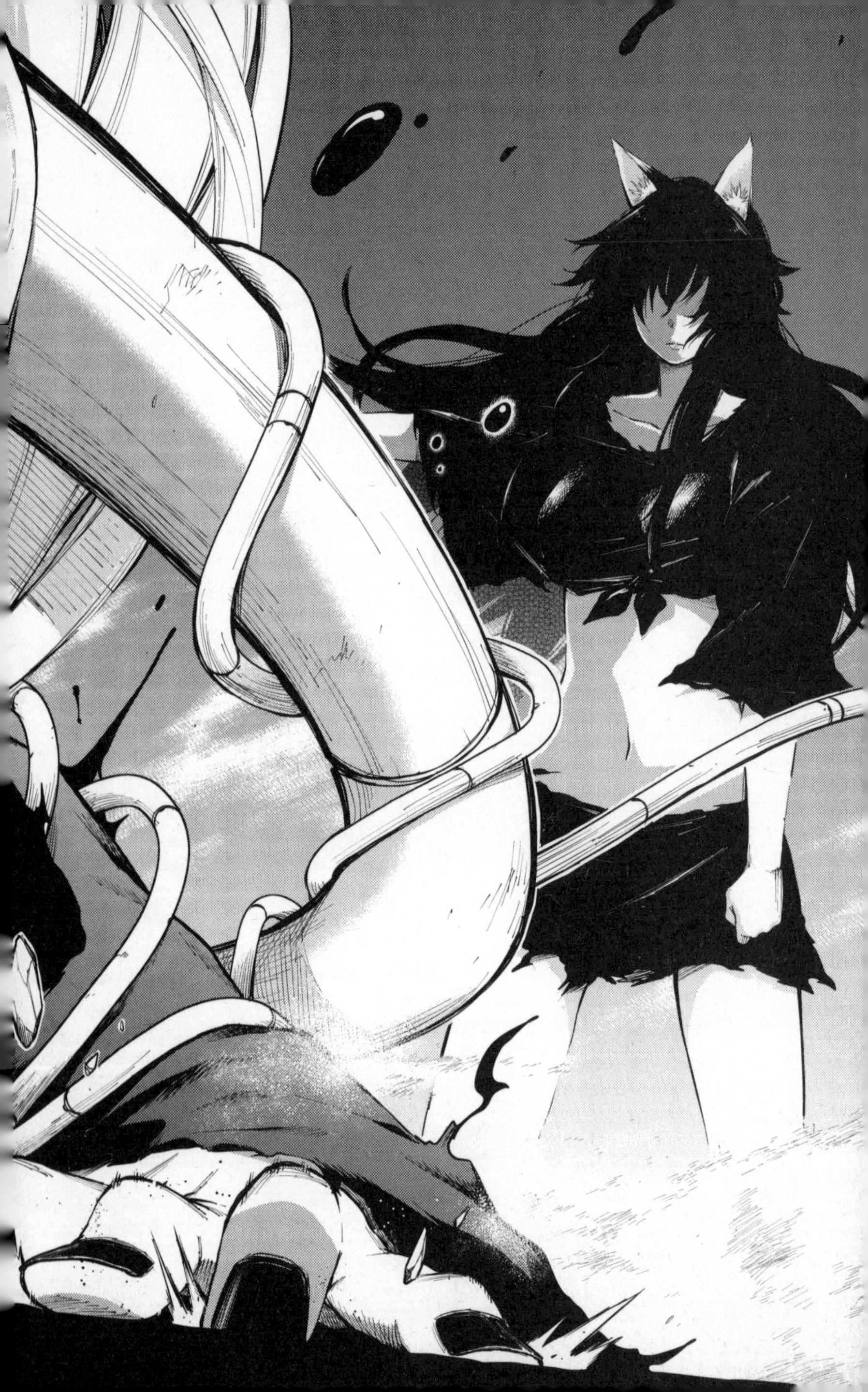

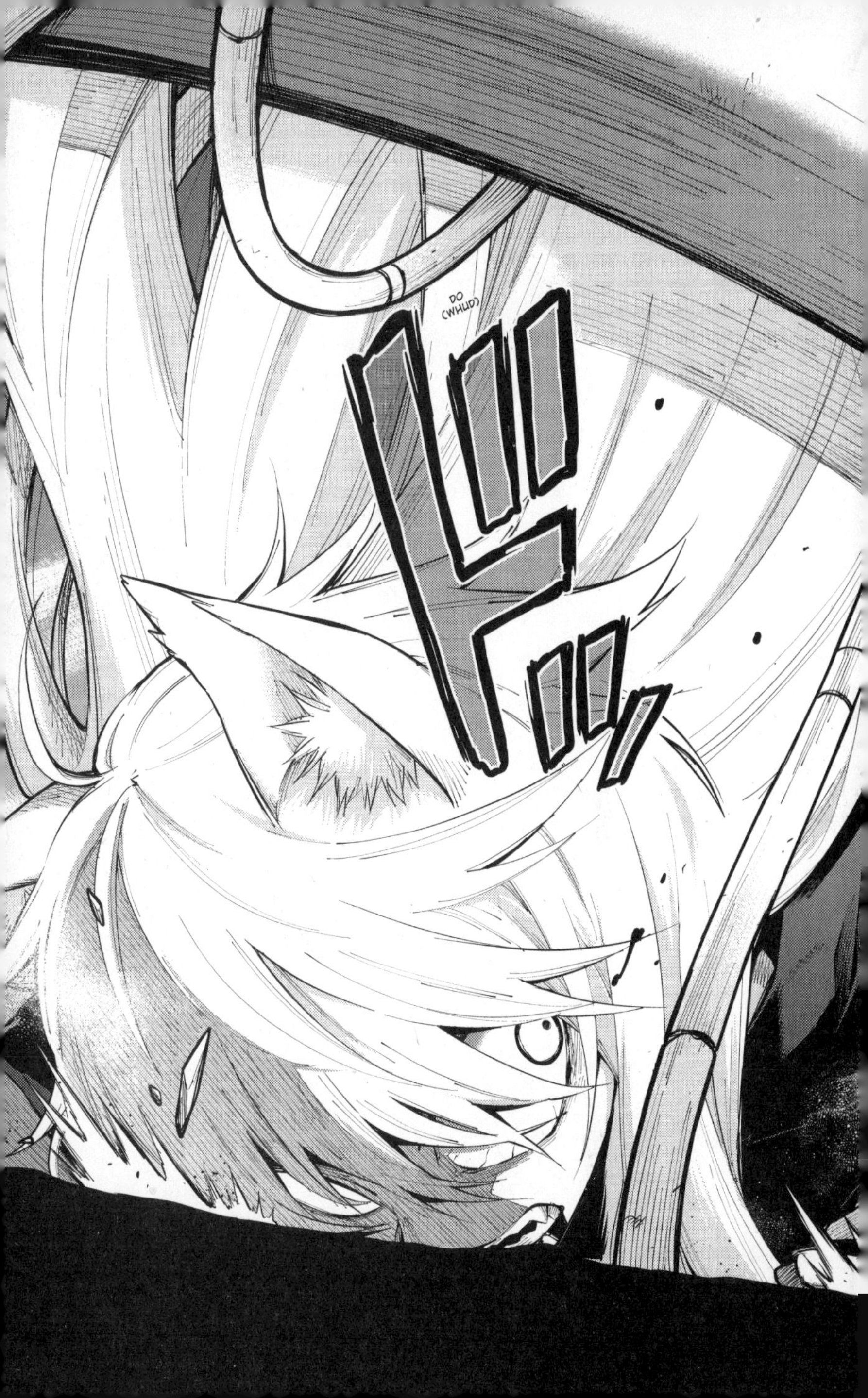
DO
(WHUD)

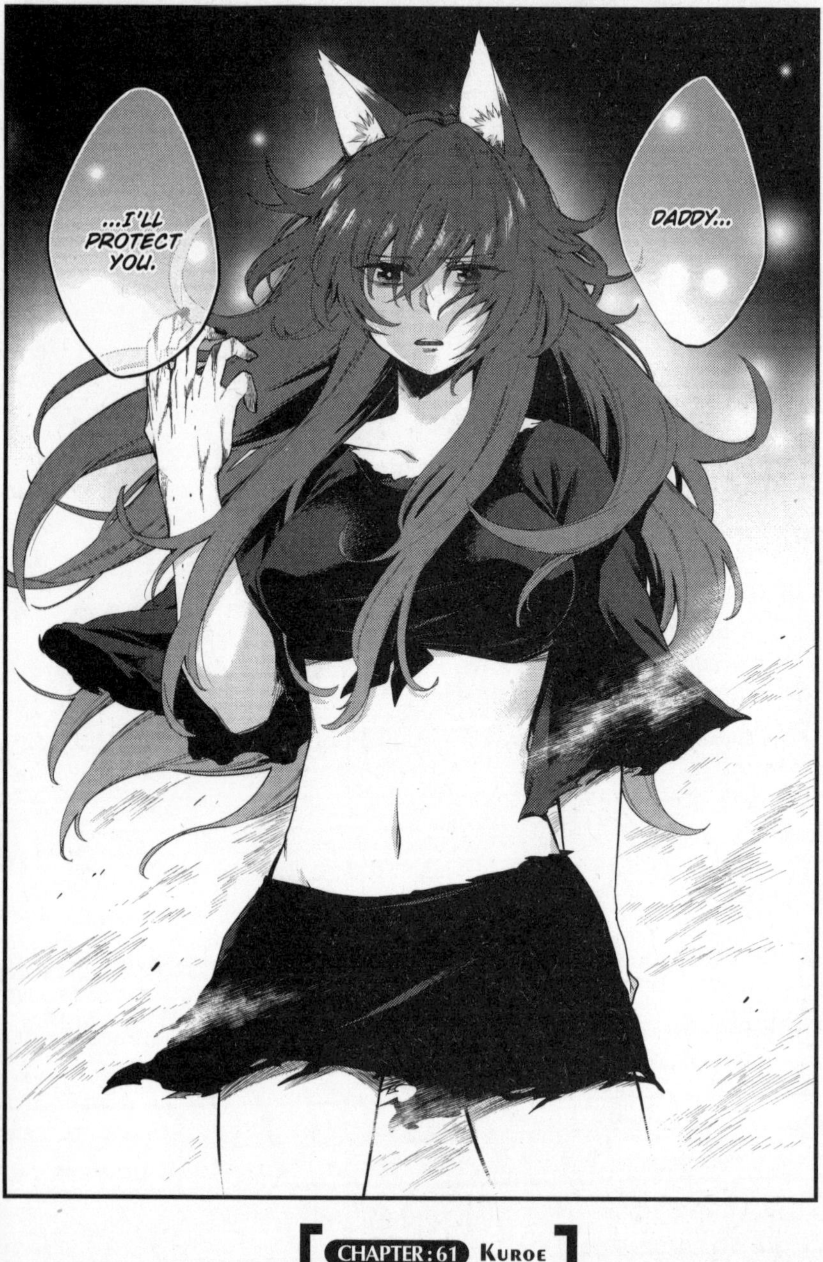
DADDY...
...I'LL PROTECT YOU.

CHAPTER: 61 Kuroe

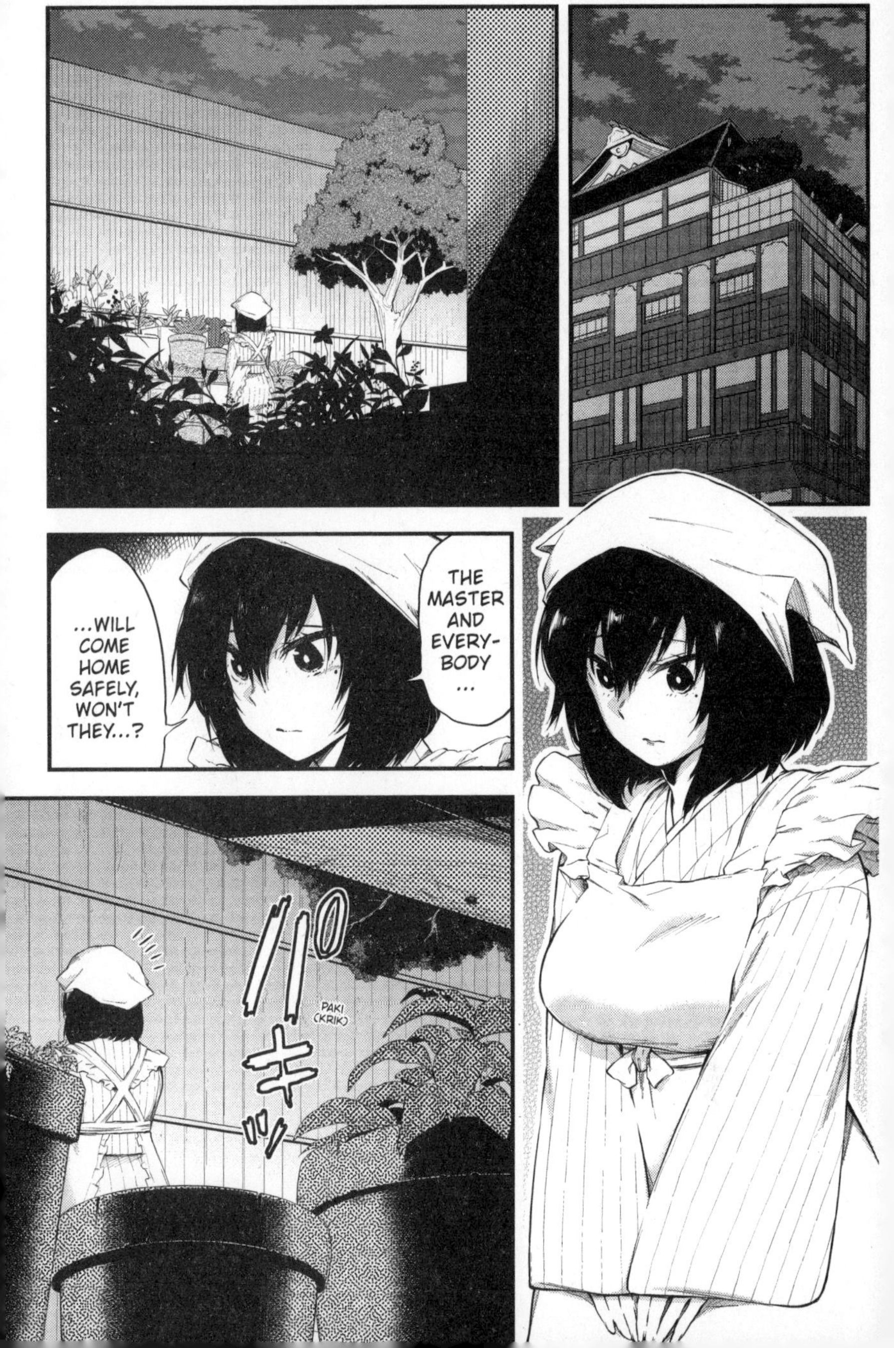
THE MASTER AND EVERY-BODY...
...WILL COME HOME SAFELY, WON'T THEY...?
PAKI (KRIK)

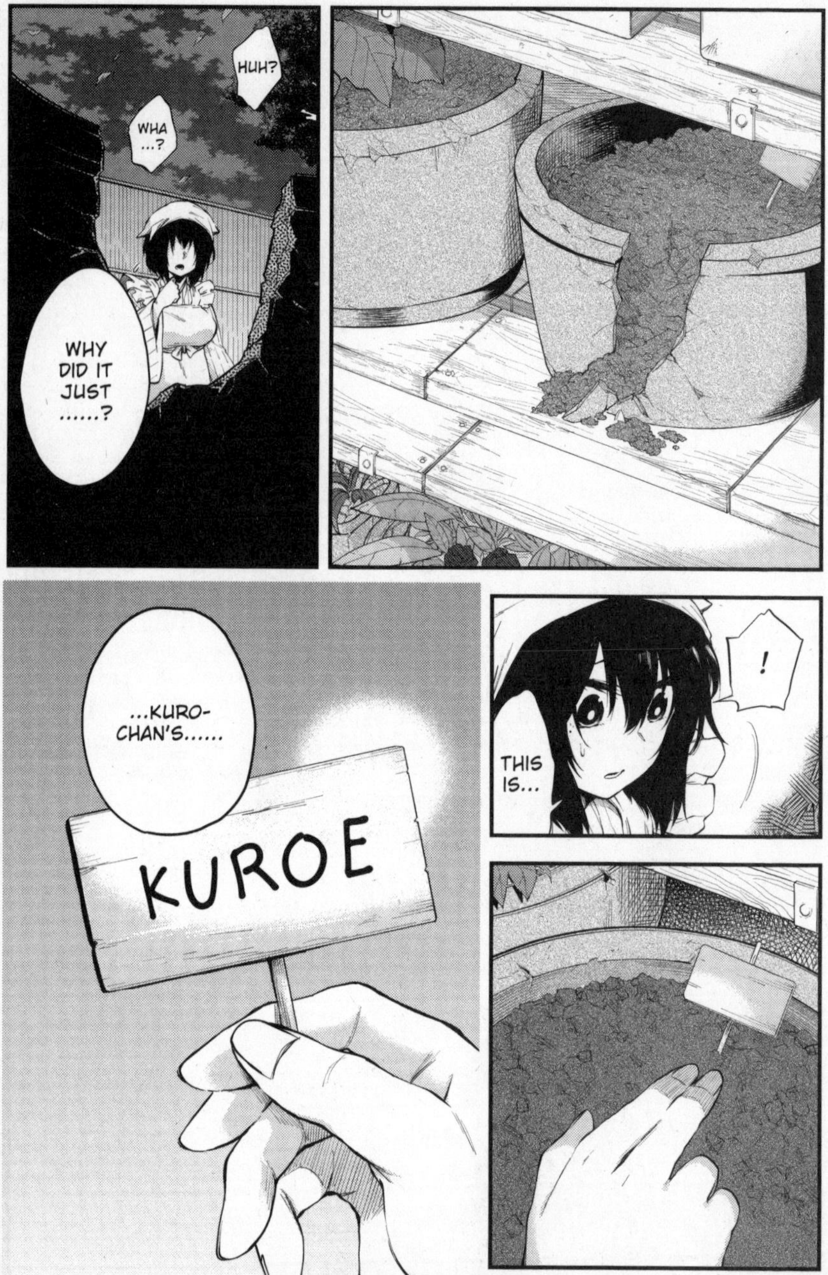
HUH?
WHA ...?
WHY DID IT JUST ......?
!
THIS IS...
...KURO-CHAN'S......
KUROE

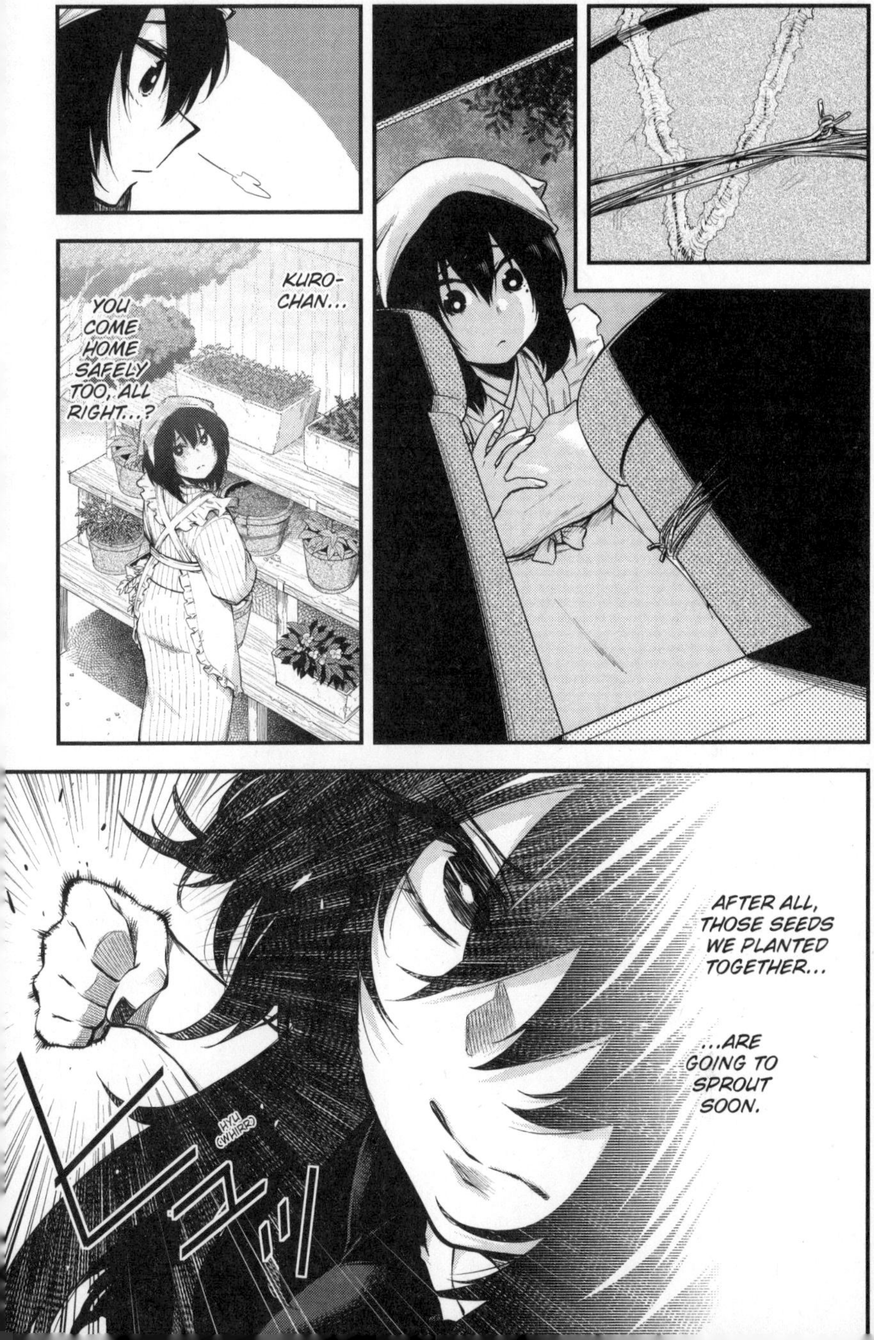
KURO-CHAN...
YOU COME HOME SAFELY TOO, ALL RIGHT...?
AFTER ALL, THOSE SEEDS WE PLANTED TOGETHER...
...ARE GOING TO SPROUT SOON.
HYU (WHIRR)

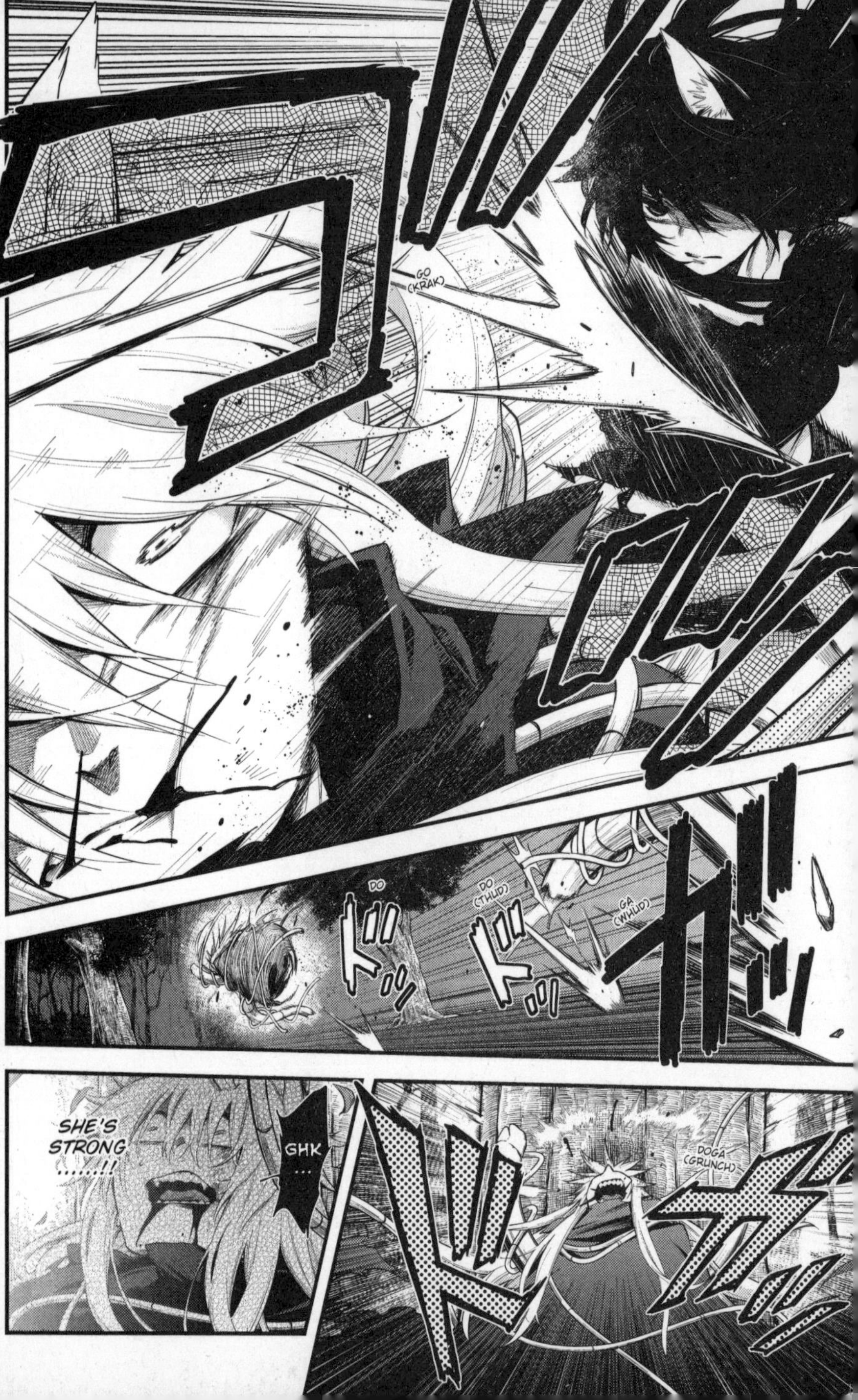
GO
(KRAK)
GA
(WHUD)
DO
(THUD)
DO
DOGA
(GRUNCH)
GHK
...
SHE'S
STRONG
......!!

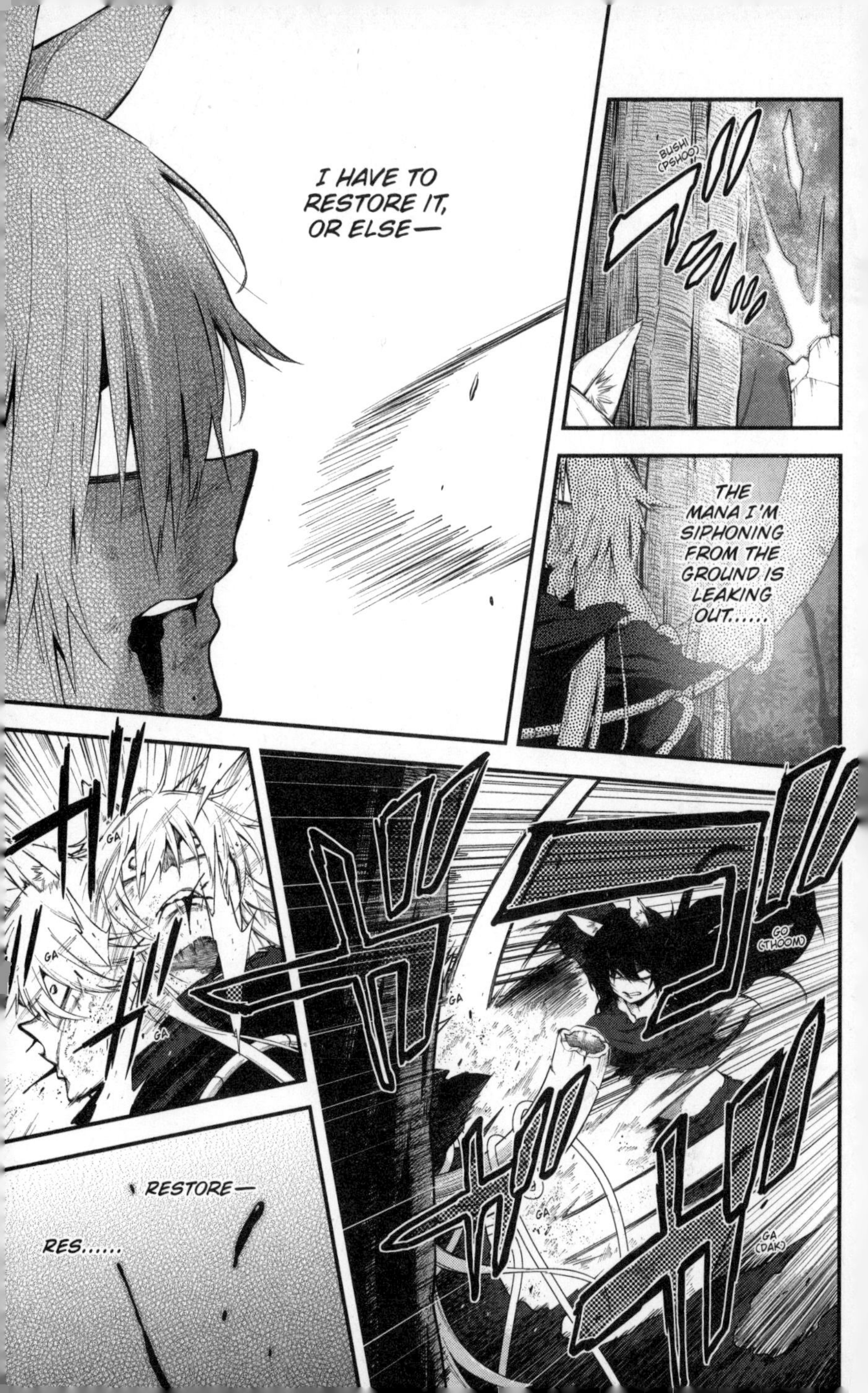
BUSHI (PSHOO)
THE MANA I'M SIPHONING FROM THE GROUND IS LEAKING OUT......
I HAVE TO RESTORE IT, OR ELSE—
GO (THOOM)
GA (DAK)
GA
GA
GA
GA
GA
RESTORE—
RES......

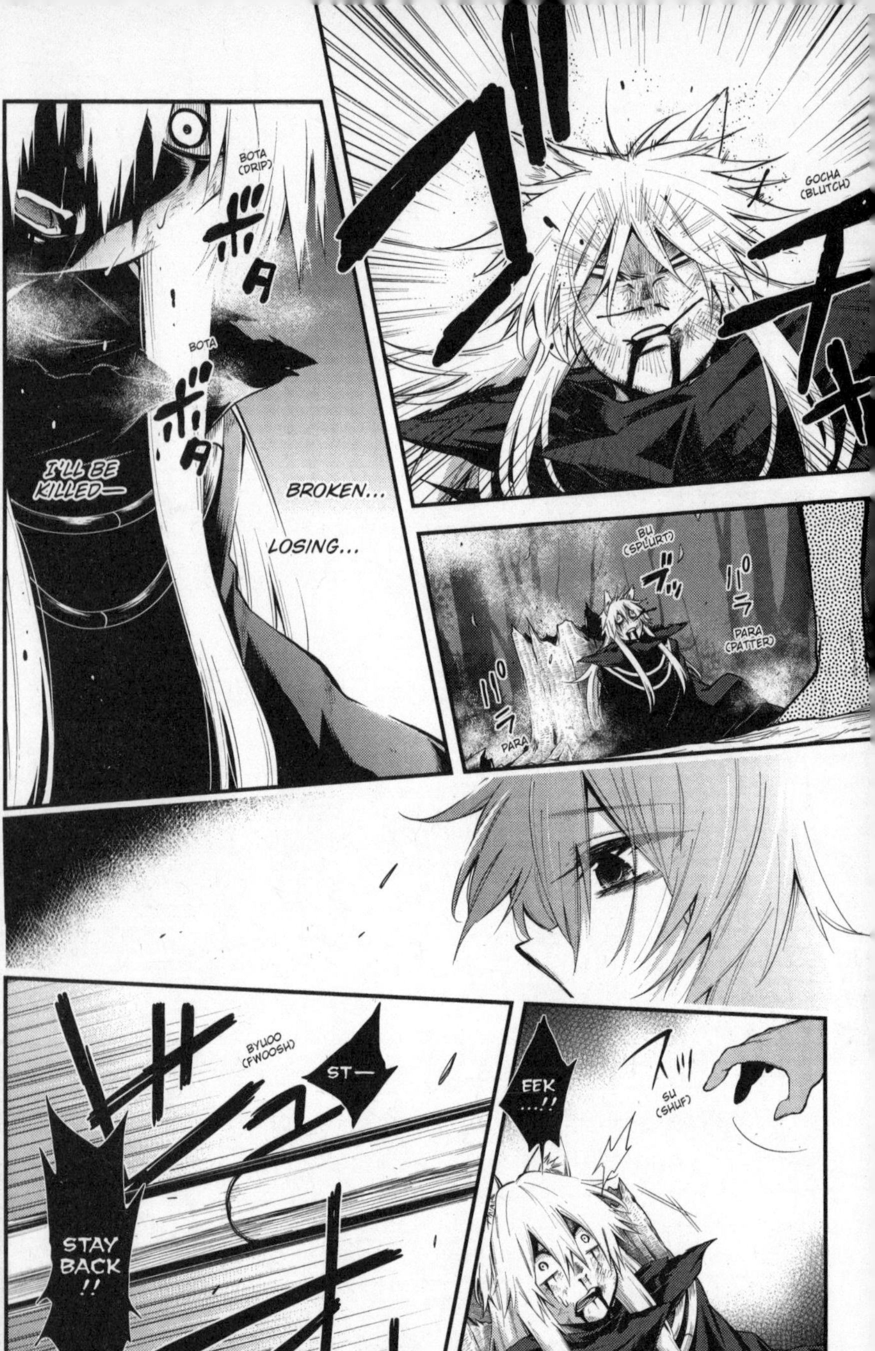
GOCHA (BLUTCH)
BU (SPLURT)
PARA (PATTER)
PARA
BOTA (DRIP)
BOTA
I'LL BE KILLED—
BROKEN...
LOSING...
SU (SHUF)
EEK ...!!
ST—
BYUOO (FWOOSH)
STAY BACK !!

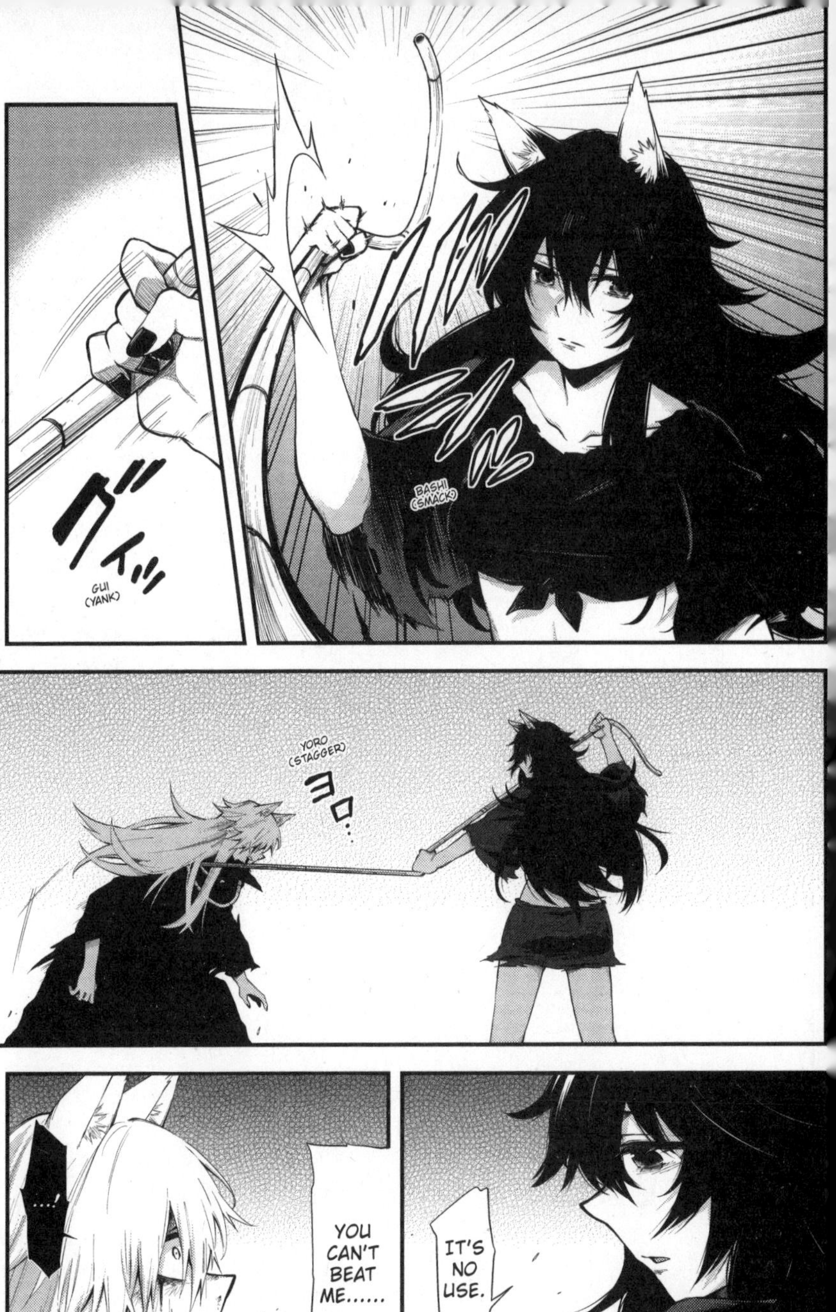
BASHI (SMACK)
GUI (YANK)
ヨロ…
YORO (STAGGER)
IT'S NO USE.
YOU CAN'T BEAT ME......
...!

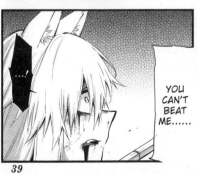

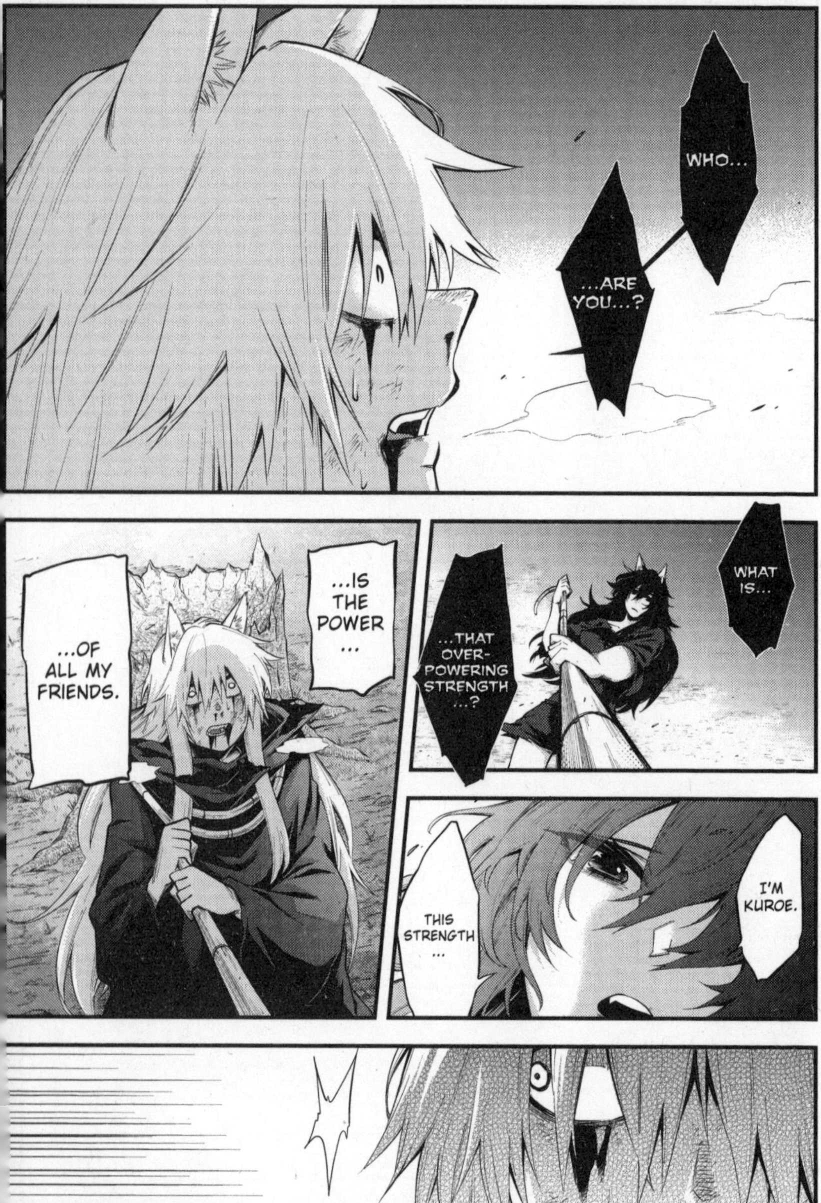
WHO...
...ARE YOU...?
WHAT IS...
...THAT OVER-POWERING STRENGTH ...?
I'M KUROE.
THIS STRENGTH ...
...IS THE POWER ...
...OF ALL MY FRIENDS.

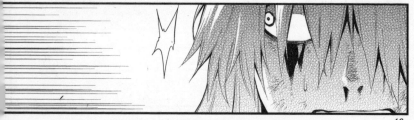

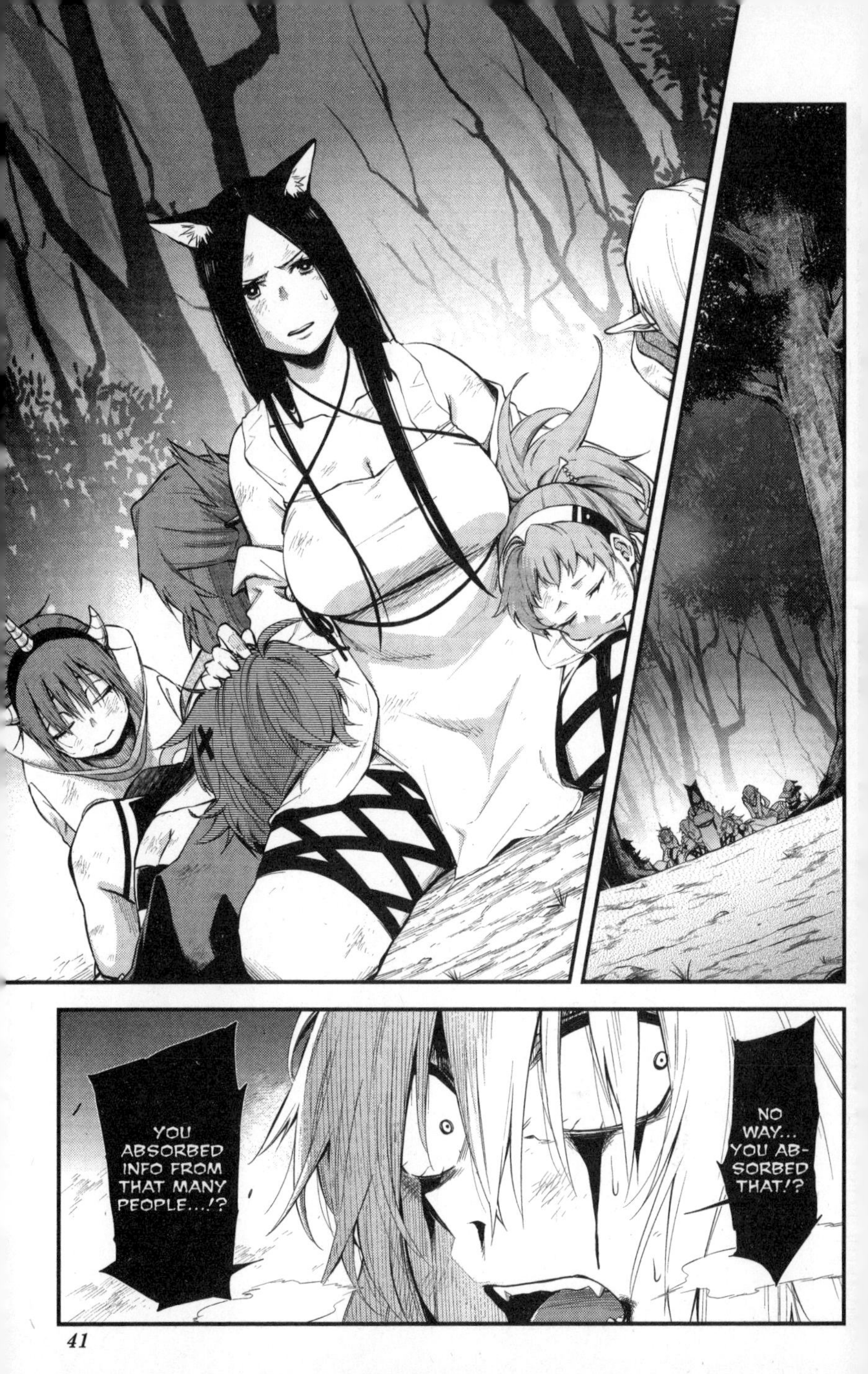
NO WAY... YOU AB-SORBED THAT!?
YOU ABSORBED INFO FROM THAT MANY PEOPLE...!?

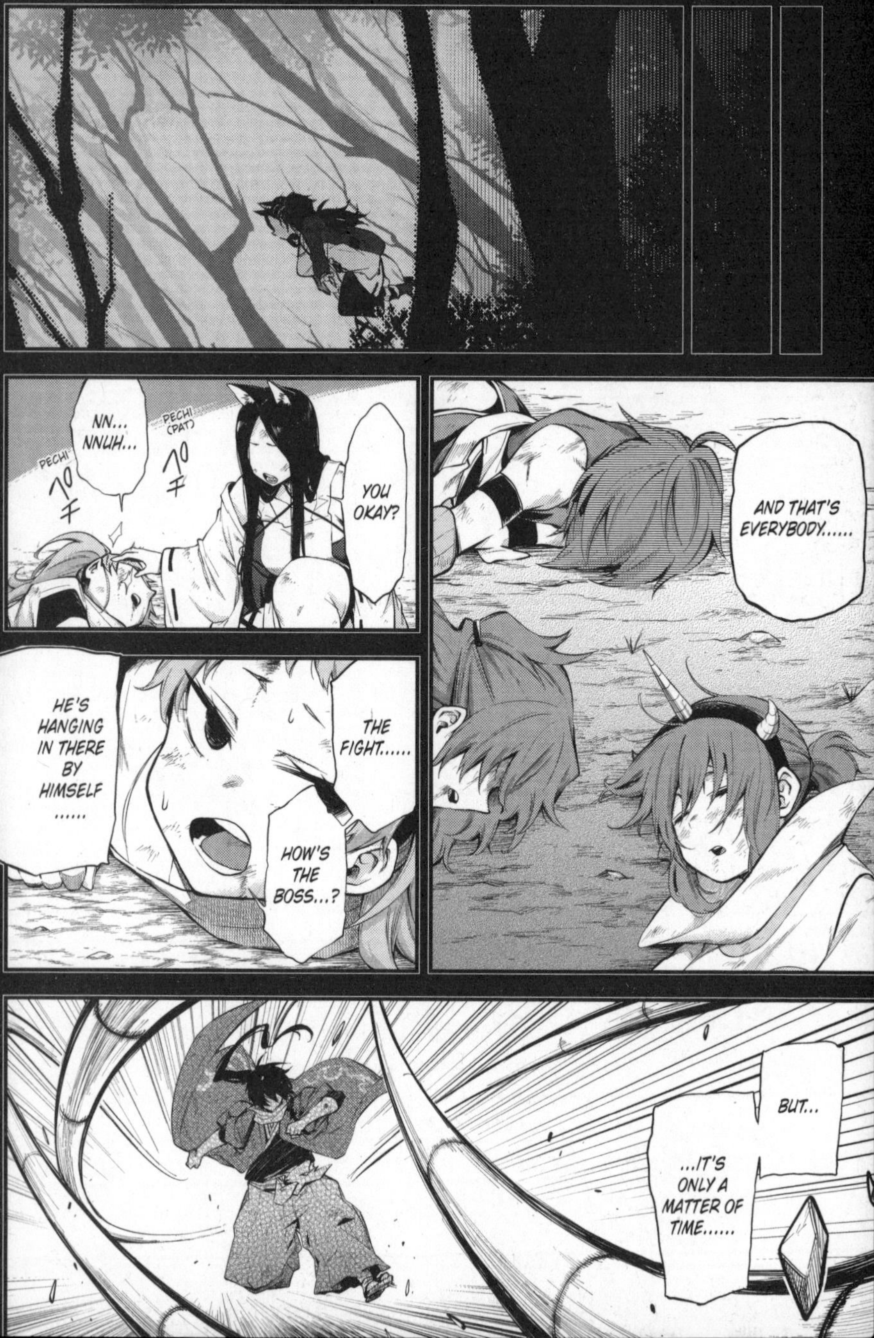
AND THAT'S EVERYBODY......
YOU OKAY?
PECHI (PAT)
NN... NNUH...
PECHI
THE FIGHT......
HOW'S THE BOSS...?
HE'S HANGING IN THERE BY HIMSELF ......
BUT...
...IT'S ONLY A MATTER OF TIME......

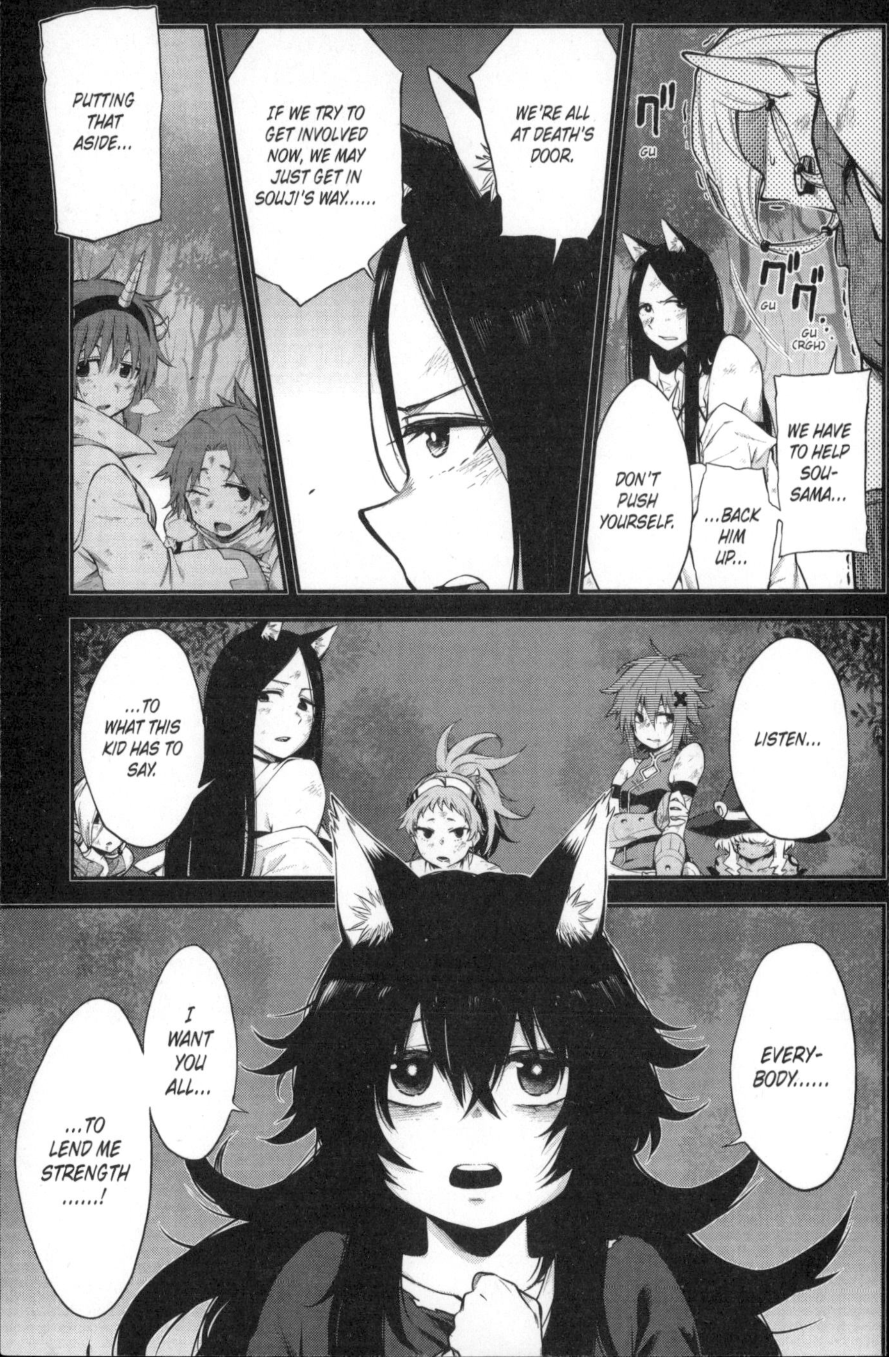
GU
GU
GU (RGH)
WE HAVE TO HELP SOU-SAMA...
...BACK HIM UP...
DON'T PUSH YOURSELF.
WE'RE ALL AT DEATH'S DOOR.
IF WE TRY TO GET INVOLVED NOW, WE MAY JUST GET IN SOUJI'S WAY......
PUTTING THAT ASIDE...
LISTEN...
...TO WHAT THIS KID HAS TO SAY.
EVERY-BODY......
I WANT YOU ALL...
...TO LEND ME STRENGTH ......!

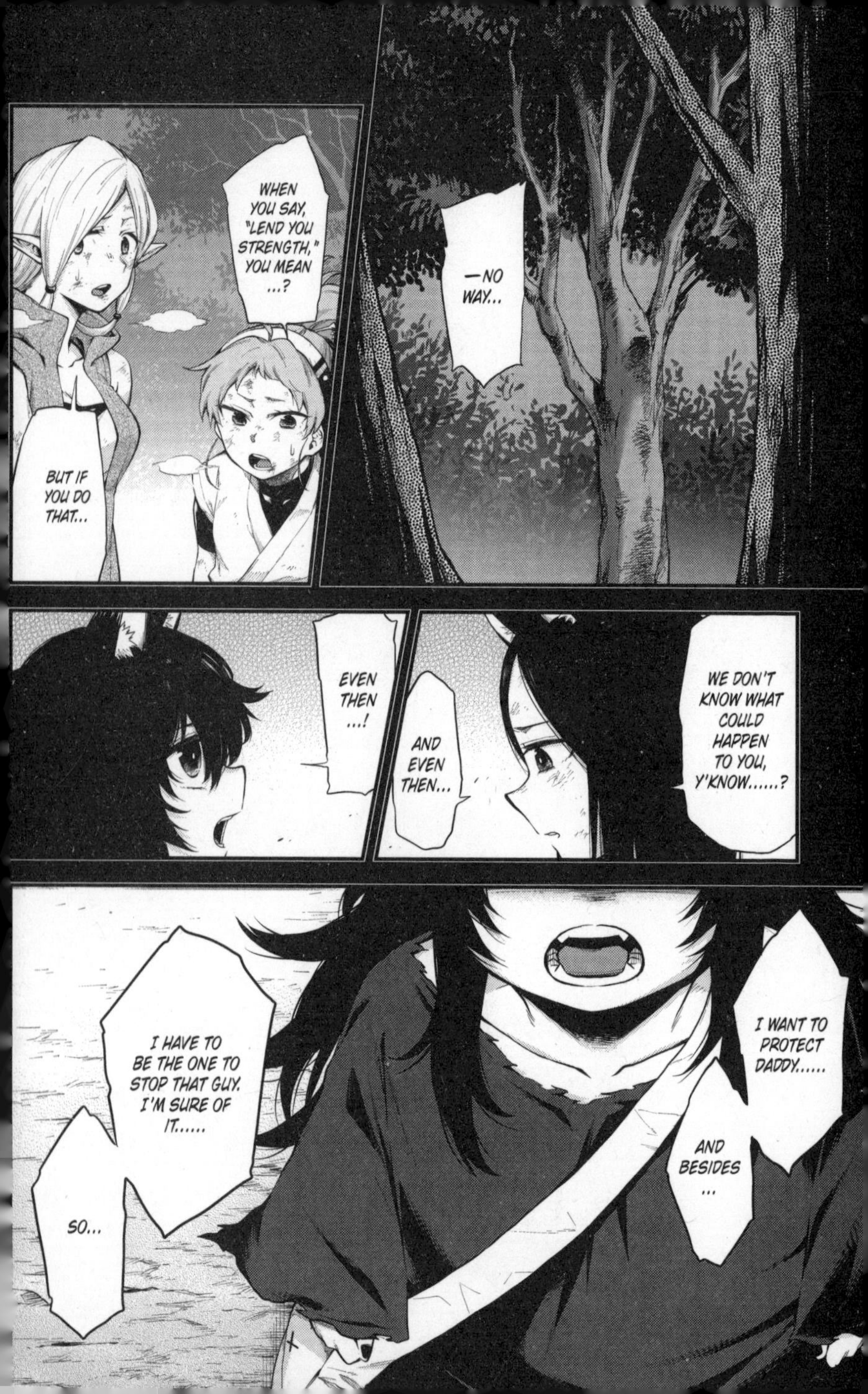
—NO WAY...
WHEN YOU SAY, "LEND YOU STRENGTH," YOU MEAN ...?
BUT IF YOU DO THAT...
WE DON'T KNOW WHAT COULD HAPPEN TO YOU, Y'KNOW......?
AND EVEN THEN...
EVEN THEN ...!
I WANT TO PROTECT DADDY......
AND BESIDES ...
I HAVE TO BE THE ONE TO STOP THAT GUY. I'M SURE OF IT......
SO...

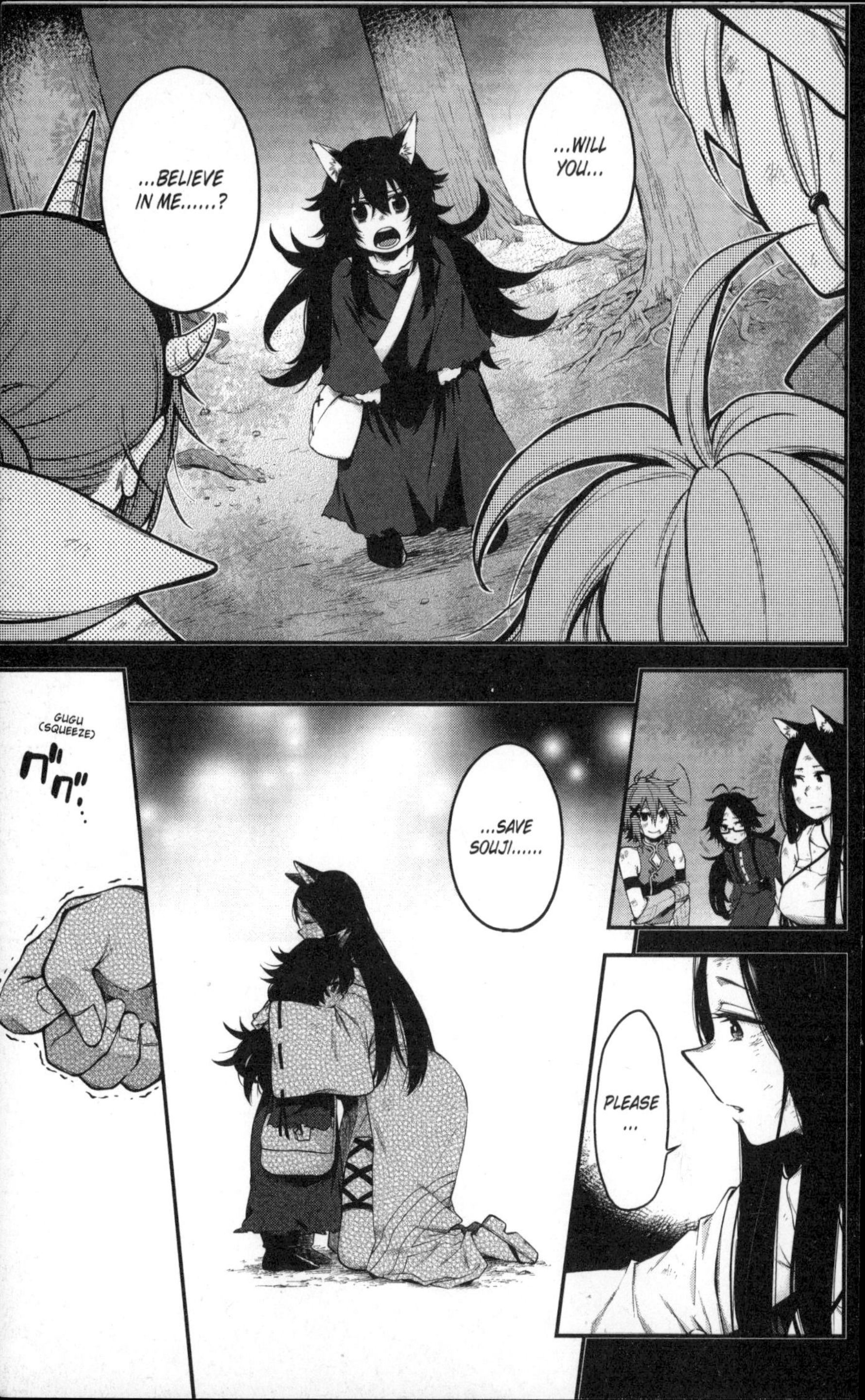
...WILL YOU...
...BELIEVE IN ME......?
PLEASE ...
...SAVE SOUJI......
GUGU (SQUEEZE)
ググ

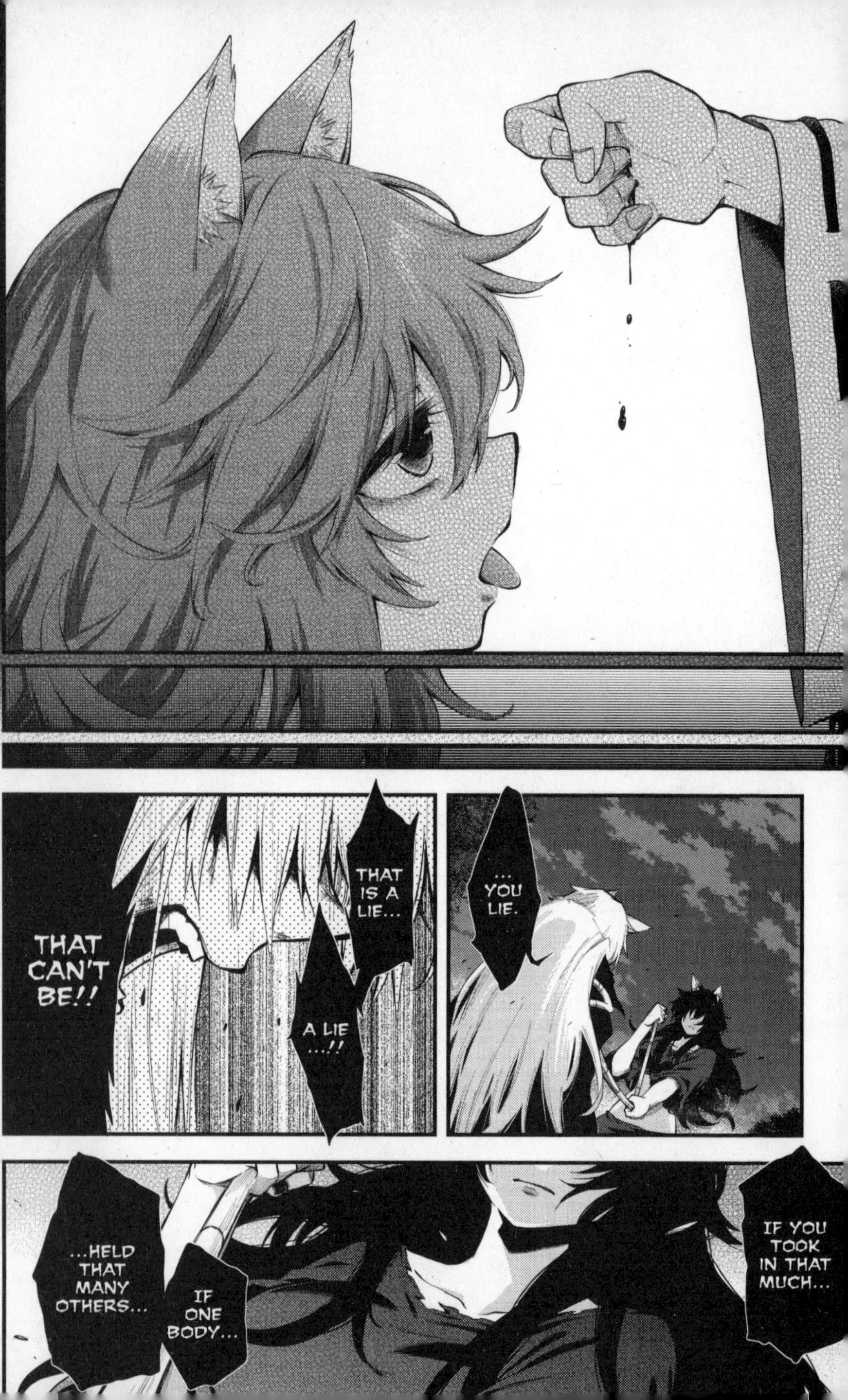
...YOU LIE.
THAT IS A LIE...
THAT CAN'T BE!!
A LIE ...!!
IF YOU TOOK IN THAT MUCH...
IF ONE BODY...
...HELD THAT MANY OTHERS...

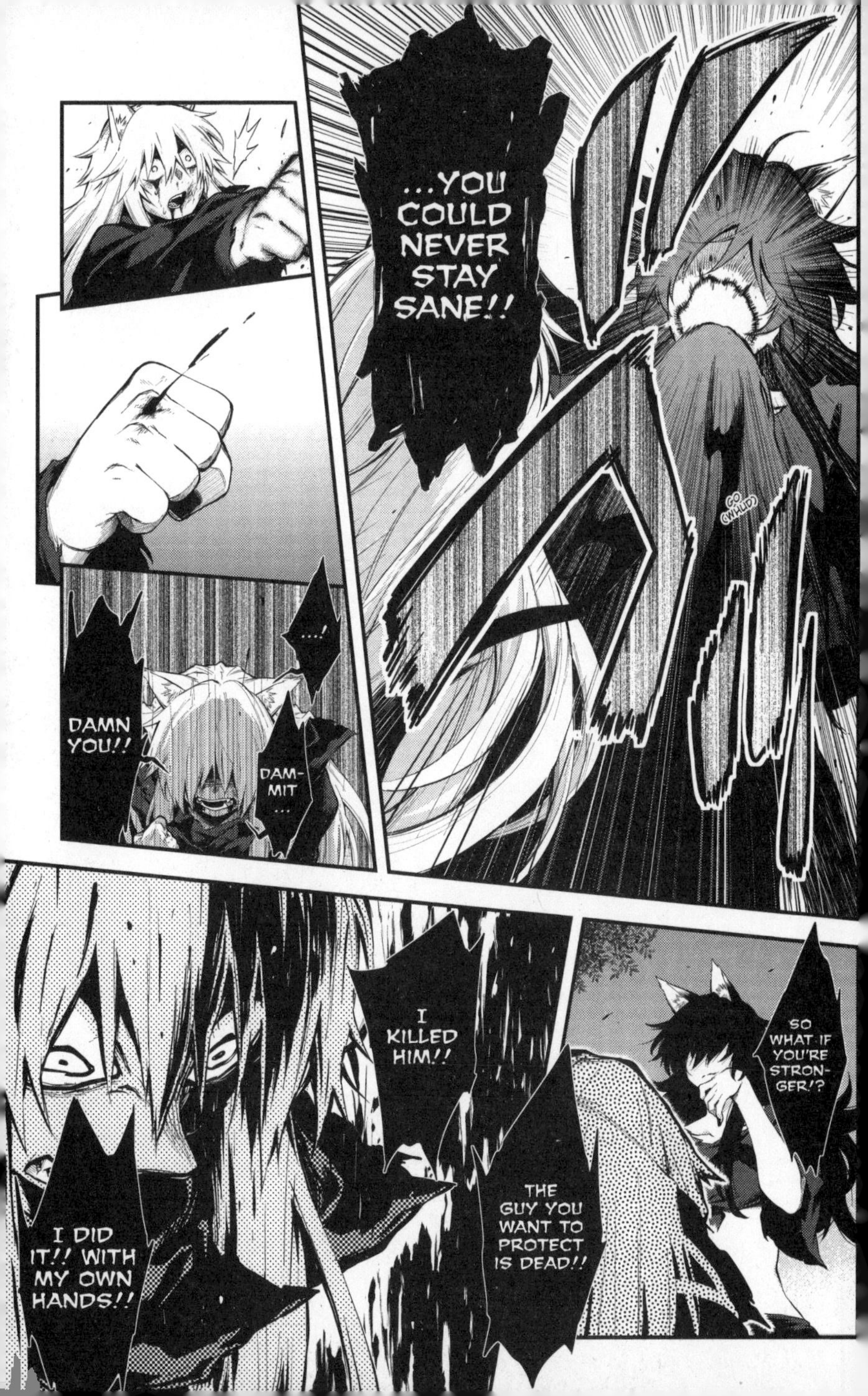

...YOU COULD NEVER STAY SANE!!
GO (WHUD)
......
DAMN YOU!!
DAM-MIT ...
SO WHAT IF YOU'RE STRONGER!?
I KILLED HIM!!
THE GUY YOU WANT TO PROTECT IS DEAD!!
I DID IT!! WITH MY OWN HANDS!!

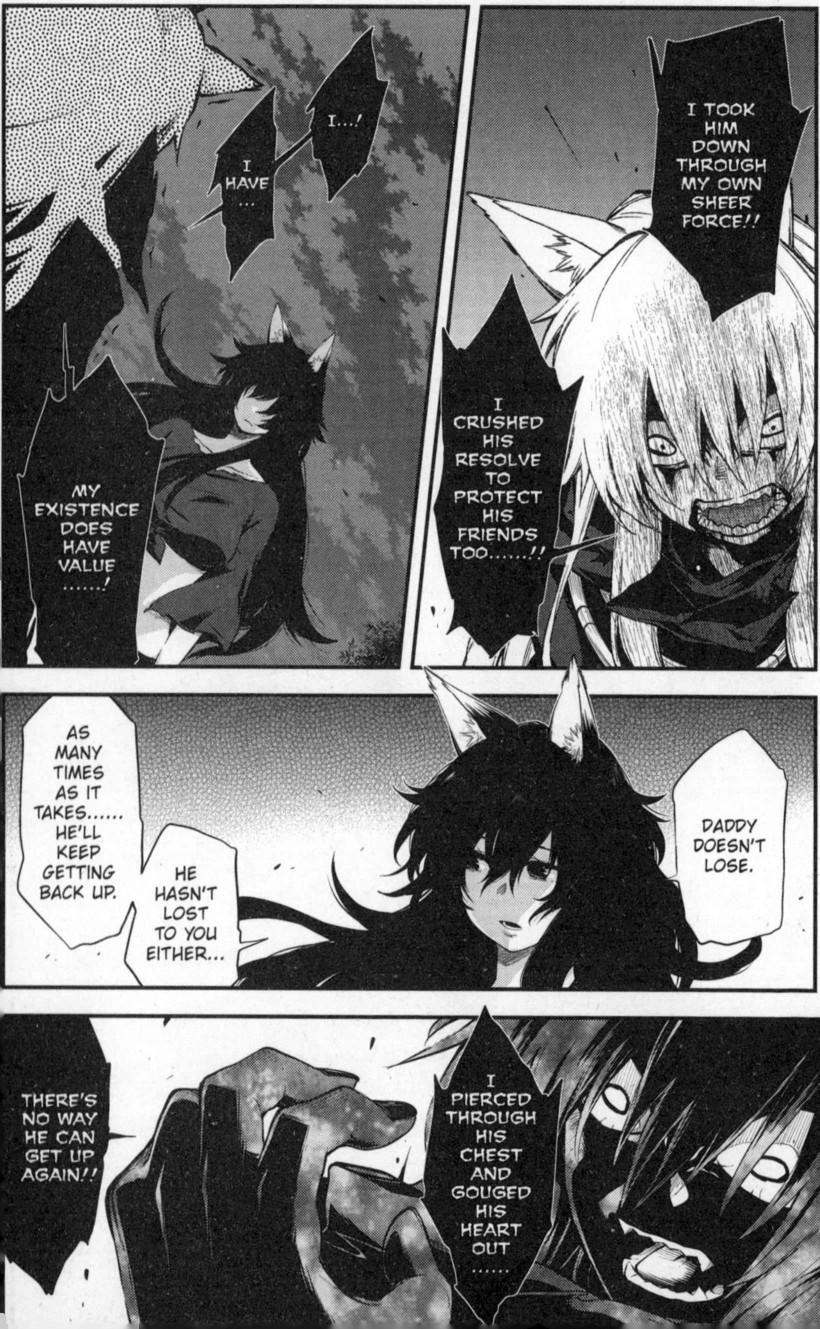
I TOOK HIM DOWN THROUGH MY OWN SHEER FORCE!!
I CRUSHED HIS RESOLVE TO PROTECT HIS FRIENDS TOO......!!
I...!
I HAVE...
MY EXISTENCE DOES HAVE VALUE......!
DADDY DOESN'T LOSE.
HE HASN'T LOST TO YOU EITHER...
AS MANY TIMES AS IT TAKES...... HE'LL KEEP GETTING BACK UP.
I PIERCED THROUGH HIS CHEST AND GOUGED HIS HEART OUT......
THERE'S NO WAY HE CAN GET UP AGAIN!!

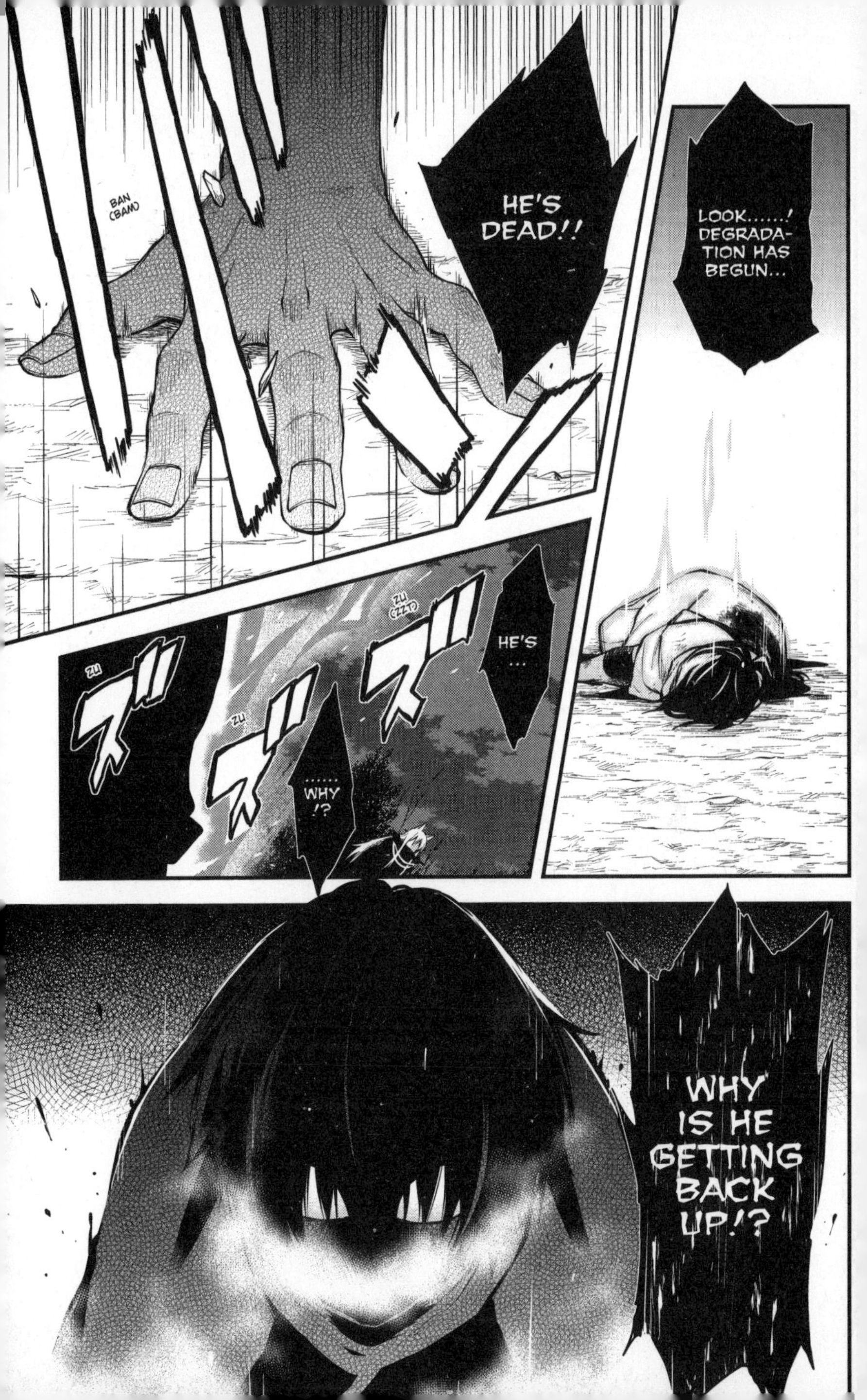
LOOK......! DEGRADATION HAS BEGUN...
BAN (BAM)
HE'S DEAD!!
HE'S ...
ZU (ZZZ)
ZU
ZU
......WHY!?
WHY IS HE GETTING BACK UP!?

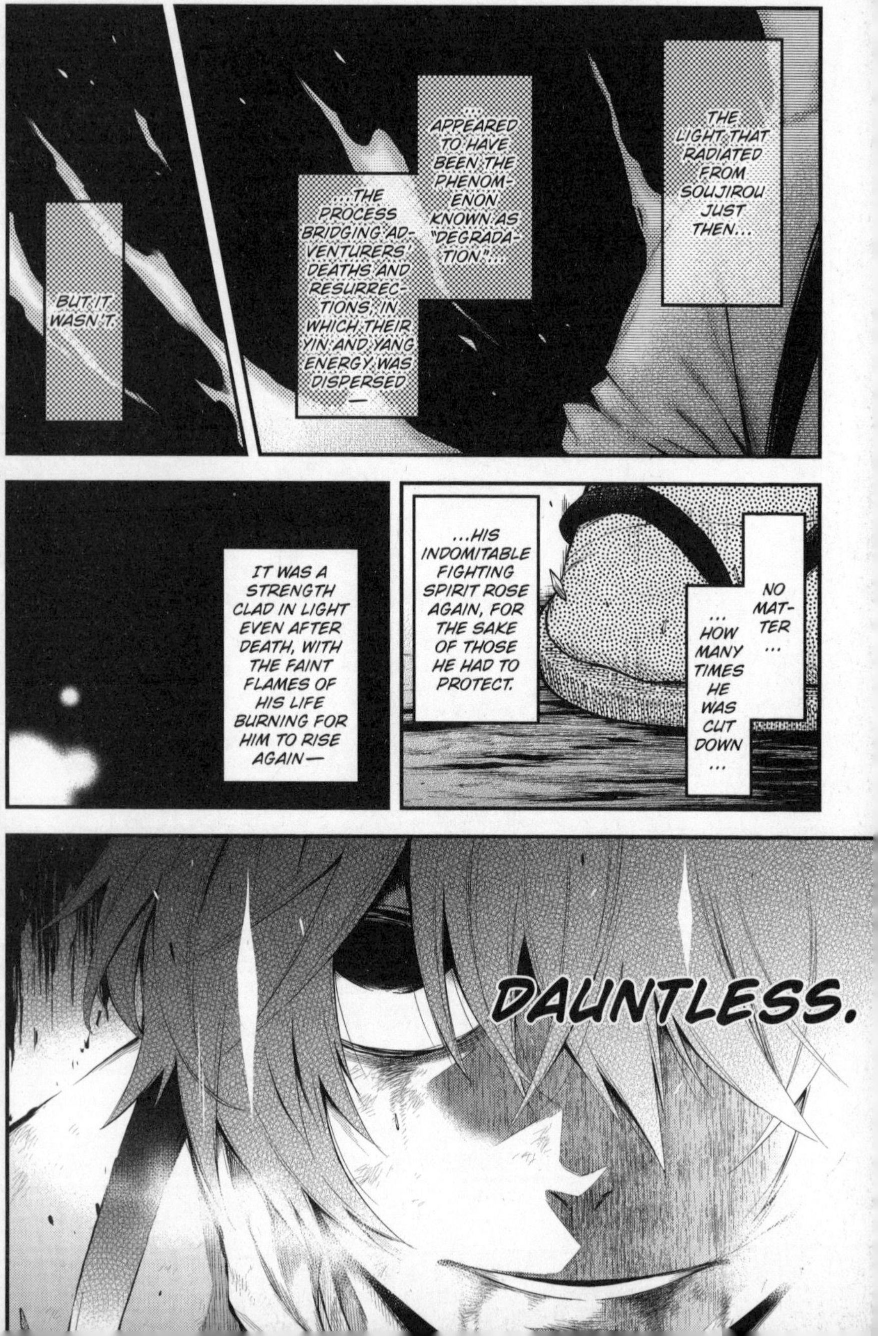
THE LIGHT THAT RADIATED FROM SOUJIROU JUST THEN...
...APPEARED TO HAVE BEEN THE PHENOMENON KNOWN AS "DEGRADATION"...
...THE PROCESS BRIDGING ADVENTURERS' DEATHS AND RESURRECTIONS, IN WHICH THEIR YIN AND YANG ENERGY WAS DISPERSED—
BUT IT WASN'T.
NO MATTER...
...HOW MANY TIMES HE WAS CUT DOWN...
...HIS INDOMITABLE FIGHTING SPIRIT ROSE AGAIN, FOR THE SAKE OF THOSE HE HAD TO PROTECT.
IT WAS A STRENGTH CLAD IN LIGHT EVEN AFTER DEATH, WITH THE FAINT FLAMES OF HIS LIFE BURNING FOR HIM TO RISE AGAIN—
DAUNTLESS.

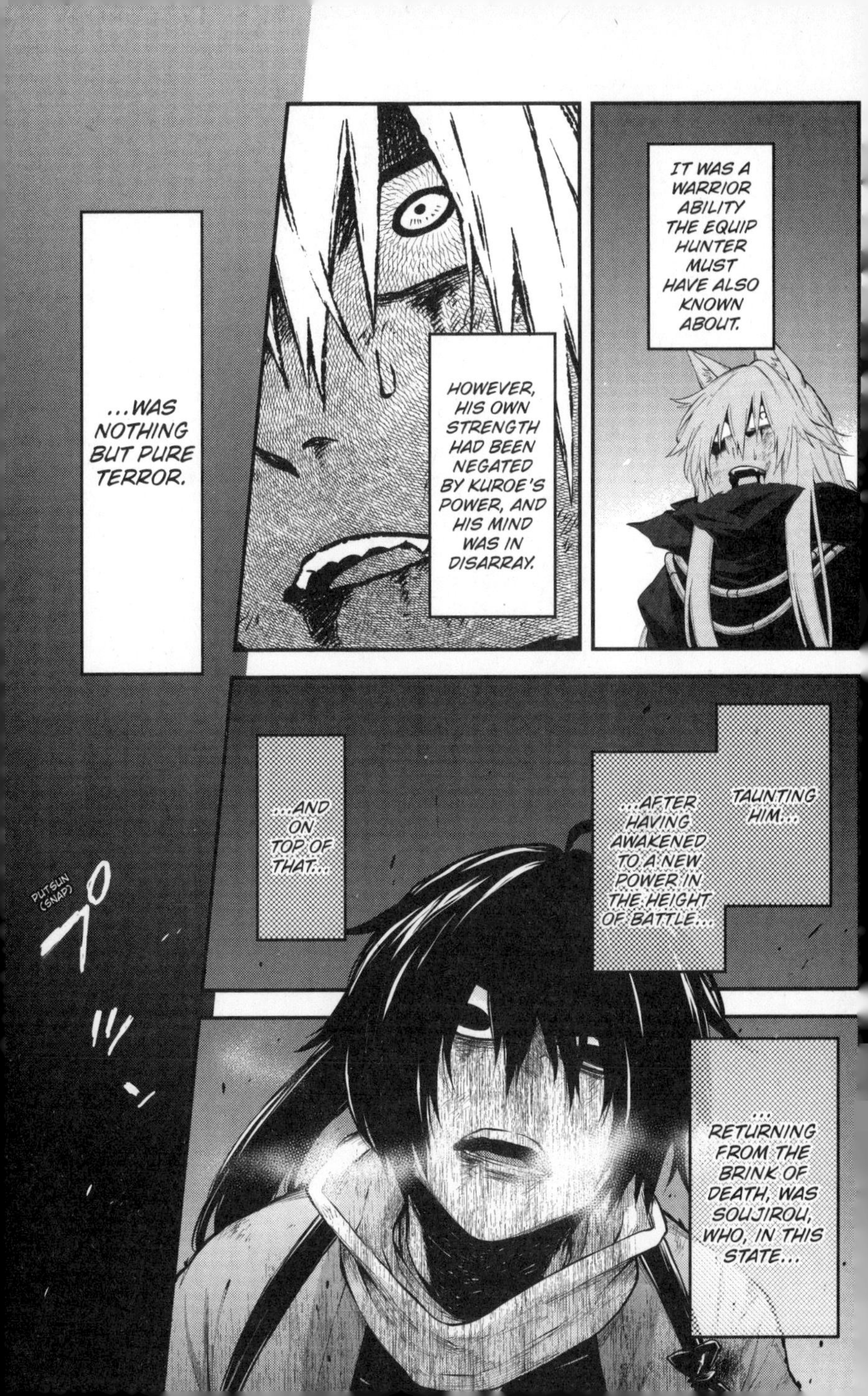
IT WAS A WARRIOR ABILITY THE EQUIP HUNTER MUST HAVE ALSO KNOWN ABOUT.
HOWEVER, HIS OWN STRENGTH HAD BEEN NEGATED BY KUROE'S POWER, AND HIS MIND WAS IN DISARRAY.
...WAS NOTHING BUT PURE TERROR.
TAUNTING HIM...
...AFTER HAVING AWAKENED TO A NEW POWER IN THE HEIGHT OF BATTLE...
...AND ON TOP OF THAT...
PUTSUN (SNAP)
... RETURNING FROM THE BRINK OF DEATH, WAS SOUJIROU, WHO, IN THIS STATE...

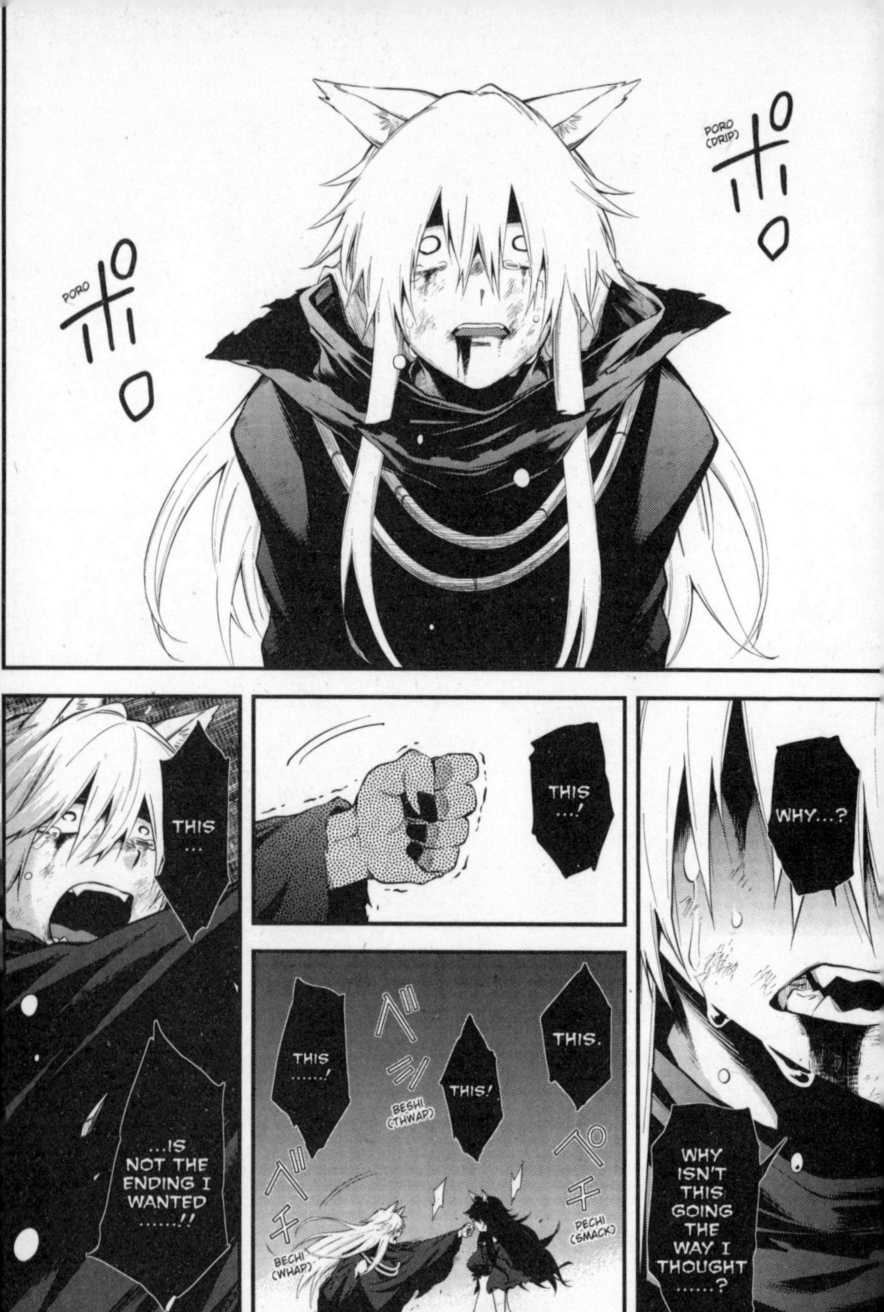
PORO (DRIP)
PORO
WHY...?
WHY ISN'T THIS GOING THE WAY I THOUGHT......?
THIS ....!
THIS.
PECHI (SMACK)
THIS!
BESHI (THWAP)
THIS......!
BECHI (WHAP)
THIS...
...IS NOT THE ENDING I WANTED......!!

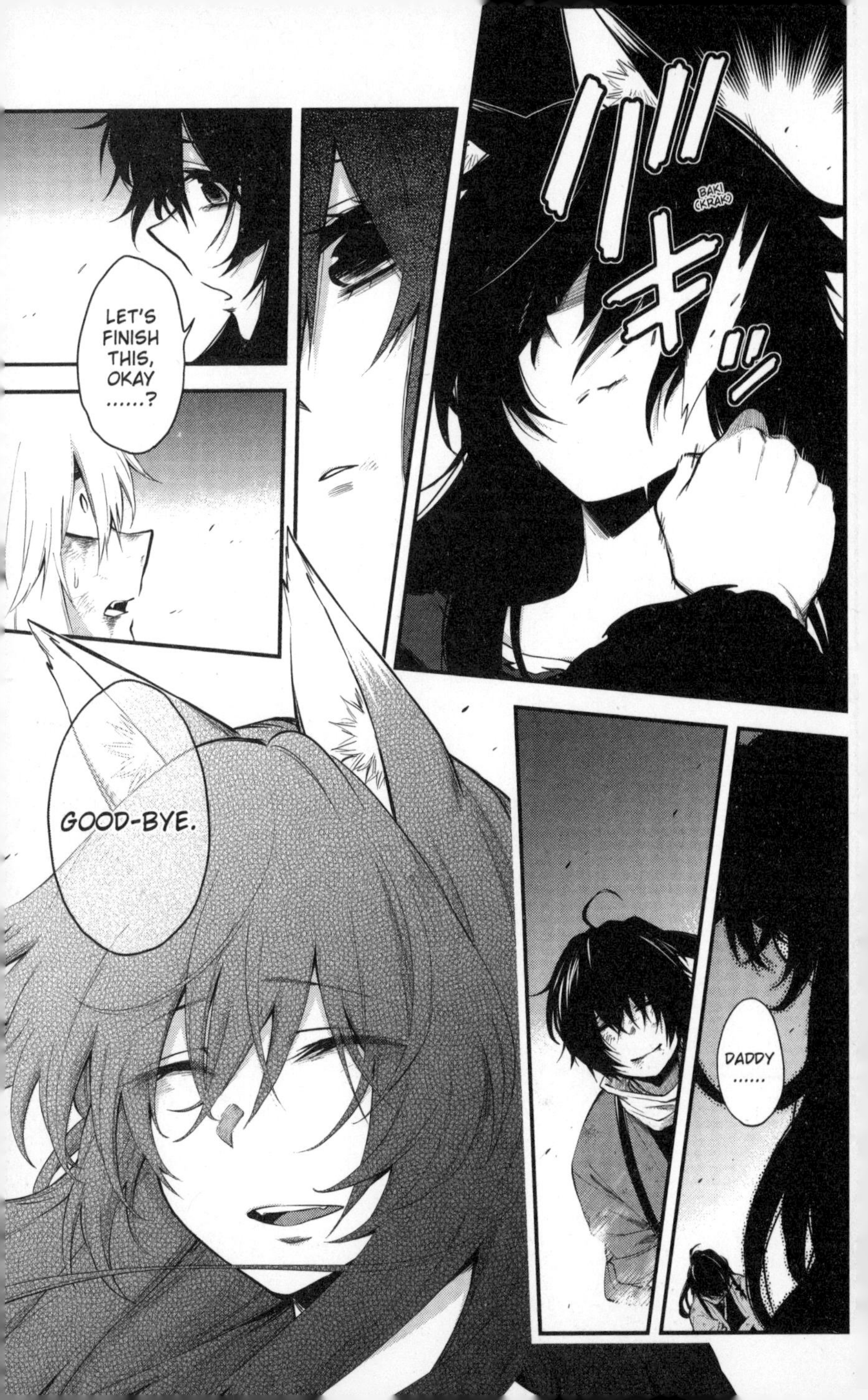
BAKI (KRAK)
LET'S FINISH THIS, OKAY ......?
DADDY ......
GOOD-BYE.

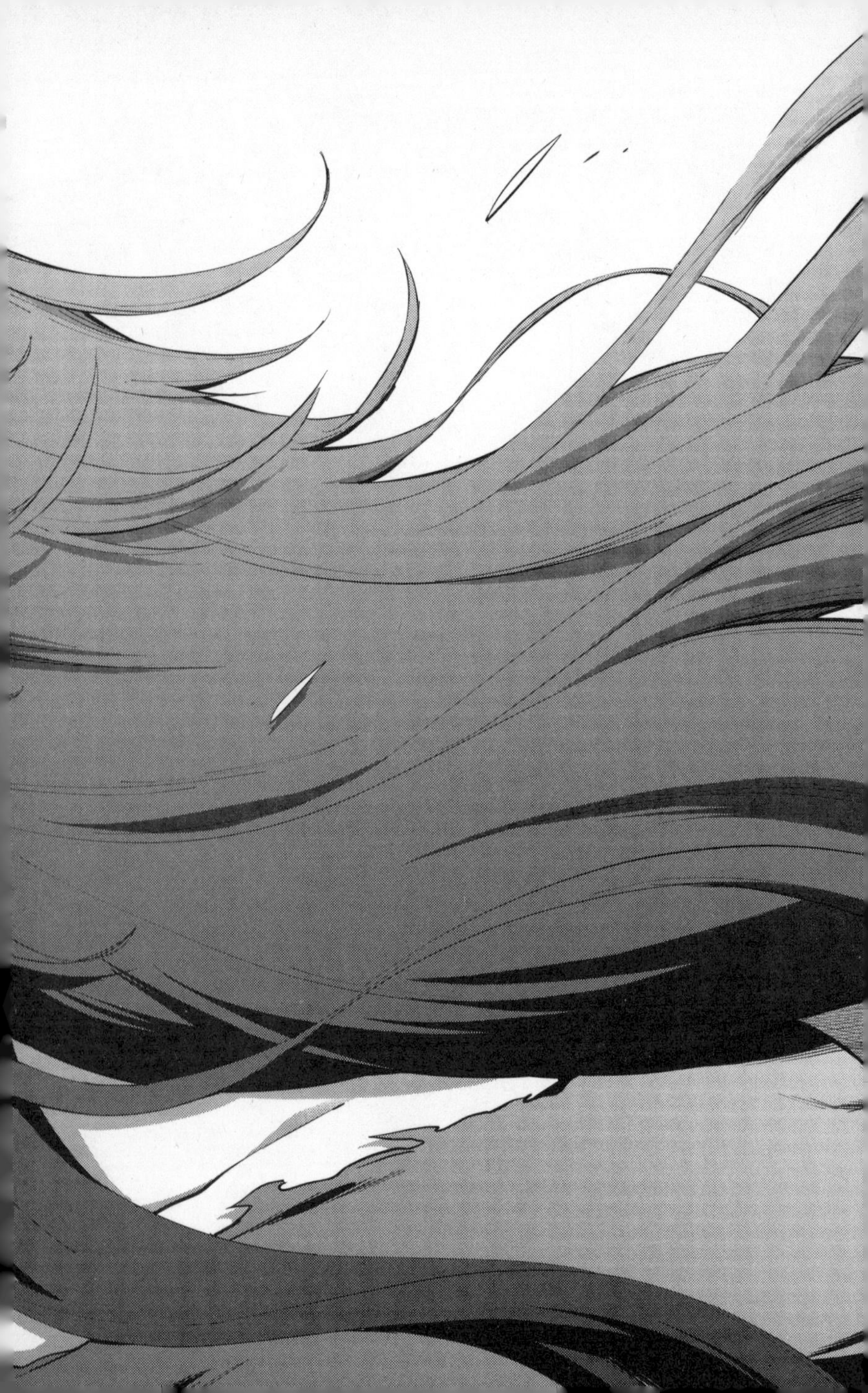

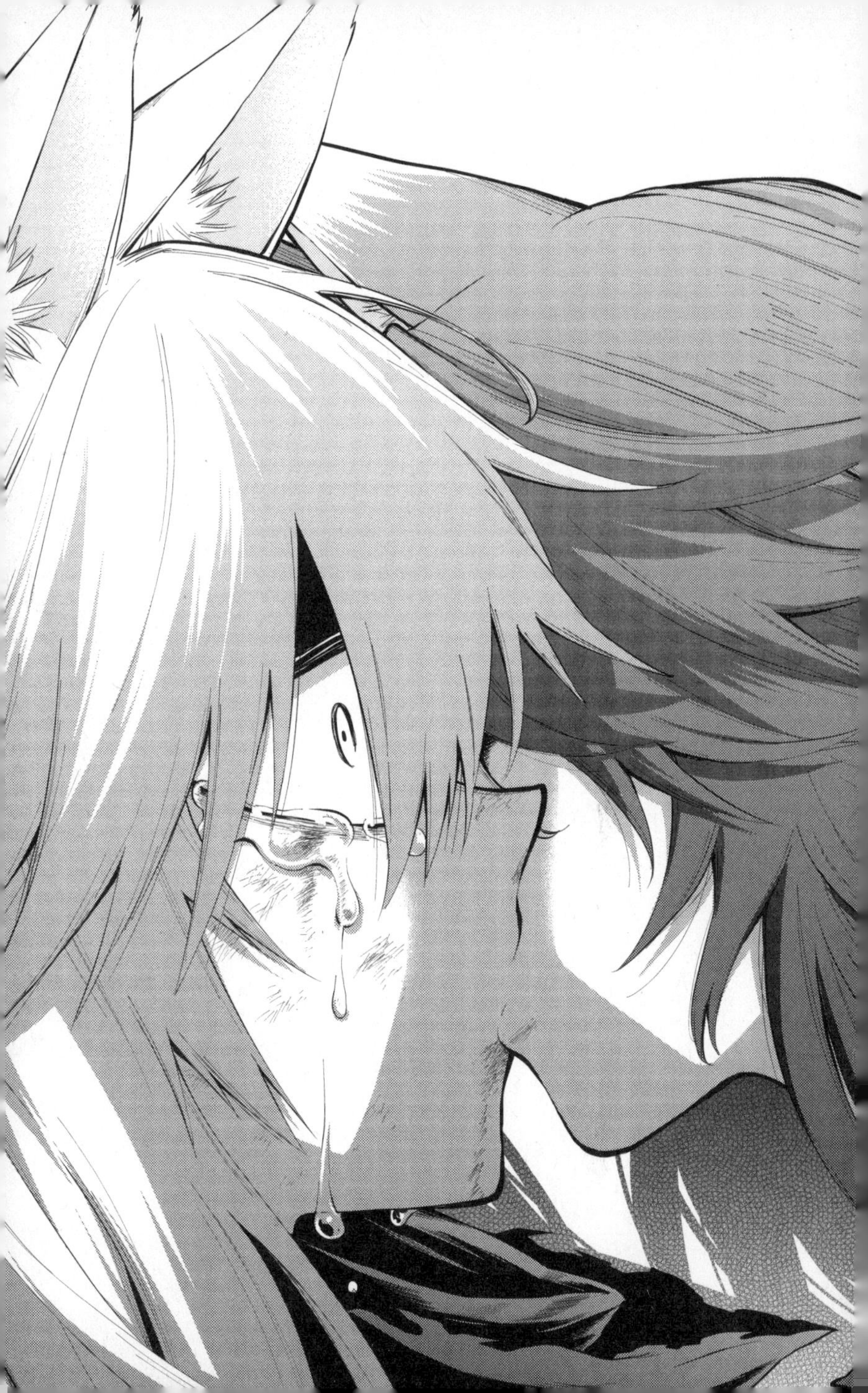

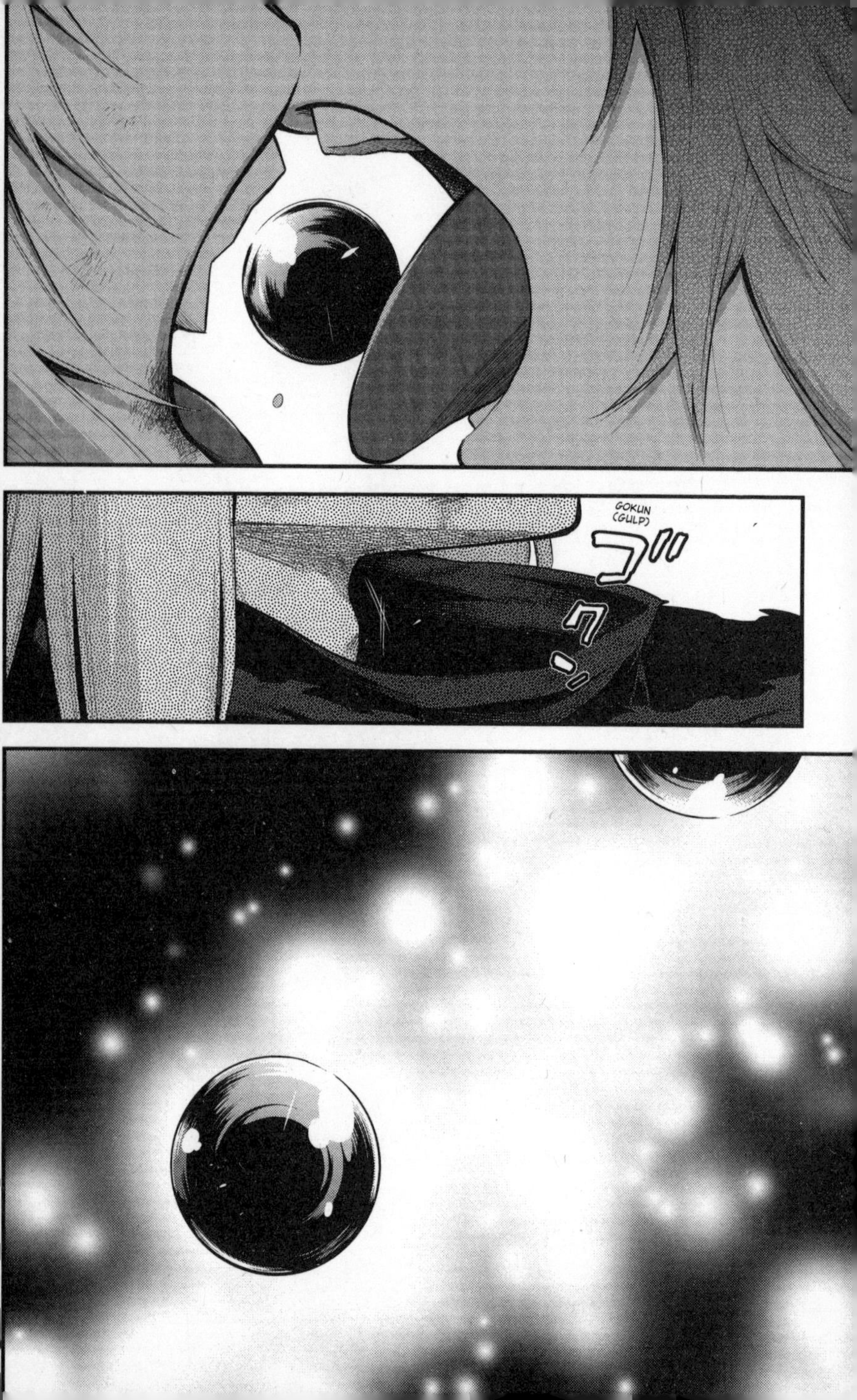
GOKUN
(GULP)

LOG HORIZON

THE WEST WIND BRIGADE

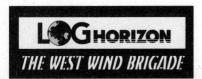

LOG HORIZON
THE WEST WIND BRIGADE

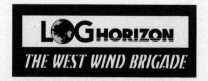

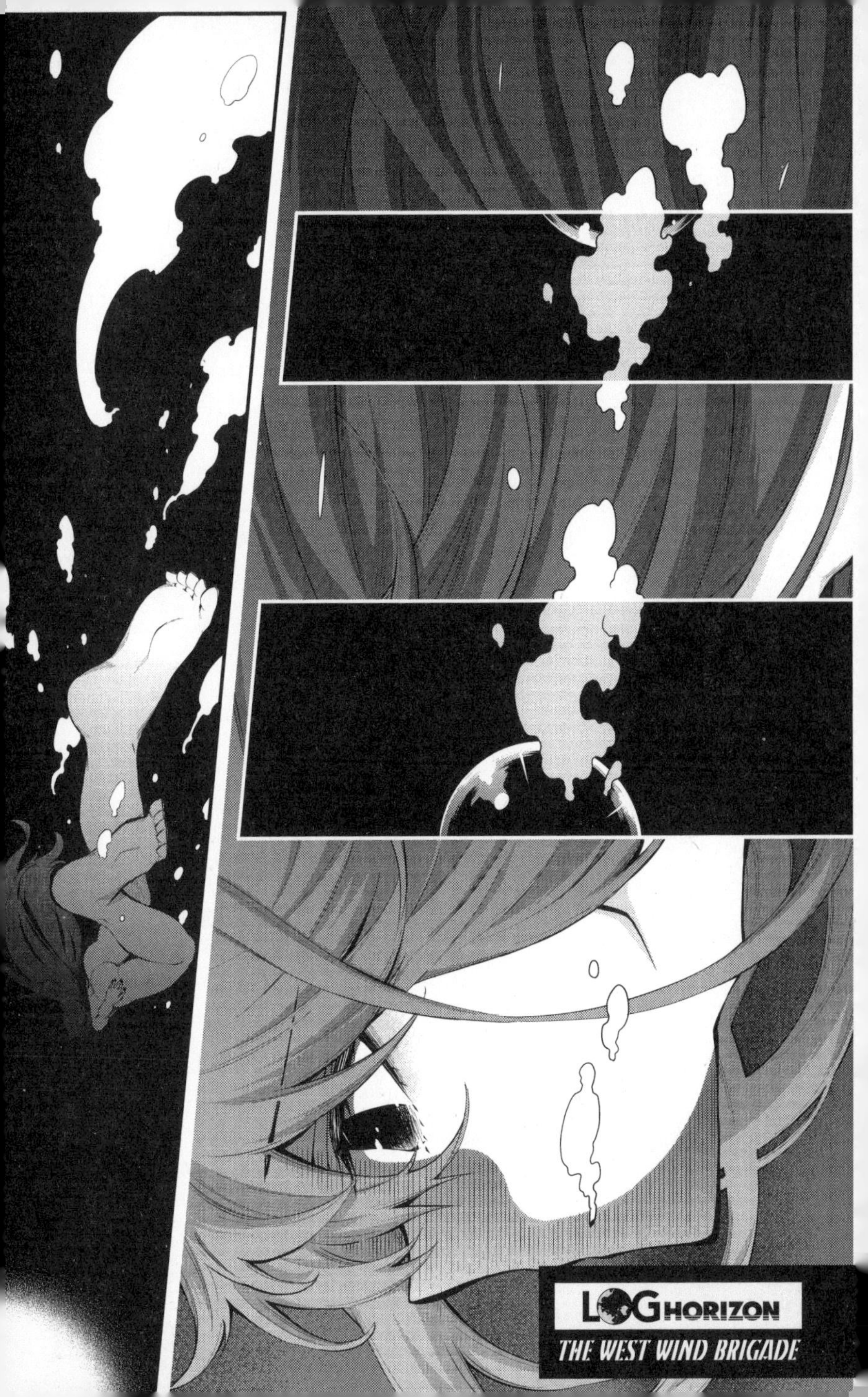
LOG HORIZON
THE WEST WIND BRIGADE

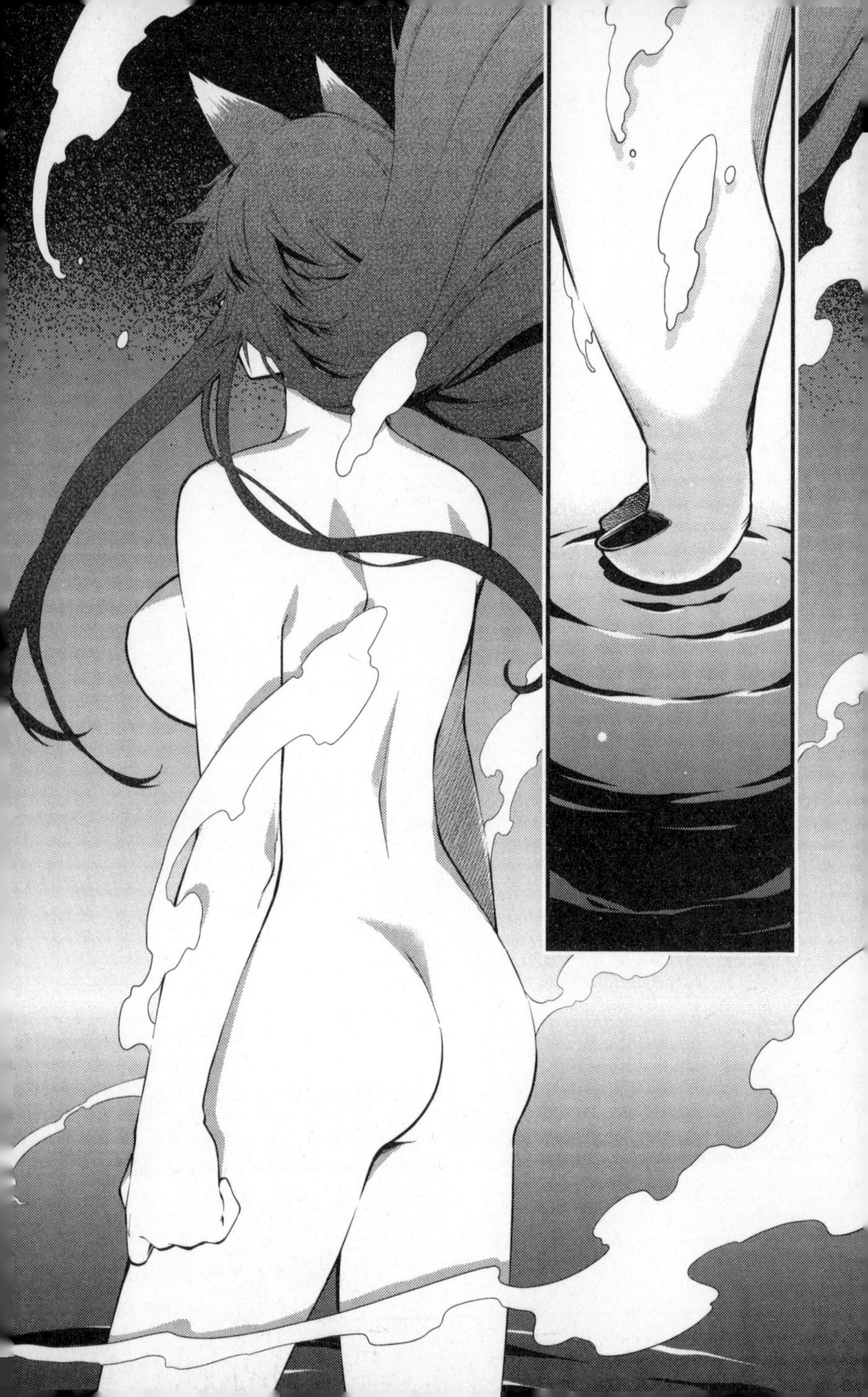

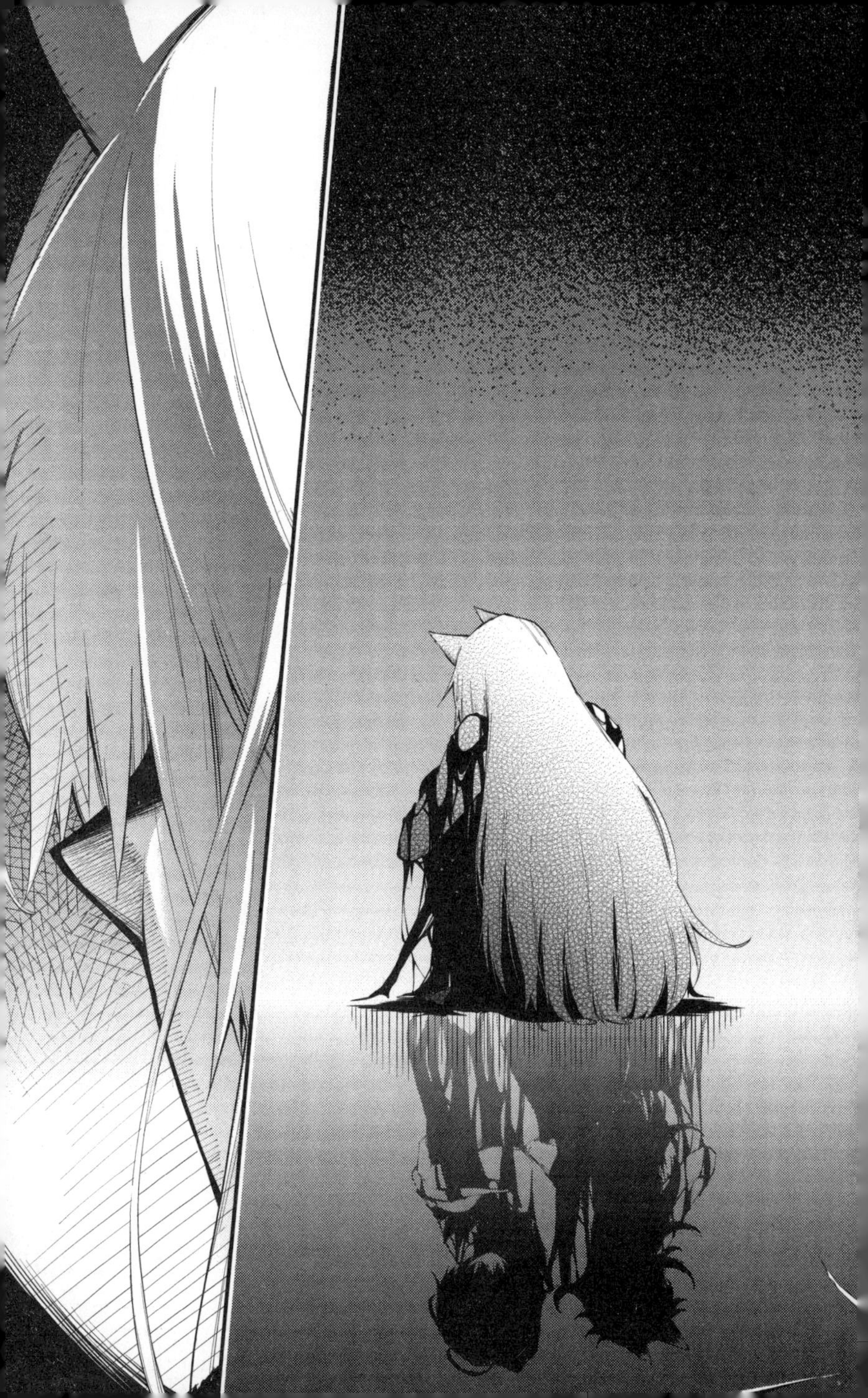

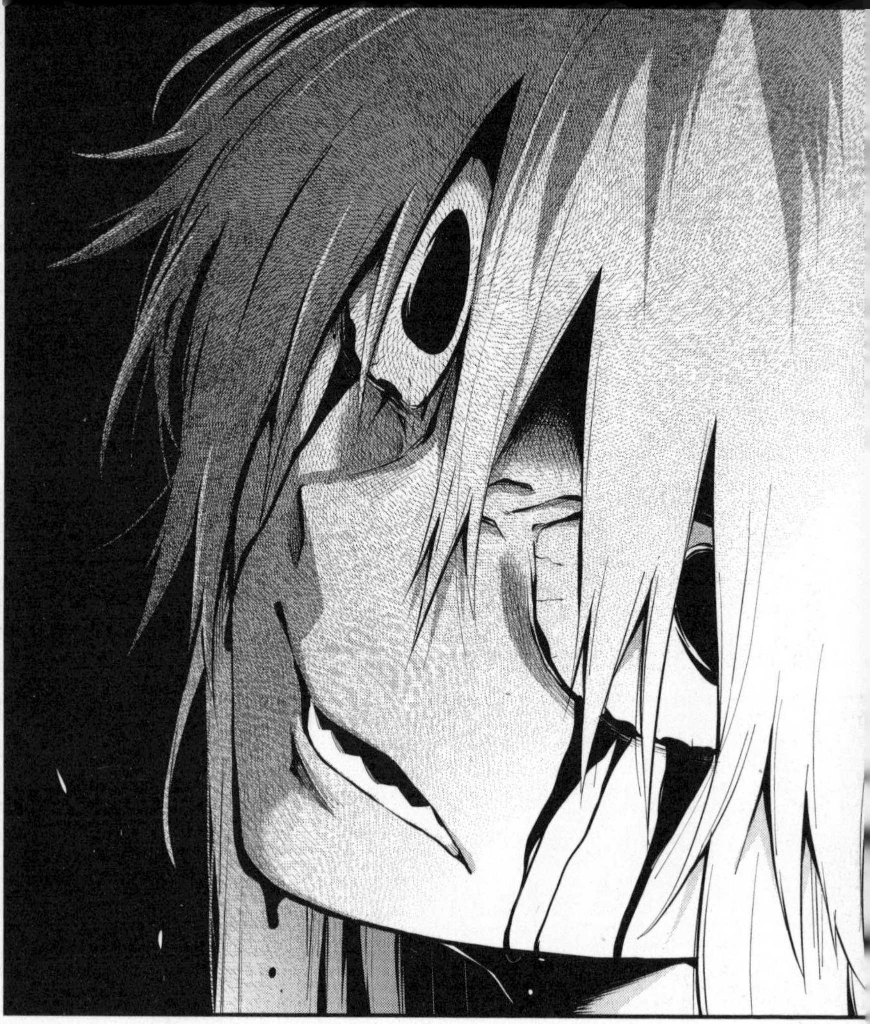

CHAPTER : 62 Even If You Hate Yourself...

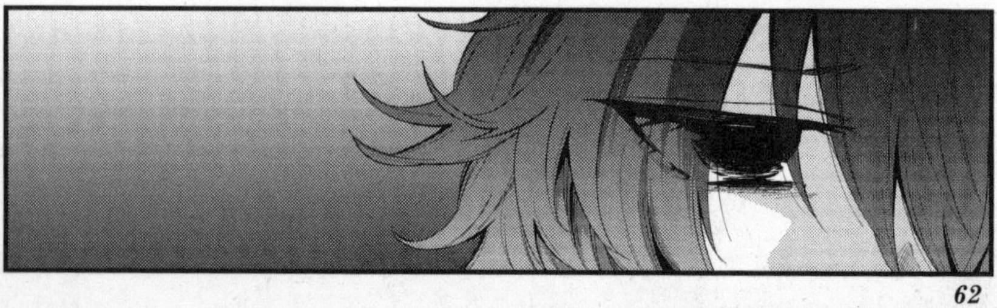

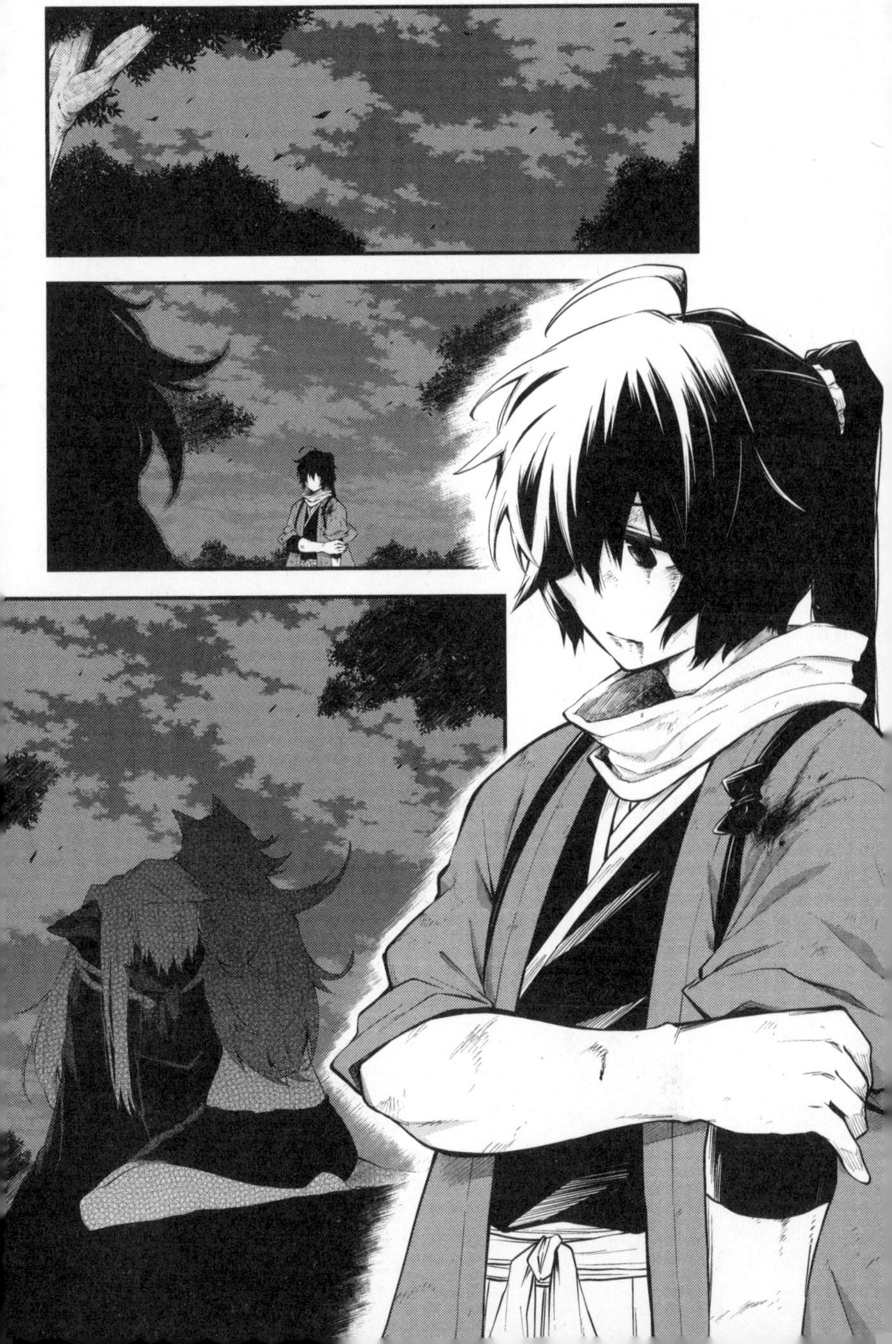

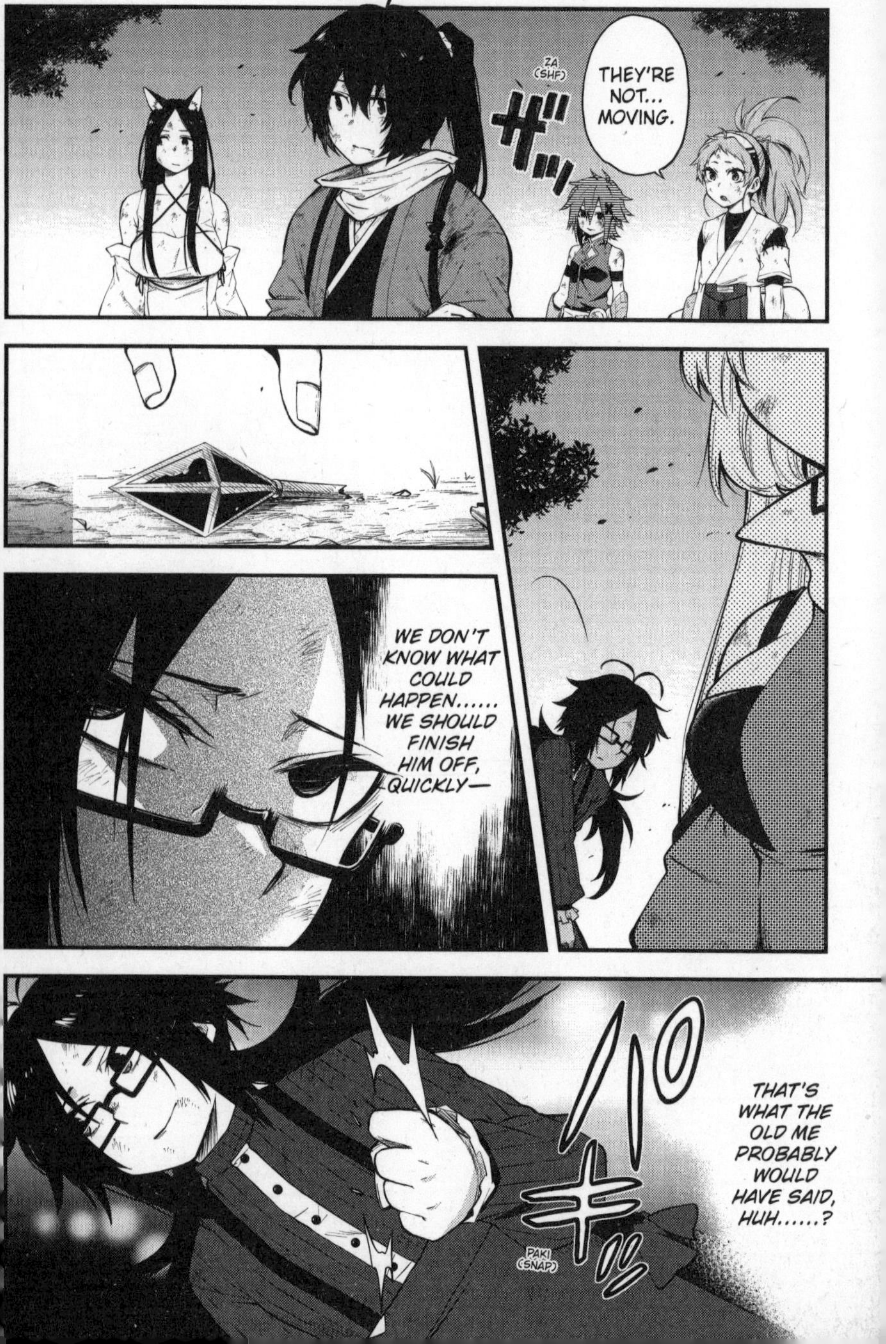
THEY'RE NOT... MOVING.
ZA (SHF)
WE DON'T KNOW WHAT COULD HAPPEN...... WE SHOULD FINISH HIM OFF, QUICKLY—
THAT'S WHAT THE OLD ME PROBABLY WOULD HAVE SAID, HUH......?
PAKI (SNAP)

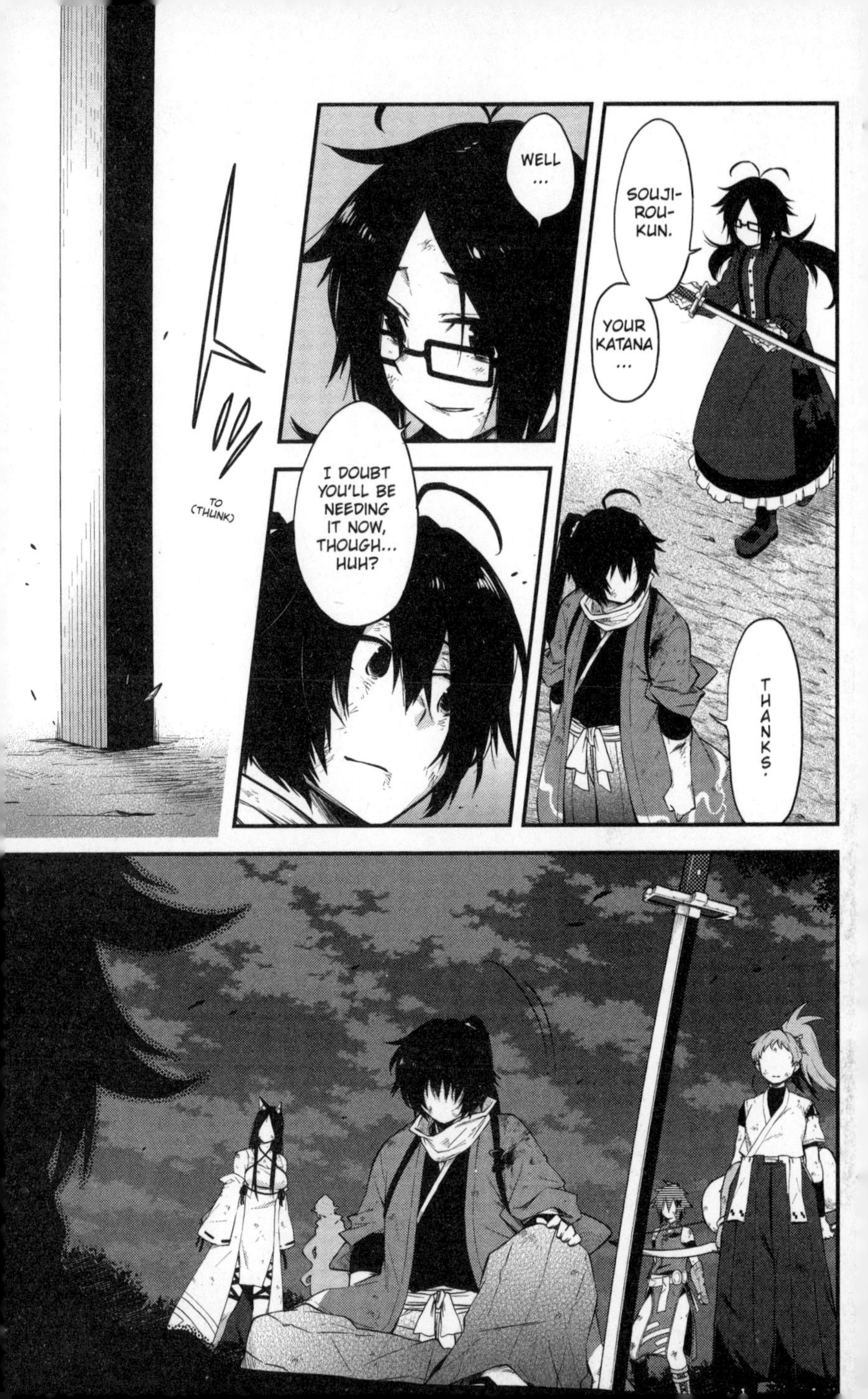
SOUJI-ROU-KUN.
YOUR KATANA...
THANKS.
WELL...
I DOUBT YOU'LL BE NEEDING IT NOW, THOUGH... HUH?
TO (THUNK)

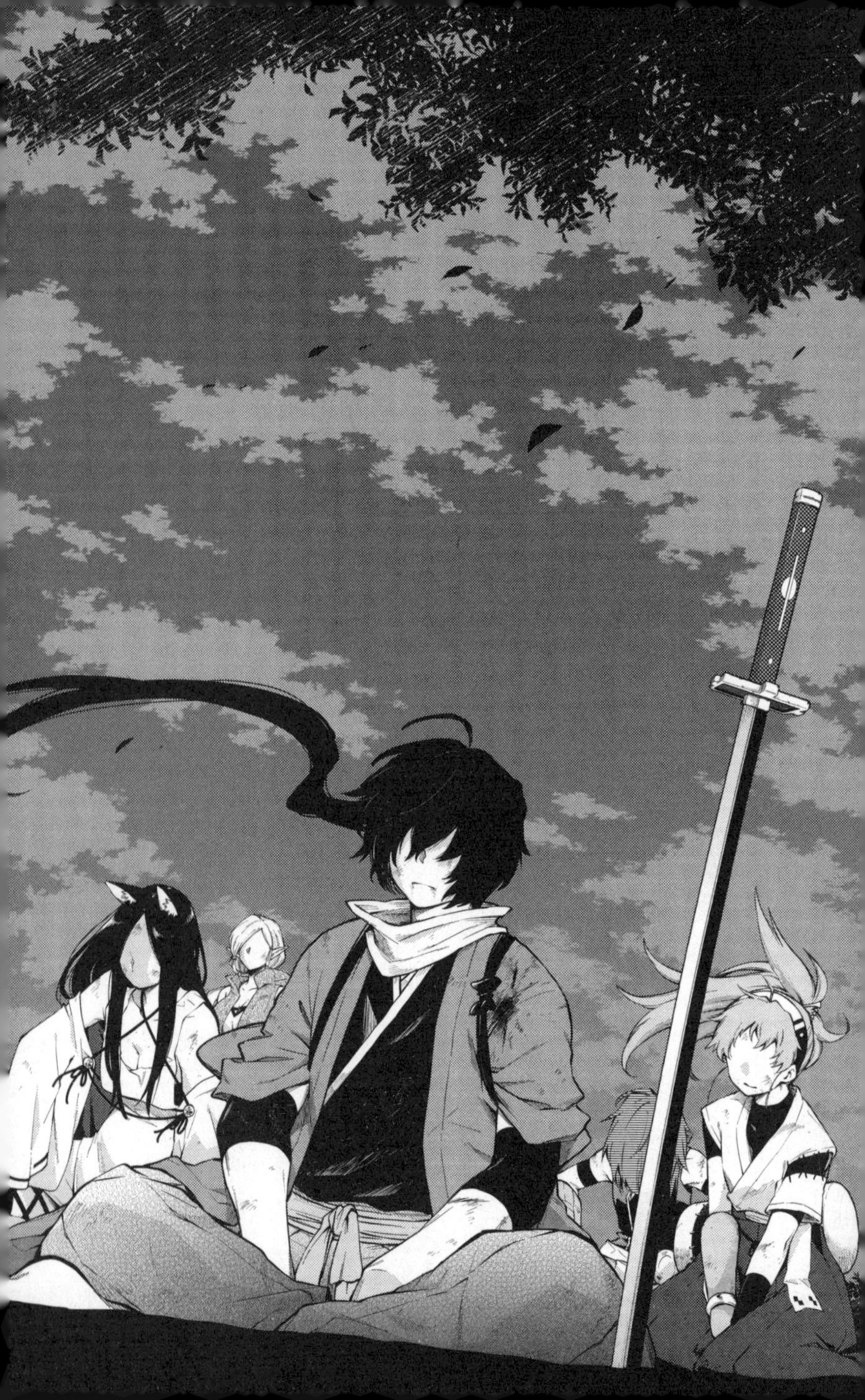

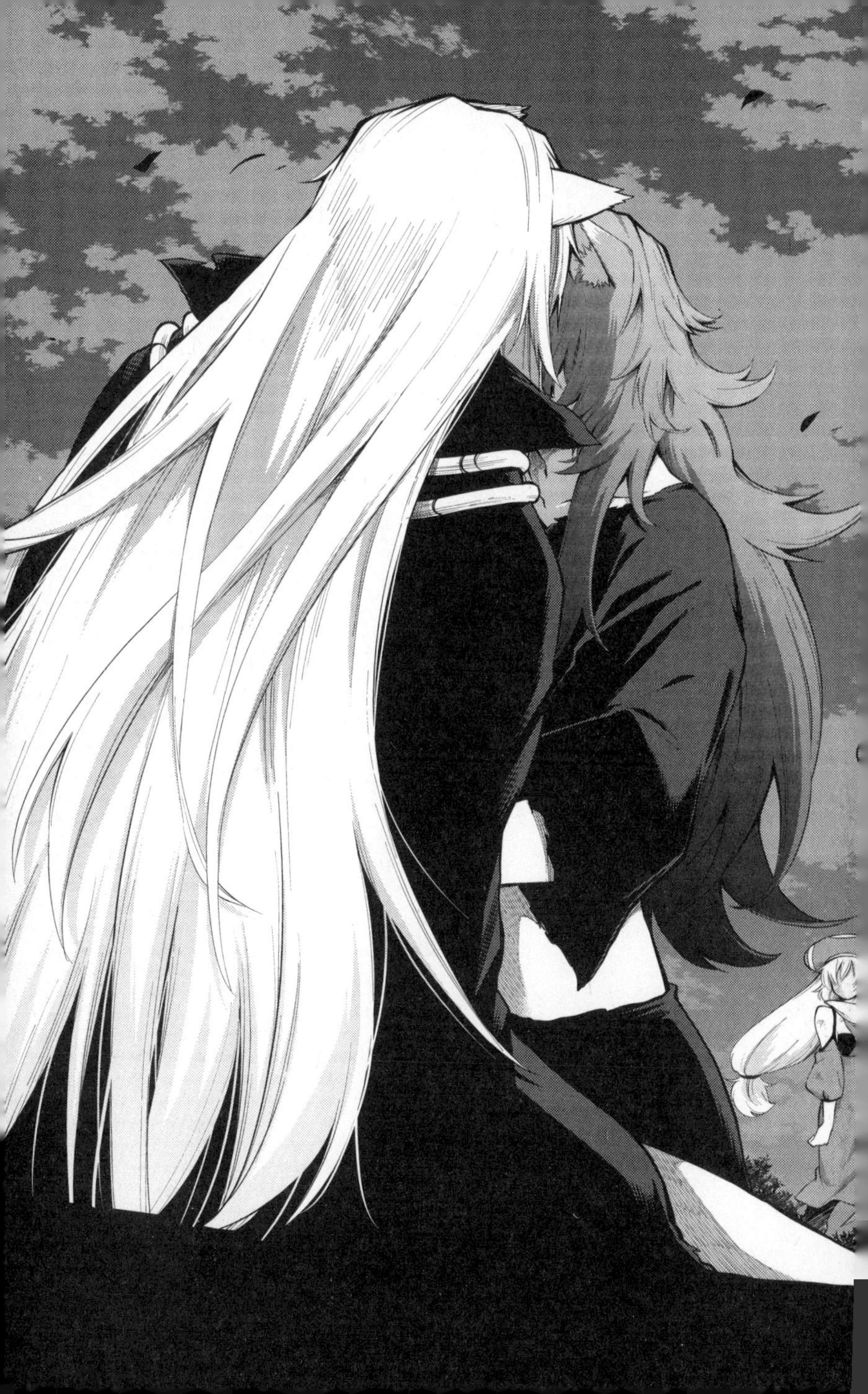

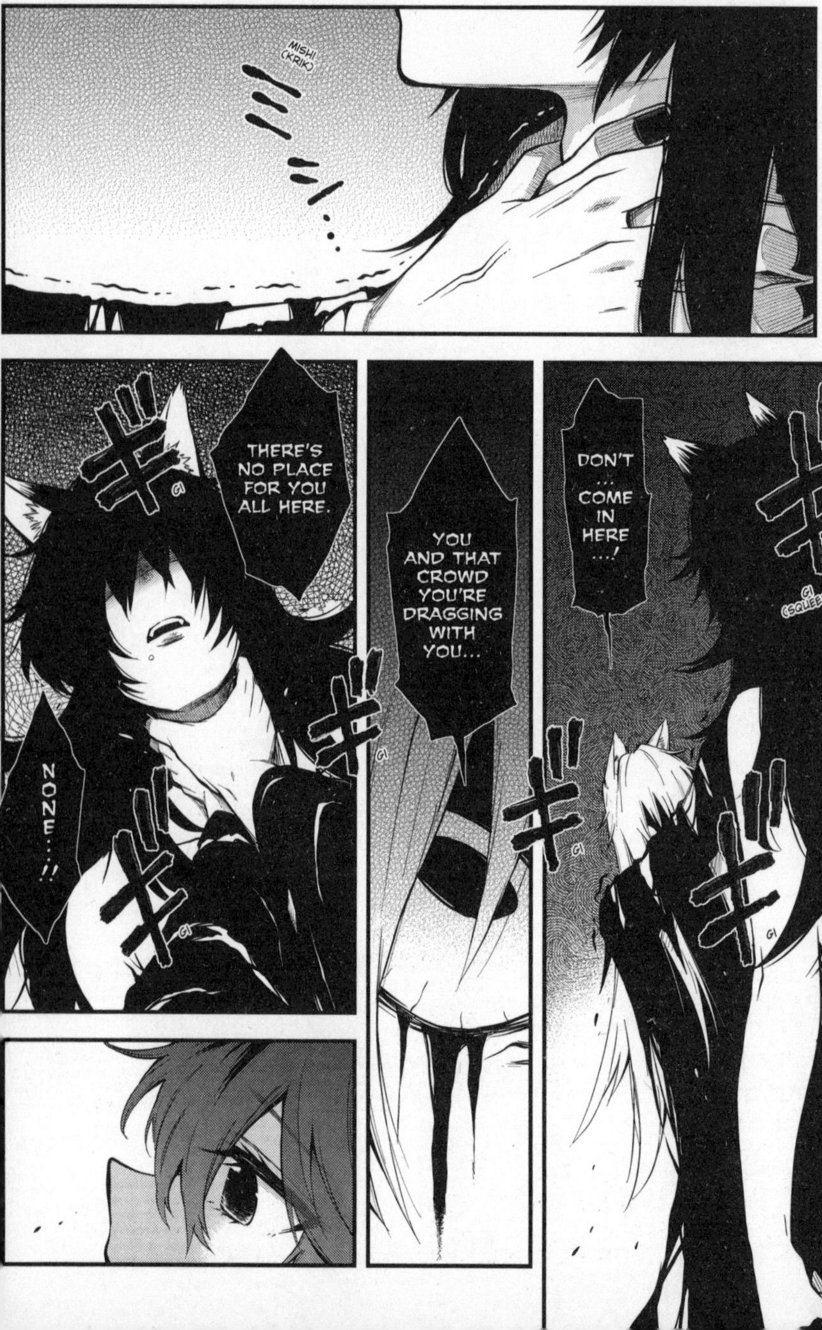
MISHI (KRIK)
DON'T ... COME IN HERE ...!
GI (SQUEEZE)
GI
GI
YOU AND THAT CROWD YOU'RE DRAGGING WITH YOU...
THERE'S NO PLACE FOR YOU ALL HERE.
GI
GI
NONE...!!
GI

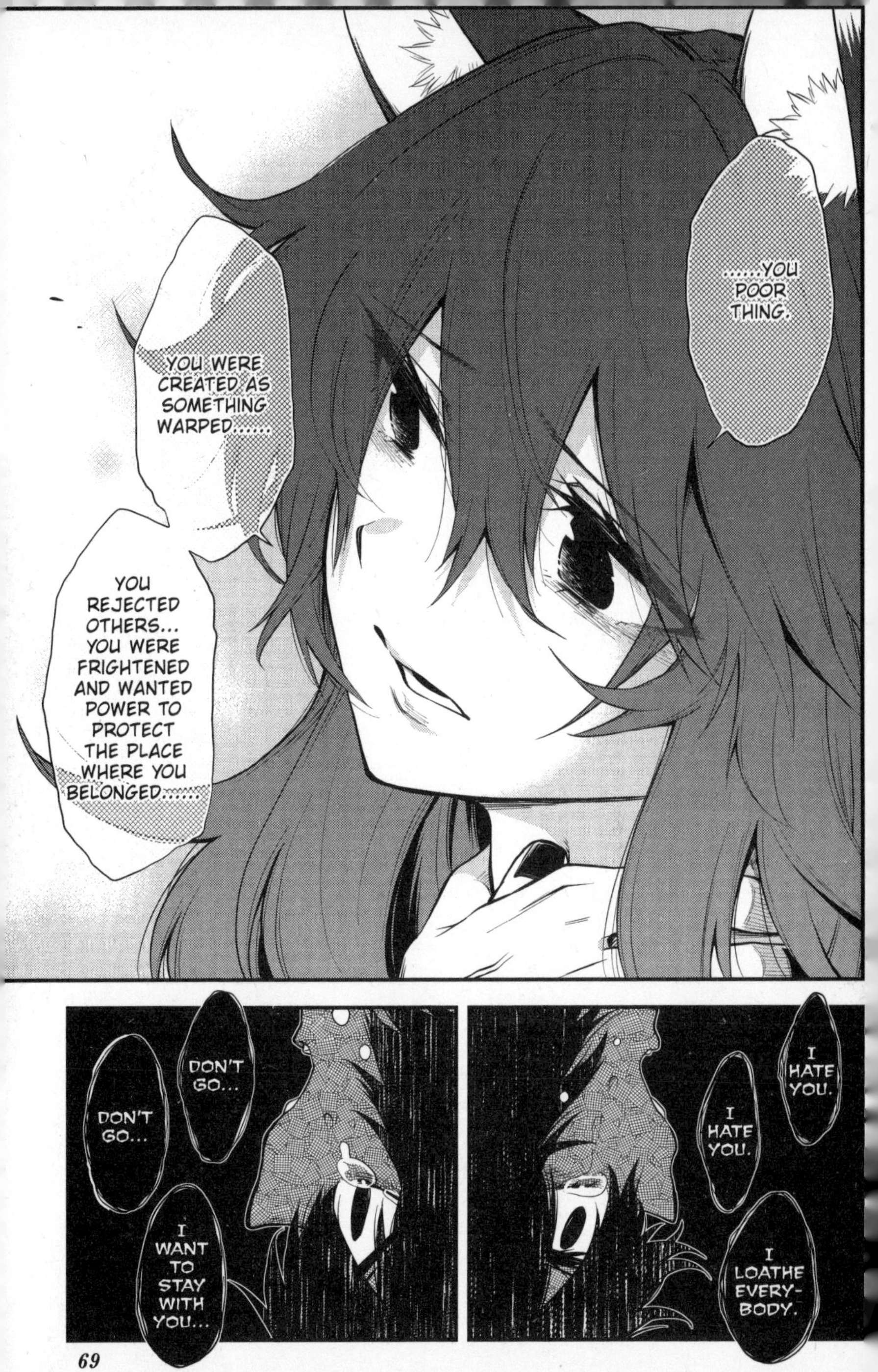

......YOU POOR THING.
YOU WERE CREATED AS SOMETHING WARPED......
YOU REJECTED OTHERS... YOU WERE FRIGHTENED AND WANTED POWER TO PROTECT THE PLACE WHERE YOU BELONGED......
I HATE YOU.
I HATE YOU.
I LOATHE EVERY-BODY.
DON'T GO...
DON'T GO...
I WANT TO STAY WITH YOU...

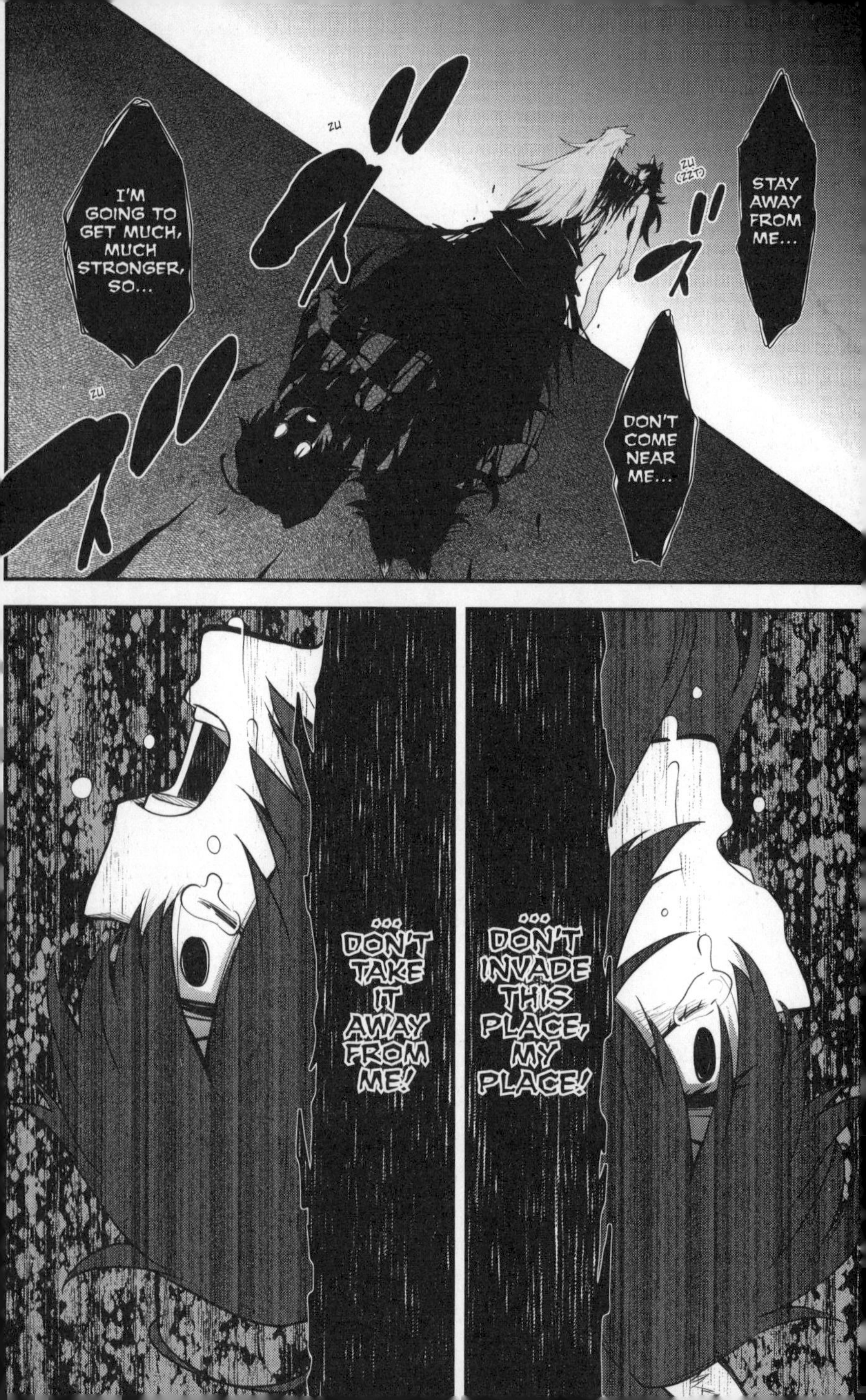
STAY AWAY FROM ME...
ZU (ZZZT)
ZU
DON'T COME NEAR ME...
I'M GOING TO GET MUCH, MUCH STRONGER, SO...
ZU
...DON'T INVADE THIS PLACE, MY PLACE!
...DON'T TAKE IT AWAY FROM ME!

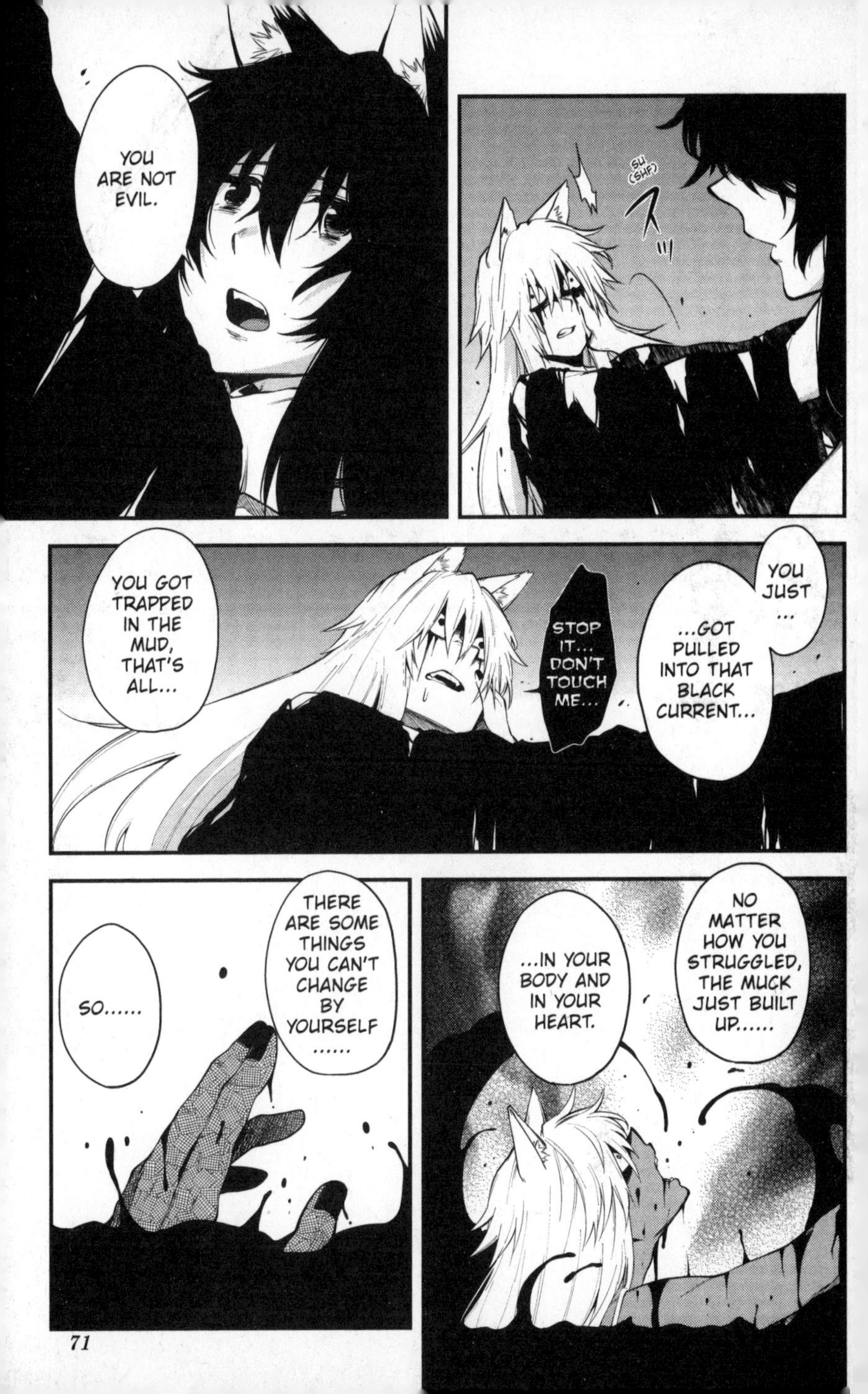
SU (SHF)
スッ
YOU ARE NOT EVIL.
YOU JUST ...
...GOT PULLED INTO THAT BLACK CURRENT...
STOP IT... DON'T TOUCH ME...
YOU GOT TRAPPED IN THE MUD, THAT'S ALL...
NO MATTER HOW YOU STRUGGLED, THE MUCK JUST BUILT UP......
...IN YOUR BODY AND IN YOUR HEART.
THERE ARE SOME THINGS YOU CAN'T CHANGE BY YOURSELF ......
SO......

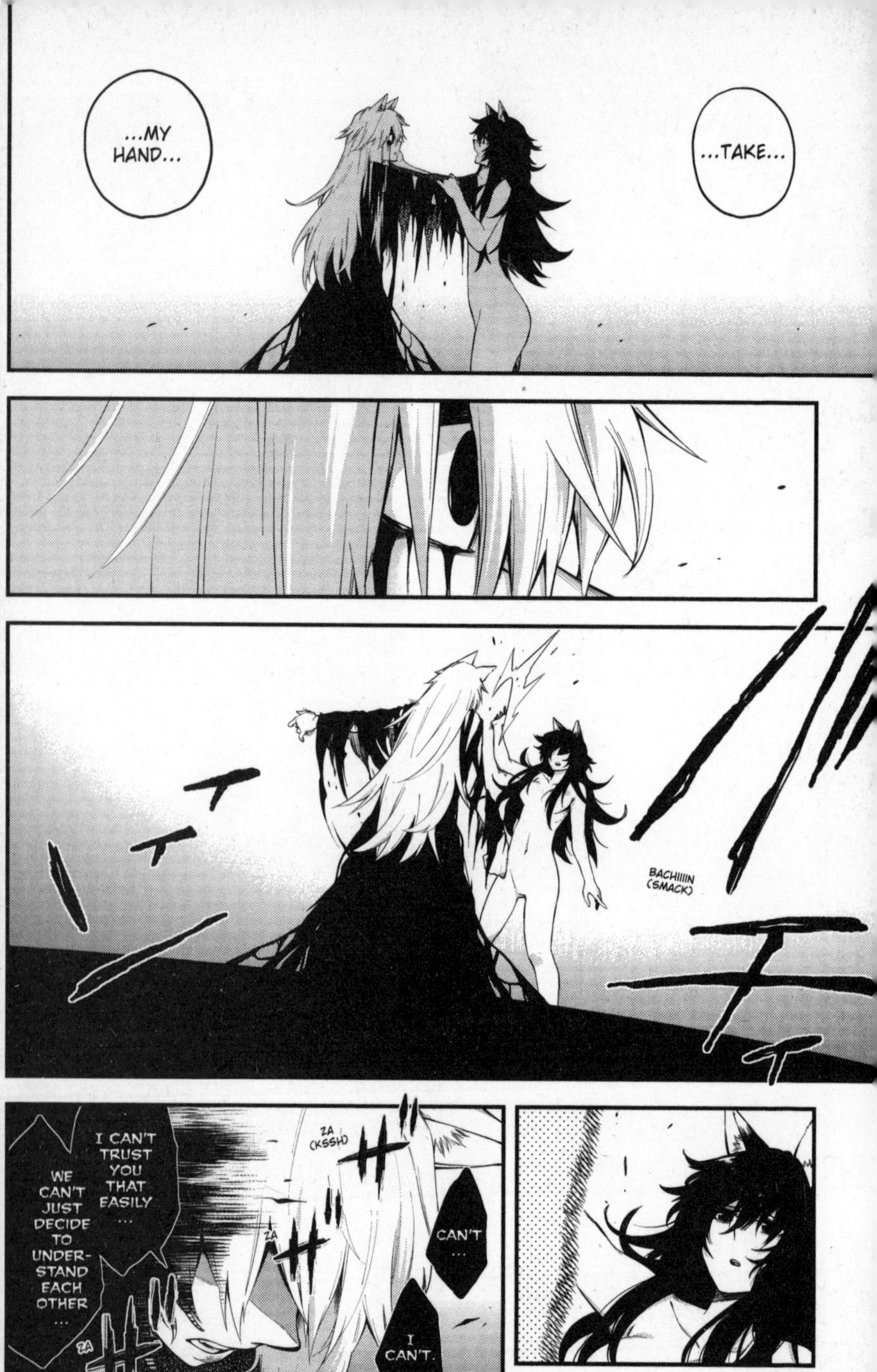
...TAKE...
...MY HAND...
BACHIIIIN (SMACK)
ZA (KSSH)
CAN'T ...
I CAN'T.
ZA
I CAN'T TRUST YOU THAT EASILY ...
WE CAN'T JUST DECIDE TO UNDER-STAND EACH OTHER ...
ZA

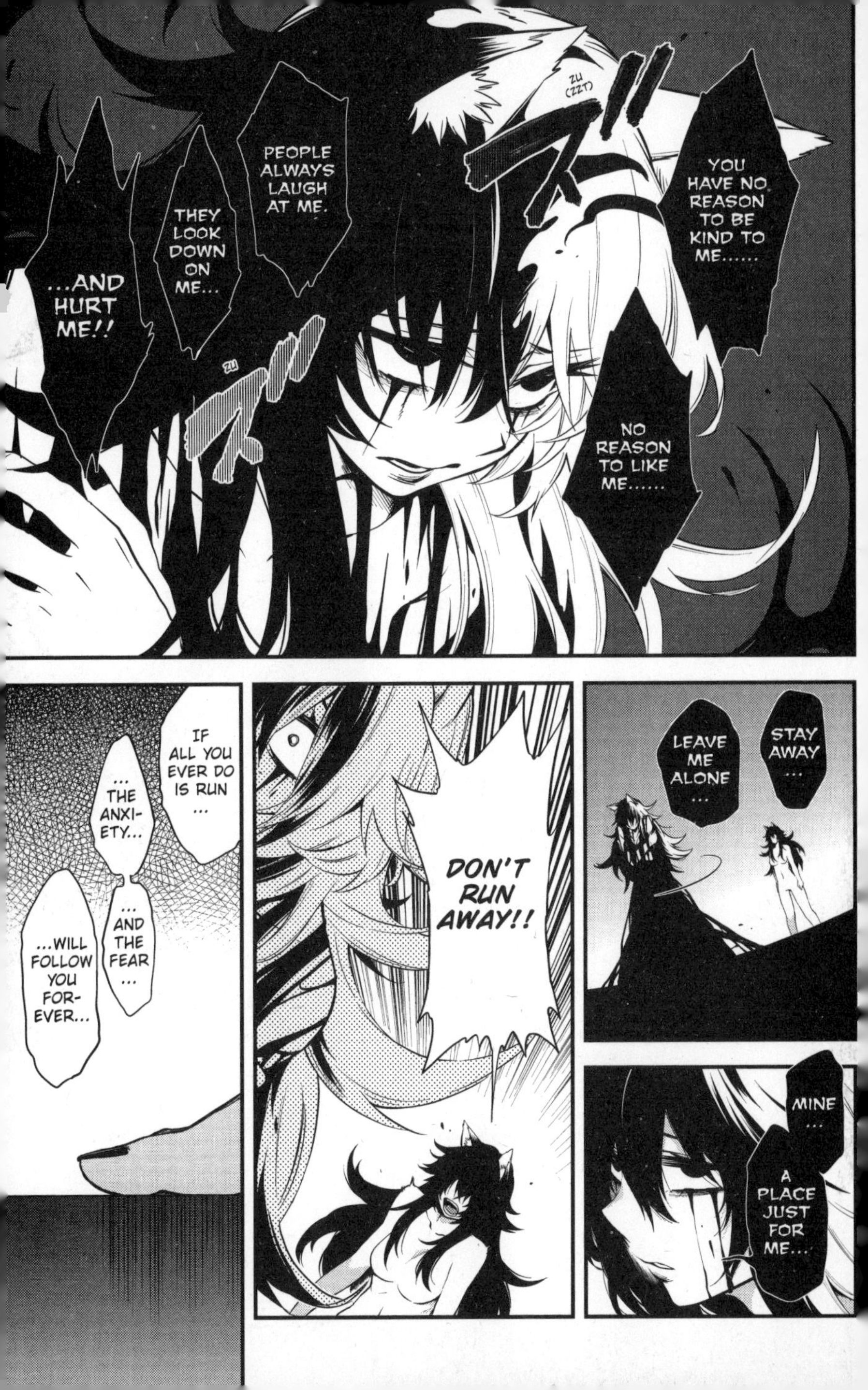
YOU HAVE NO REASON TO BE KIND TO ME......
NO REASON TO LIKE ME......
ZU (ZZZT)
PEOPLE ALWAYS LAUGH AT ME.
THEY LOOK DOWN ON ME...
ZU
...AND HURT ME!!
STAY AWAY ...
LEAVE ME ALONE ...
MINE ...
A PLACE JUST FOR ME...
DON'T RUN AWAY!!
IF ALL YOU EVER DO IS RUN ...
... THE ANXIETY...
... AND THE FEAR ...
...WILL FOLLOW YOU FOREVER...

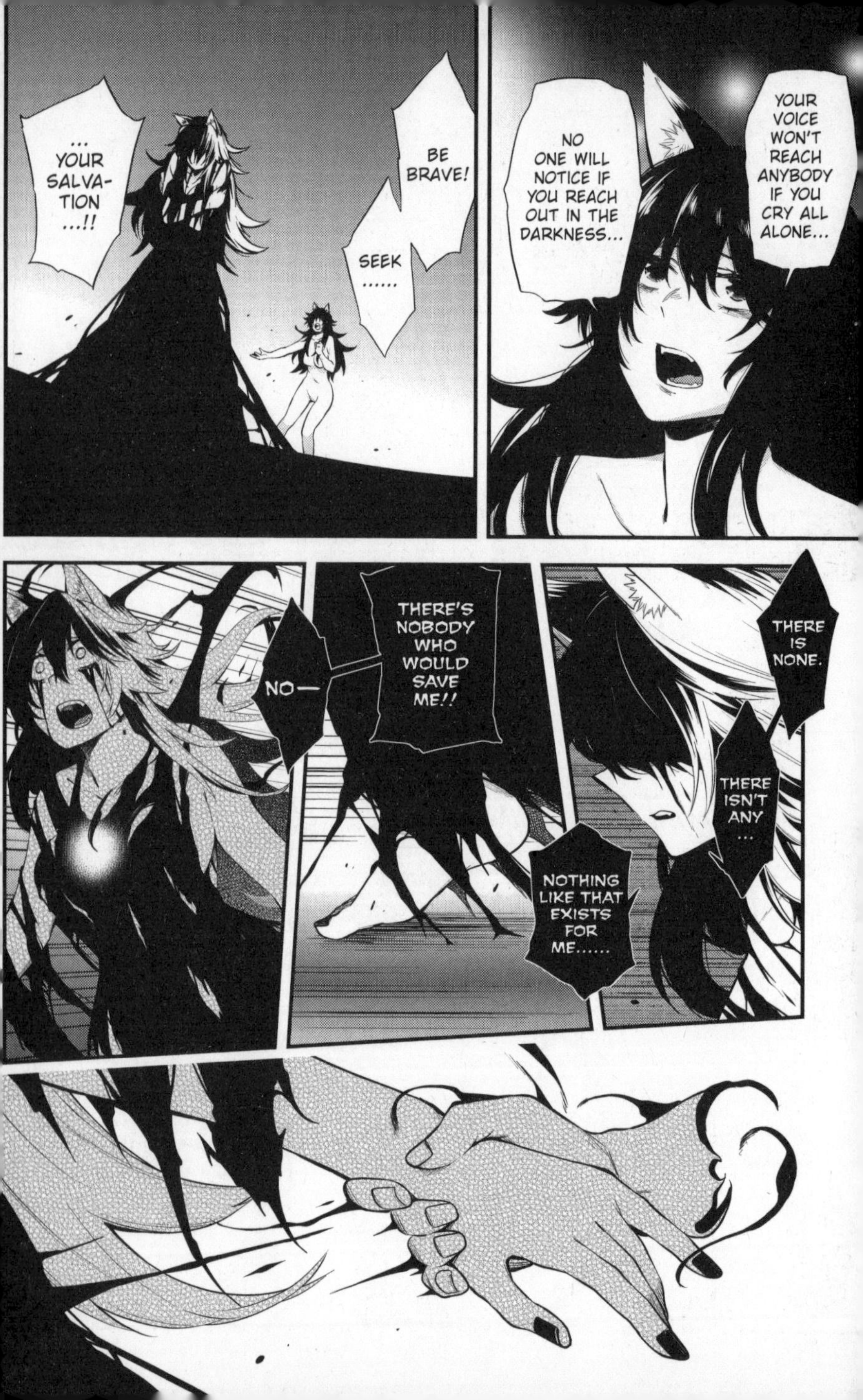
YOUR VOICE WON'T REACH ANYBODY IF YOU CRY ALL ALONE...
NO ONE WILL NOTICE IF YOU REACH OUT IN THE DARKNESS...
BE BRAVE!
SEEK ......
... YOUR SALVATION ...!!
THERE IS NONE.
THERE ISN'T ANY ...
NOTHING LIKE THAT EXISTS FOR ME......
THERE'S NOBODY WHO WOULD SAVE ME!!
NO—

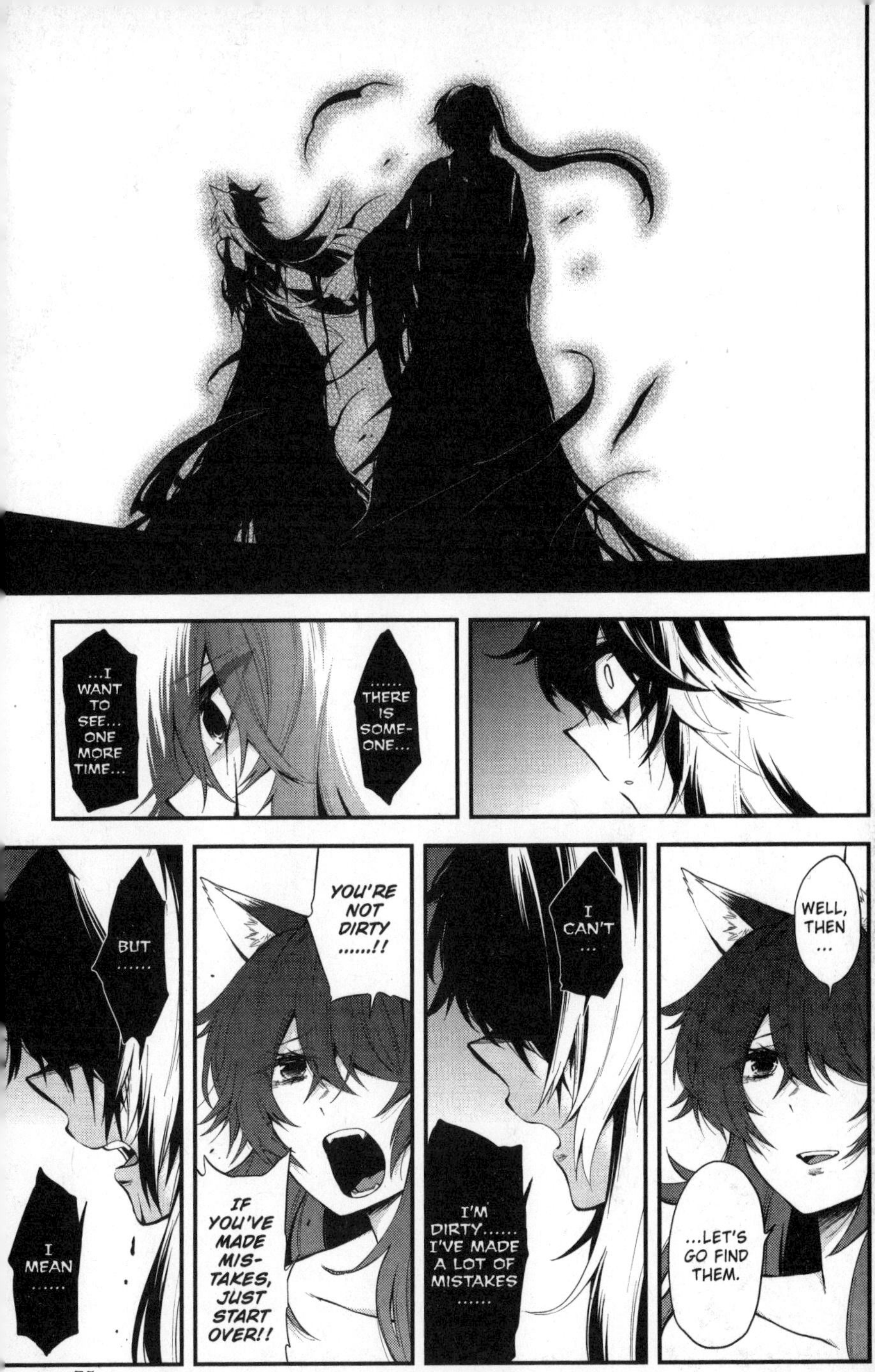
......THERE IS SOME-ONE...
...I WANT TO SEE... ONE MORE TIME...
WELL, THEN ...
...LET'S GO FIND THEM.
I CAN'T ...
I'M DIRTY...... I'VE MADE A LOT OF MISTAKES ......
YOU'RE NOT DIRTY ......!!
IF YOU'VE MADE MIS-TAKES, JUST START OVER!!
BUT ......
I MEAN ......

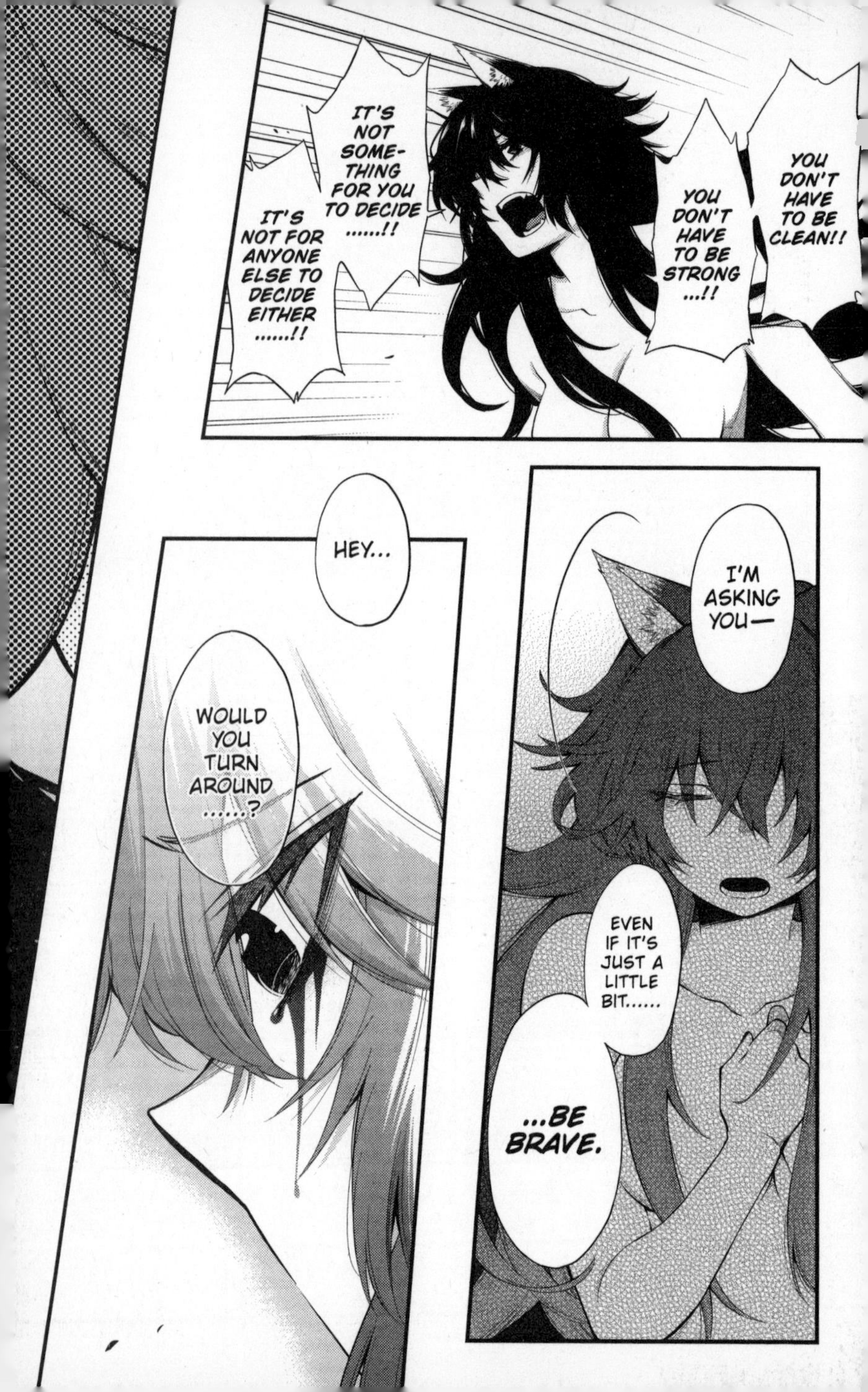
YOU DON'T HAVE TO BE CLEAN!!
YOU DON'T HAVE TO BE STRONG...!!
IT'S NOT SOMETHING FOR YOU TO DECIDE......!!
IT'S NOT FOR ANYONE ELSE TO DECIDE EITHER......!!
I'M ASKING YOU—
EVEN IF IT'S JUST A LITTLE BIT......
...BE BRAVE.
HEY...
WOULD YOU TURN AROUND......?

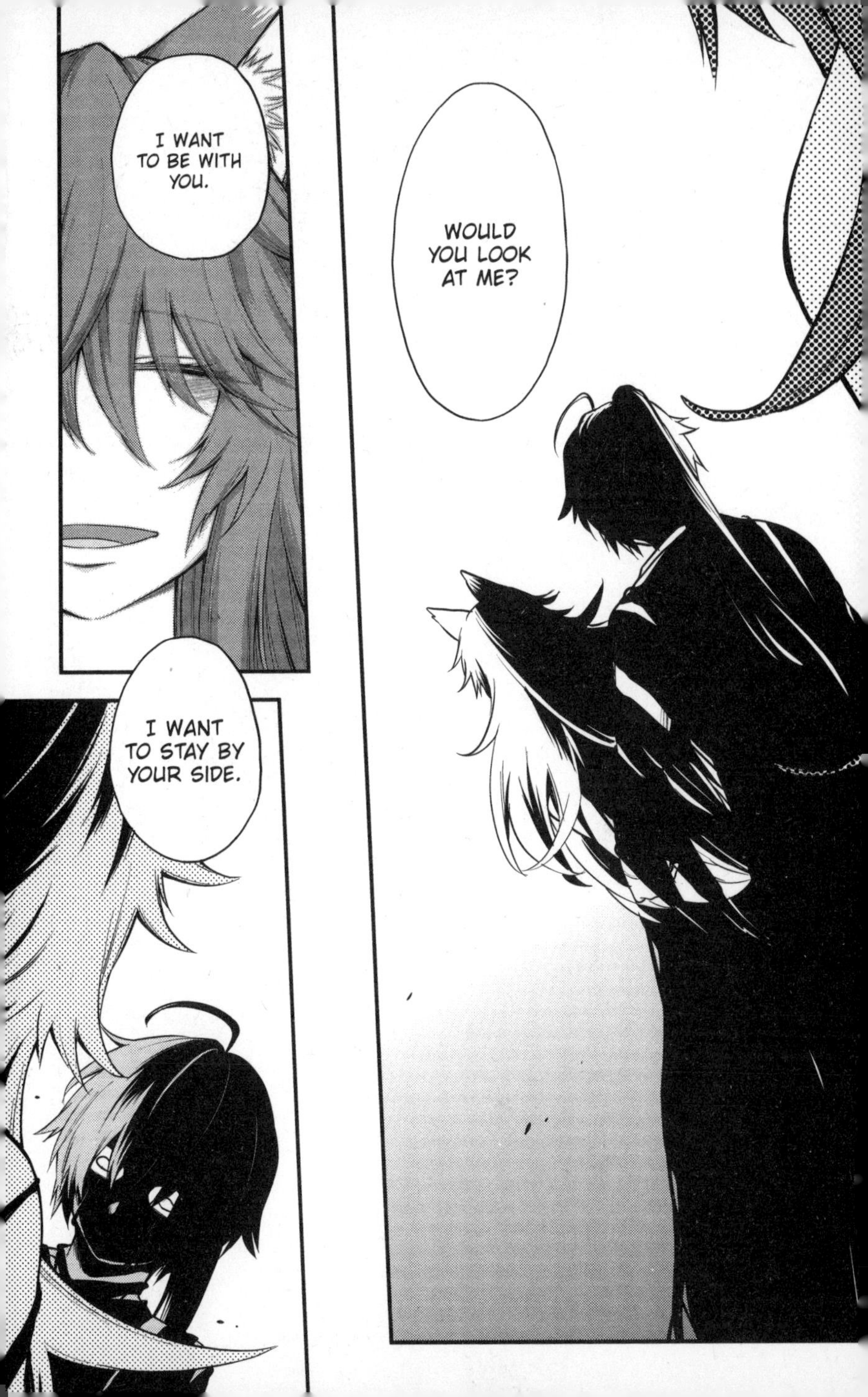
WOULD YOU LOOK AT ME?
I WANT TO BE WITH YOU.
I WANT TO STAY BY YOUR SIDE.

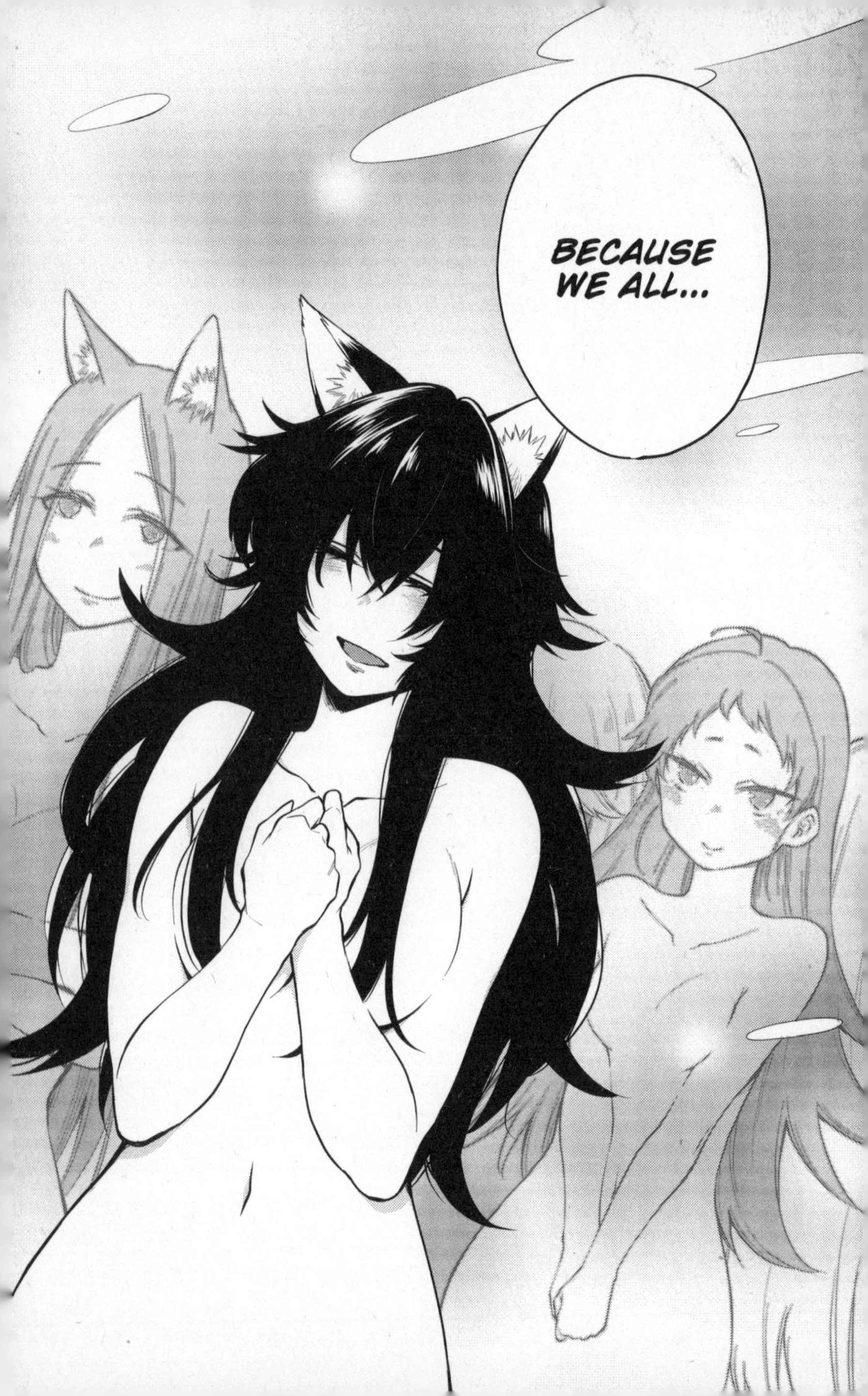
BECAUSE WE ALL...

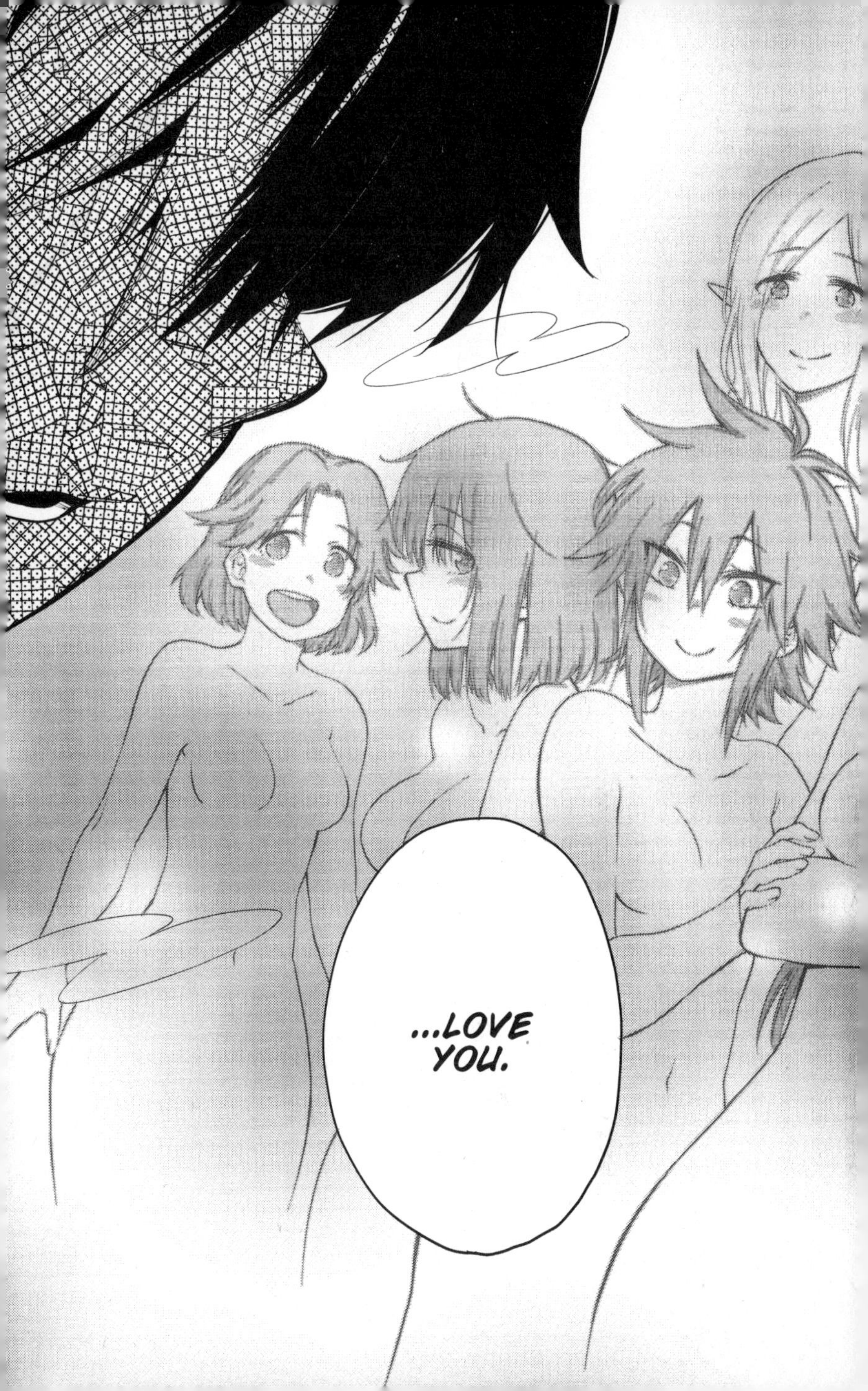
...LOVE YOU.

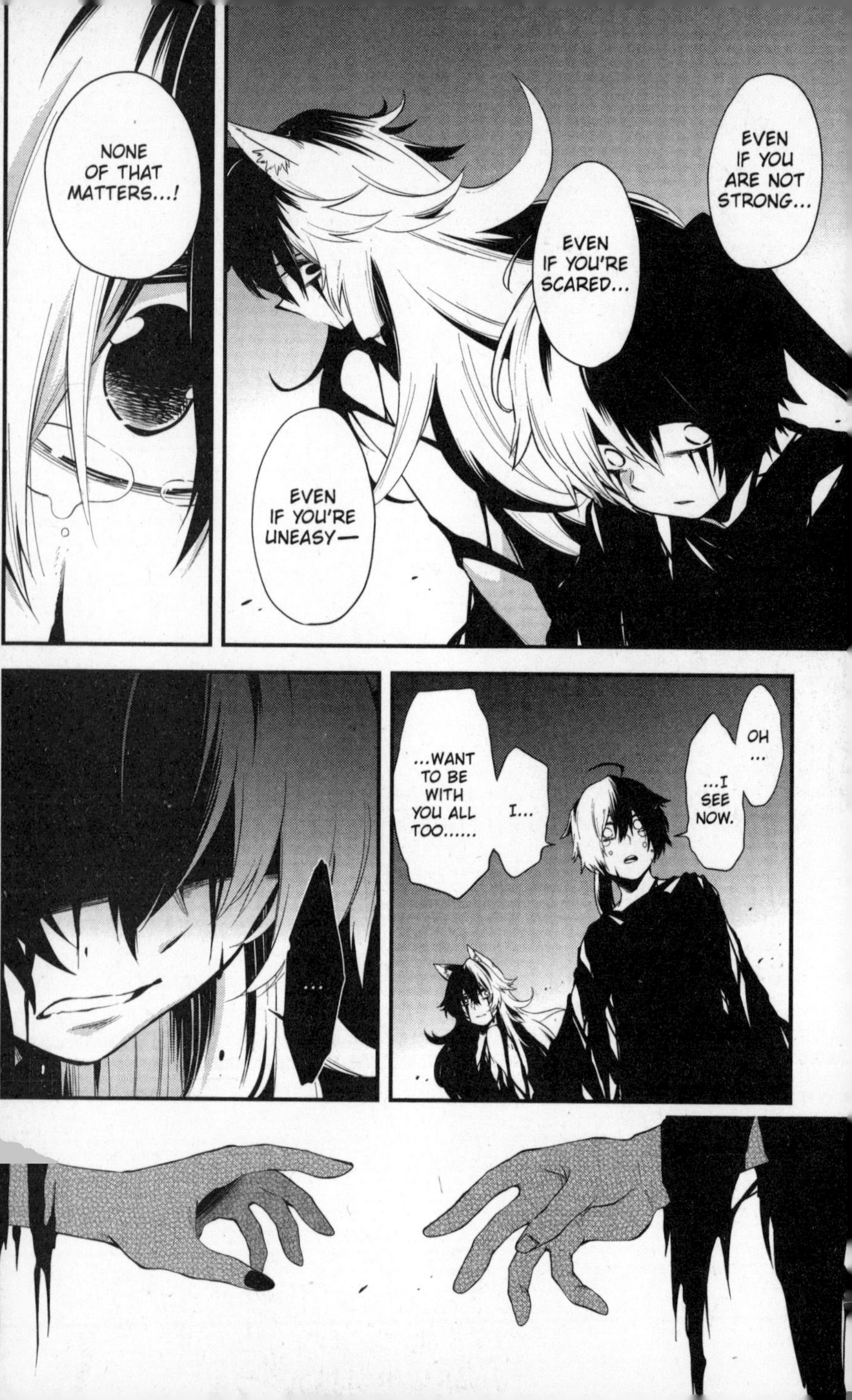
EVEN IF YOU ARE NOT STRONG...
EVEN IF YOU'RE SCARED...
EVEN IF YOU'RE UNEASY—
NONE OF THAT MATTERS...!
OH ...
...I SEE NOW.
I...
...WANT TO BE WITH YOU ALL TOO......
...

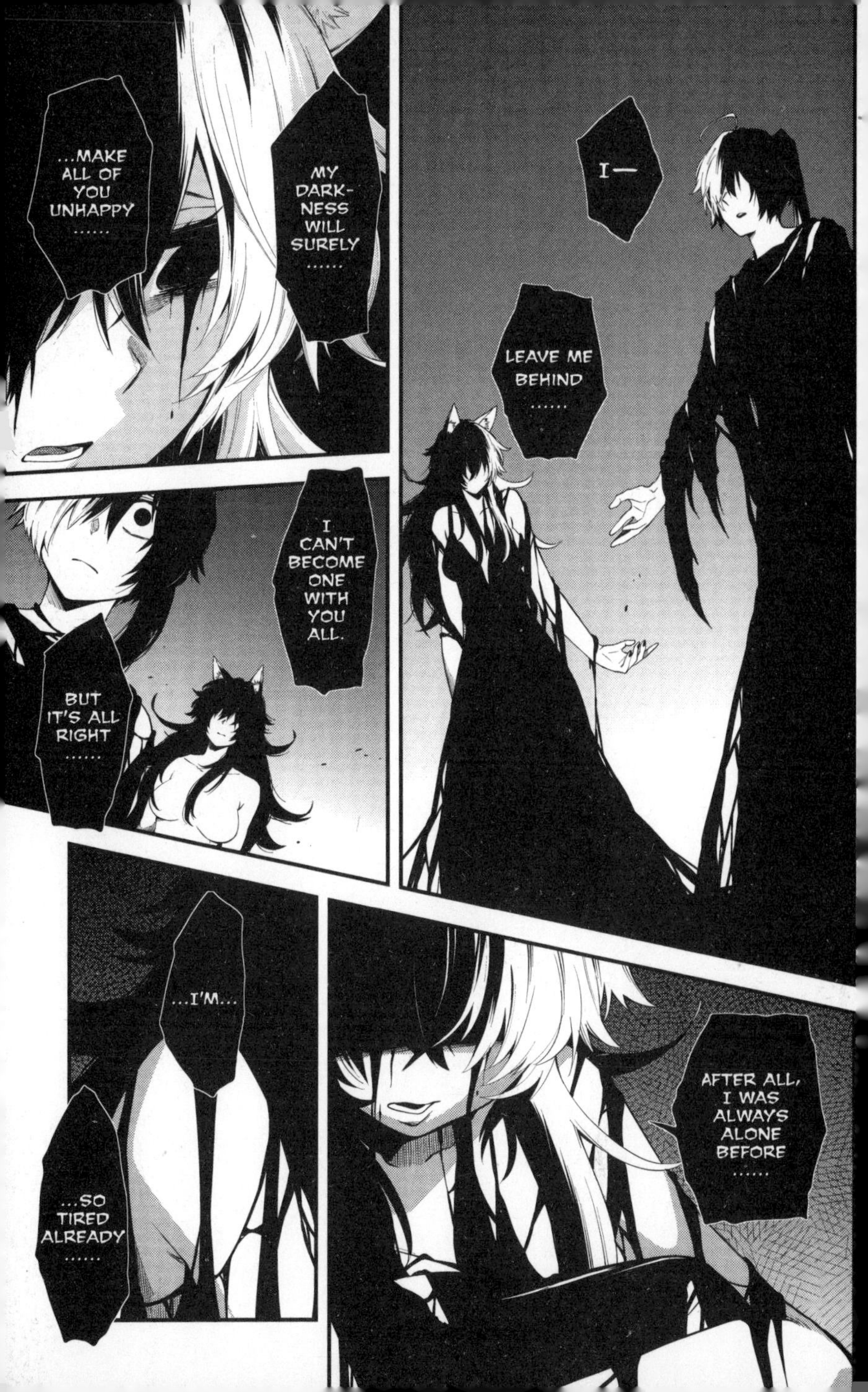
I—
LEAVE ME BEHIND ......
MY DARKNESS WILL SURELY ......
...MAKE ALL OF YOU UNHAPPY ......
I CAN'T BECOME ONE WITH YOU ALL.
BUT IT'S ALL RIGHT ......
AFTER ALL, I WAS ALWAYS ALONE BEFORE ......
...I'M...
...SO TIRED ALREADY ......

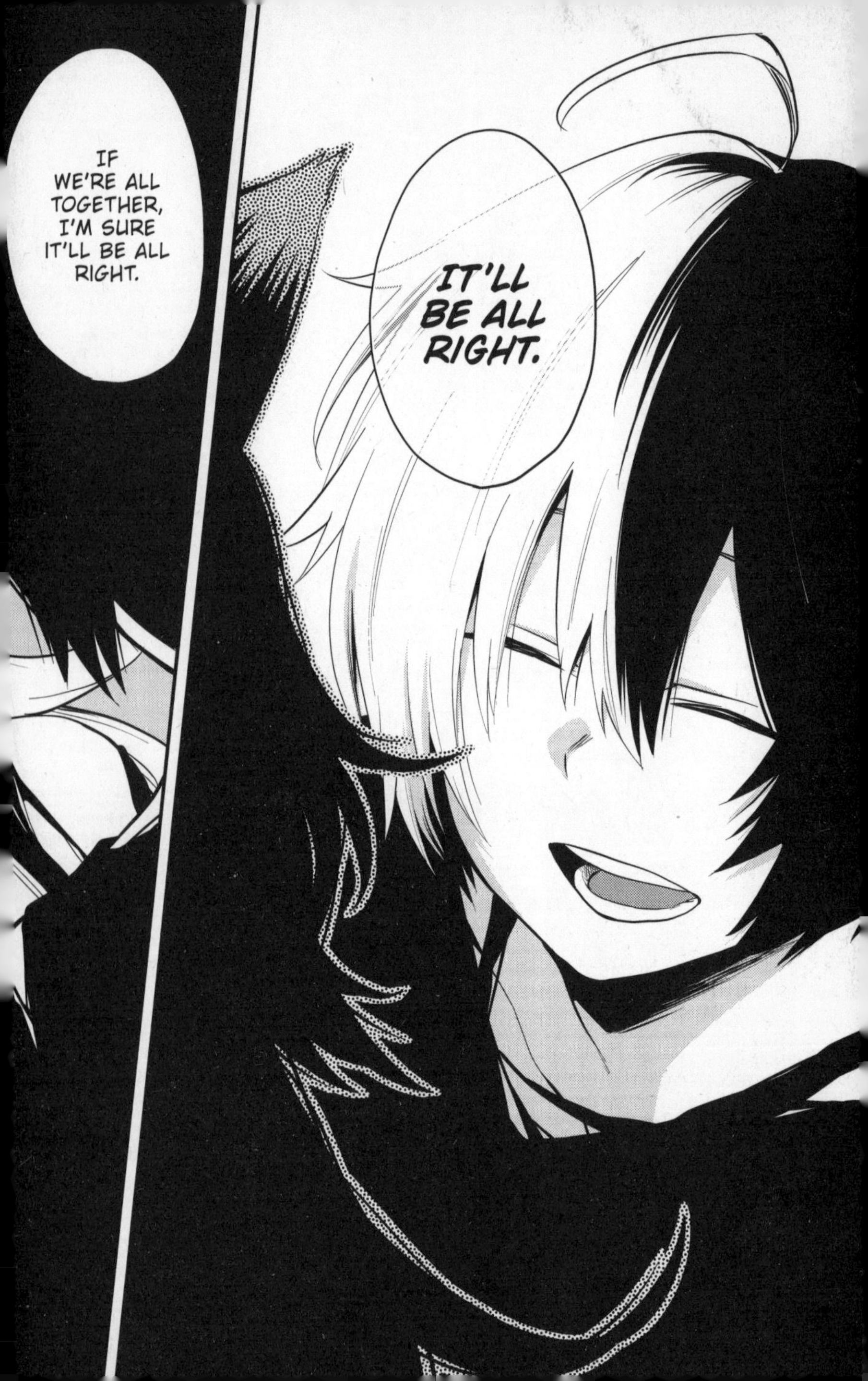
IT'LL BE ALL RIGHT.
IF WE'RE ALL TOGETHER, I'M SURE IT'LL BE ALL RIGHT.

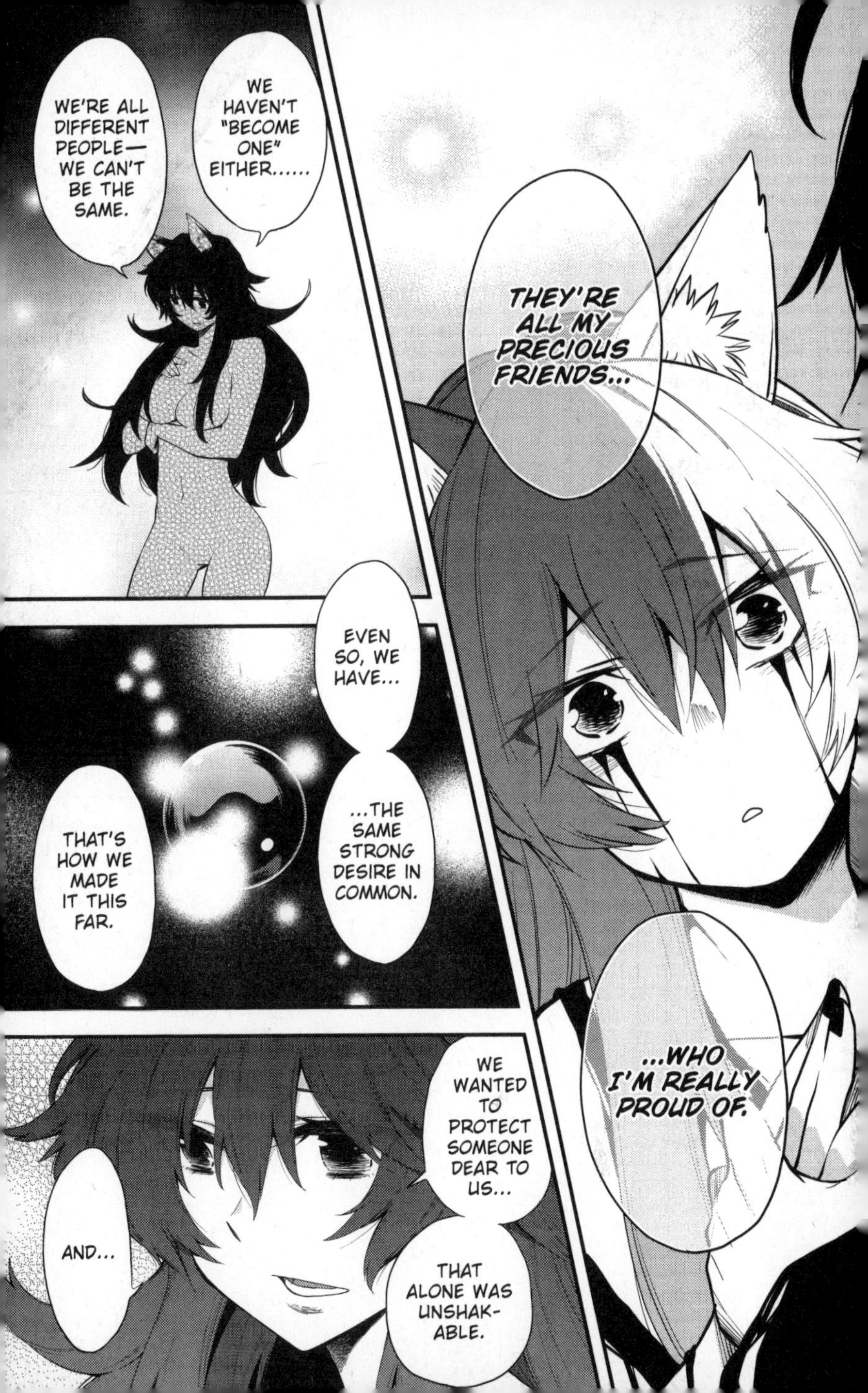
THEY'RE ALL MY PRECIOUS FRIENDS...
...WHO I'M REALLY PROUD OF.
WE HAVEN'T "BECOME ONE" EITHER......
WE'RE ALL DIFFERENT PEOPLE— WE CAN'T BE THE SAME.
EVEN SO, WE HAVE...
...THE SAME STRONG DESIRE IN COMMON.
THAT'S HOW WE MADE IT THIS FAR.
WE WANTED TO PROTECT SOMEONE DEAR TO US...
THAT ALONE WAS UNSHAK-ABLE.
AND...

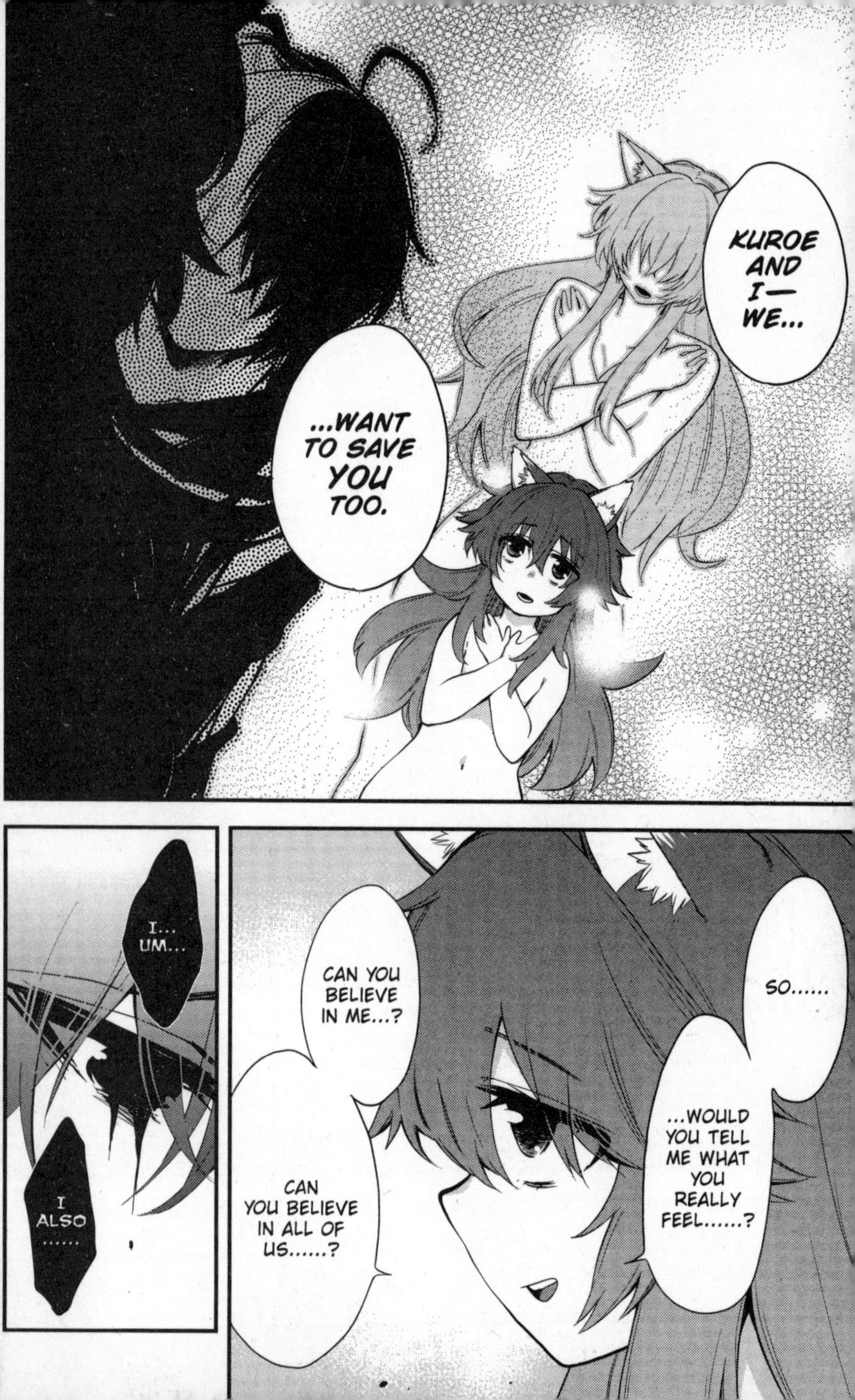
KUROE AND I— WE...
...WANT TO SAVE YOU TOO.
SO......
...WOULD YOU TELL ME WHAT YOU REALLY FEEL......?
CAN YOU BELIEVE IN ME...?
CAN YOU BELIEVE IN ALL OF US......?
I... UM...
I ALSO ......

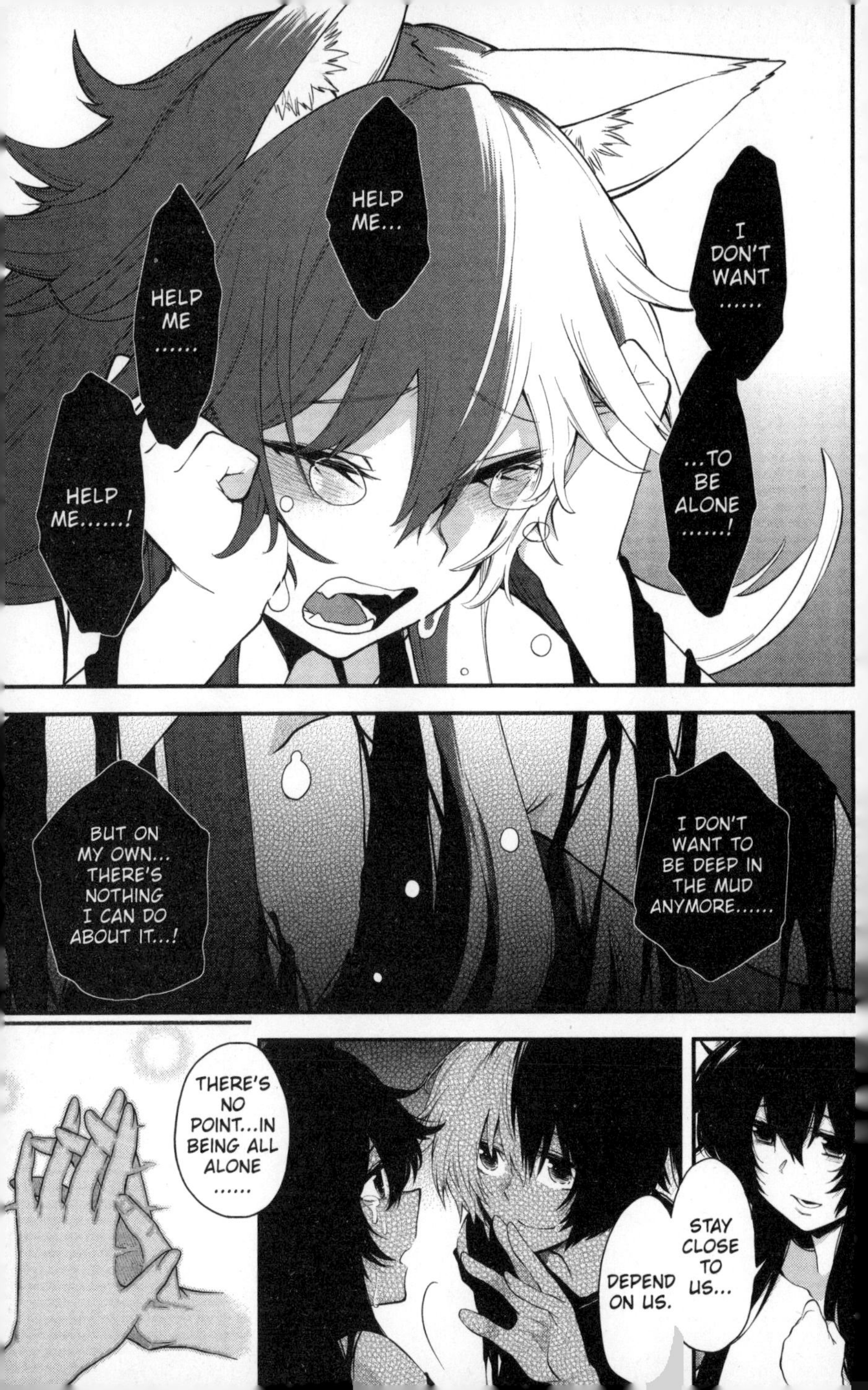
I DON'T WANT ......
...TO BE ALONE ......!
HELP ME...
HELP ME ......
HELP ME......!
I DON'T WANT TO BE DEEP IN THE MUD ANYMORE......
BUT ON MY OWN... THERE'S NOTHING I CAN DO ABOUT IT...!
STAY CLOSE TO US...
DEPEND ON US.
THERE'S NO POINT...IN BEING ALL ALONE ......

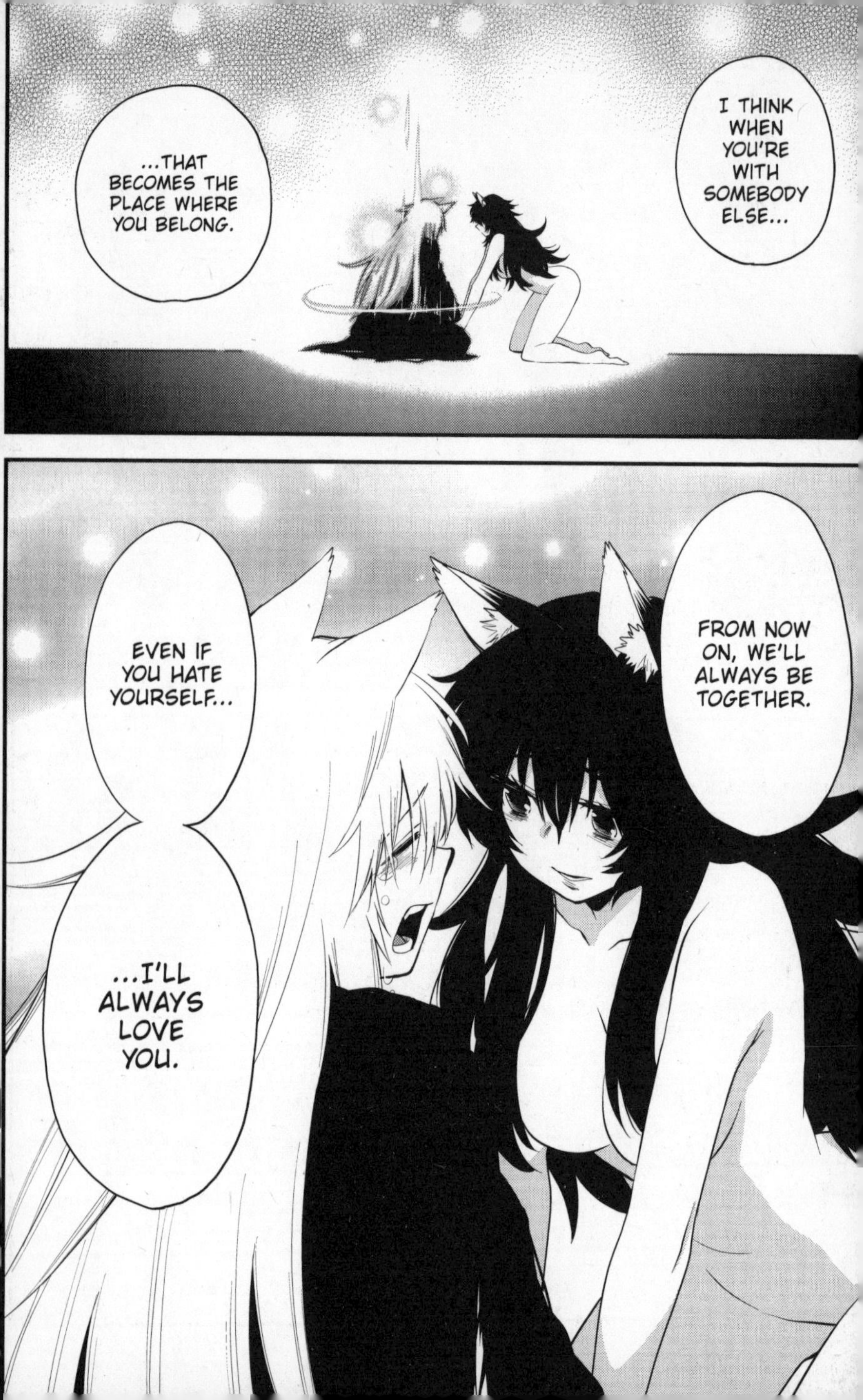
I THINK WHEN YOU'RE WITH SOMEBODY ELSE...
...THAT BECOMES THE PLACE WHERE YOU BELONG.
FROM NOW ON, WE'LL ALWAYS BE TOGETHER.
EVEN IF YOU HATE YOURSELF...
...I'LL ALWAYS LOVE YOU.

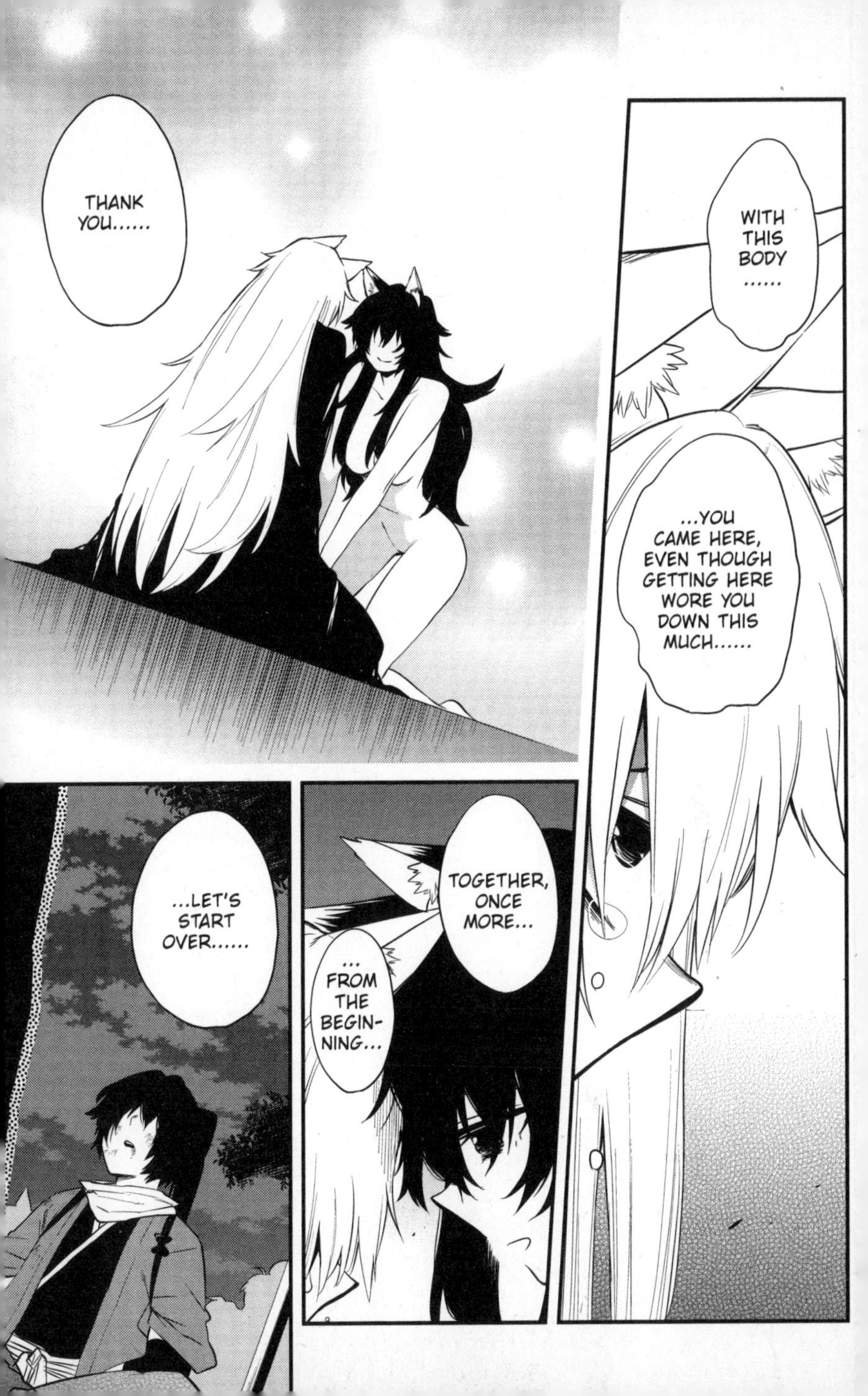
WITH THIS BODY ......
...YOU CAME HERE, EVEN THOUGH GETTING HERE WORE YOU DOWN THIS MUCH......
THANK YOU......
TOGETHER, ONCE MORE...
... FROM THE BEGIN-NING...
...LET'S START OVER......

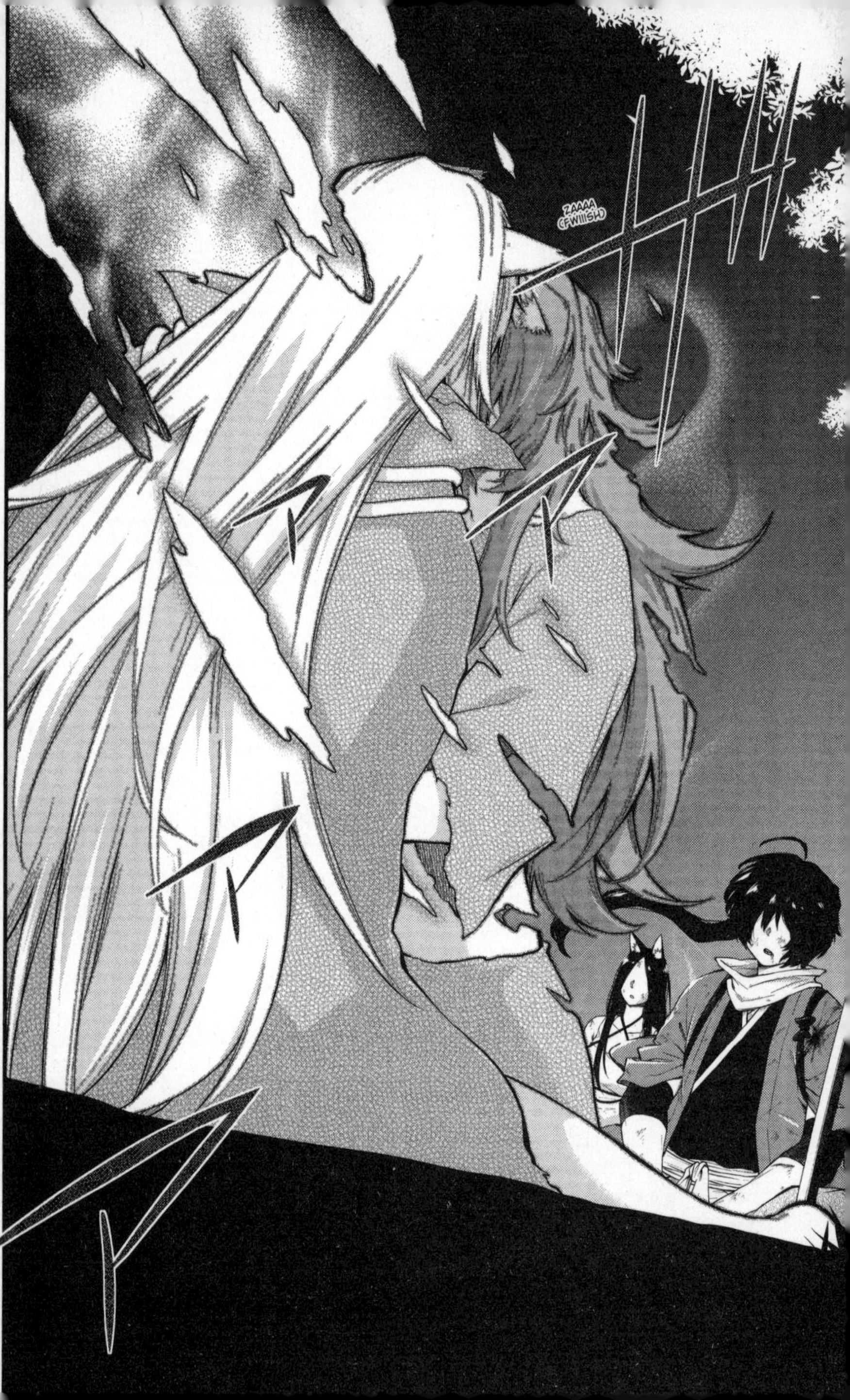
ZAAAA (FWIIIISH)

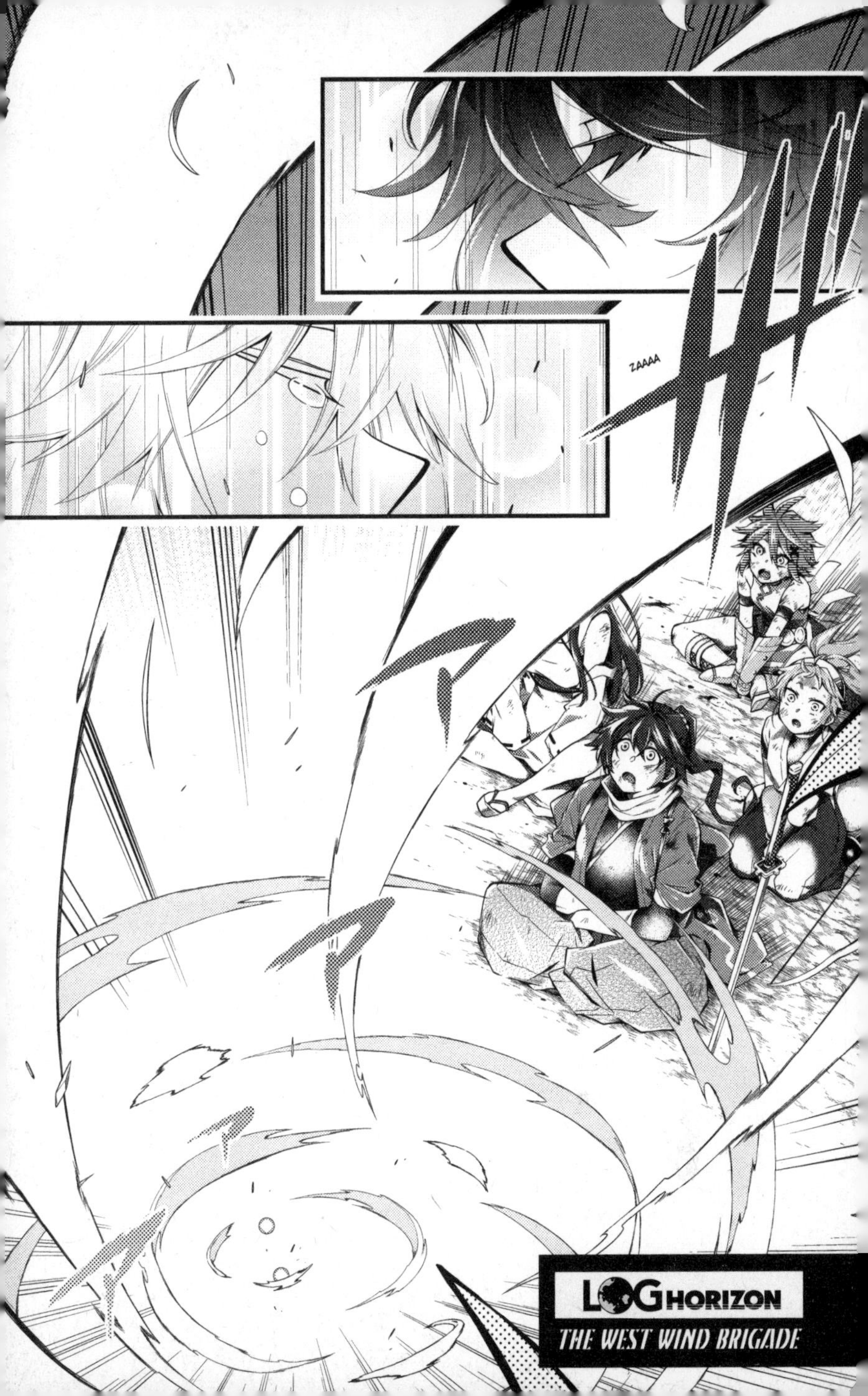

ZAAAA
LOG HORIZON
THE WEST WIND BRIGADE

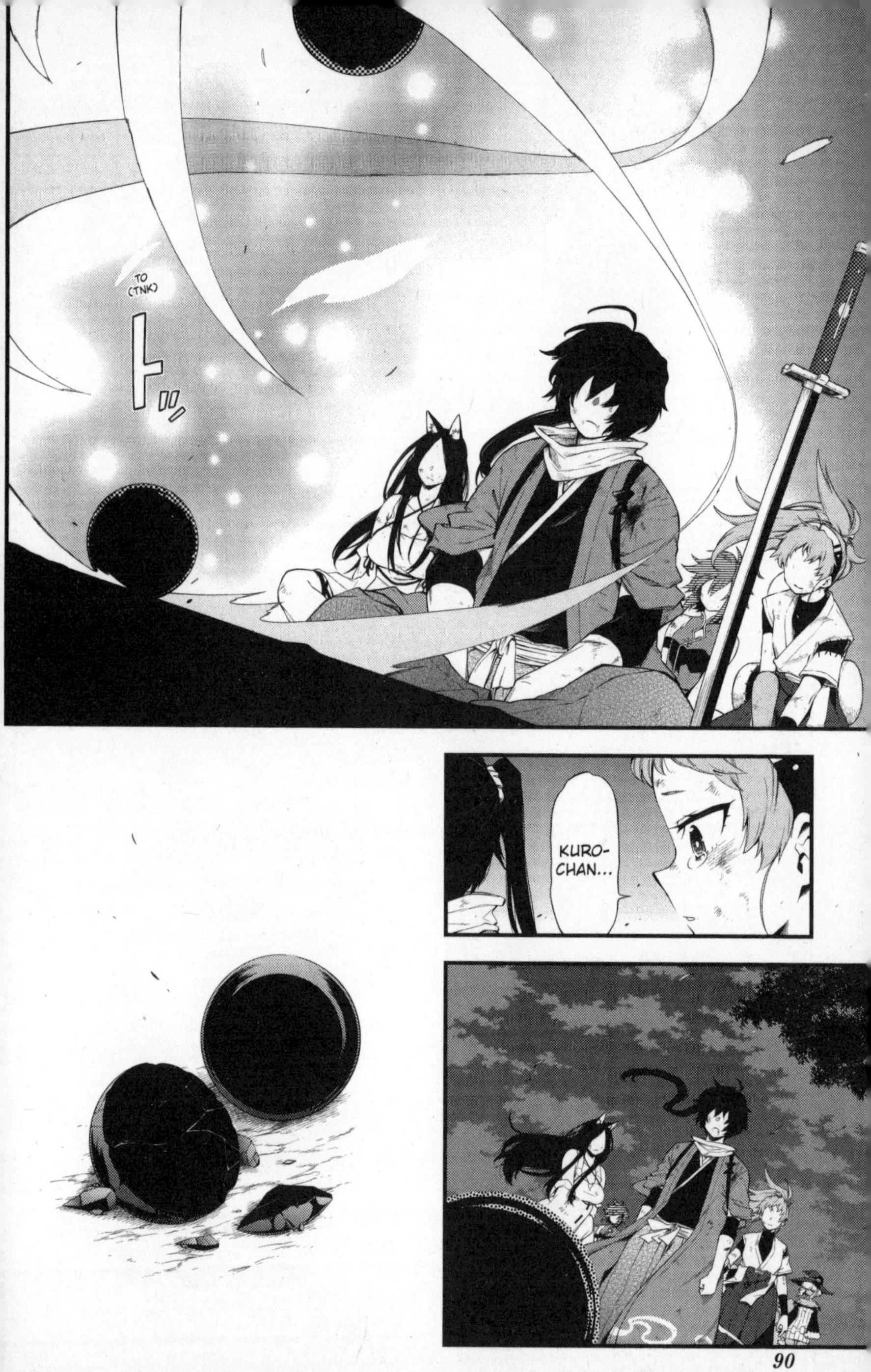
TO
(TNK)
トッ
KURO-
CHAN...

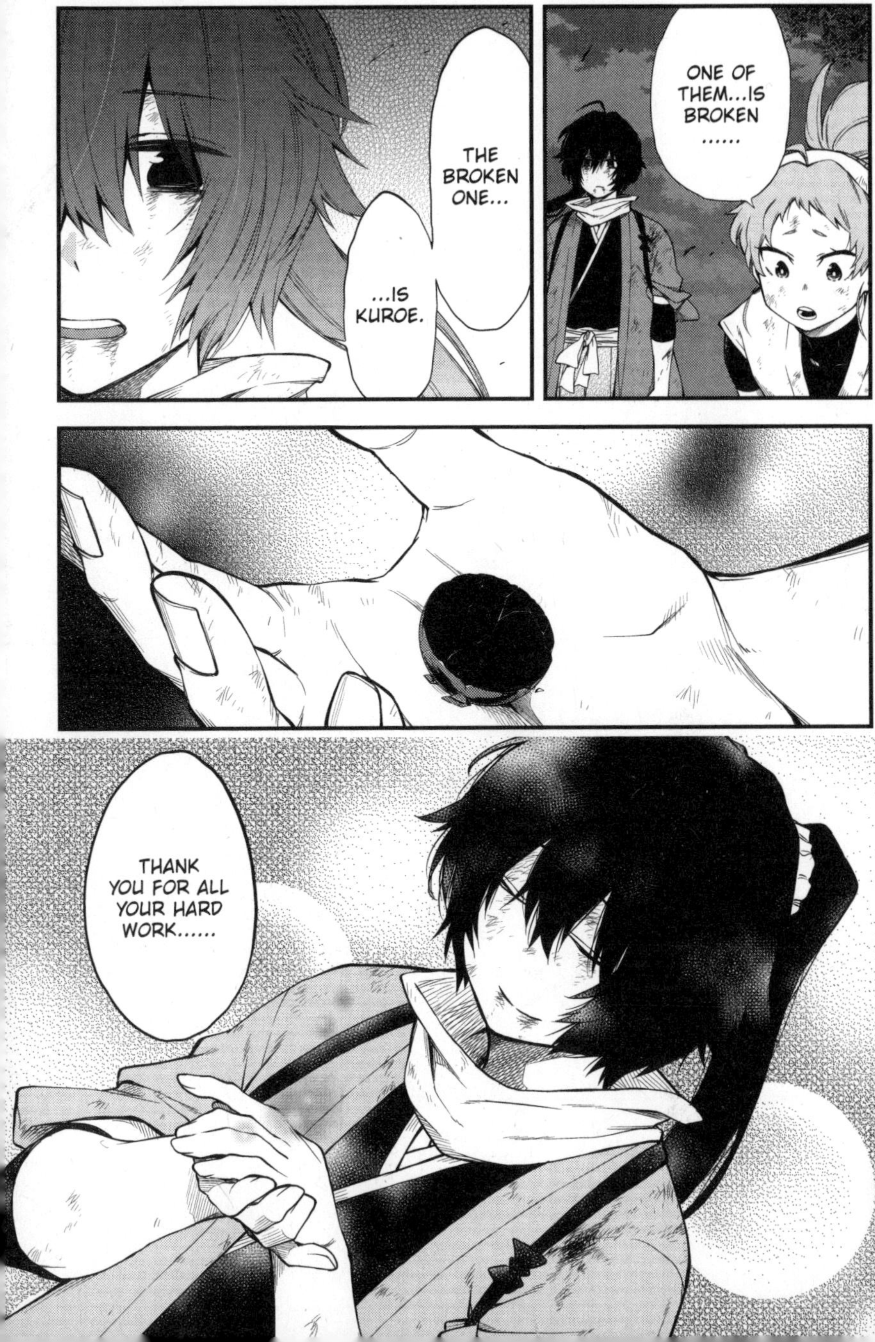
ONE OF THEM...IS BROKEN ......
THE BROKEN ONE...
...IS KUROE.
THANK YOU FOR ALL YOUR HARD WORK......

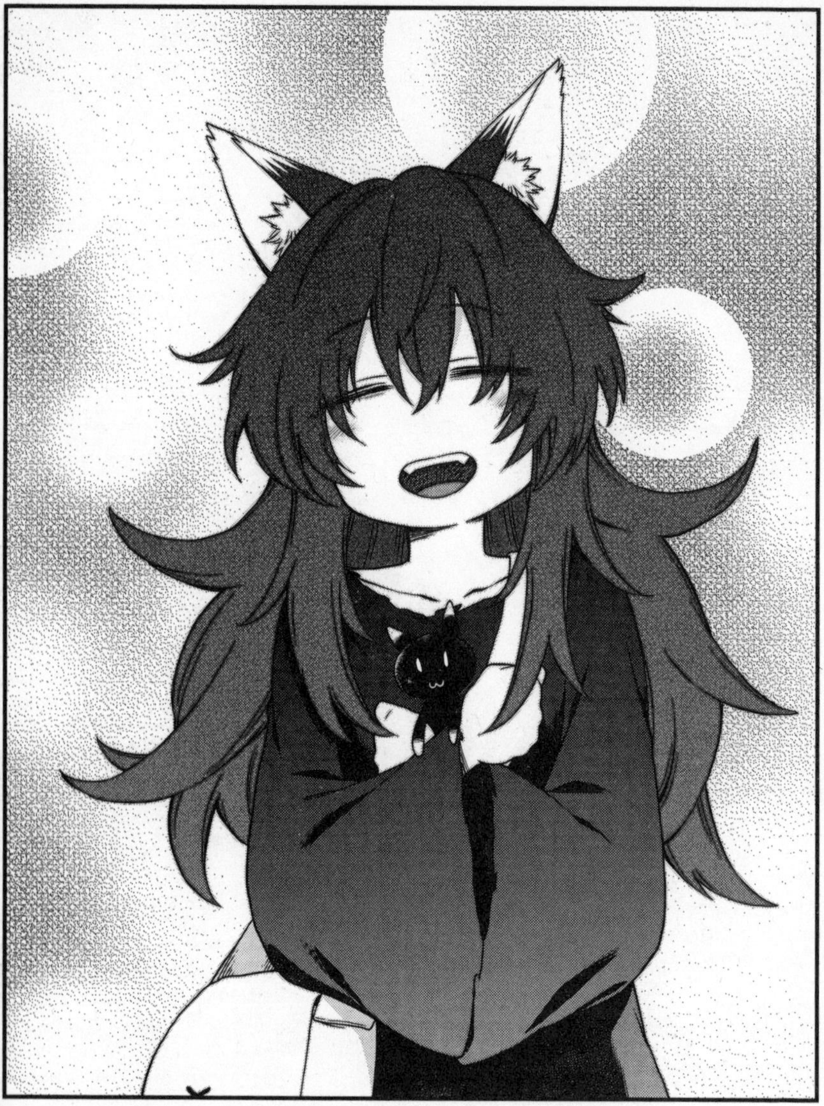

CHAPTER: 63 Someday, Again, for Sure...

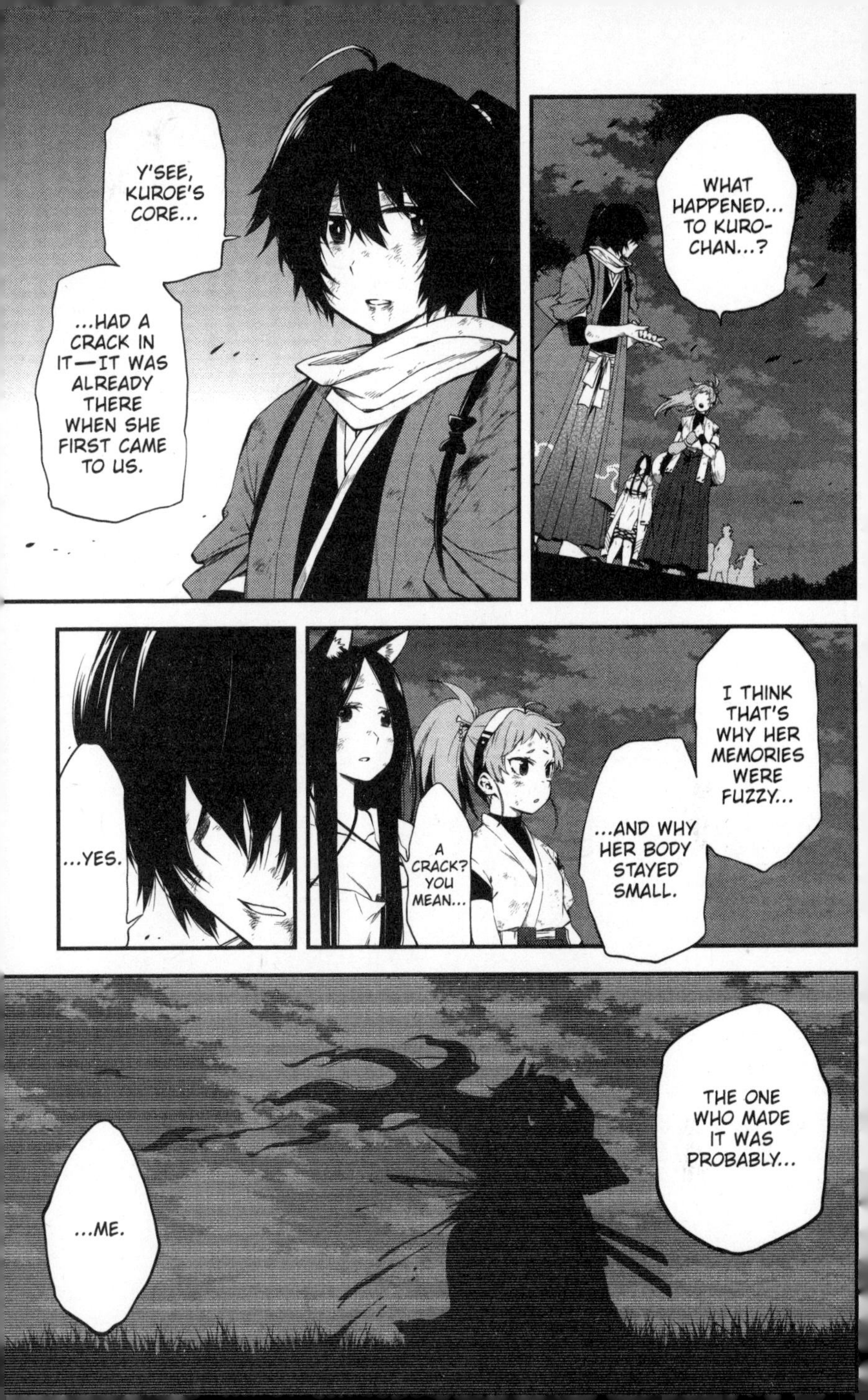
WHAT HAPPENED... TO KURO-CHAN...?
Y'SEE, KUROE'S CORE...
...HAD A CRACK IN IT—IT WAS ALREADY THERE WHEN SHE FIRST CAME TO US.
I THINK THAT'S WHY HER MEMORIES WERE FUZZY...
...AND WHY HER BODY STAYED SMALL.
A CRACK? YOU MEAN...
...YES.
THE ONE WHO MADE IT WAS PROBABLY...
...ME.

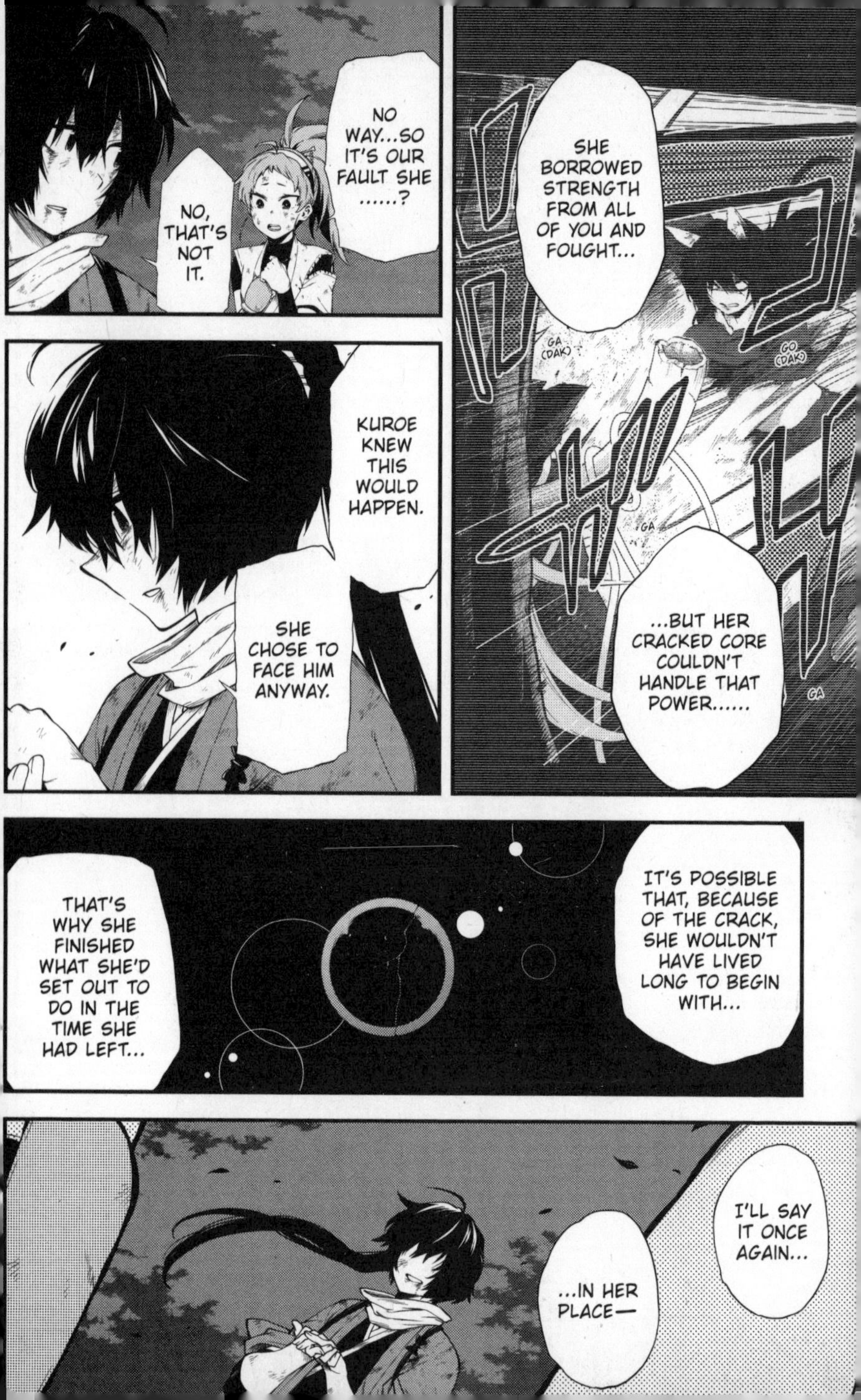
SHE BORROWED STRENGTH FROM ALL OF YOU AND FOUGHT...
GO (DAK)
GA (DAK)
GA
...BUT HER CRACKED CORE COULDN'T HANDLE THAT POWER......
GA
NO WAY...SO IT'S OUR FAULT SHE ......?
NO, THAT'S NOT IT.
KUROE KNEW THIS WOULD HAPPEN.
SHE CHOSE TO FACE HIM ANYWAY.
IT'S POSSIBLE THAT, BECAUSE OF THE CRACK, SHE WOULDN'T HAVE LIVED LONG TO BEGIN WITH...
THAT'S WHY SHE FINISHED WHAT SHE'D SET OUT TO DO IN THE TIME SHE HAD LEFT...
I'LL SAY IT ONCE AGAIN...
...IN HER PLACE—

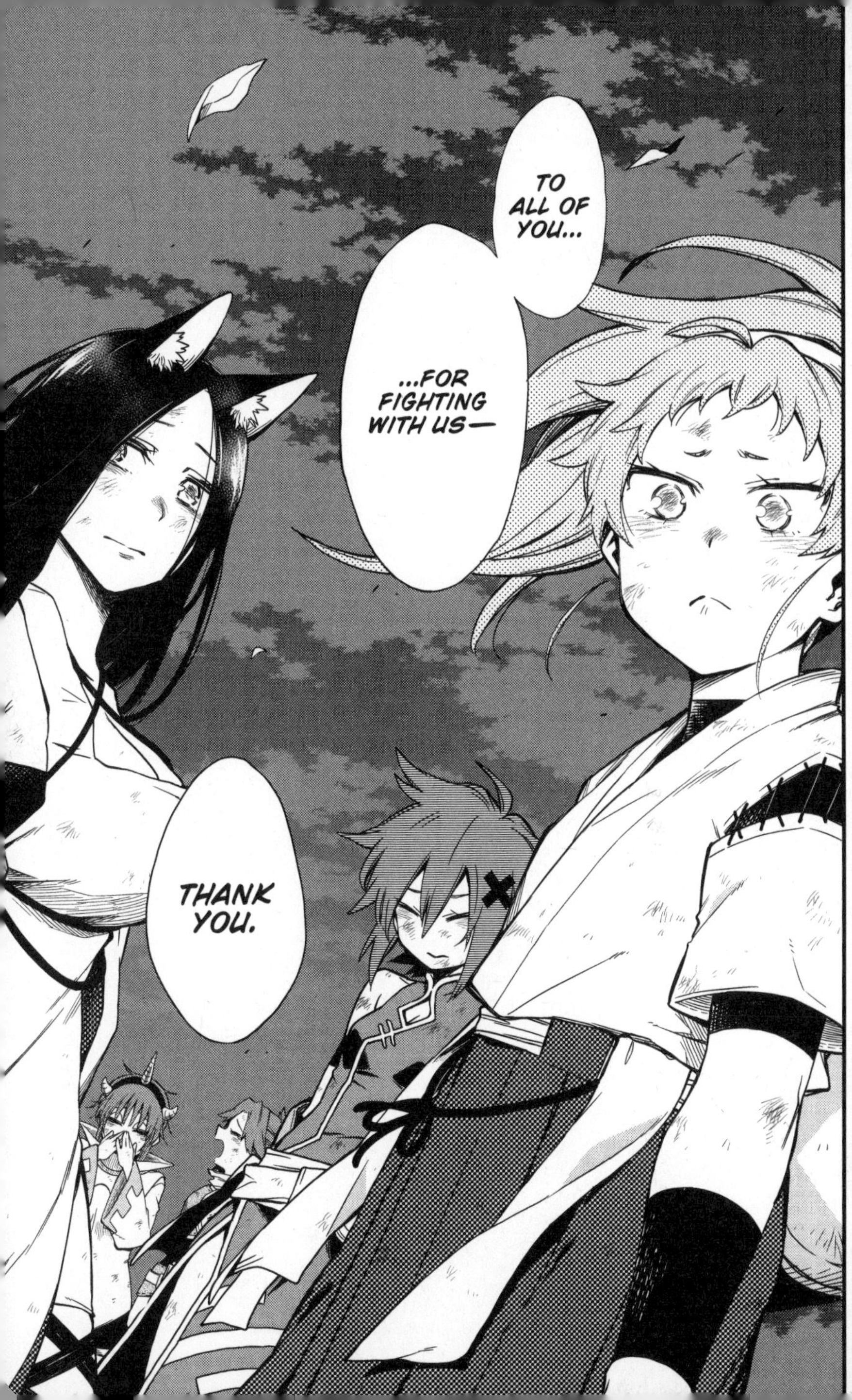
TO ALL OF YOU...
...FOR FIGHTING WITH US—
THANK YOU.

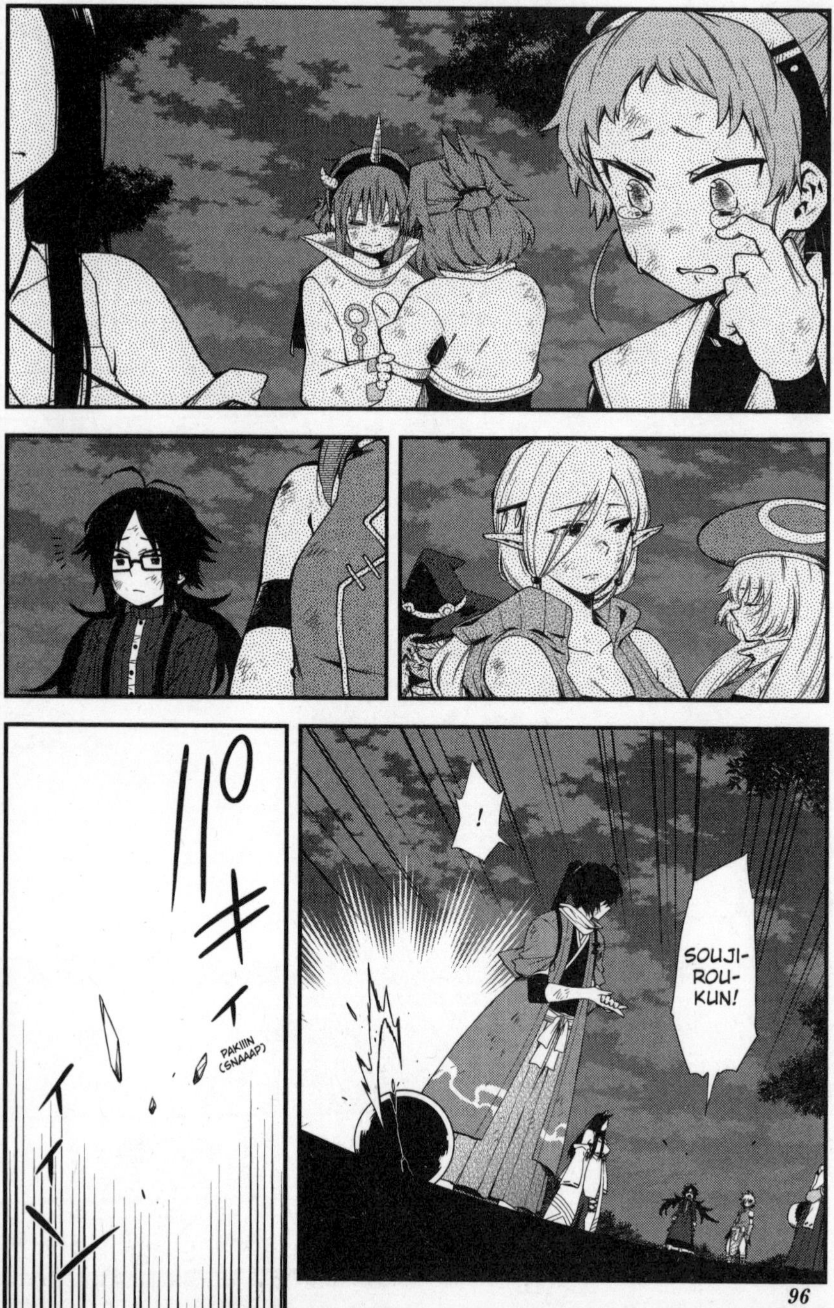
!
SOUJI-
ROU-
KUN!
PAKIIIN
(SNAAAP)

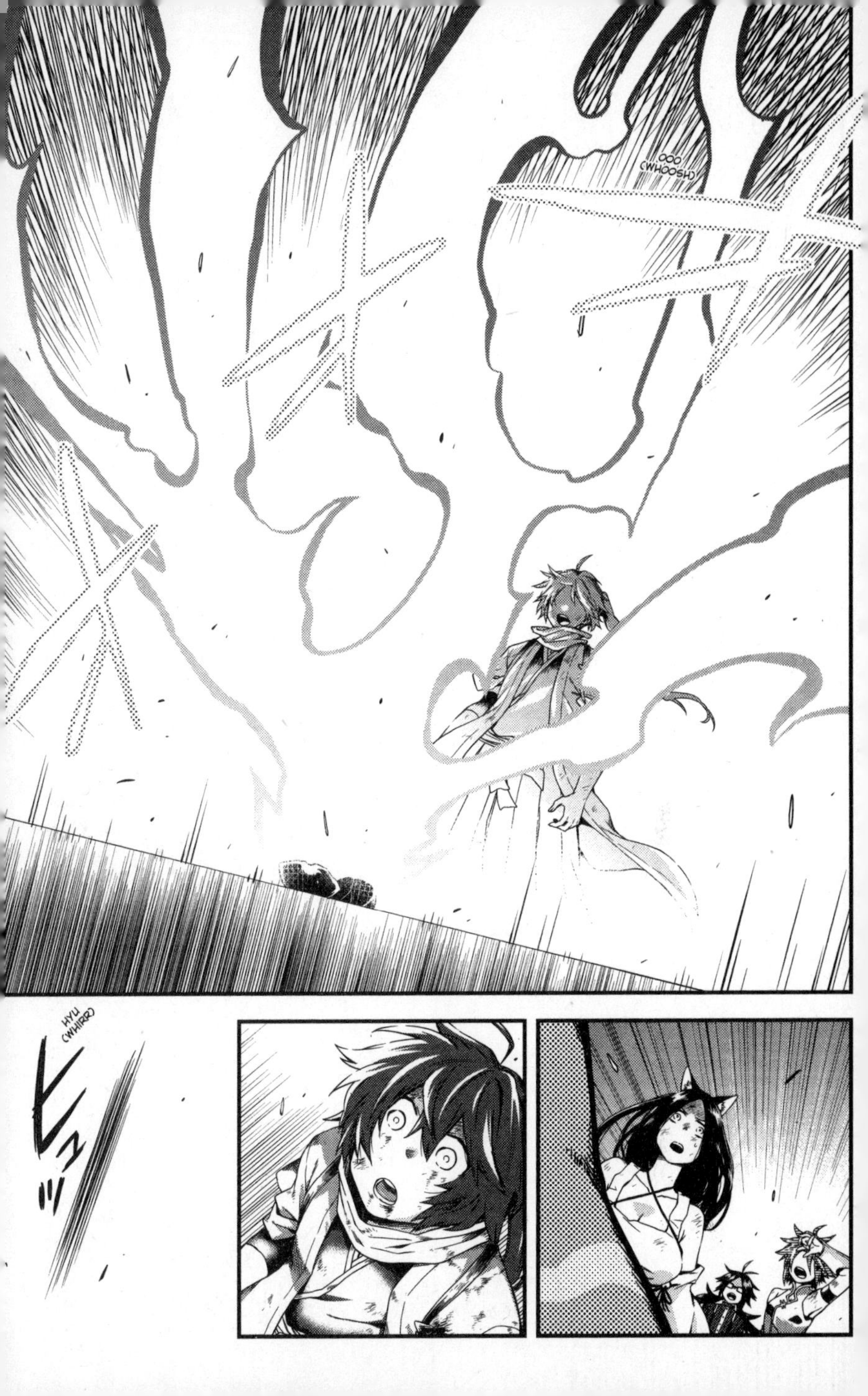
OOO (WHOOSH)
HYU (WHIRR)

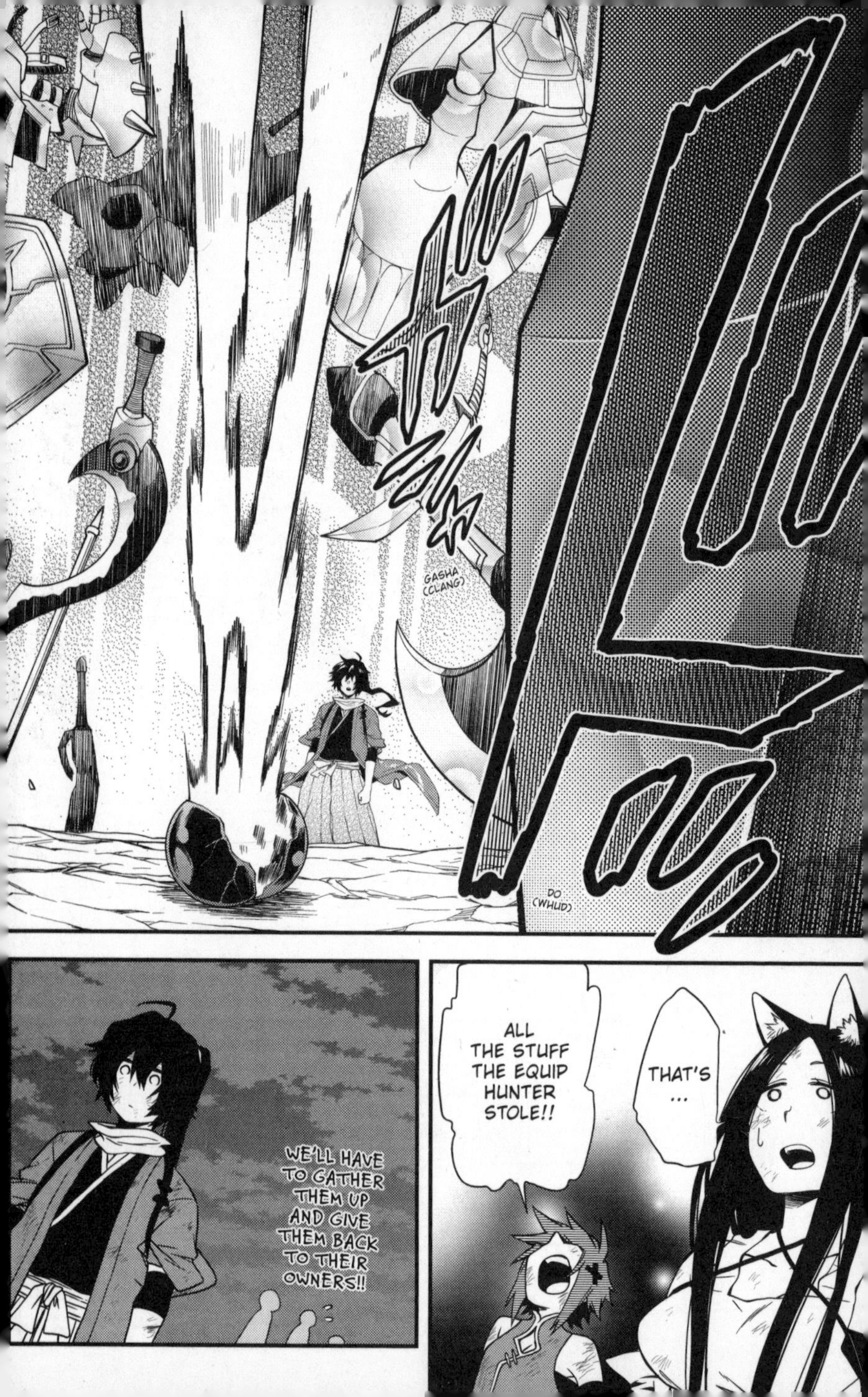
GASHA (CLANG)
DO (WHUD)
THAT'S ...
ALL THE STUFF THE EQUIP HUNTER STOLE!!
WE'LL HAVE TO GATHER THEM UP AND GIVE THEM BACK TO THEIR OWNERS!!

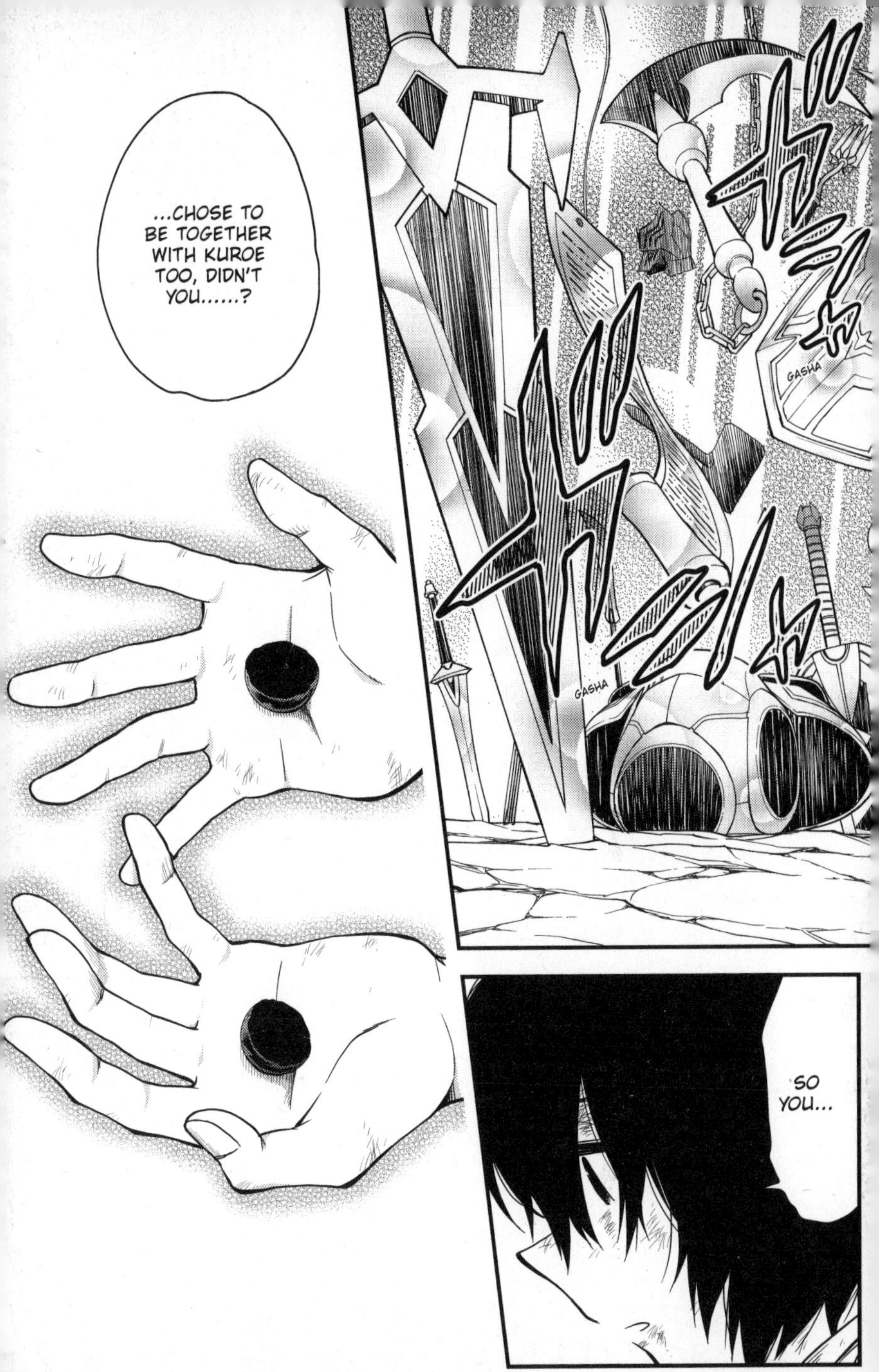
GASHA
GASHA
SO YOU...
...CHOSE TO BE TOGETHER WITH KUROE TOO, DIDN'T YOU......?

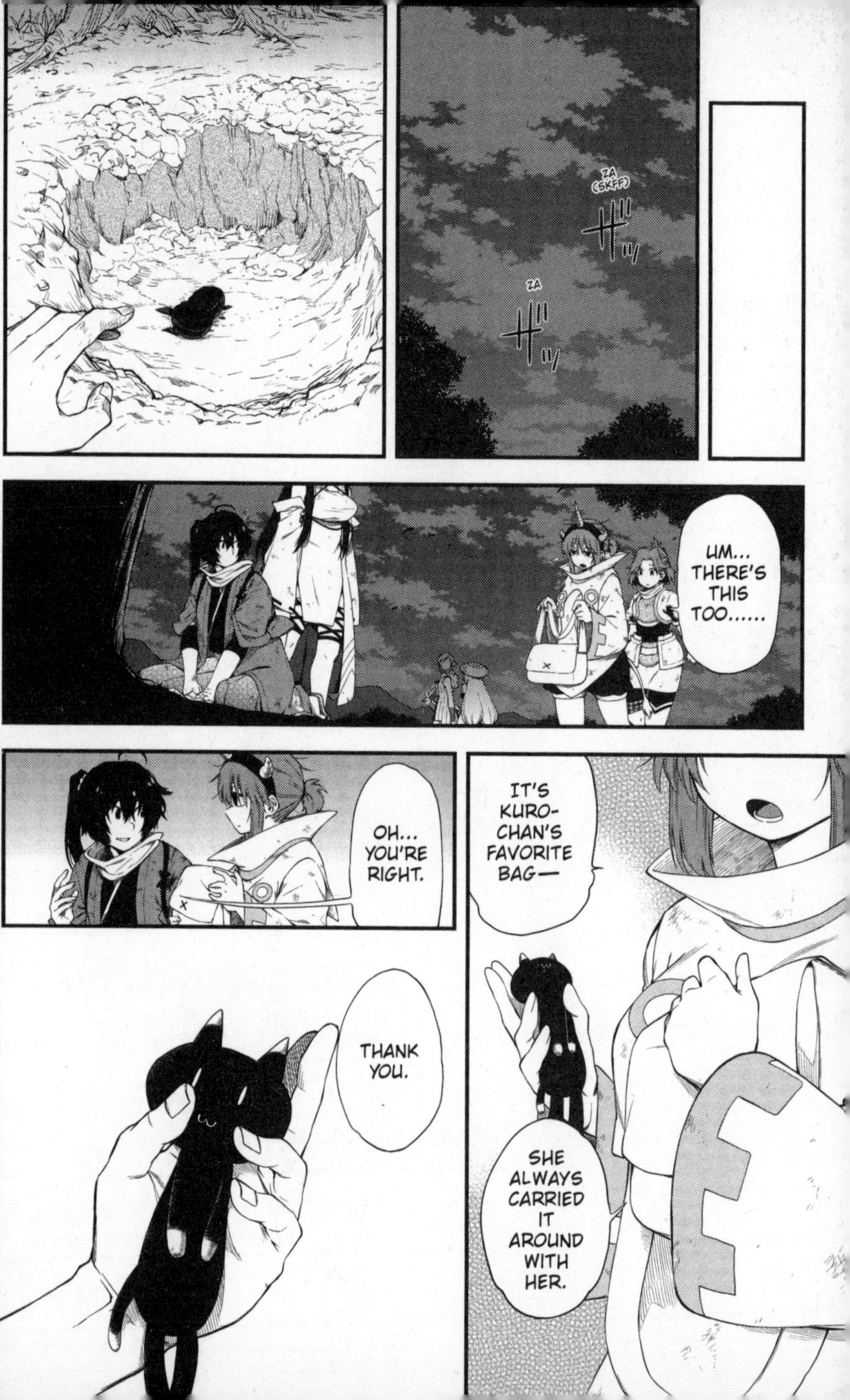
ZA (SKFF)
ZA
UM... THERE'S THIS TOO......
IT'S KURO-CHAN'S FAVORITE BAG—
SHE ALWAYS CARRIED IT AROUND WITH HER.
OH... YOU'RE RIGHT.
THANK YOU.

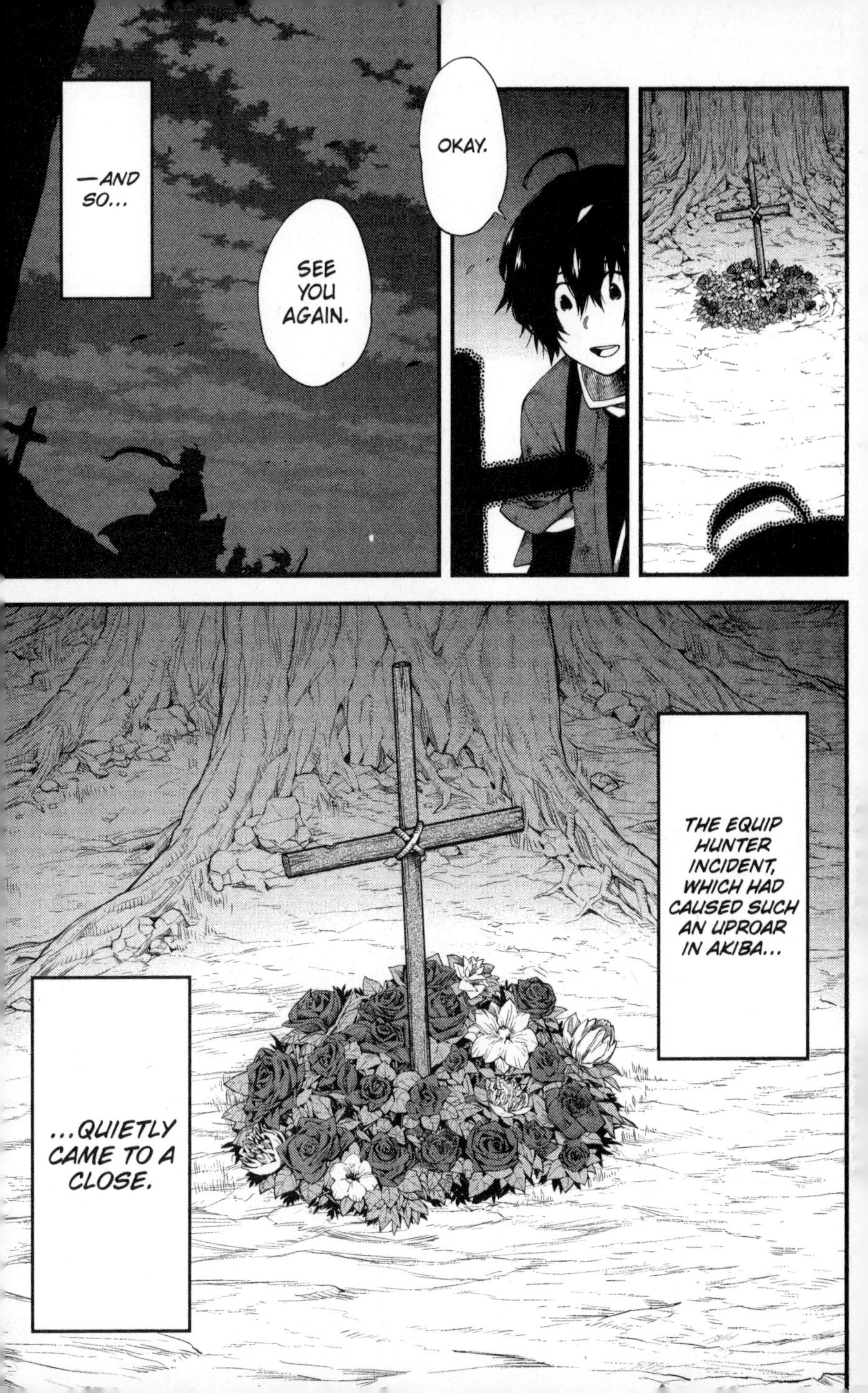
OKAY.
SEE YOU AGAIN.
—AND SO...
THE EQUIP HUNTER INCIDENT, WHICH HAD CAUSED SUCH AN UPROAR IN AKIBA...
...QUIETLY CAME TO A CLOSE.

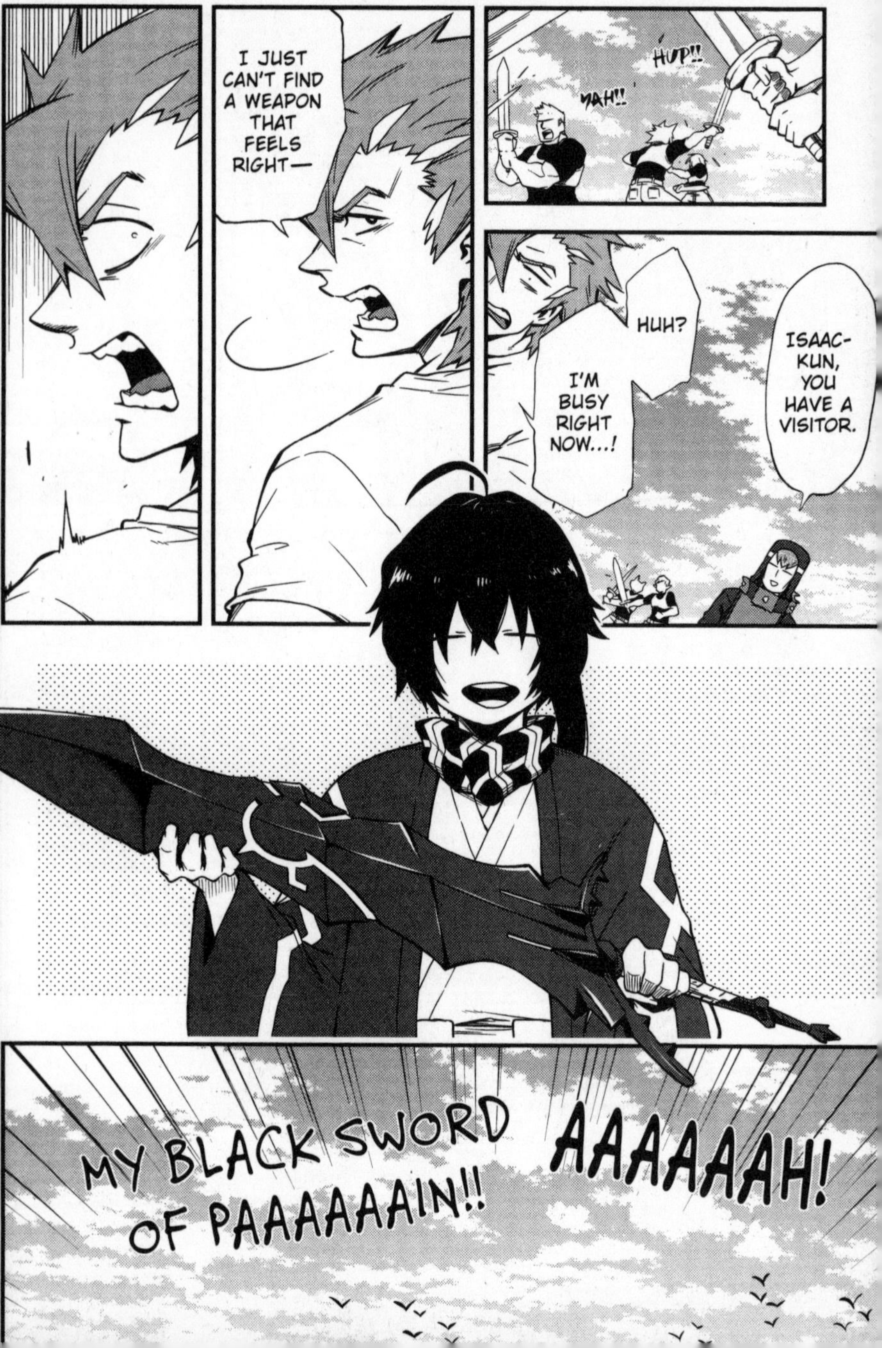
HUP!!
YAH!!
ISAAC-KUN, YOU HAVE A VISITOR.
HUH?
I'M BUSY RIGHT NOW...!
I JUST CAN'T FIND A WEAPON THAT FEELS RIGHT—
AAAAAAH!
MY BLACK SWORD OF PAAAAAAIN!!

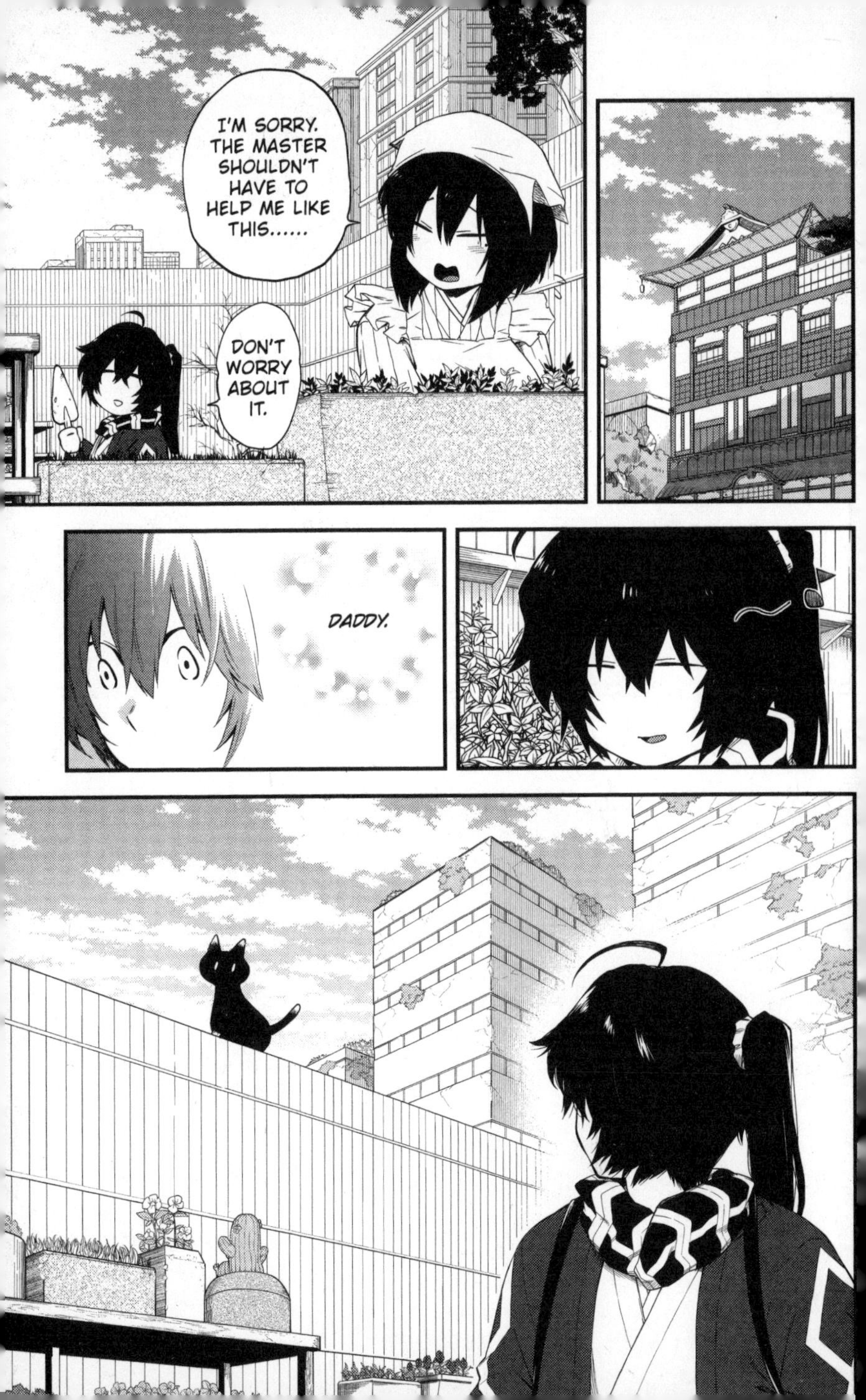
I'M SORRY. THE MASTER SHOULDN'T HAVE TO HELP ME LIKE THIS......
DON'T WORRY ABOUT IT.
DADDY.

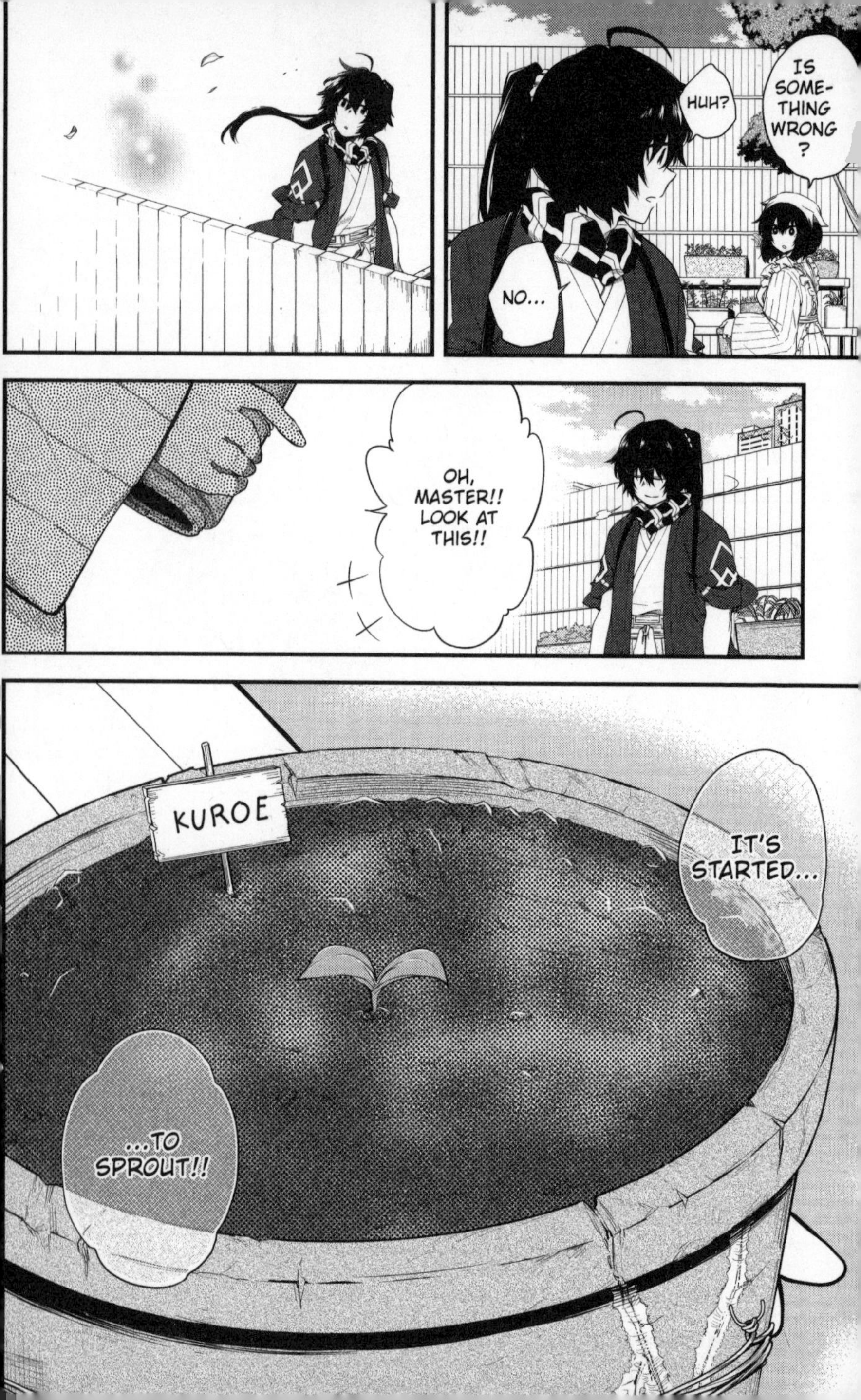
IS SOME-THING WRONG?
HUH?
NO...
OH, MASTER!! LOOK AT THIS!!
KUROE
IT'S STARTED...
...TO SPROUT!!

LOG HORIZON
THE WEST WIND BRIGADE

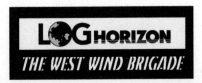

LOG HORIZON

THE WEST WIND BRIGADE

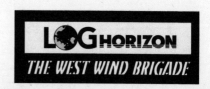

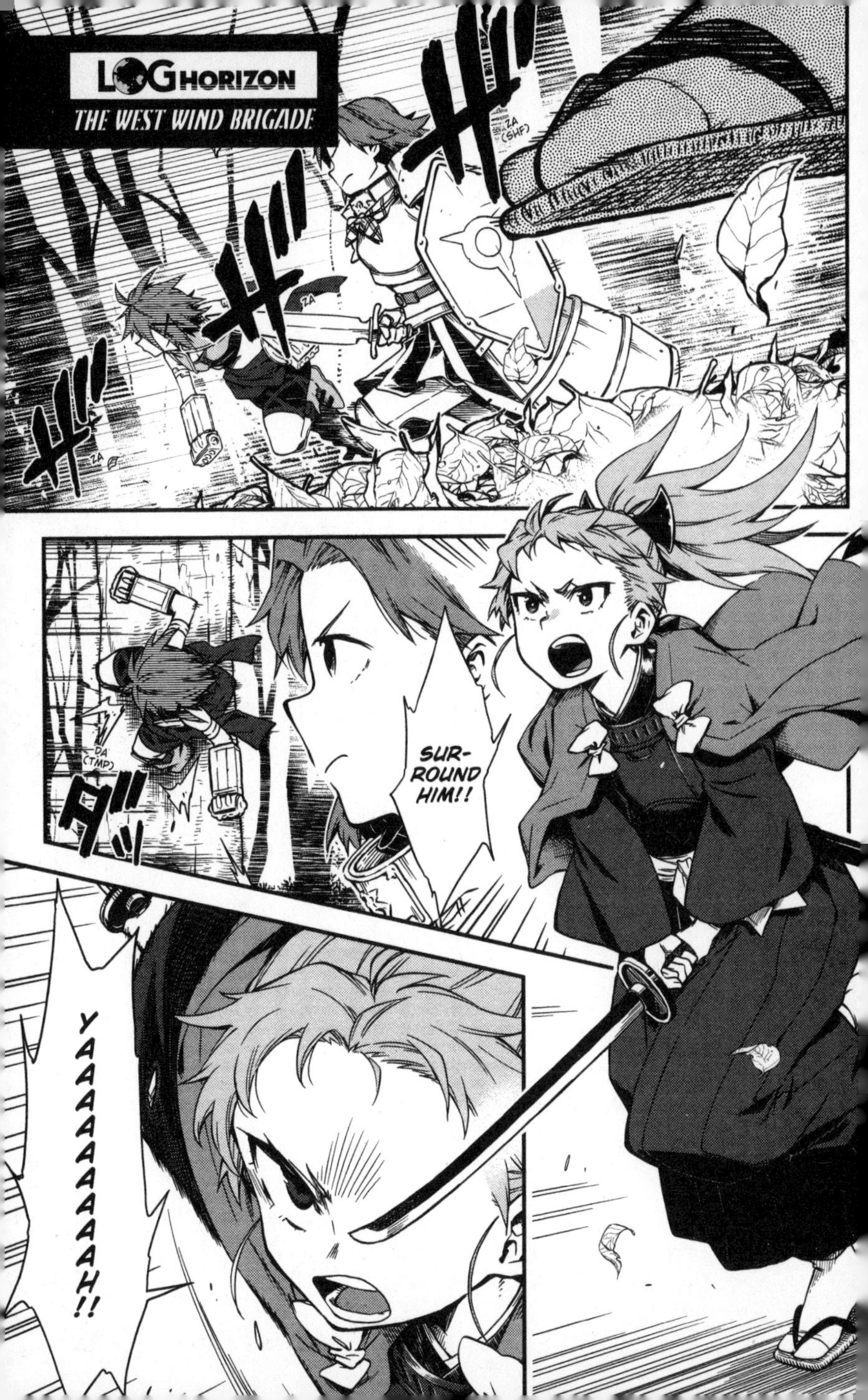
LOG HORIZON
THE WEST WIND BRIGADE
ZA (SHF)
ZA
ZA
SUR-ROUND HIM!!
DA (TMP)
YAAAAAAAAAAAH!!

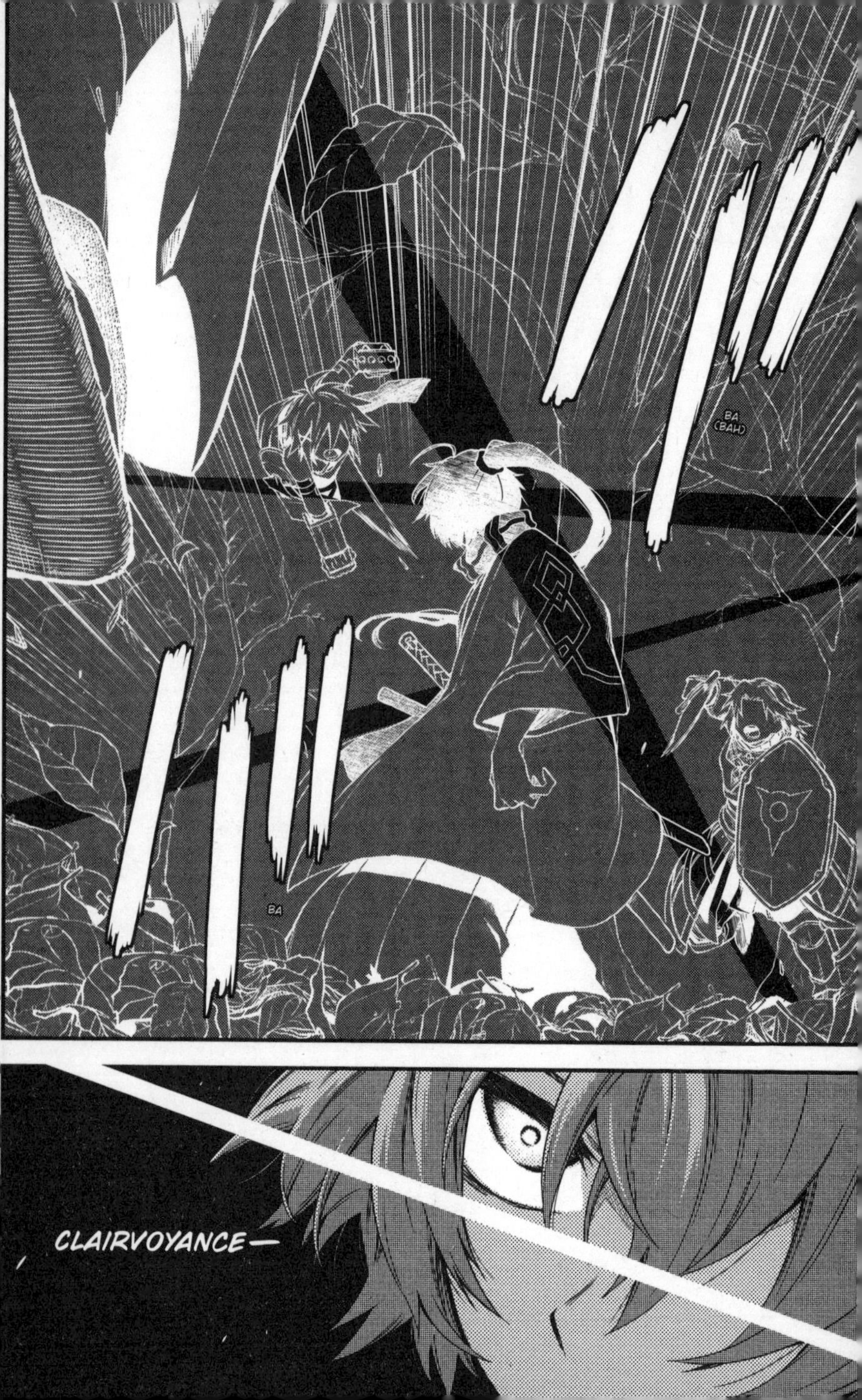
BA
(BAH)
BA
CLAIRVOYANCE—

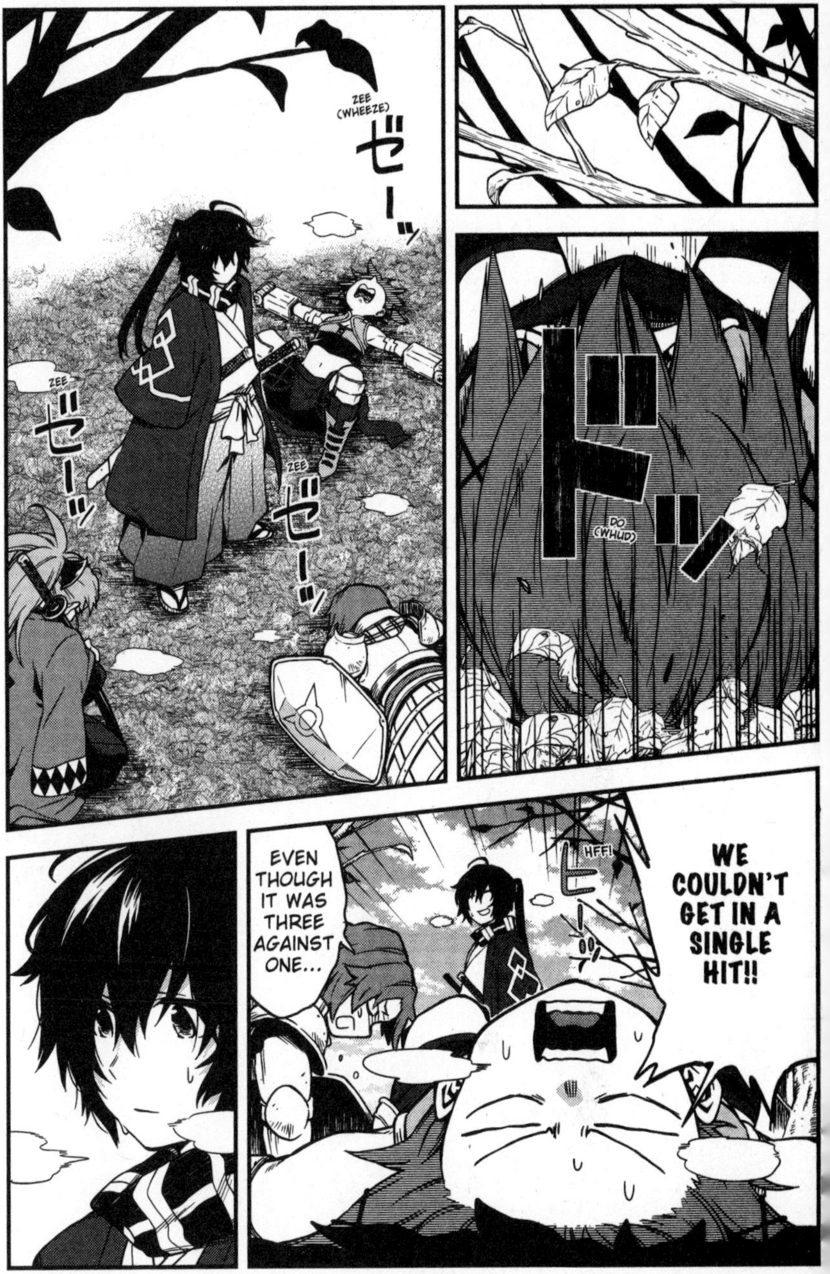
DO
(WHUD)
ドドッ
ZEE
(WHEEZE)
ゼーッ
ZEE
ゼーッ
ZEE
ゼーッ
WE COULDN'T GET IN A SINGLE HIT!!
HFF!
ヒーッ
EVEN THOUGH IT WAS THREE AGAINST ONE...

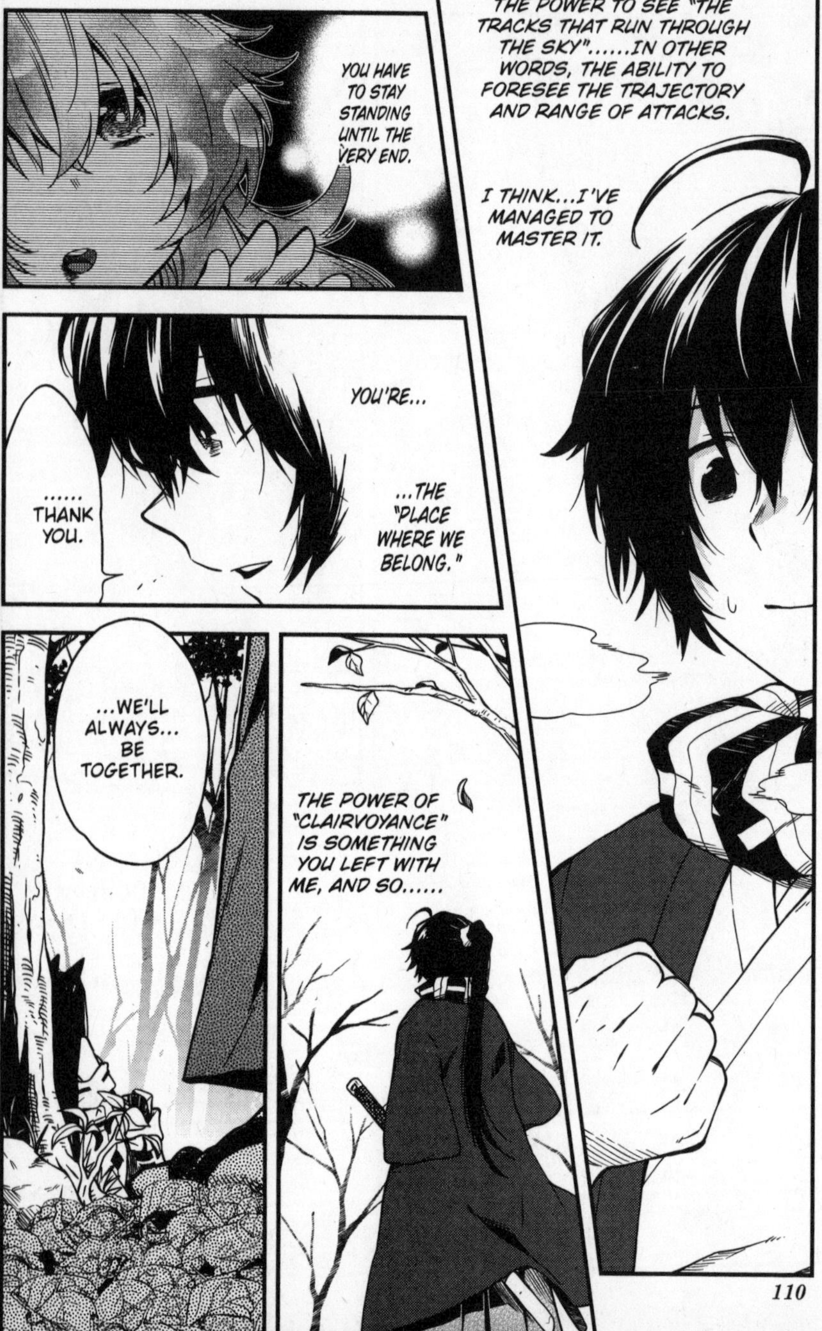
THE POWER TO SEE "THE TRACKS THAT RUN THROUGH THE SKY"......IN OTHER WORDS, THE ABILITY TO FORESEE THE TRAJECTORY AND RANGE OF ATTACKS.
I THINK...I'VE MANAGED TO MASTER IT.
YOU HAVE TO STAY STANDING UNTIL THE VERY END.
YOU'RE...
...THE "PLACE WHERE WE BELONG."
......THANK YOU.
THE POWER OF "CLAIRVOYANCE" IS SOMETHING YOU LEFT WITH ME, AND SO......
...WE'LL ALWAYS... BE TOGETHER.

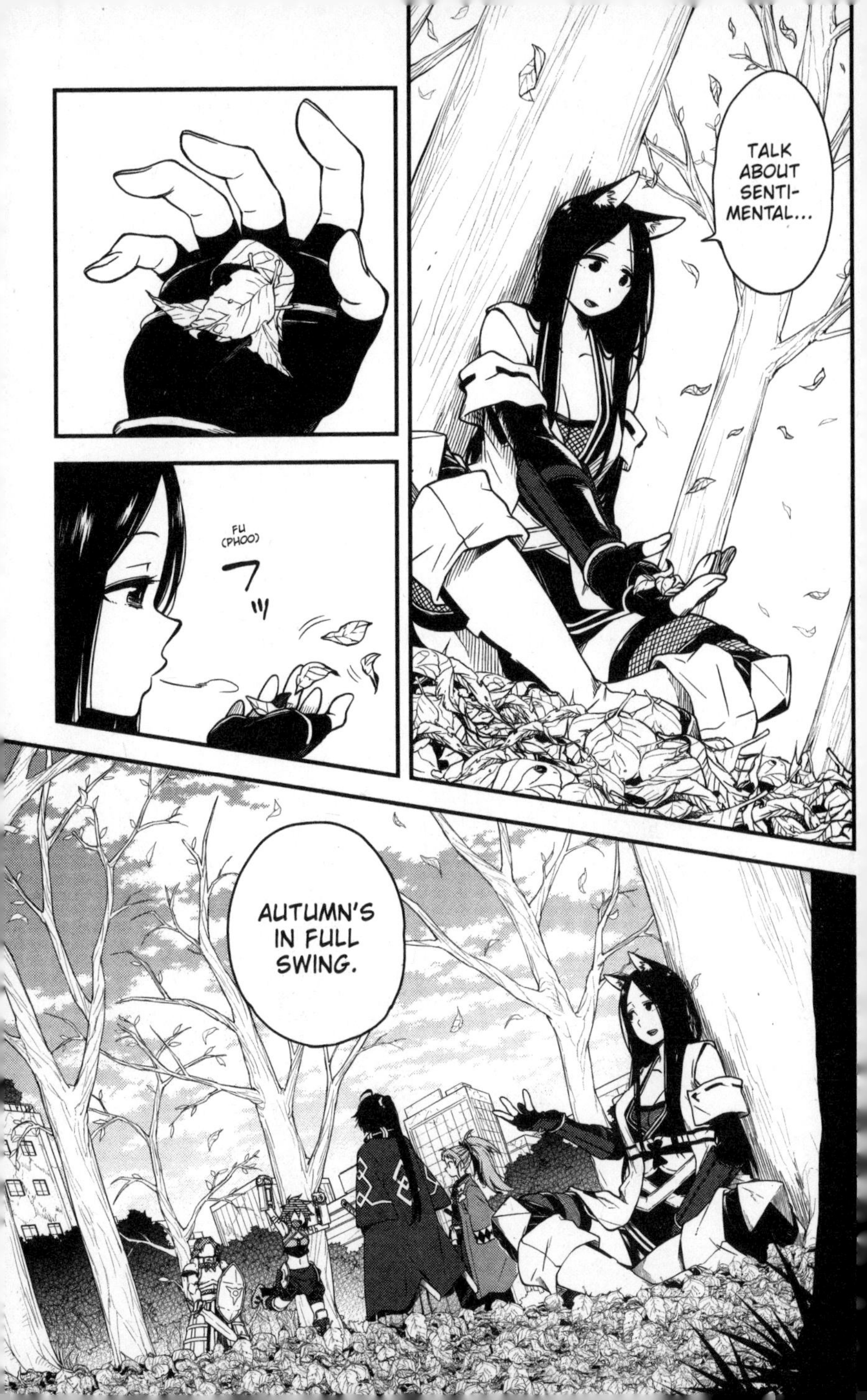
TALK ABOUT SENTI-MENTAL...
FU (PHOO)
フッ
AUTUMN'S IN FULL SWING.

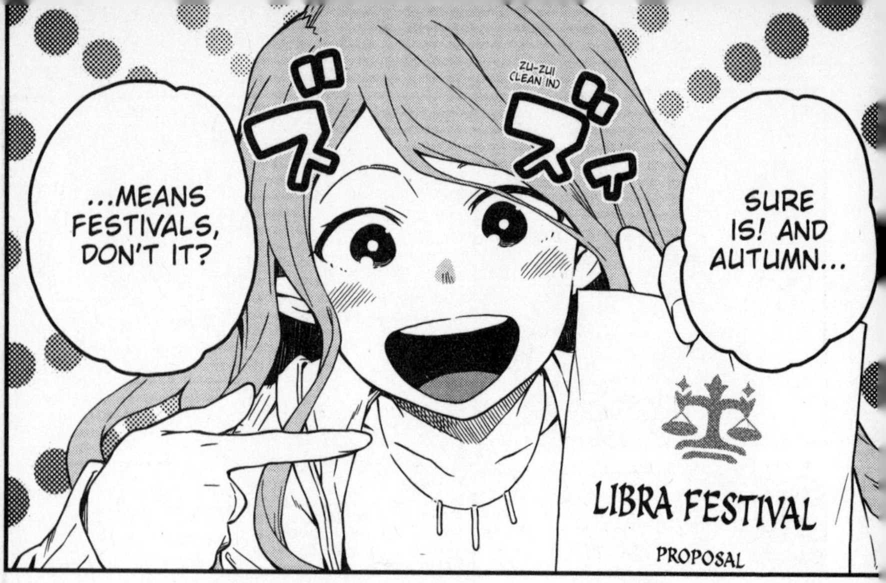
SURE IS! AND AUTUMN...
ZU-ZUI (CLEAN IN)
...MEANS FESTIVALS, DON'T IT?
LIBRA FESTIVAL
PROPOSAL

CHAPTER: 64 The Libra Festival

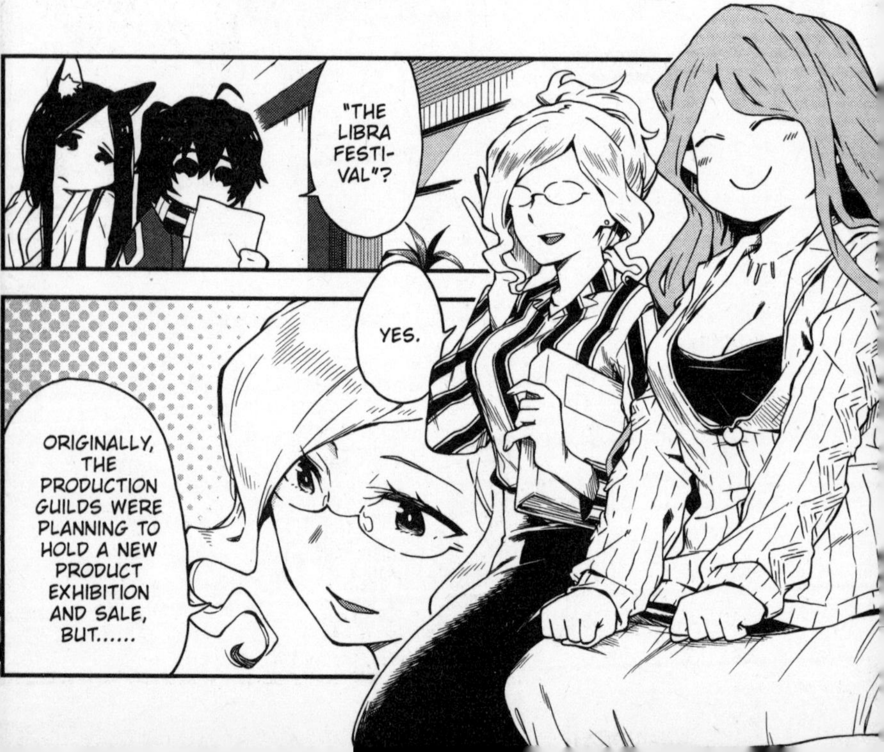
"THE LIBRA FESTI-VAL"?
YES.
ORIGINALLY, THE PRODUCTION GUILDS WERE PLANNING TO HOLD A NEW PRODUCT EXHIBITION AND SALE, BUT......

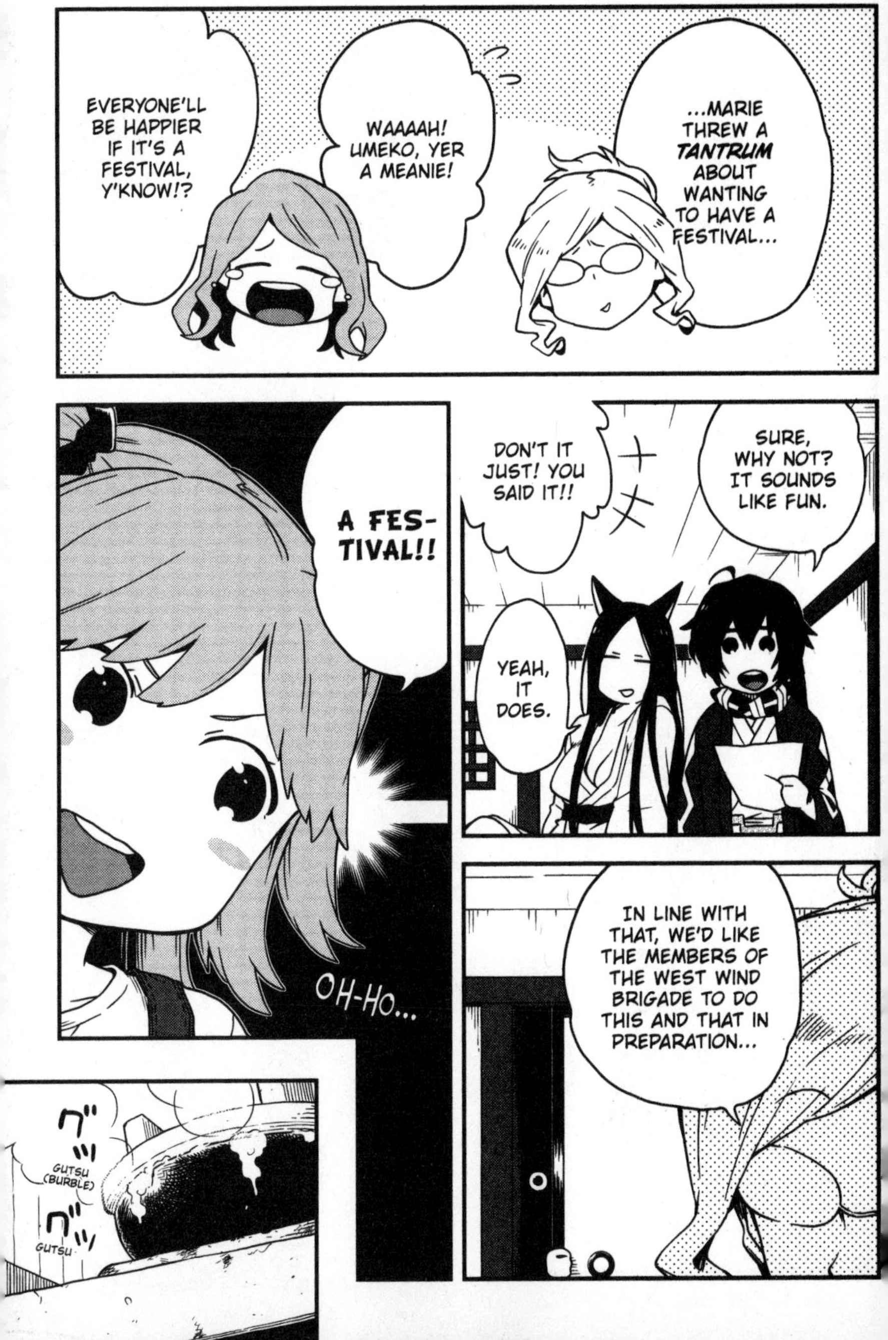
...MARIE THREW A *TANTRUM* ABOUT WANTING TO HAVE A FESTIVAL...
WAAAAH! UMEKO, YER A MEANIE!
EVERYONE'LL BE HAPPIER IF IT'S A FESTIVAL, Y'KNOW!?
SURE, WHY NOT? IT SOUNDS LIKE FUN.
DON'T IT JUST! YOU SAID IT!!
YEAH, IT DOES.
IN LINE WITH THAT, WE'D LIKE THE MEMBERS OF THE WEST WIND BRIGADE TO DO THIS AND THAT IN PREPARATION...
A FES-TIVAL!!
OH-HO...
グツ
GUTSU (BURBLE)
グツ
GUTSU

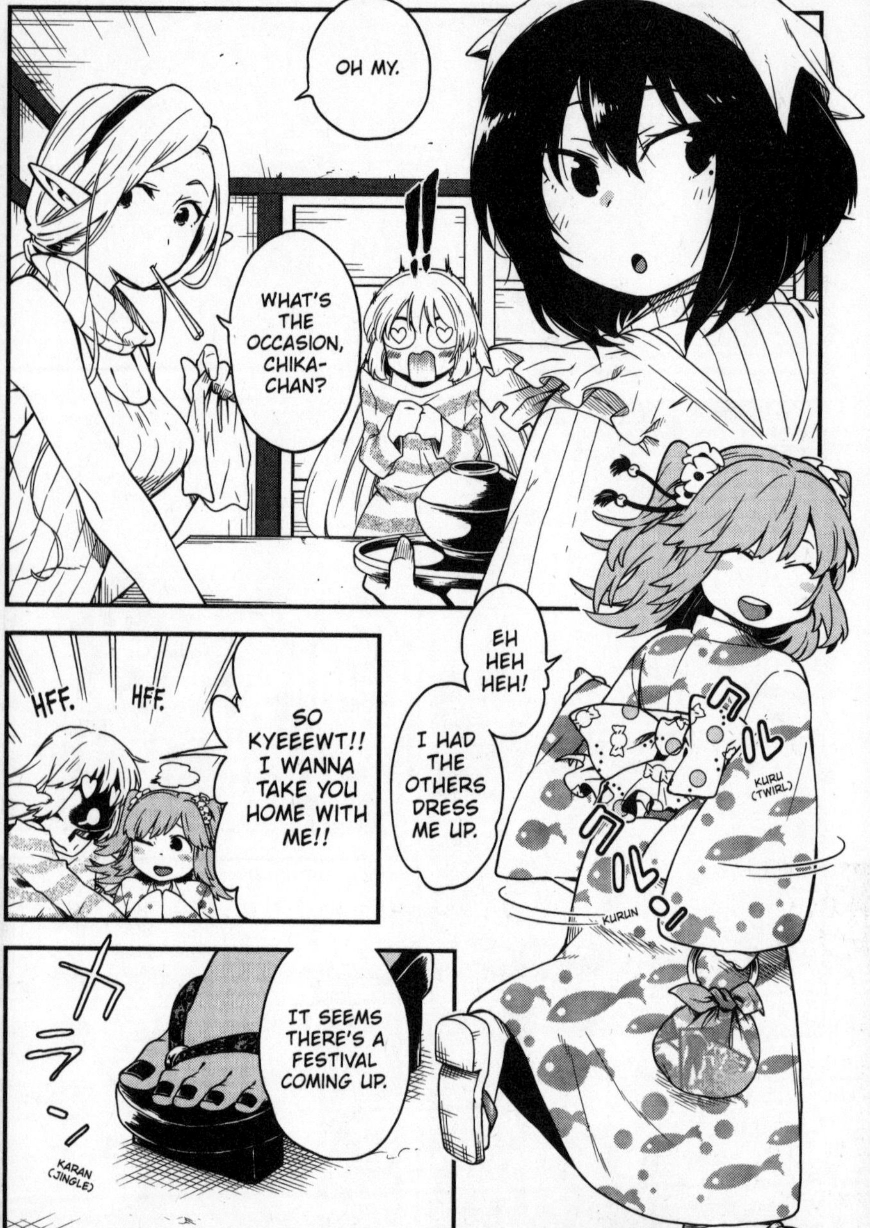
OH MY.
WHAT'S THE OCCASION, CHIKA-CHAN?
EH HEH HEH!
I HAD THE OTHERS DRESS ME UP.
KURU (TWIRL)
KURUN
HFF. HFF.
SO KYEEEWT!! I WANNA TAKE YOU HOME WITH ME!!
IT SEEMS THERE'S A FESTIVAL COMING UP.
KARAN (JINGLE)

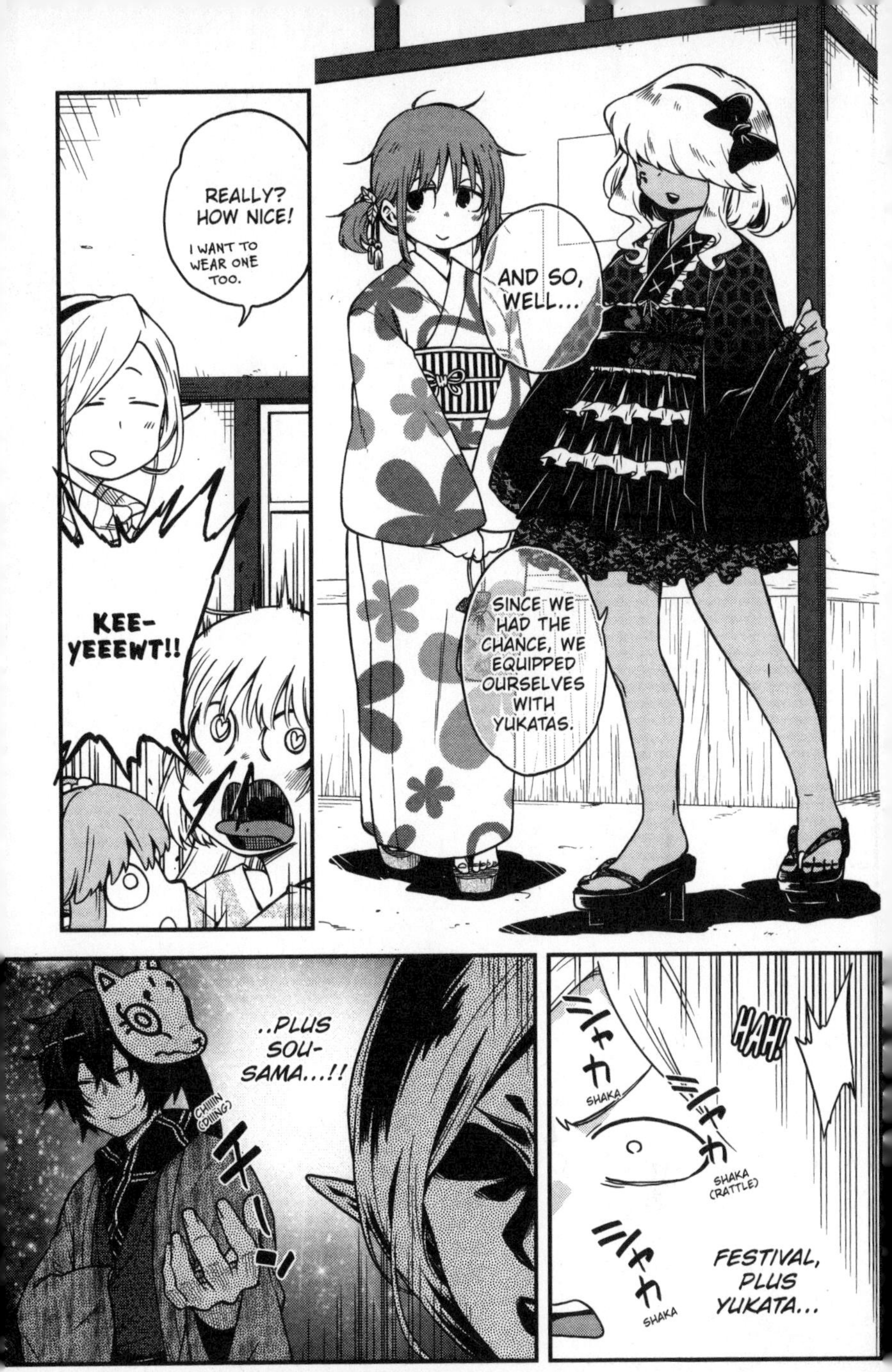
AND SO, WELL...
SINCE WE HAD THE CHANCE, WE EQUIPPED OURSELVES WITH YUKATAS.
REALLY? HOW NICE!
I WANT TO WEAR ONE TOO.
KEE-YEEEWT!!
HAH!
シャカ
SHAKA
シャカ
SHAKA (RATTLE)
シャカ
SHAKA
FESTIVAL, PLUS YUKATA...
..PLUS SOU-SAMA...!!
CHIIIN (DIING)

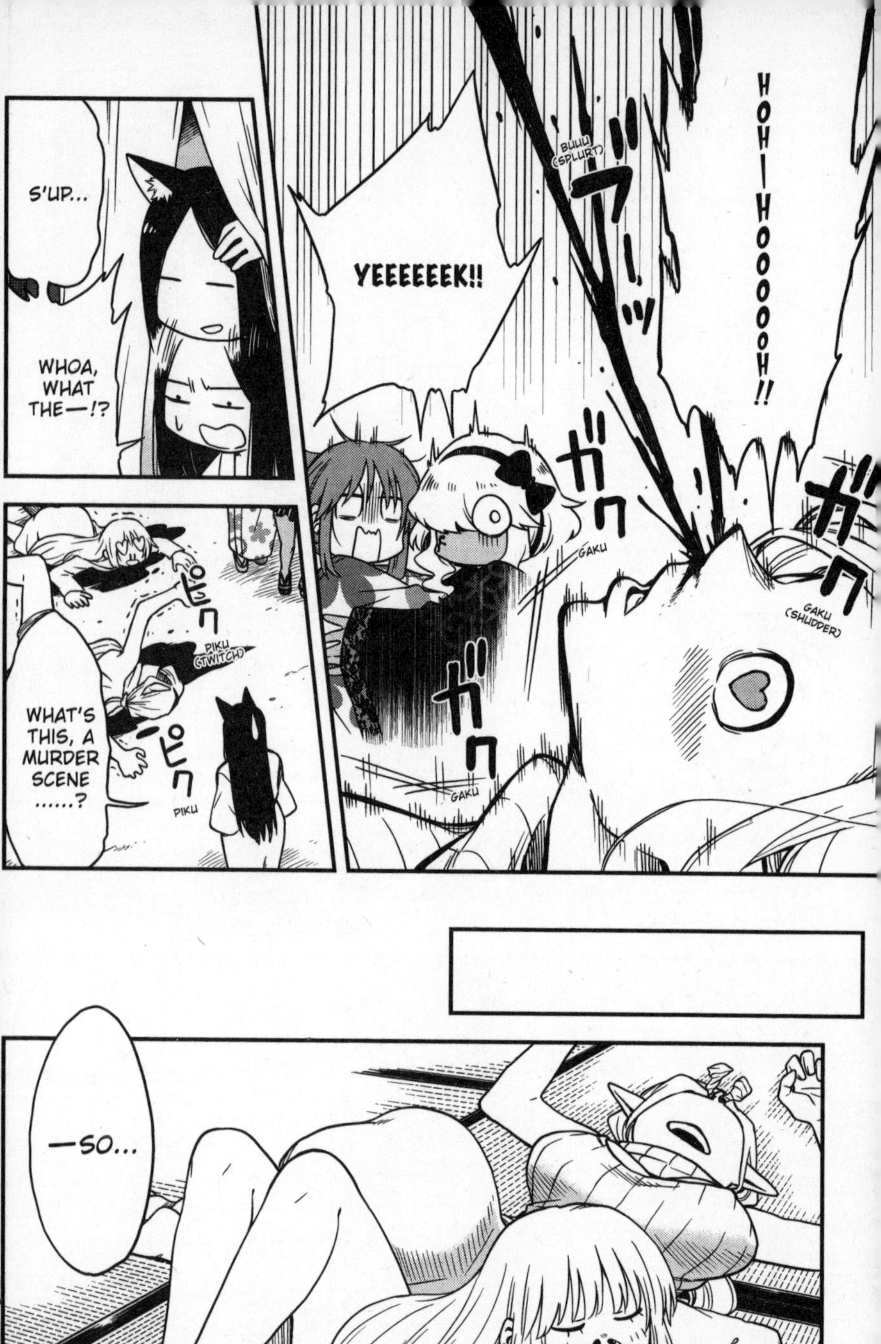
HOHIHOOOOOOH!!
BUUU (SPLURT)
YEEEEEEK!!
GAKU (SHUDDER)
GAKU
GAKU
S'UP...
WHOA, WHAT THE—!?
PIKU (TWITCH)
PIKU
WHAT'S THIS, A MURDER SCENE ......?
—SO...

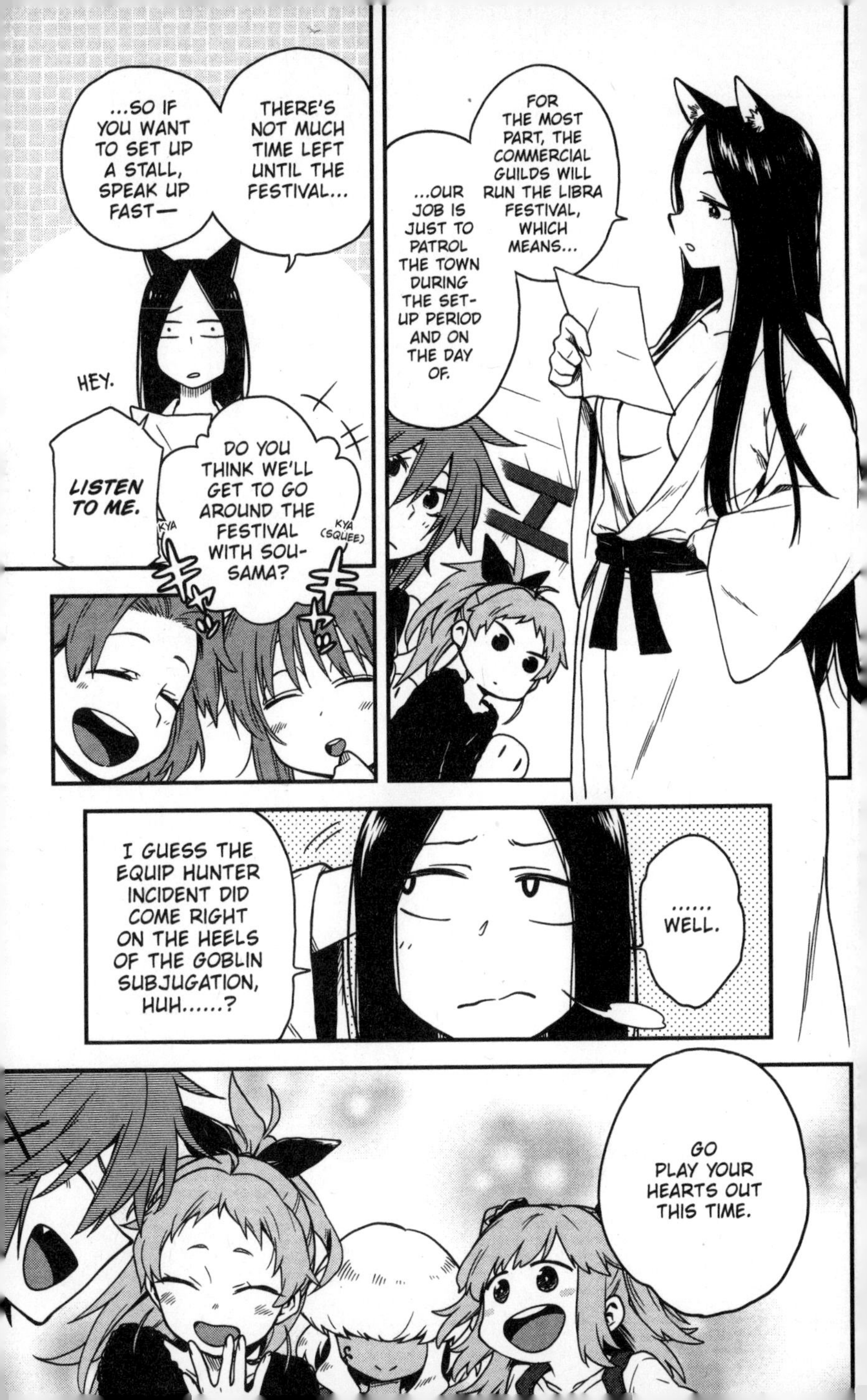

FOR THE MOST PART, THE COMMERCIAL GUILDS WILL RUN THE LIBRA FESTIVAL, WHICH MEANS...
...OUR JOB IS JUST TO PATROL THE TOWN DURING THE SET-UP PERIOD AND ON THE DAY OF.
THERE'S NOT MUCH TIME LEFT UNTIL THE FESTIVAL...
...SO IF YOU WANT TO SET UP A STALL, SPEAK UP FAST—
HEY.
DO YOU THINK WE'LL GET TO GO AROUND THE FESTIVAL WITH SOU-SAMA?
LISTEN TO ME.
KYA (SQUEE)
KYA
......WELL.
I GUESS THE EQUIP HUNTER INCIDENT DID COME RIGHT ON THE HEELS OF THE GOBLIN SUBJUGATION, HUH......?
GO PLAY YOUR HEARTS OUT THIS TIME.

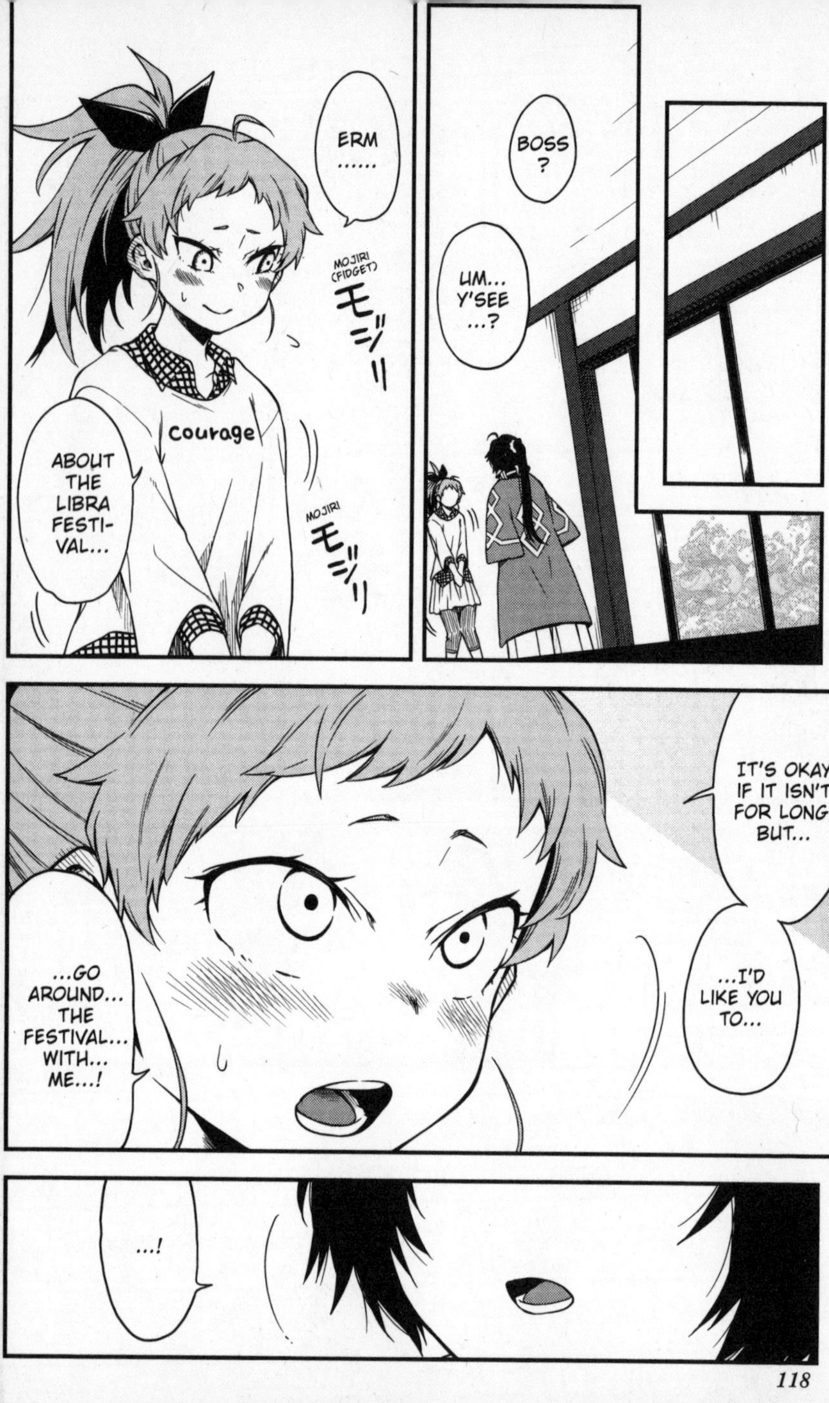
BOSS?
UM... Y'SEE...?
ERM......
MOJIRI (FIDGET)
モジリ
Courage
ABOUT THE LIBRA FESTI-VAL...
MOJIRI
モジリ
IT'S OKAY IF IT ISN'T FOR LONG, BUT...
...I'D LIKE YOU TO...
...GO AROUND... THE FESTIVAL... WITH... ME...!
...!

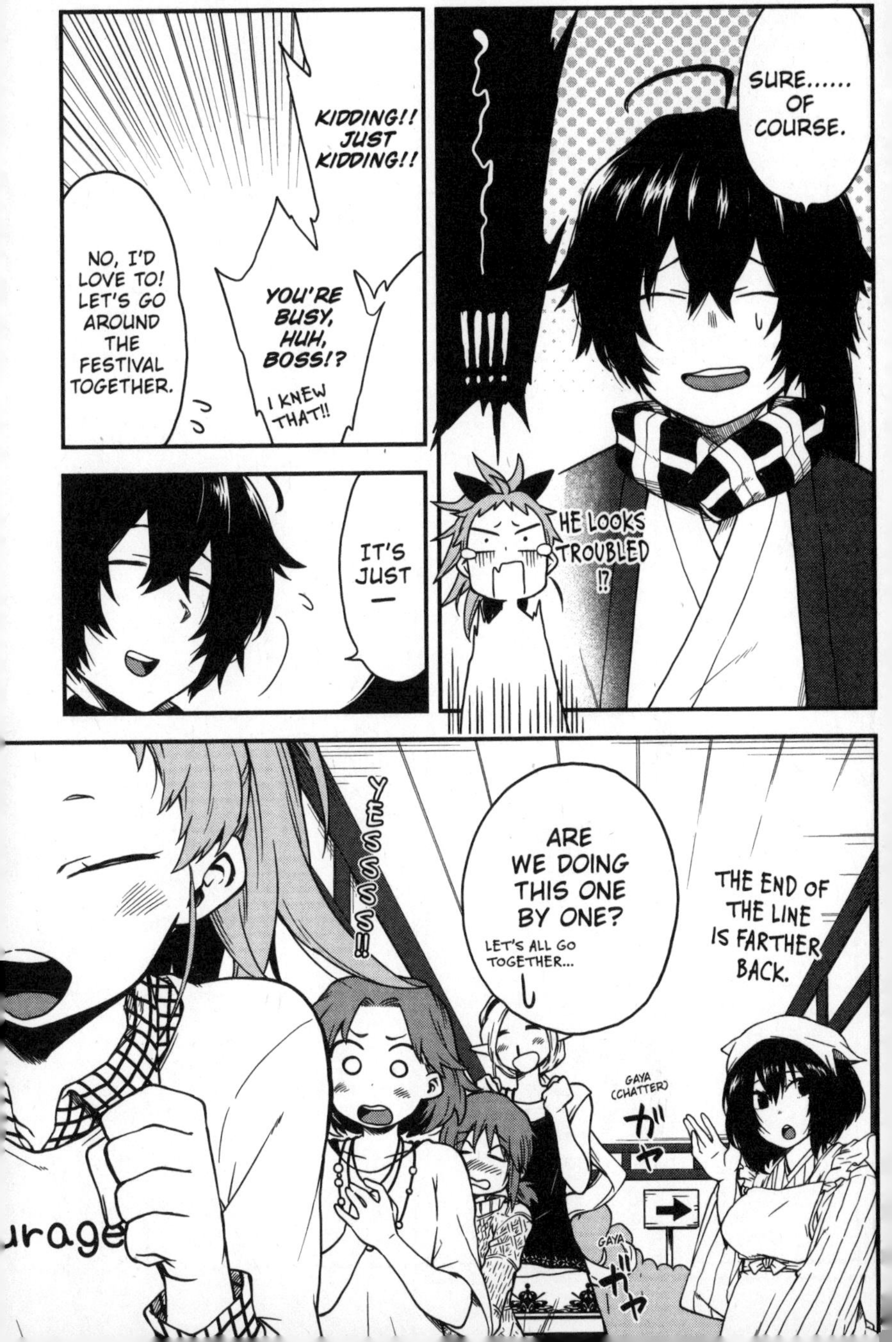
SURE...... OF COURSE.
!!!!
HE LOOKS TROUBLED!?
KIDDING!! JUST KIDDING!!
YOU'RE BUSY, HUH, BOSS!?
I KNEW THAT!!
NO, I'D LOVE TO! LET'S GO AROUND THE FESTIVAL TOGETHER.
IT'S JUST—
THE END OF THE LINE IS FARTHER BACK.
ARE WE DOING THIS ONE BY ONE?
LET'S ALL GO TOGETHER...
YESSSSS!!
GAYA (CHATTER)
ガヤ
GAYA
ガヤ

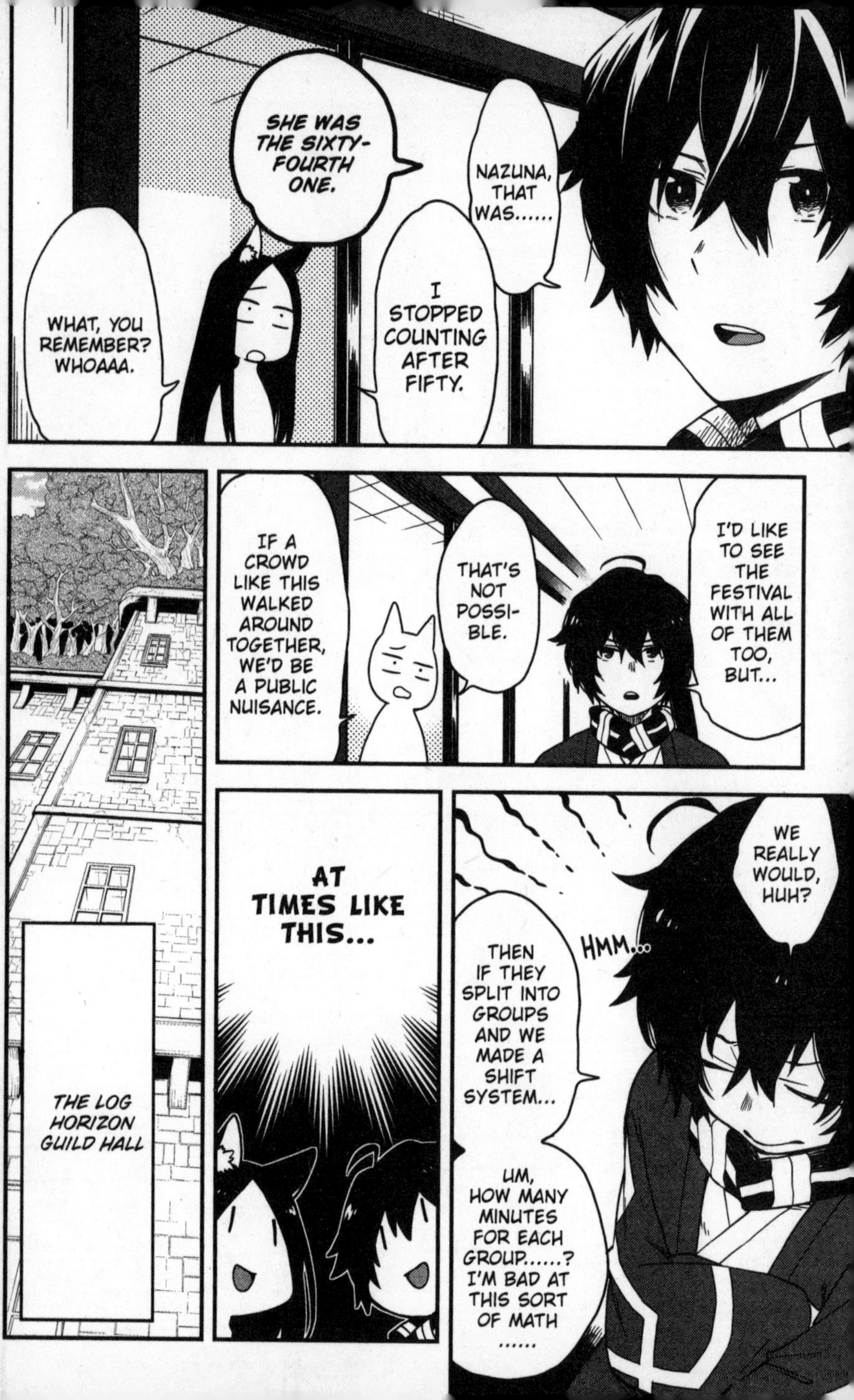
NAZUNA, THAT WAS......
SHE WAS THE SIXTY-FOURTH ONE.
I STOPPED COUNTING AFTER FIFTY.
WHAT, YOU REMEMBER? WHOAAA.
I'D LIKE TO SEE THE FESTIVAL WITH ALL OF THEM TOO, BUT...
THAT'S NOT POSSIBLE.
IF A CROWD LIKE THIS WALKED AROUND TOGETHER, WE'D BE A PUBLIC NUISANCE.
WE REALLY WOULD, HUH?
HMM...
THEN IF THEY SPLIT INTO GROUPS AND WE MADE A SHIFT SYSTEM...
UM, HOW MANY MINUTES FOR EACH GROUP......? I'M BAD AT THIS SORT OF MATH ......
AT TIMES LIKE THIS...
THE LOG HORIZON GUILD HALL

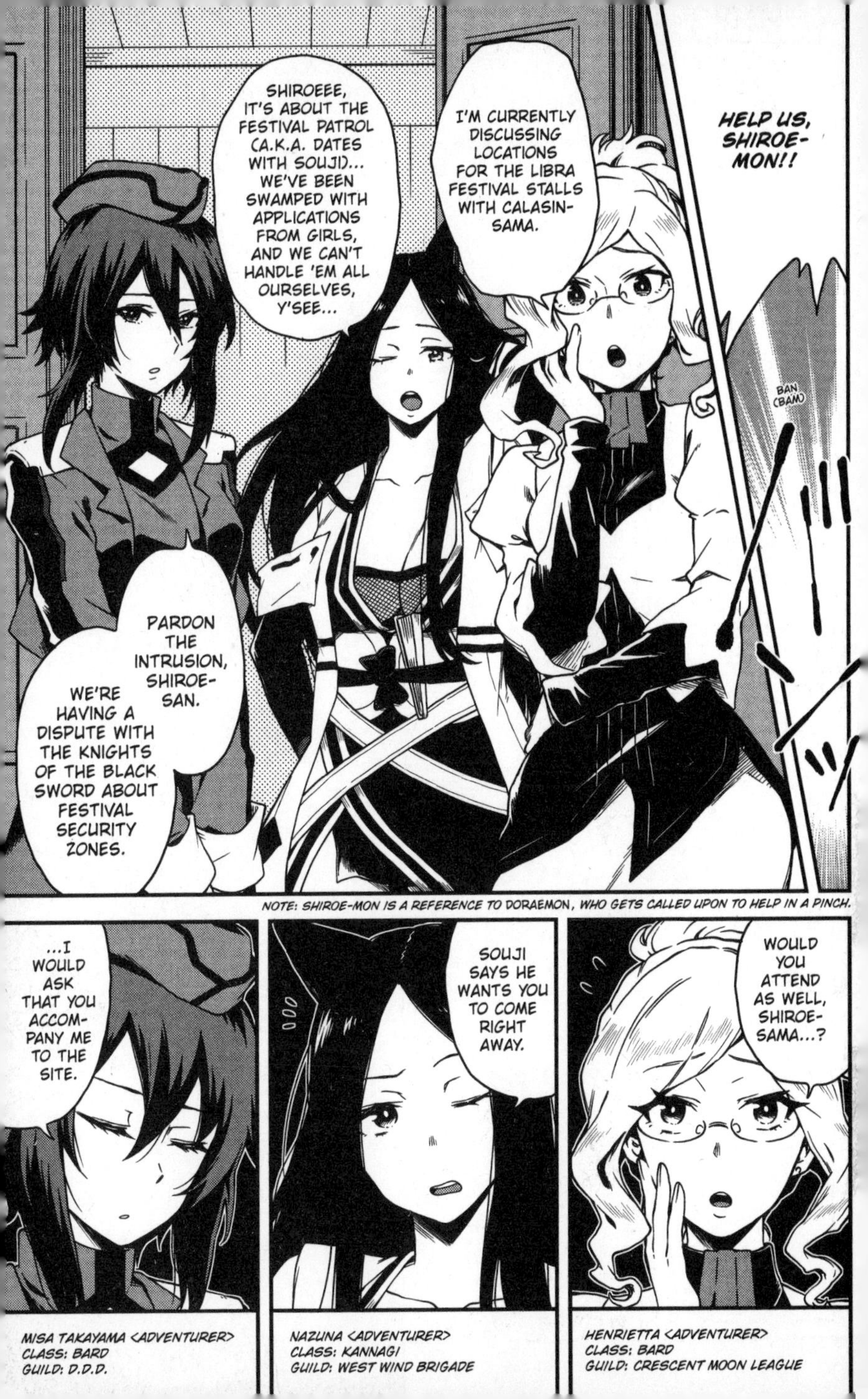
HELP US, SHIROE-MON!!
BAN (BAM)
I'M CURRENTLY DISCUSSING LOCATIONS FOR THE LIBRA FESTIVAL STALLS WITH CALASIN-SAMA.
SHIROEEE, IT'S ABOUT THE FESTIVAL PATROL (A.K.A. DATES WITH SOUJI)... WE'VE BEEN SWAMPED WITH APPLICATIONS FROM GIRLS, AND WE CAN'T HANDLE 'EM ALL OURSELVES, Y'SEE...
PARDON THE INTRUSION, SHIROE-SAN.
WE'RE HAVING A DISPUTE WITH THE KNIGHTS OF THE BLACK SWORD ABOUT FESTIVAL SECURITY ZONES.
WOULD YOU ATTEND AS WELL, SHIROE-SAMA...?
HENRIETTA <ADVENTURER>
CLASS: BARD
GUILD: CRESCENT MOON LEAGUE
SOUJI SAYS HE WANTS YOU TO COME RIGHT AWAY.
NAZUNA <ADVENTURER>
CLASS: KANNAGI
GUILD: WEST WIND BRIGADE
...I WOULD ASK THAT YOU ACCOMPANY ME TO THE SITE.
MISA TAKAYAMA <ADVENTURER>
CLASS: BARD
GUILD: D.D.D.
NOTE: SHIROE-MON IS A REFERENCE TO DORAEMON, WHO GETS CALLED UPON TO HELP IN A PINCH.

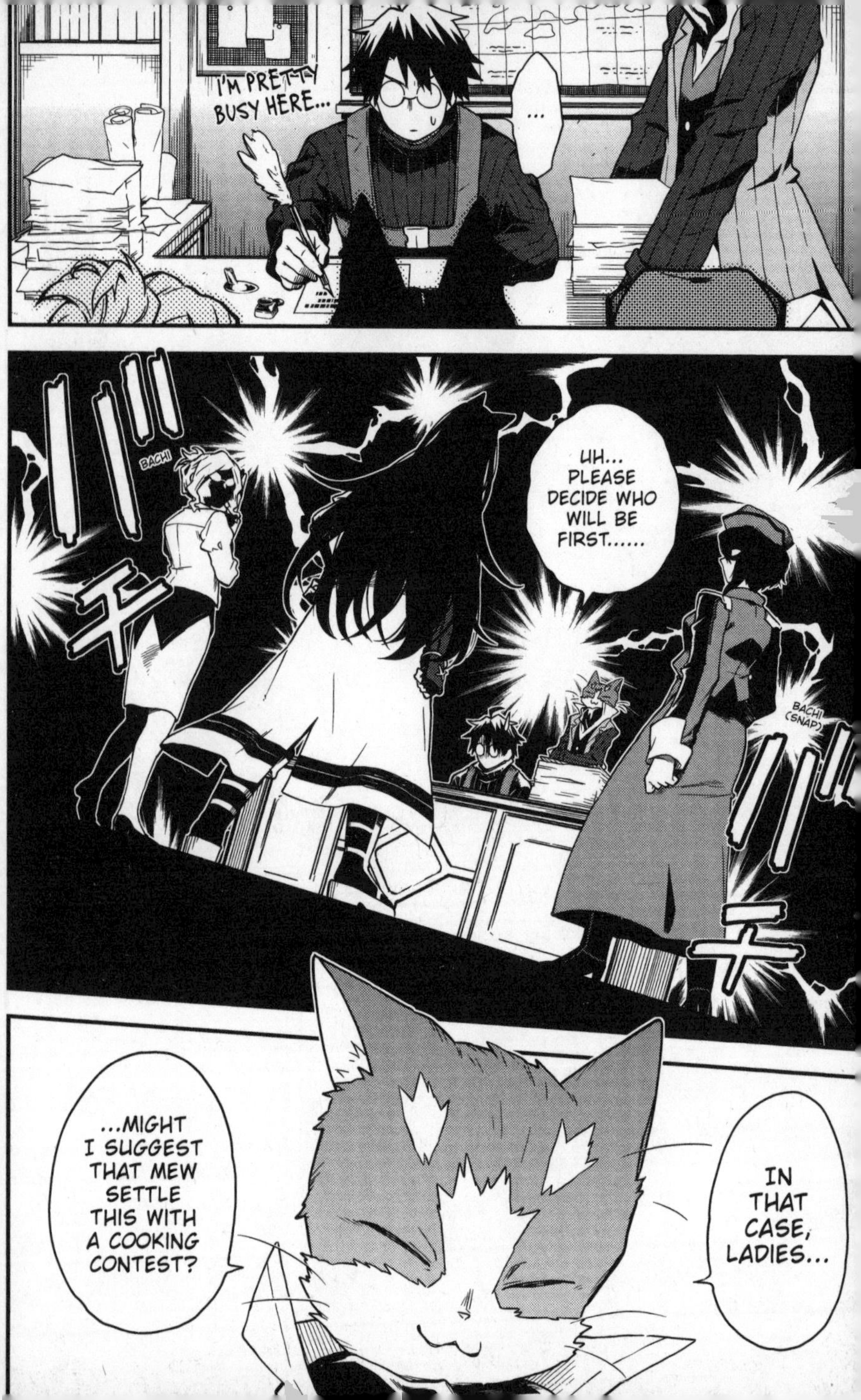
...
I'M PRETTY BUSY HERE...
UH... PLEASE DECIDE WHO WILL BE FIRST......
BACHI (SNAP)
BACHI
IN THAT CASE, LADIES...
...MIGHT I SUGGEST THAT MEW SETTLE THIS WITH A COOKING CONTEST?

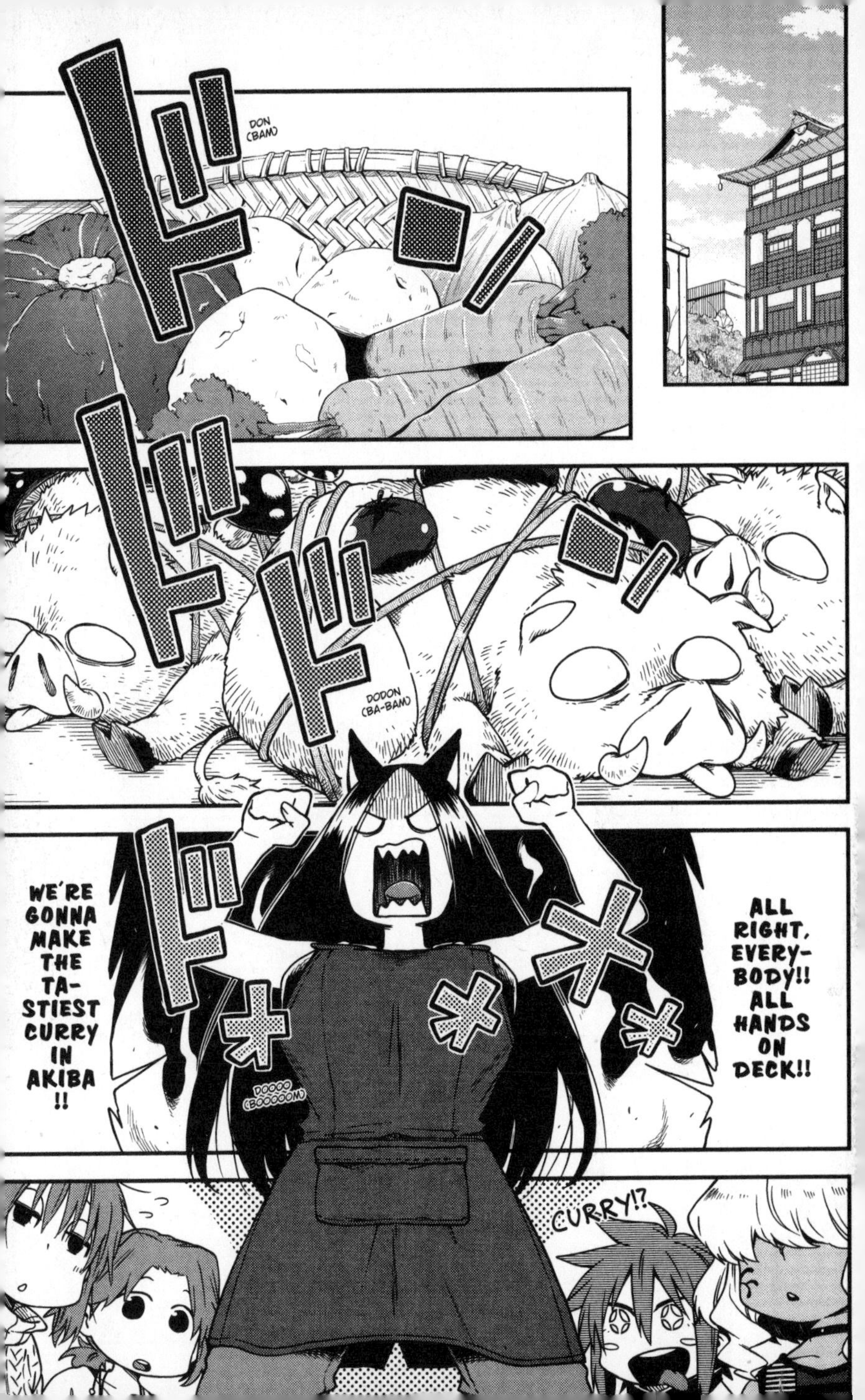

DON (BAM)
DODON (BA-BAM)
ALL RIGHT, EVERYBODY!! ALL HANDS ON DECK!!
WE'RE GONNA MAKE THE TASTIEST CURRY IN AKIBA!!
DOOOO (BOOOOOM)
CURRY!?

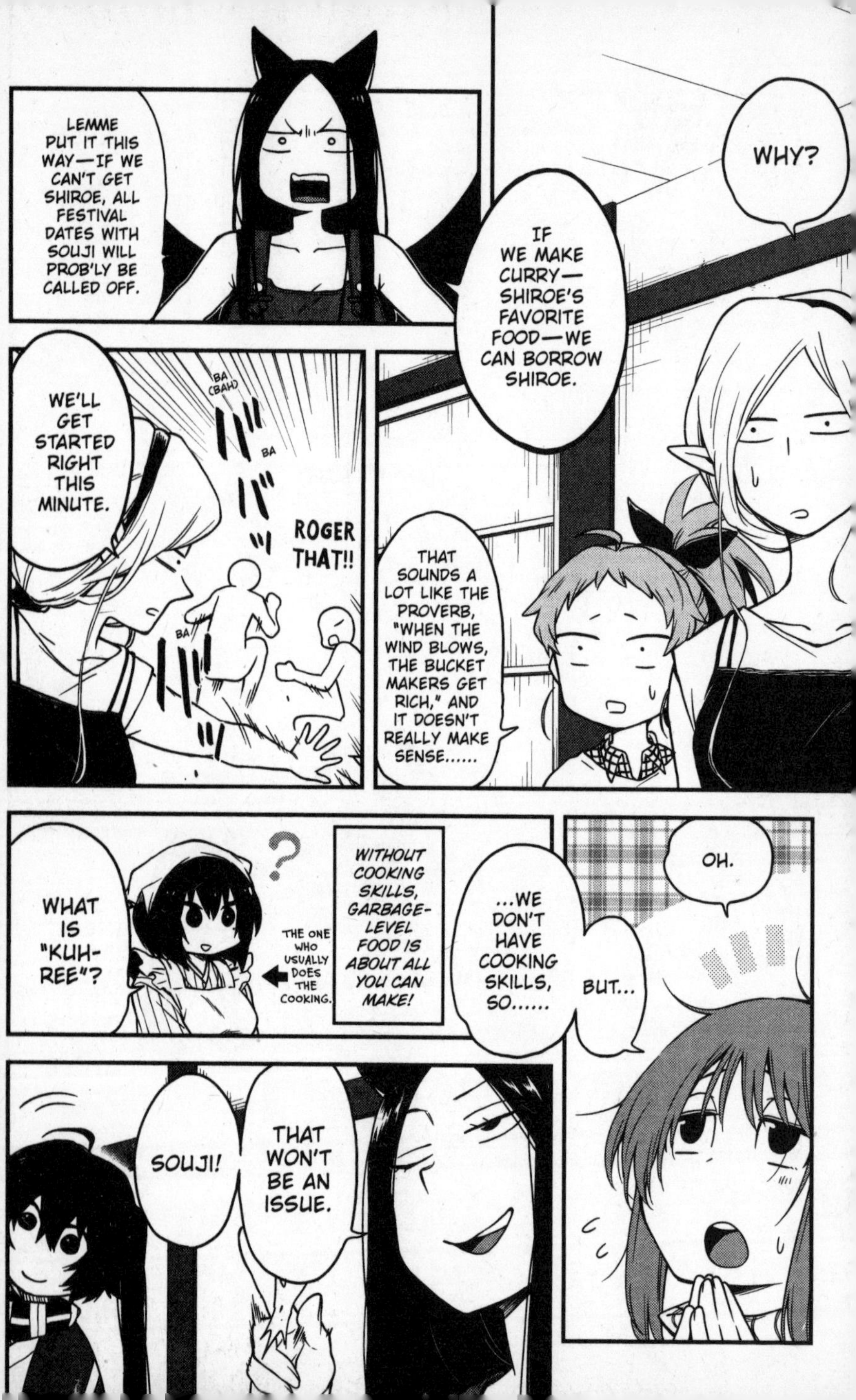
IF WE MAKE CURRY—SHIROE'S FAVORITE FOOD—WE CAN BORROW SHIROE.
WHY?
LEMME PUT IT THIS WAY—IF WE CAN'T GET SHIROE, ALL FESTIVAL DATES WITH SOUJI WILL PROB'LY BE CALLED OFF.
THAT SOUNDS A LOT LIKE THE PROVERB, "WHEN THE WIND BLOWS, THE BUCKET MAKERS GET RICH," AND IT DOESN'T REALLY MAKE SENSE......
ROGER THAT!!
BA
BA (BAH)
BA
WE'LL GET STARTED RIGHT THIS MINUTE.
OH.
BUT...
...WE DON'T HAVE COOKING SKILLS, SO......
WITHOUT COOKING SKILLS, GARBAGE-LEVEL FOOD IS ABOUT ALL YOU CAN MAKE!
THE ONE WHO USUALLY DOES THE COOKING.
?
WHAT IS "KUH-REE"?
THAT WON'T BE AN ISSUE.
SOUJI!

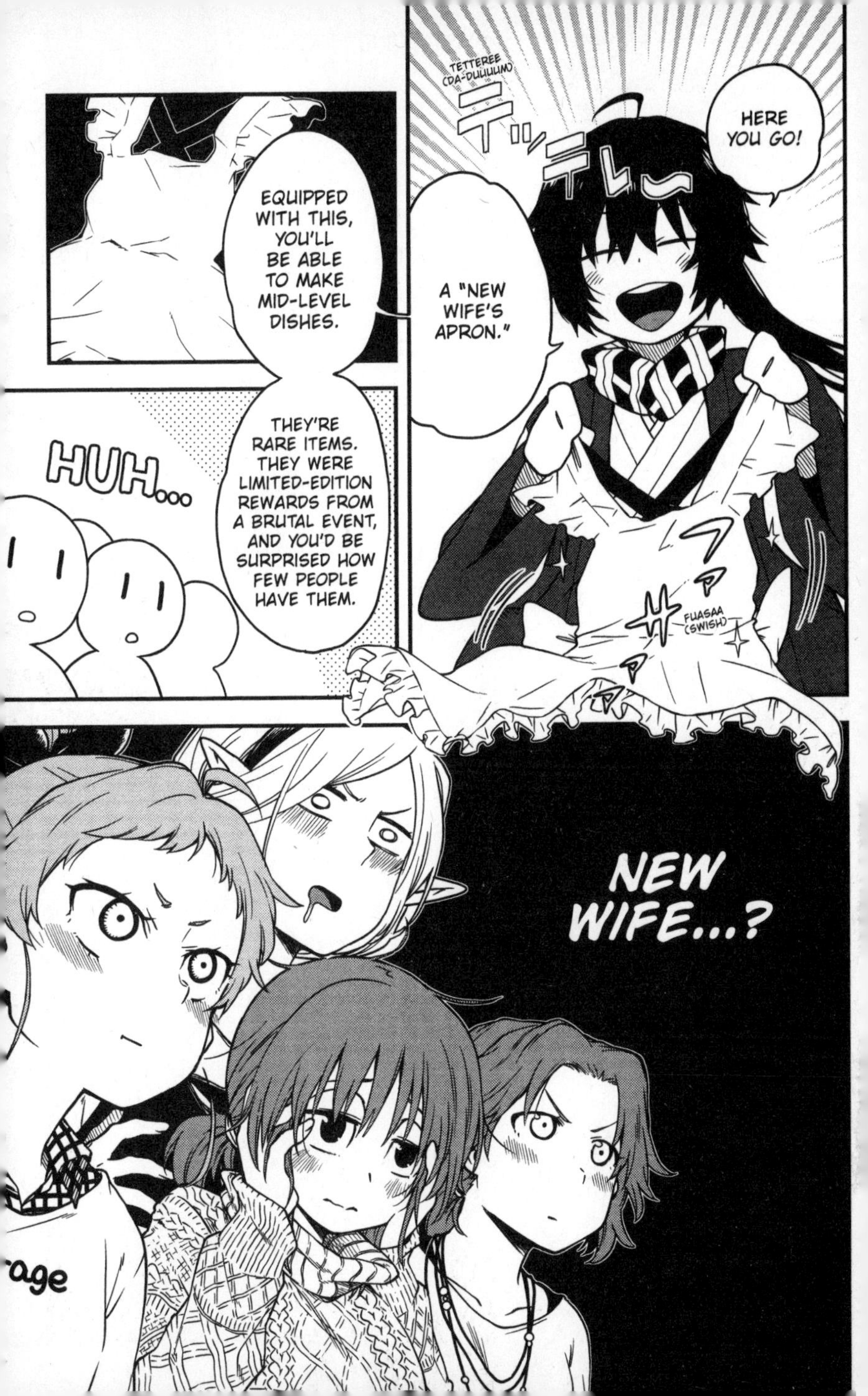

TETTEREE (DA-DUUUUM)
HERE YOU GO!
A "NEW WIFE'S APRON."
FUASAA (SWISH)
EQUIPPED WITH THIS, YOU'LL BE ABLE TO MAKE MID-LEVEL DISHES.
THEY'RE RARE ITEMS. THEY WERE LIMITED-EDITION REWARDS FROM A BRUTAL EVENT, AND YOU'D BE SURPRISED HOW FEW PEOPLE HAVE THEM.
HUH...
NEW WIFE...?
rage

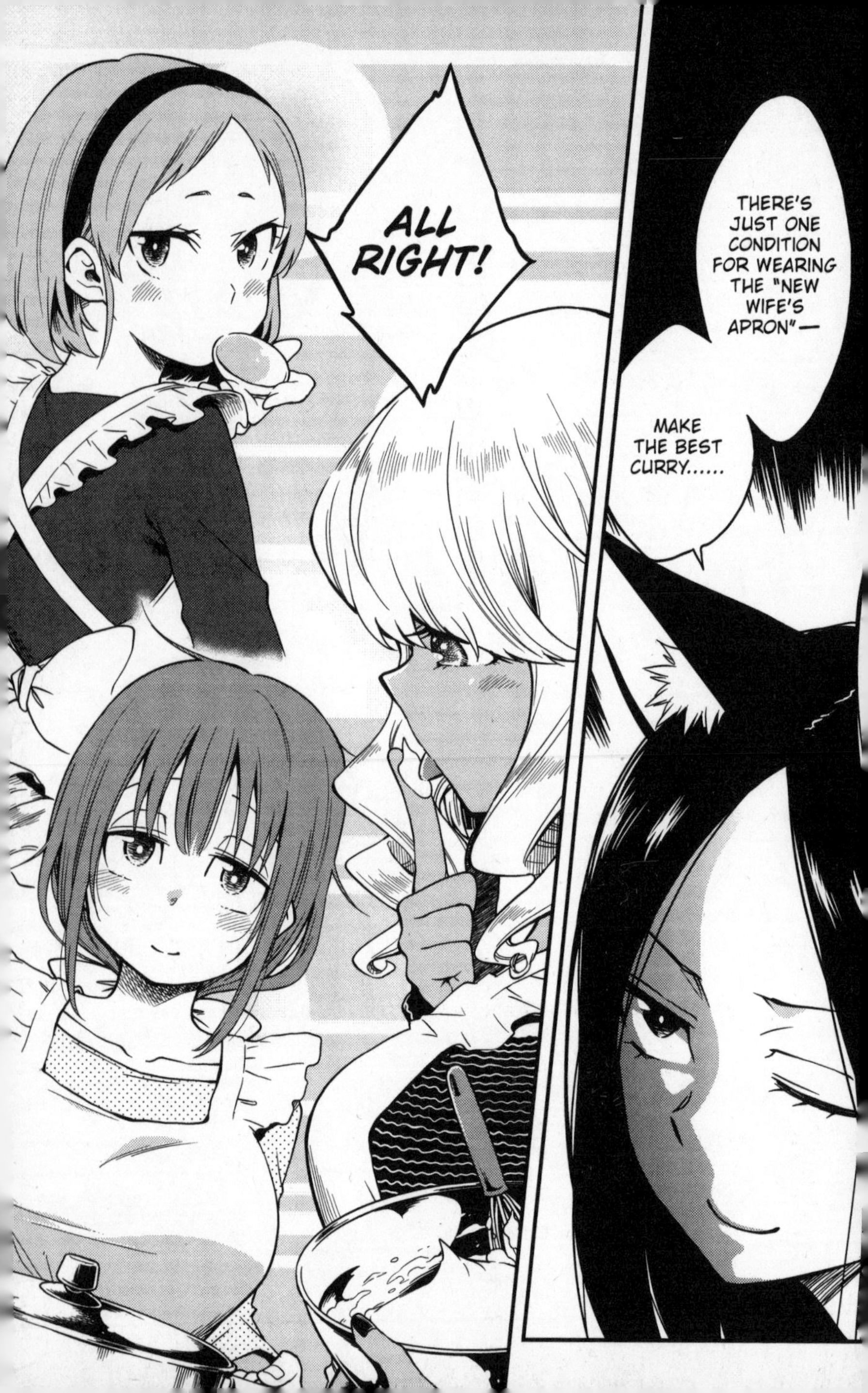
THERE'S JUST ONE CONDITION FOR WEARING THE "NEW WIFE'S APRON"—
MAKE THE BEST CURRY......
ALL RIGHT!

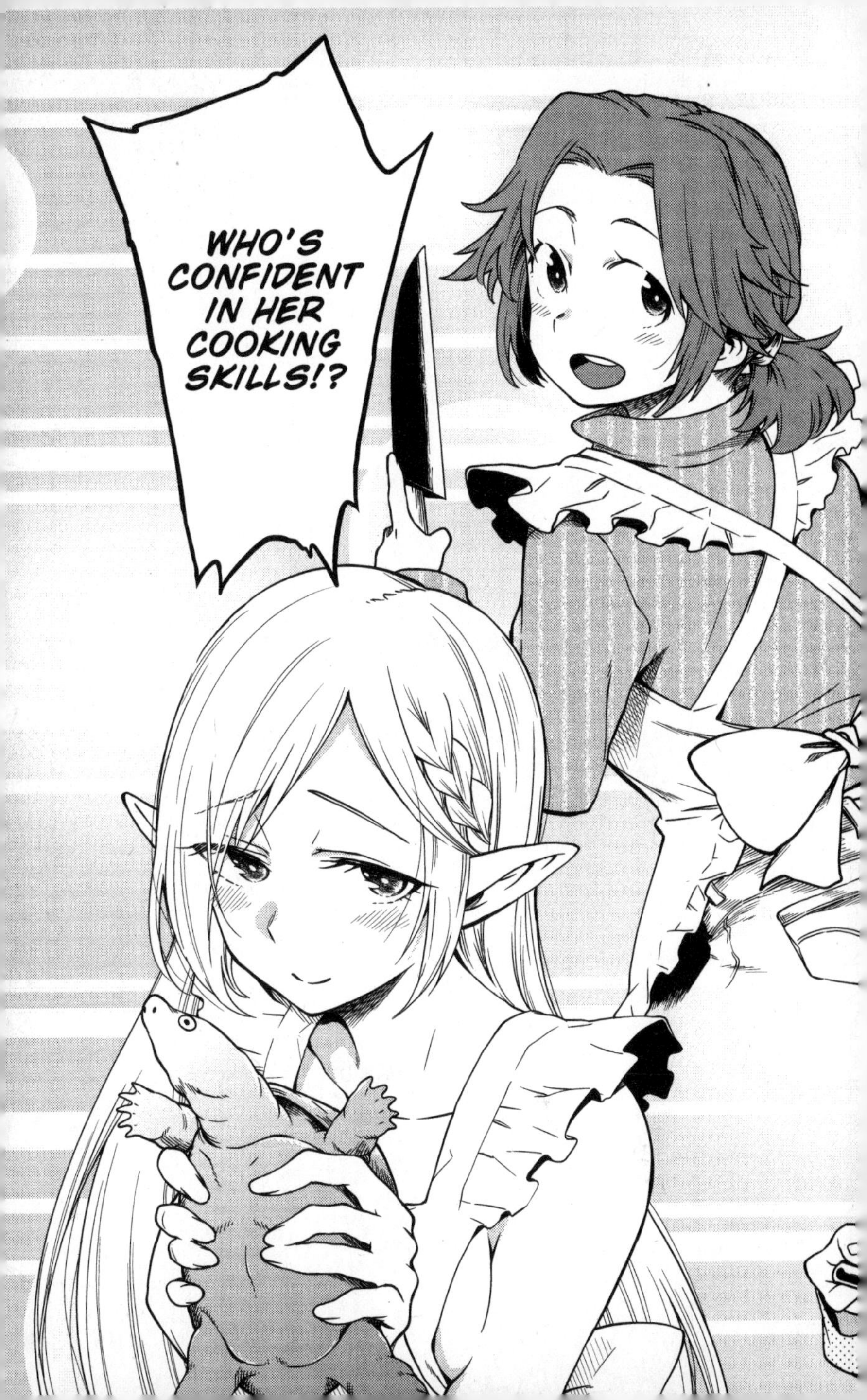
WHO'S CONFIDENT IN HER COOKING SKILLS!?

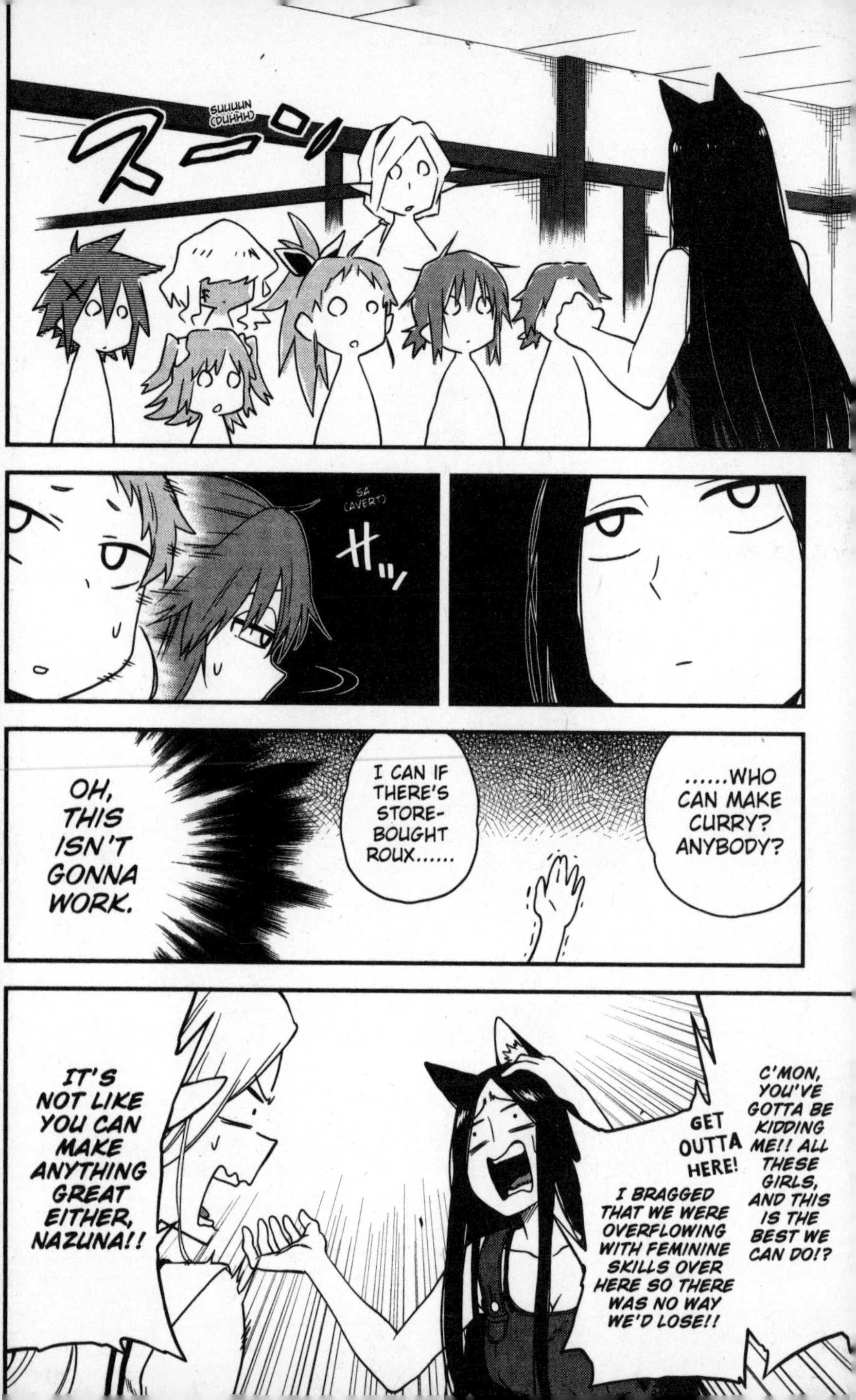
SUUUUN (DUHHH)
SA (AVERT)
......WHO CAN MAKE CURRY? ANYBODY?
I CAN IF THERE'S STORE-BOUGHT ROUX......
OH, THIS ISN'T GONNA WORK.
C'MON, YOU'VE GOTTA BE KIDDING ME!! ALL THESE GIRLS, AND THIS IS THE BEST WE CAN DO!?
GET OUTTA HERE!
I BRAGGED THAT WE WERE OVERFLOWING WITH FEMININE SKILLS OVER HERE SO THERE WAS NO WAY WE'D LOSE!!
IT'S NOT LIKE YOU CAN MAKE ANYTHING GREAT EITHER, NAZUNA!!

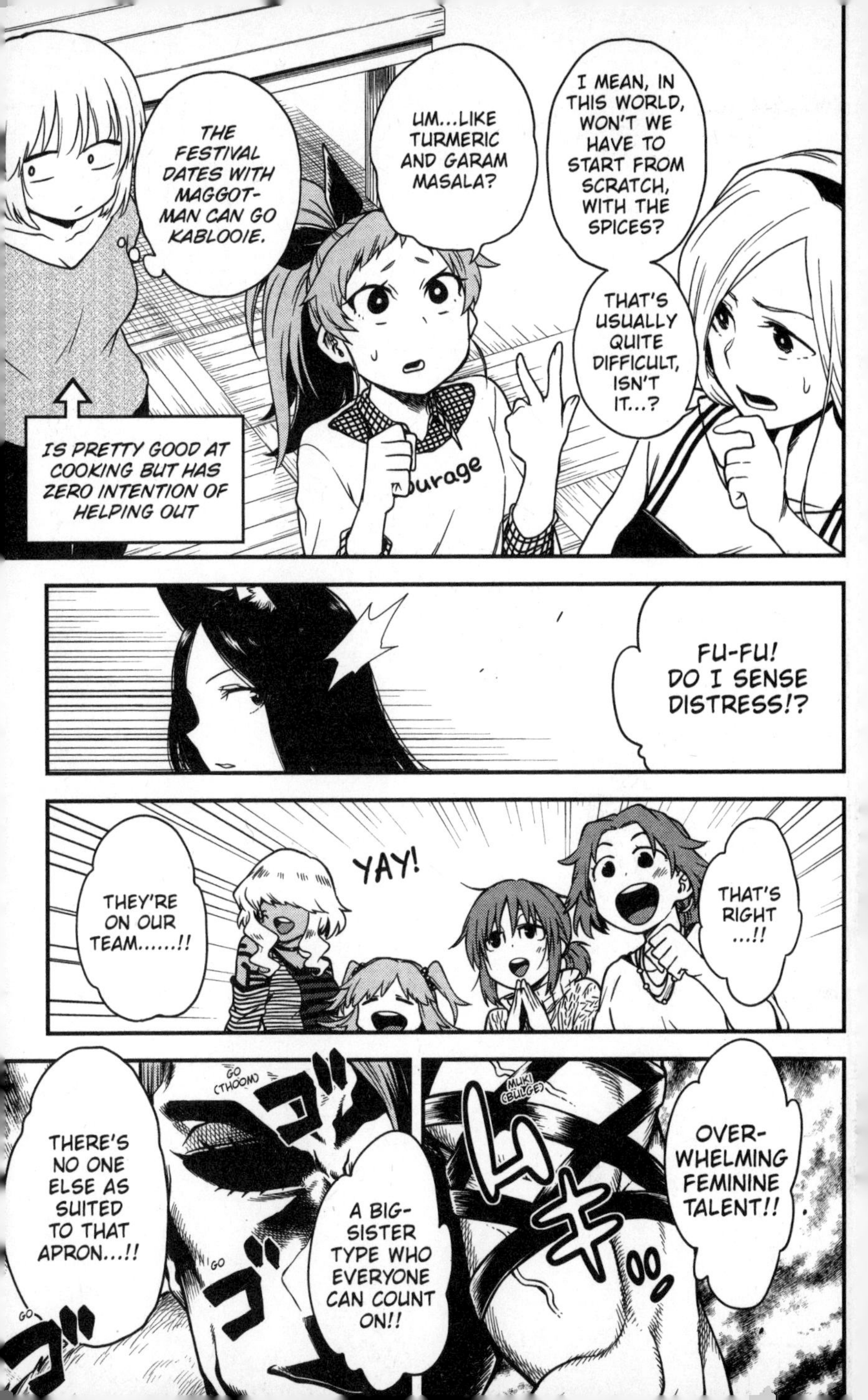
I MEAN, IN THIS WORLD, WON'T WE HAVE TO START FROM SCRATCH, WITH THE SPICES?
UM...LIKE TURMERIC AND GARAM MASALA?
THAT'S USUALLY QUITE DIFFICULT, ISN'T IT...?
THE FESTIVAL DATES WITH MAGGOT-MAN CAN GO KABLOOIE.
IS PRETTY GOOD AT COOKING BUT HAS ZERO INTENTION OF HELPING OUT
FU-FU! DO I SENSE DISTRESS!?
THAT'S RIGHT ...!!
YAY!
THEY'RE ON OUR TEAM......!!
OVER-WHELMING FEMININE TALENT!!
MUKI (BULGE)
A BIG-SISTER TYPE WHO EVERYONE CAN COUNT ON!!
GO (THOOM)
THERE'S NO ONE ELSE AS SUITED TO THAT APRON...!!
GO
GO

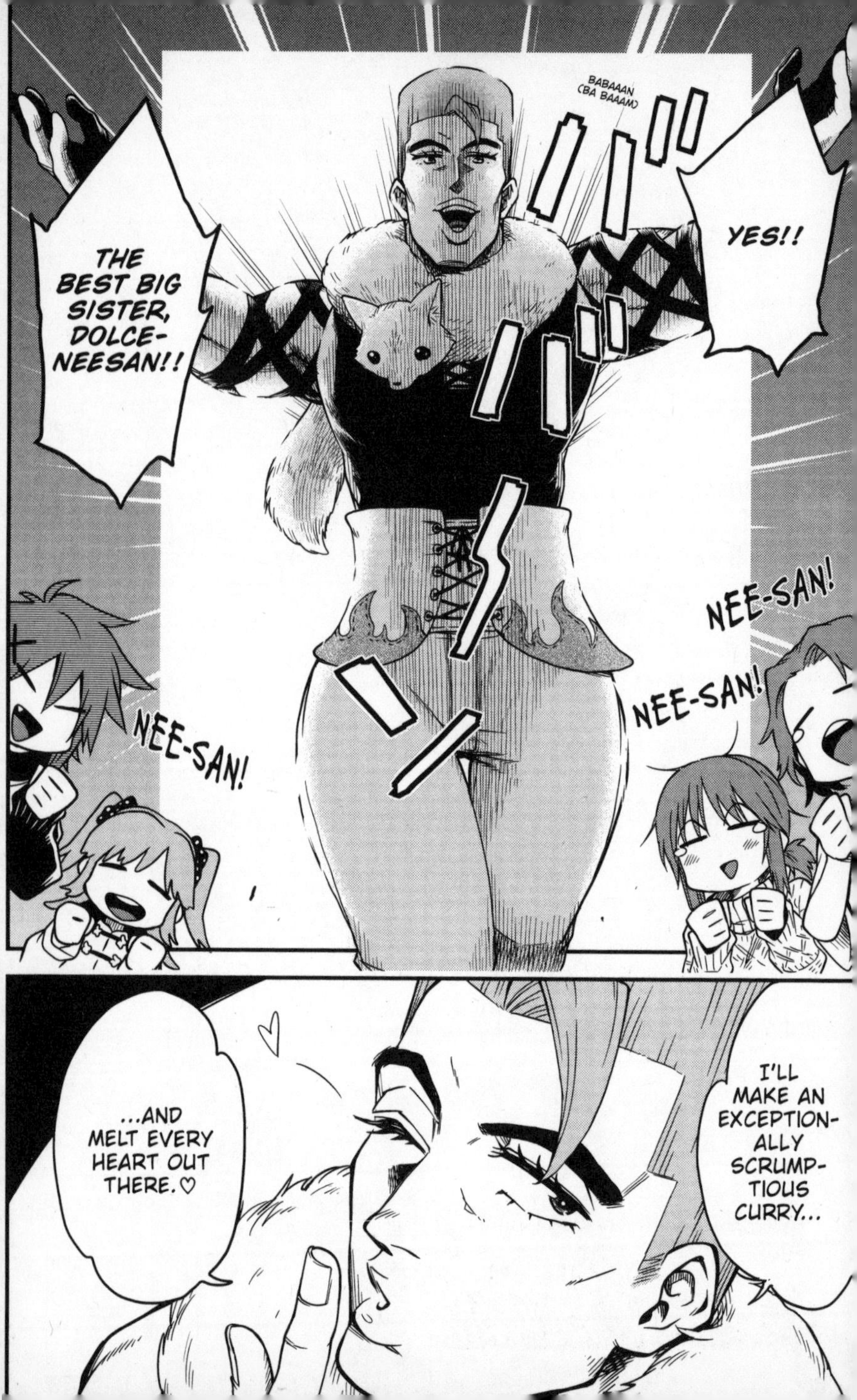
YES!!
BABAAAN (BA BAAAM)
THE BEST BIG SISTER, DOLCE-NEESAN!!
NEE-SAN!
NEE-SAN!
NEE-SAN!
I'LL MAKE AN EXCEPTION-ALLY SCRUMP-TIOUS CURRY...
...AND MELT EVERY HEART OUT THERE.♡

LOG HORIZON

THE WEST WIND BRIGADE

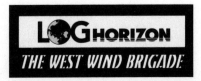

LOG HORIZON
THE WEST WIND BRIGADE

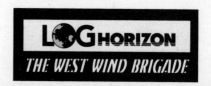

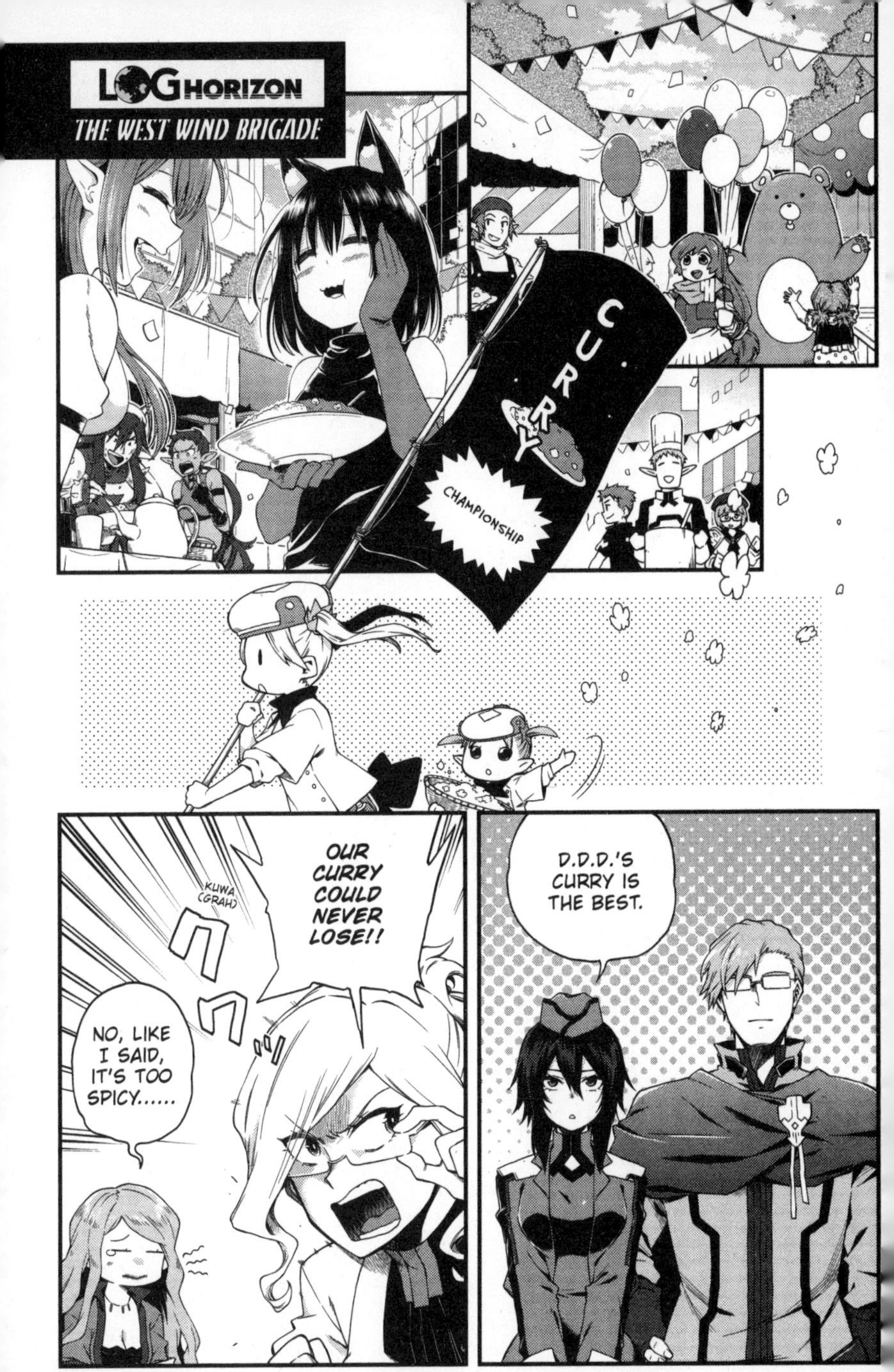
LOG HORIZON
THE WEST WIND BRIGADE
CURRY
CHAMPIONSHIP
D.D.D.'S CURRY IS THE BEST.
OUR CURRY COULD NEVER LOSE!!
KUWA (GRAH)
NO, LIKE I SAID, IT'S TOO SPICY......

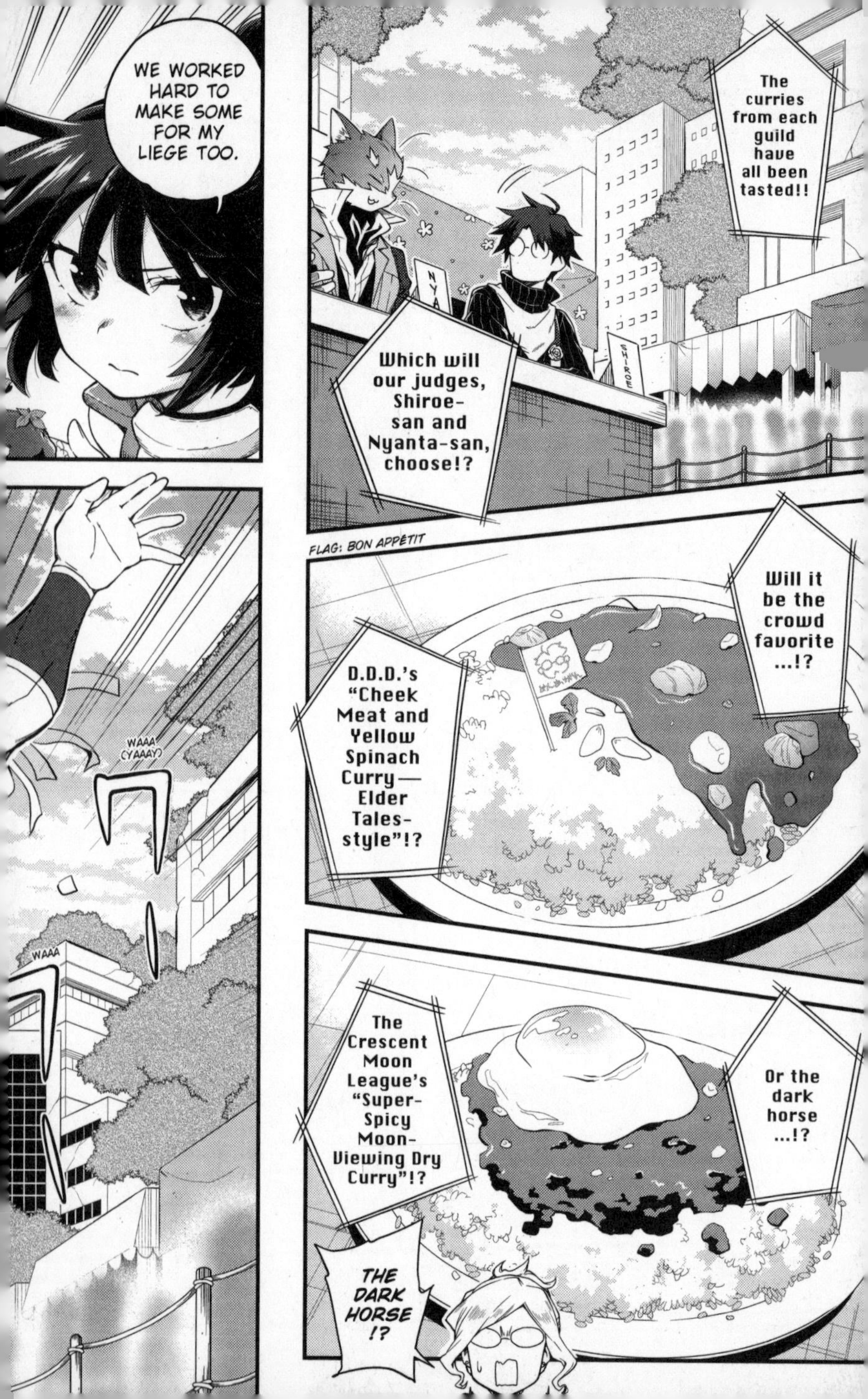
The curries from each guild have all been tasted!!
Which will our judges, Shiroe-san and Nyanta-san, choose!?
NYA
SHIROE
FLAG: BON APPÉTIT
WE WORKED HARD TO MAKE SOME FOR MY LIEGE TOO.
Will it be the crowd favorite ...!?
D.D.D.'s "Cheek Meat and Yellow Spinach Curry—Elder Tales-style"!?
Or the dark horse ...!?
The Crescent Moon League's "Super-Spicy Moon-Viewing Dry Curry"!?
THE DARK HORSE !?
WAAA (YAAAY)
WAAA

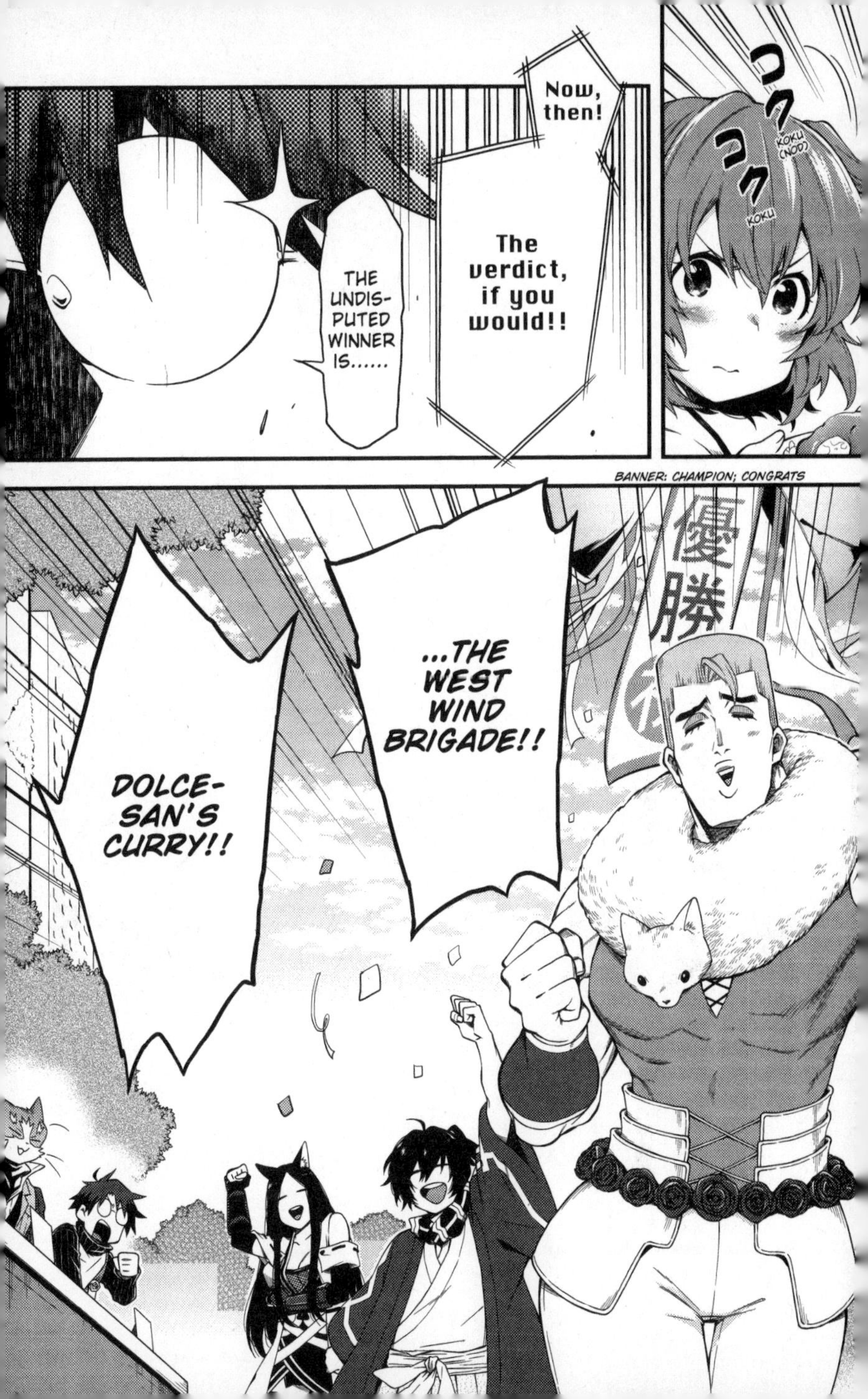
KOKU (NOD)
KOKU
Now, then!
The verdict, if you would!!
THE UNDISPUTED WINNER IS......
BANNER: CHAMPION; CONGRATS
優勝
...THE WEST WIND BRIGADE!!
DOLCE-SAN'S CURRY!!

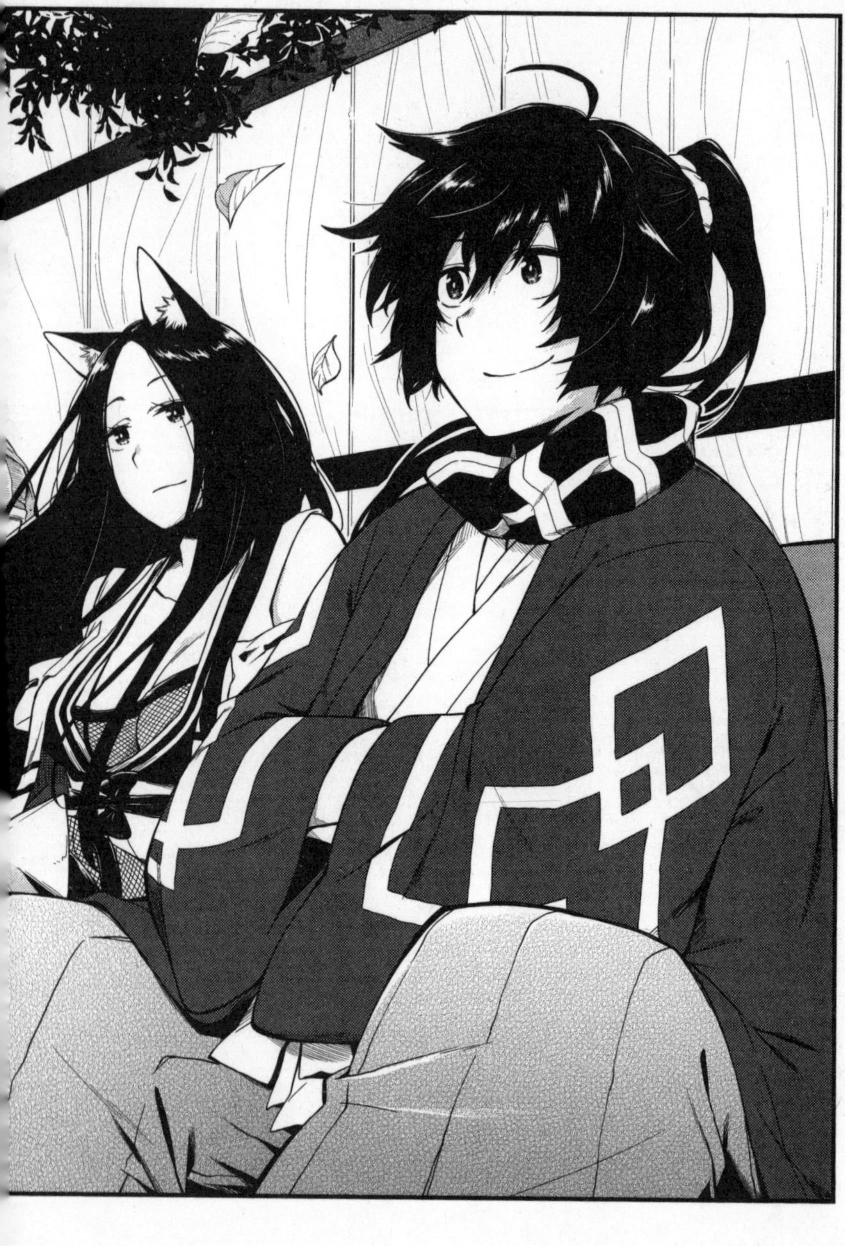

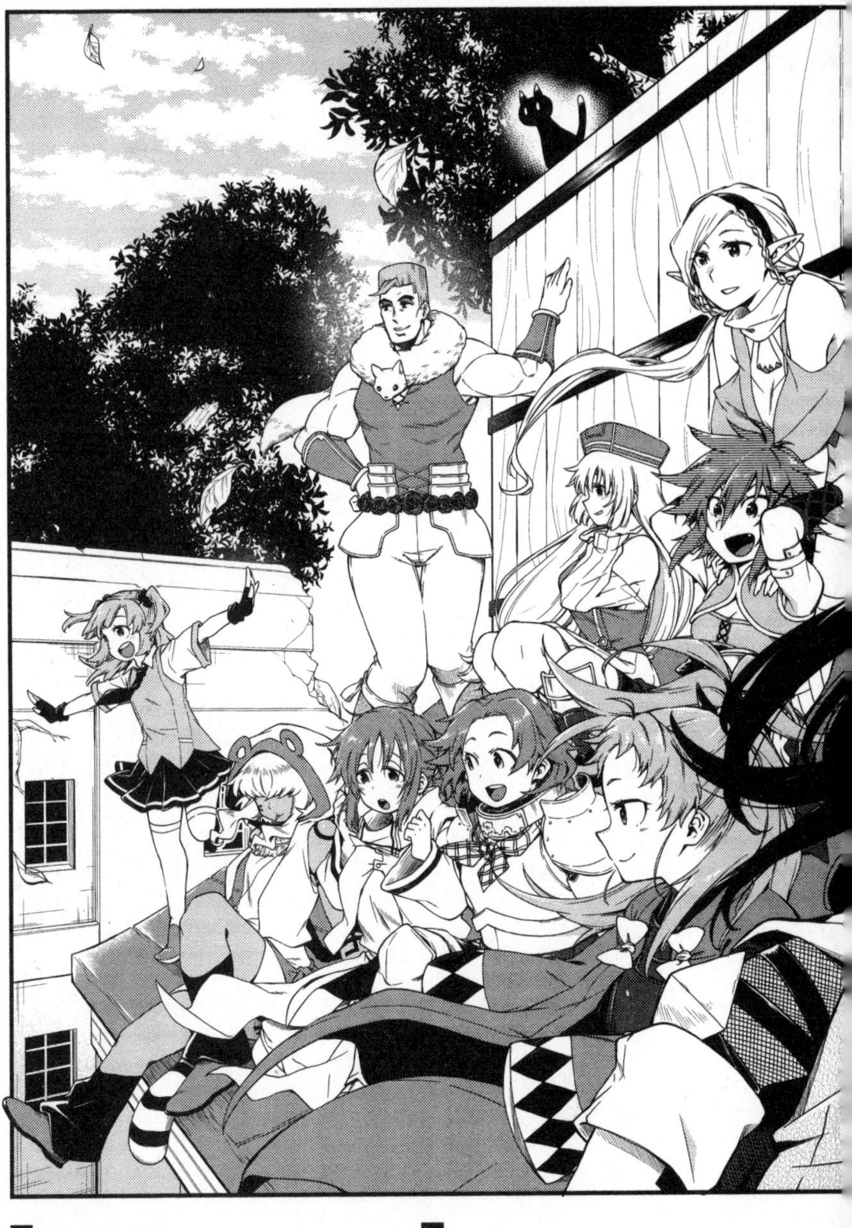

CHAPTER: 65 Beyond the Horizon

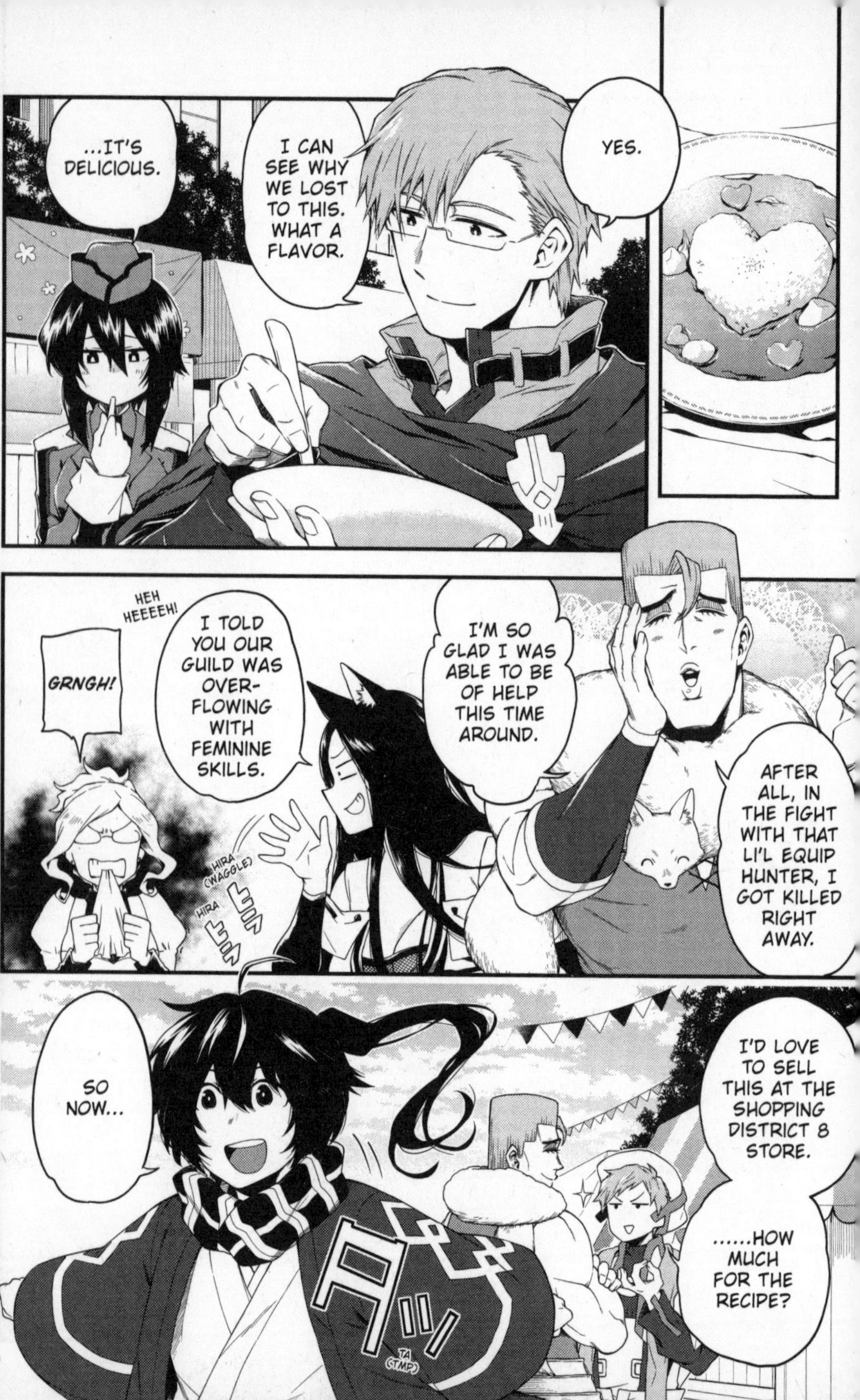
YES.
I CAN SEE WHY WE LOST TO THIS. WHAT A FLAVOR.
...IT'S DELICIOUS.
I'M SO GLAD I WAS ABLE TO BE OF HELP THIS TIME AROUND.
AFTER ALL, IN THE FIGHT WITH THAT LI'L EQUIP HUNTER, I GOT KILLED RIGHT AWAY.
I TOLD YOU OUR GUILD WAS OVER-FLOWING WITH FEMININE SKILLS.
HEH HEEEEH!
GRNGH!
HIRA (WAGGLE)
HIRA
I'D LOVE TO SELL THIS AT THE SHOPPING DISTRICT 8 STORE.
......HOW MUCH FOR THE RECIPE?
SO NOW...
TA (TMP)

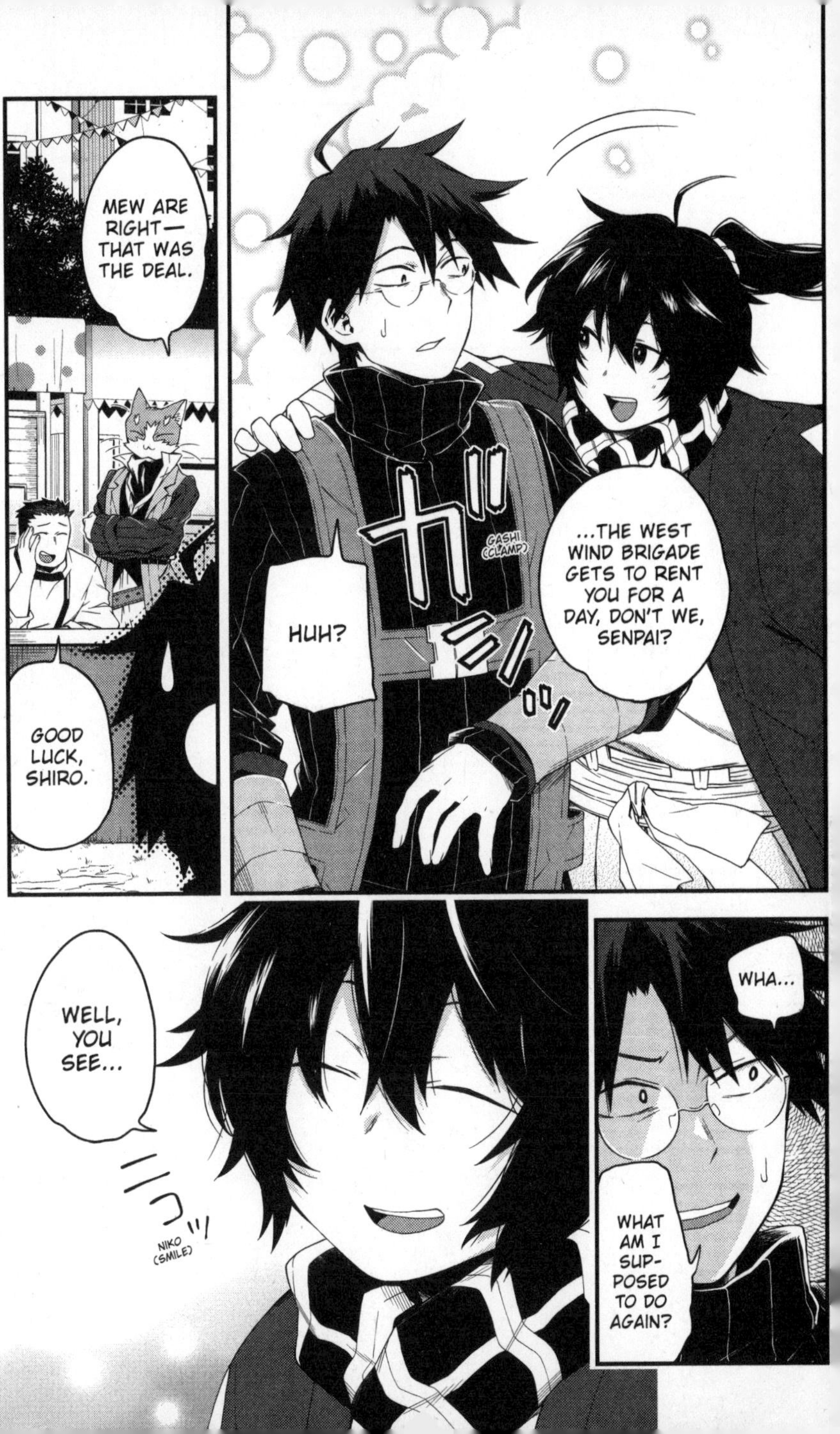
...THE WEST WIND BRIGADE GETS TO RENT YOU FOR A DAY, DON'T WE, SENPAI?
GASHI (CLAMP)
HUH?
MEW ARE RIGHT—THAT WAS THE DEAL.
GOOD LUCK, SHIRO.
WHA...
WHAT AM I SUP-POSED TO DO AGAIN?
WELL, YOU SEE...
NIKO (SMILE)

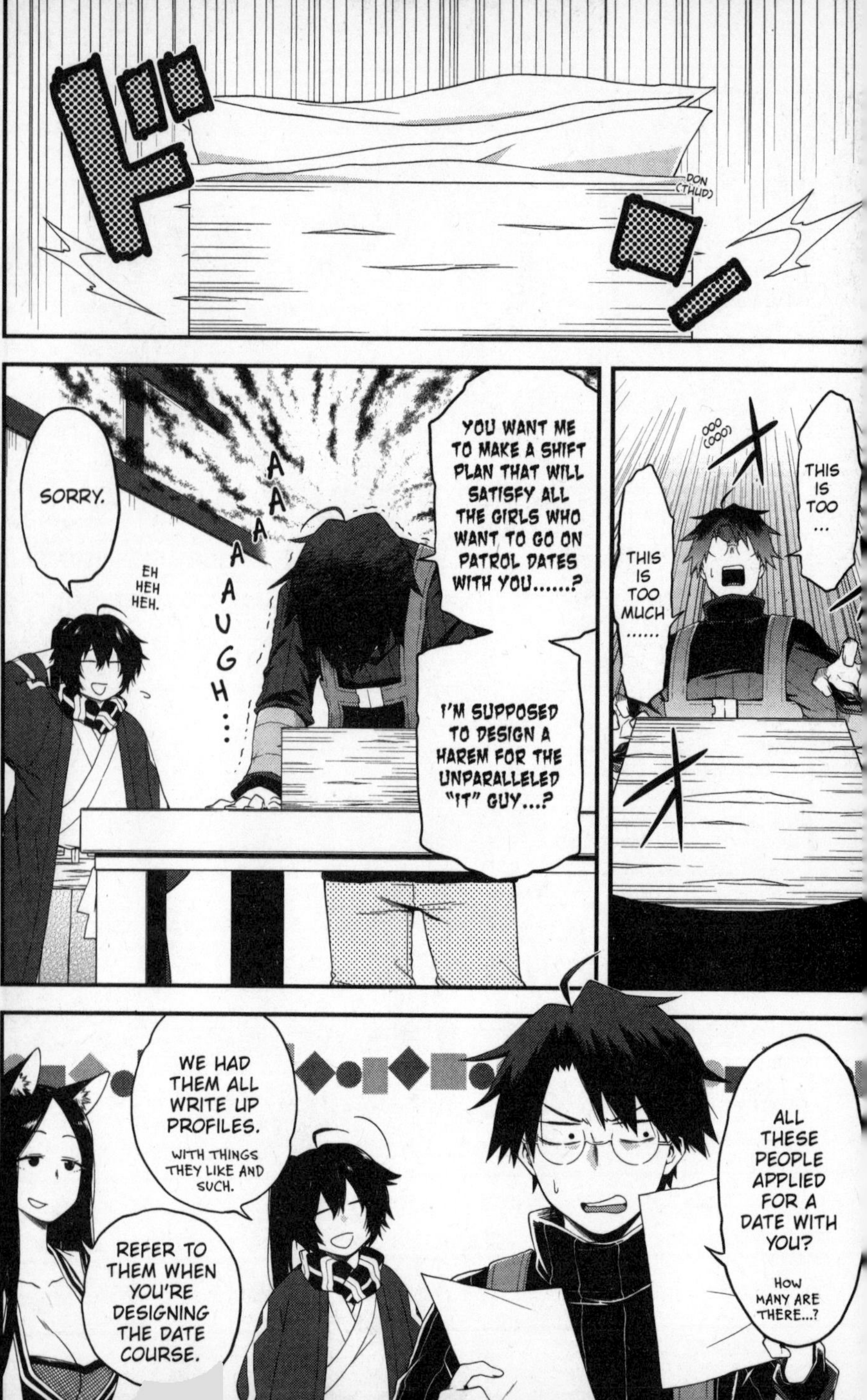
DON (THUD)
OOO (OOO)
THIS IS TOO ...
THIS IS TOO MUCH ......
YOU WANT ME TO MAKE A SHIFT PLAN THAT WILL SATISFY ALL THE GIRLS WHO WANT TO GO ON PATROL DATES WITH YOU......?
I'M SUPPOSED TO DESIGN A HAREM FOR THE UNPARALLELED "IT" GUY...?
AAAAAAUGH...
SORRY.
EH HEH HEH.
ALL THESE PEOPLE APPLIED FOR A DATE WITH YOU?
HOW MANY ARE THERE...?
WE HAD THEM ALL WRITE UP PROFILES.
WITH THINGS THEY LIKE AND SUCH.
REFER TO THEM WHEN YOU'RE DESIGNING THE DATE COURSE.

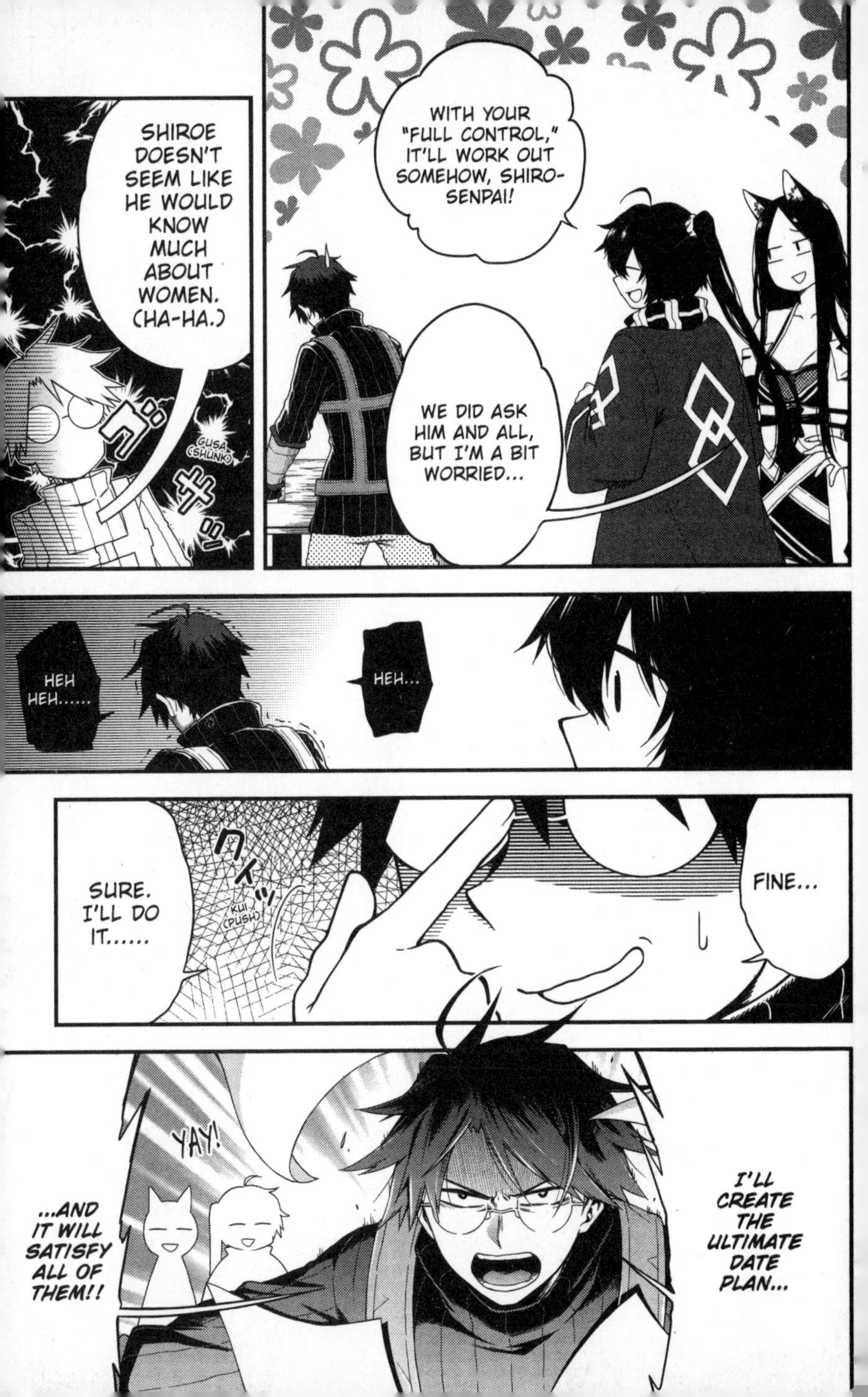
WITH YOUR "FULL CONTROL," IT'LL WORK OUT SOMEHOW, SHIRO-SENPAI!
WE DID ASK HIM AND ALL, BUT I'M A BIT WORRIED...
SHIROE DOESN'T SEEM LIKE HE WOULD KNOW MUCH ABOUT WOMEN. (HA-HA.)
GUSA (SHUNK)
HEH...
HEH HEH......
FINE...
KUI (PUSH)
SURE. I'LL DO IT......
I'LL CREATE THE ULTIMATE DATE PLAN...
YAY!
...AND IT WILL SATISFY ALL OF THEM!!

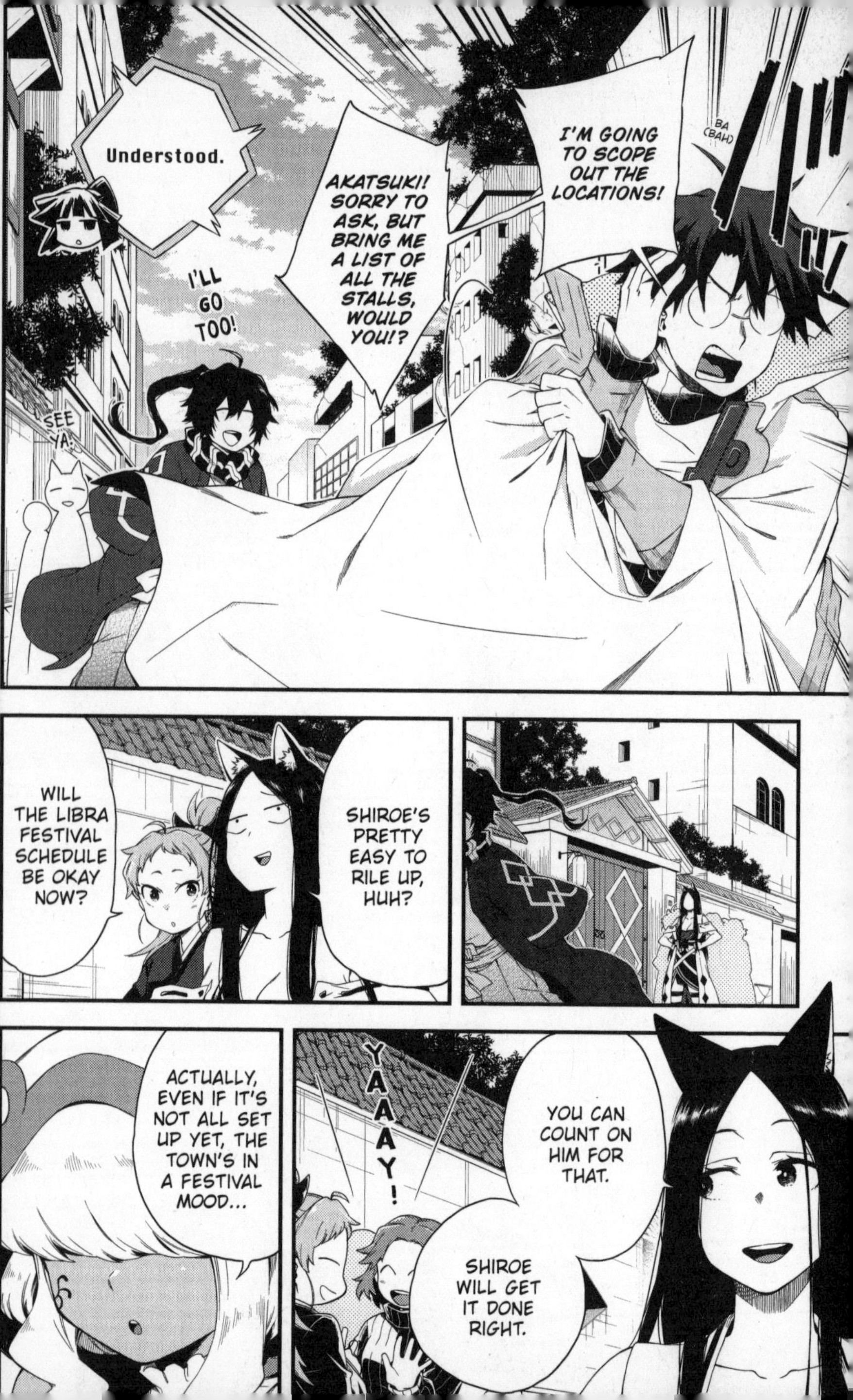
BA (BAH)
I'M GOING TO SCOPE OUT THE LOCATIONS!
AKATSUKI! SORRY TO ASK, BUT BRING ME A LIST OF ALL THE STALLS, WOULD YOU!?
Understood.
I'LL GO TOO!
SEE YA!
SHIROE'S PRETTY EASY TO RILE UP, HUH?
WILL THE LIBRA FESTIVAL SCHEDULE BE OKAY NOW?
YOU CAN COUNT ON HIM FOR THAT.
YAAAY!
SHIROE WILL GET IT DONE RIGHT.
ACTUALLY, EVEN IF IT'S NOT ALL SET UP YET, THE TOWN'S IN A FESTIVAL MOOD...

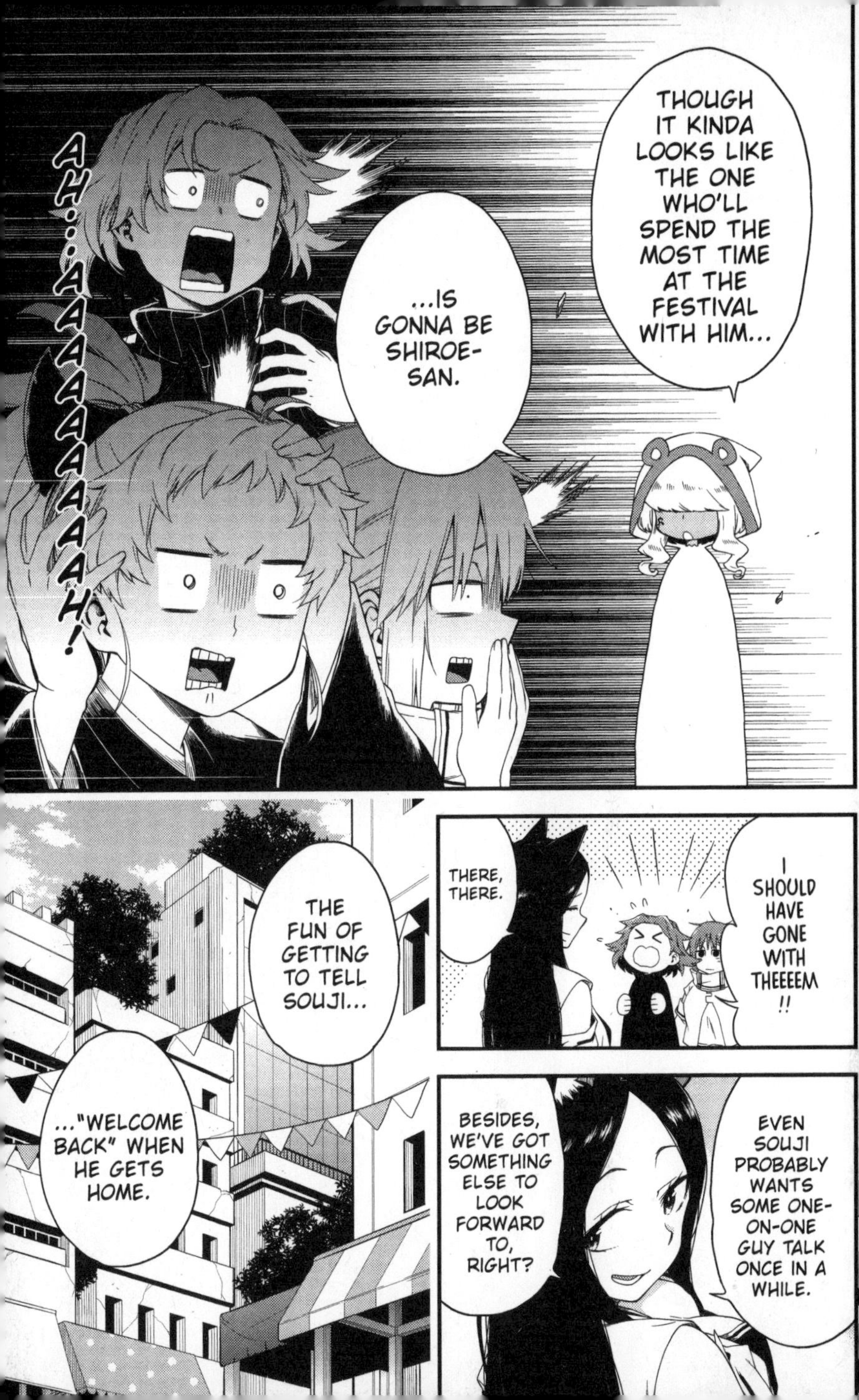
THOUGH IT KINDA LOOKS LIKE THE ONE WHO'LL SPEND THE MOST TIME AT THE FESTIVAL WITH HIM...
...IS GONNA BE SHIROE-SAN.
AH..AAAAAAAAAAAAAH!
I SHOULD HAVE GONE WITH THEEEEM!!
THERE, THERE.
EVEN SOUJI PROBABLY WANTS SOME ONE-ON-ONE GUY TALK ONCE IN A WHILE.
BESIDES, WE'VE GOT SOMETHING ELSE TO LOOK FORWARD TO, RIGHT?
THE FUN OF GETTING TO TELL SOUJI...
..."WELCOME BACK" WHEN HE GETS HOME.

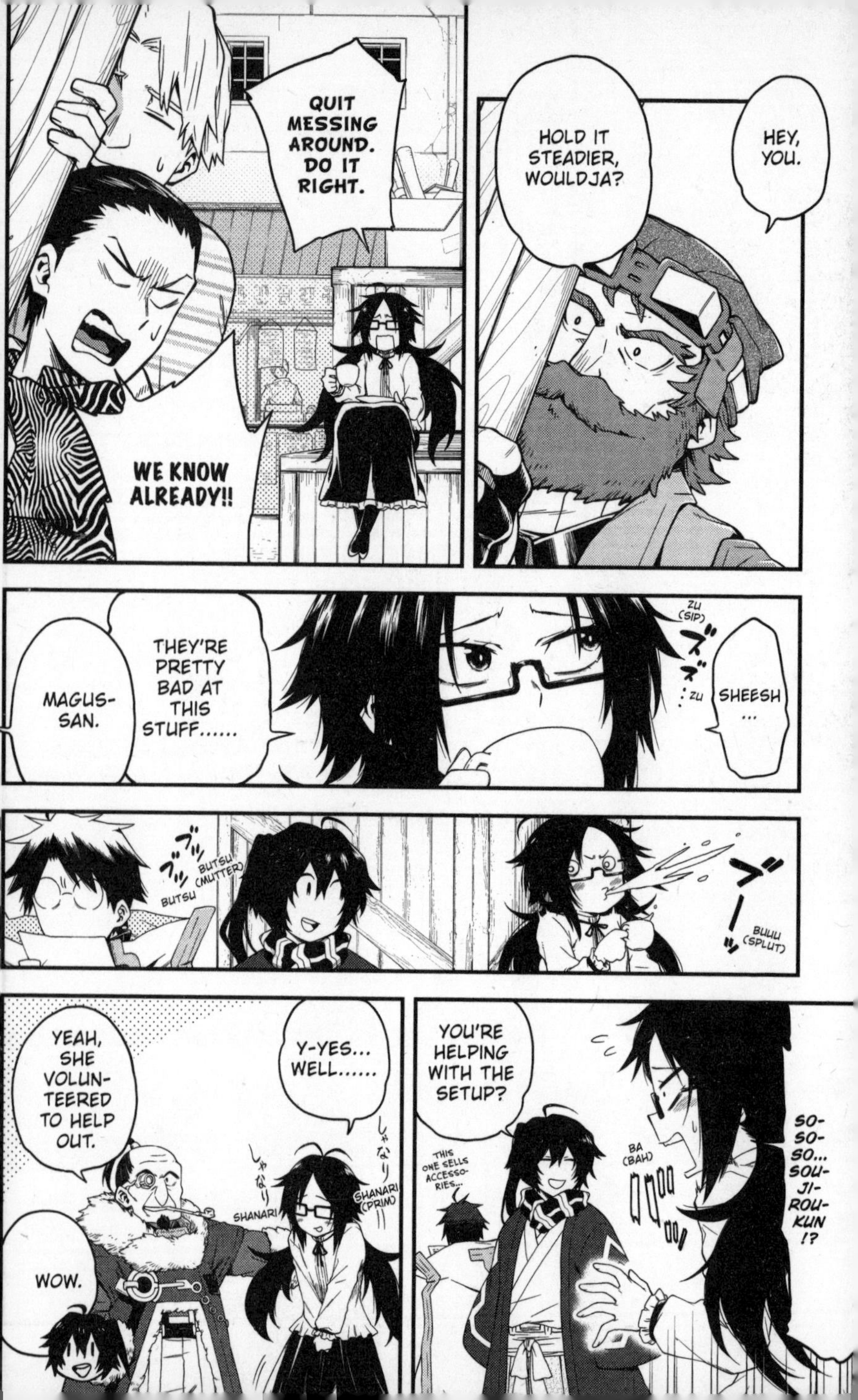
HEY, YOU.
HOLD IT STEADIER, WOULDJA?
QUIT MESSING AROUND. DO IT RIGHT.
WE KNOW ALREADY!!
ZU (SIP)
ZU
SHEESH...
THEY'RE PRETTY BAD AT THIS STUFF......
MAGUS-SAN.
BUUU (SPLUT)
BUTSU (MUTTER)
BUTSU
SO-SO-SO... SOUJI-ROU-KUN!?
BA (BAH)
YOU'RE HELPING WITH THE SETUP?
THIS ONE SELLS ACCESSORIES...
Y-YES... WELL......
SHANARI (PRIM)
SHANARI
YEAH, SHE VOLUN-TEERED TO HELP OUT.
WOW.

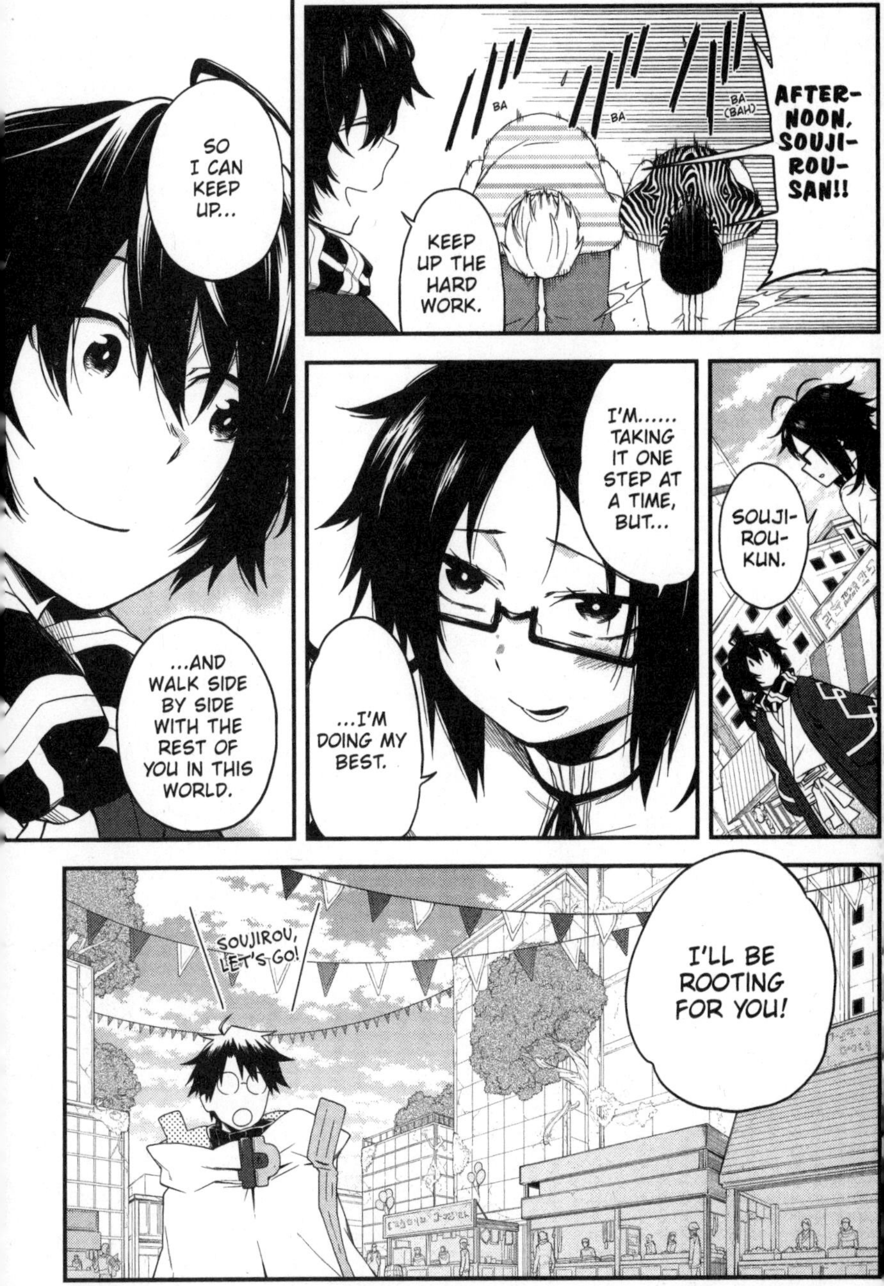
AFTER-NOON, SOUJI-ROU-SAN!!
BA (BAH)
BA
BA
KEEP UP THE HARD WORK.
SOUJI-ROU-KUN.
I'M...... TAKING IT ONE STEP AT A TIME, BUT...
...I'M DOING MY BEST.
SO I CAN KEEP UP...
...AND WALK SIDE BY SIDE WITH THE REST OF YOU IN THIS WORLD.
I'LL BE ROOTING FOR YOU!
SOUJIROU, LET'S GO!

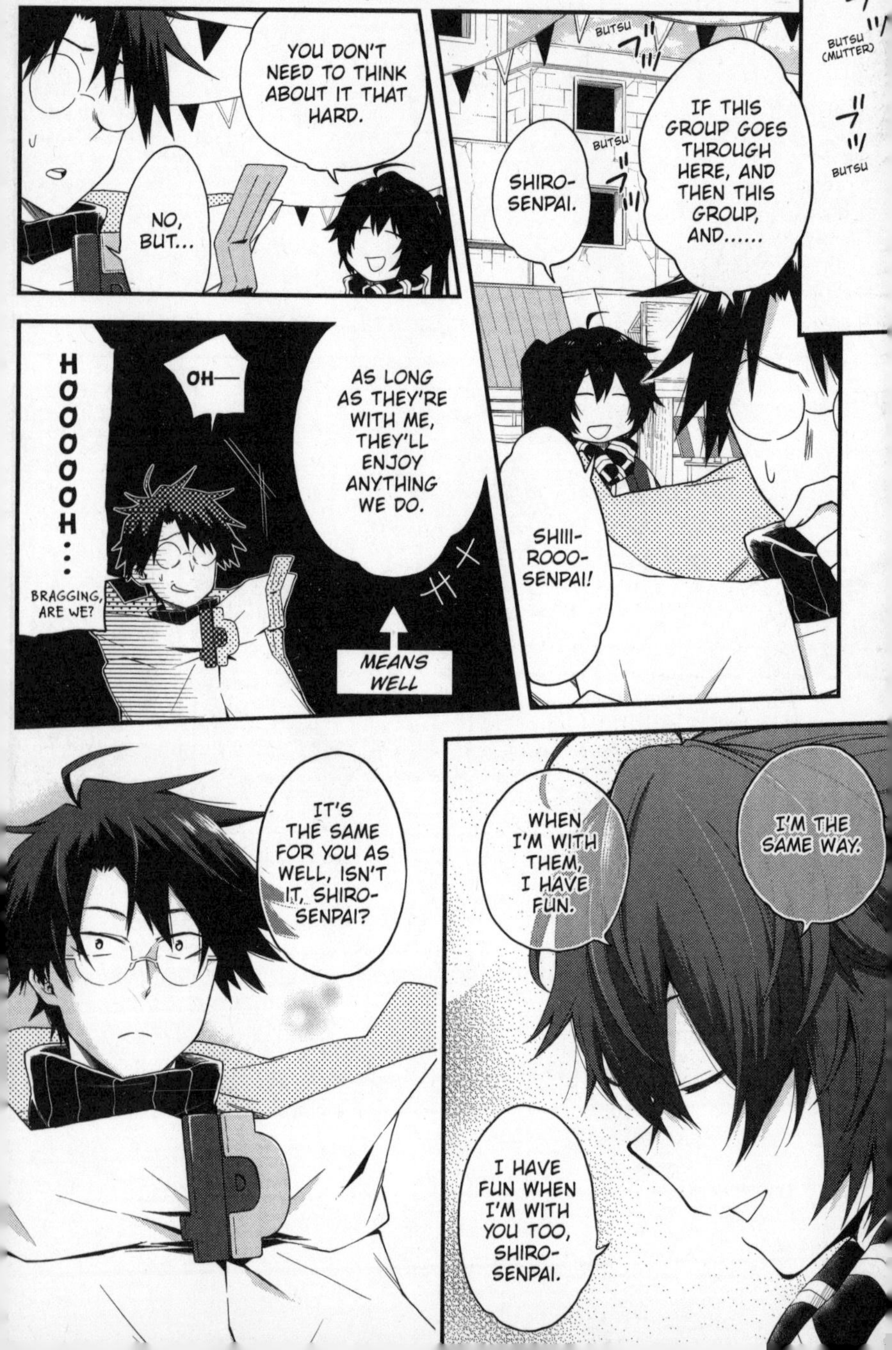
BUTSU
BUTSU (MUTTER)
BUTSU
BUTSU
IF THIS GROUP GOES THROUGH HERE, AND THEN THIS GROUP, AND......
SHIRO-SENPAI.
SHIII-ROOO-SENPAI!
YOU DON'T NEED TO THINK ABOUT IT THAT HARD.
NO, BUT...
AS LONG AS THEY'RE WITH ME, THEY'LL ENJOY ANYTHING WE DO.
OH—
HOOOOOOH...
BRAGGING, ARE WE?
MEANS WELL
I'M THE SAME WAY.
WHEN I'M WITH THEM, I HAVE FUN.
I HAVE FUN WHEN I'M WITH YOU TOO, SHIRO-SENPAI.
IT'S THE SAME FOR YOU AS WELL, ISN'T IT, SHIRO-SENPAI?

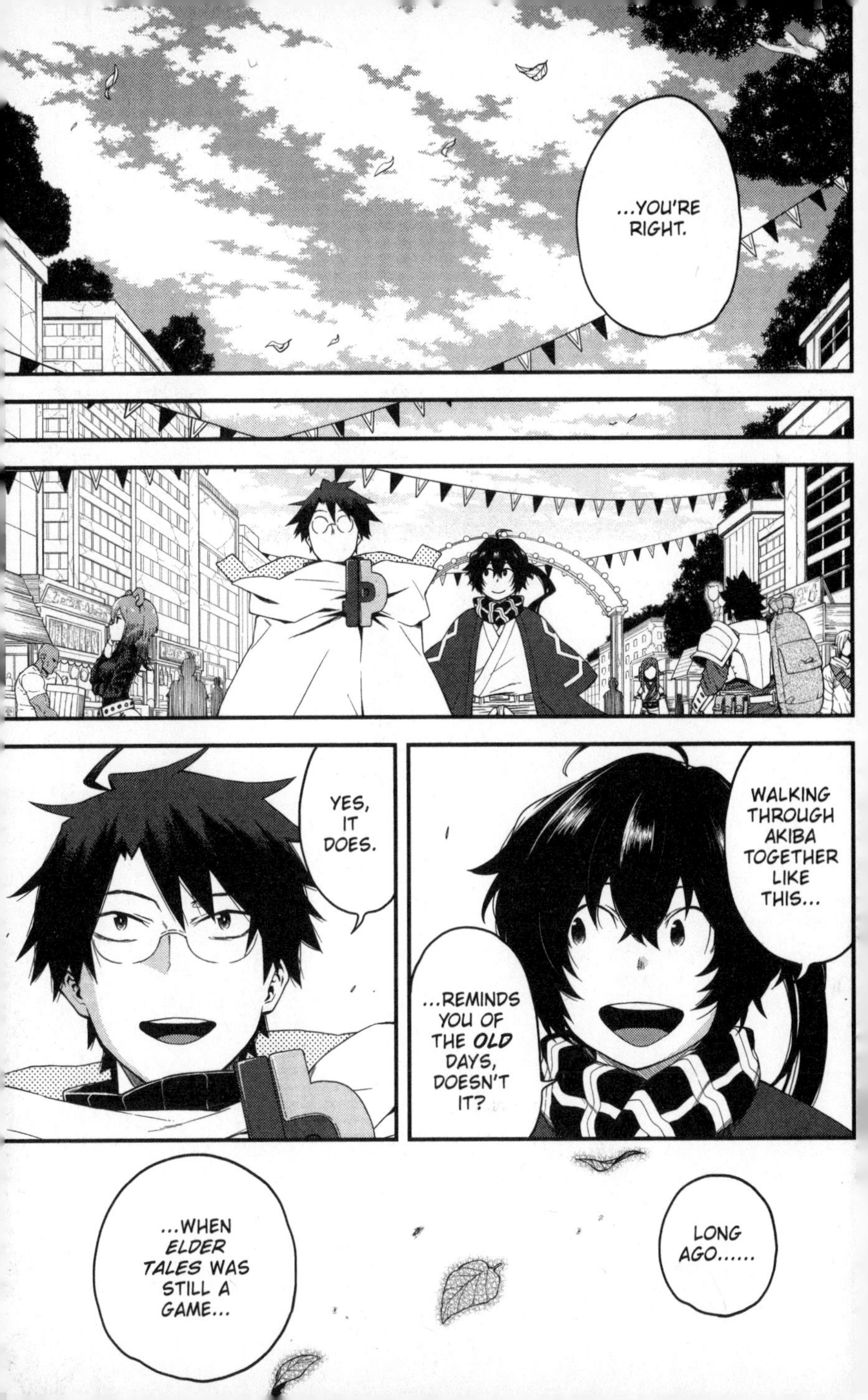
...YOU'RE RIGHT.
WALKING THROUGH AKIBA TOGETHER LIKE THIS...
...REMINDS YOU OF THE *OLD* DAYS, DOESN'T IT?
YES, IT DOES.
LONG AGO......
...WHEN *ELDER TALES* WAS STILL A GAME...

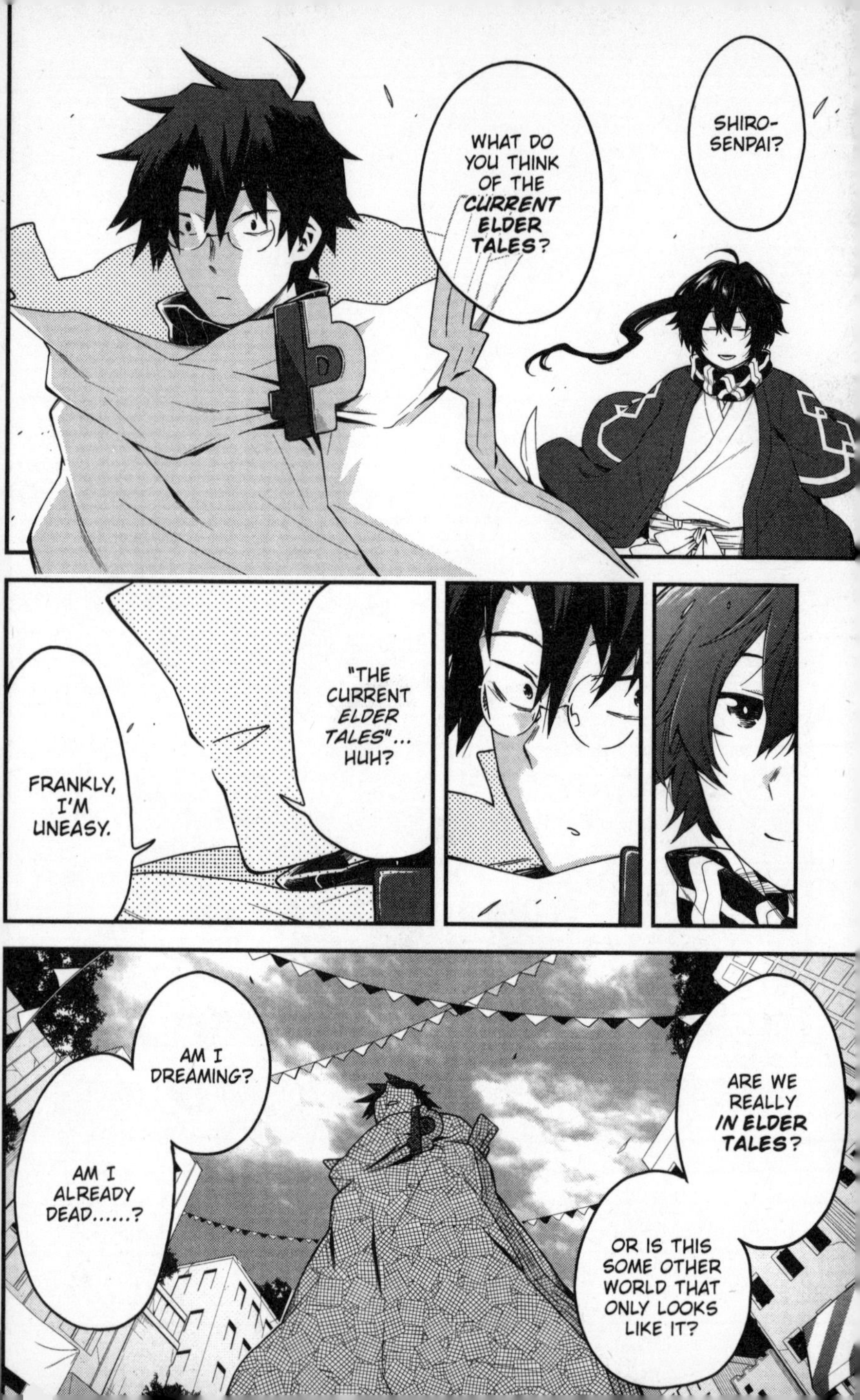
SHIRO-SENPAI?
WHAT DO YOU THINK OF THE CURRENT ELDER TALES?
"THE CURRENT ELDER TALES"... HUH?
FRANKLY, I'M UNEASY.
ARE WE REALLY IN ELDER TALES?
OR IS THIS SOME OTHER WORLD THAT ONLY LOOKS LIKE IT?
AM I DREAMING?
AM I ALREADY DEAD......?

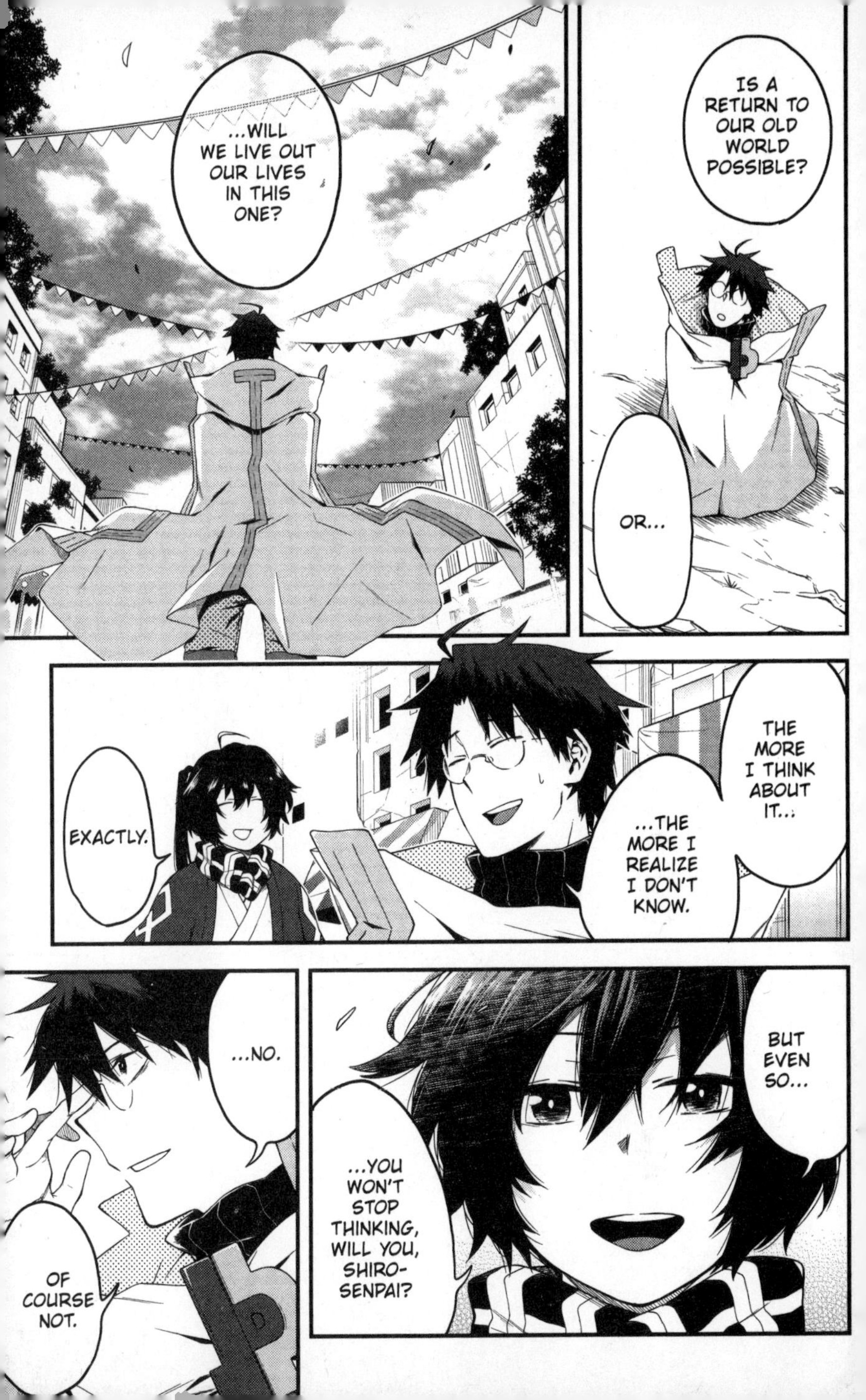
IS A RETURN TO OUR OLD WORLD POSSIBLE?
OR...
...WILL WE LIVE OUT OUR LIVES IN THIS ONE?
THE MORE I THINK ABOUT IT...
...THE MORE I REALIZE I DON'T KNOW.
EXACTLY.
BUT EVEN SO...
...YOU WON'T STOP THINKING, WILL YOU, SHIRO-SENPAI?
...NO.
OF COURSE NOT.

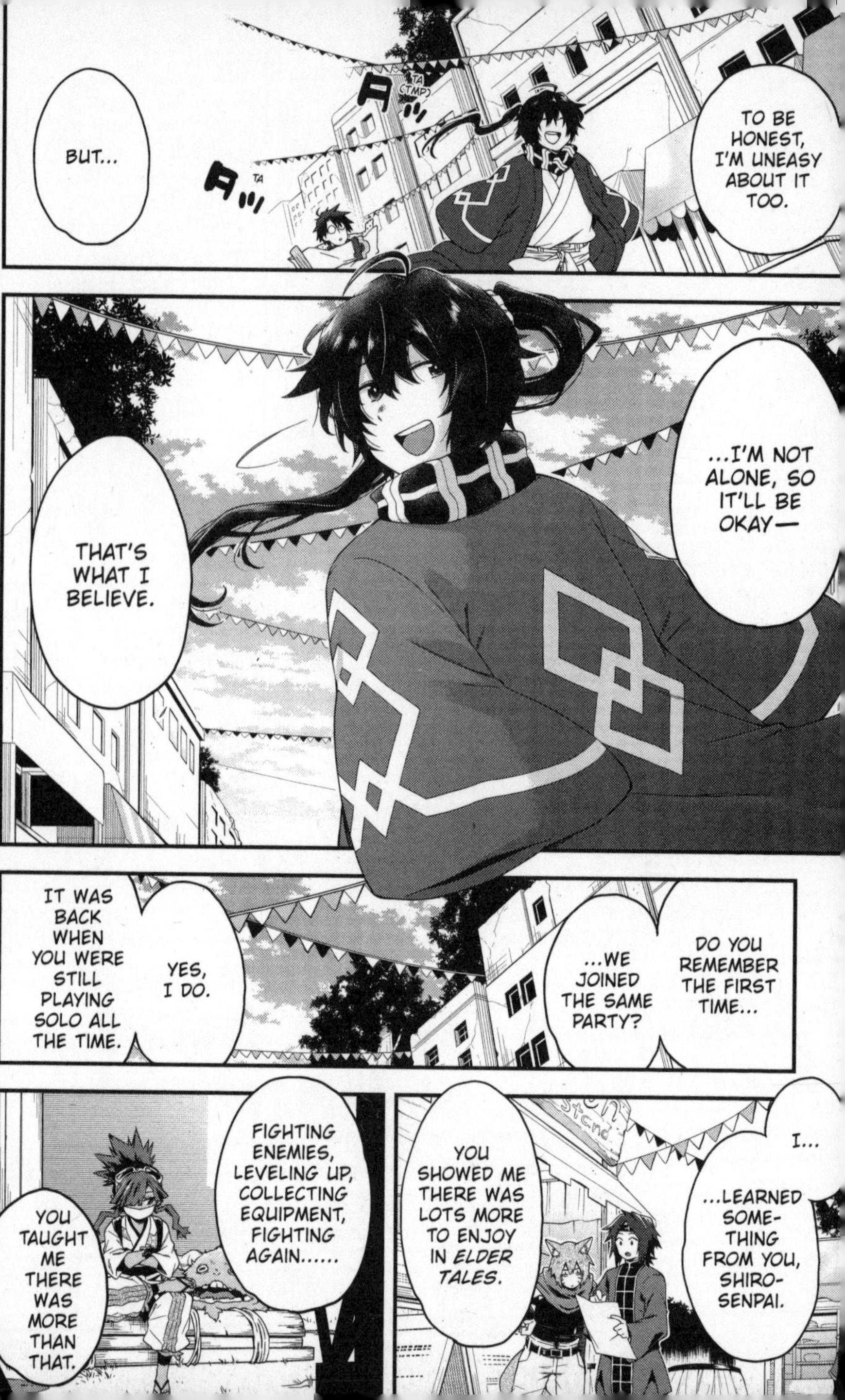
TO BE HONEST, I'M UNEASY ABOUT IT TOO.
TA (TMP)
TA
BUT...
...I'M NOT ALONE, SO IT'LL BE OKAY—
THAT'S WHAT I BELIEVE.
DO YOU REMEMBER THE FIRST TIME...
...WE JOINED THE SAME PARTY?
YES, I DO.
IT WAS BACK WHEN YOU WERE STILL PLAYING SOLO ALL THE TIME.
I...
...LEARNED SOME-THING FROM YOU, SHIRO-SENPAI.
YOU SHOWED ME THERE WAS LOTS MORE TO ENJOY IN *ELDER TALES*.
FIGHTING ENEMIES, LEVELING UP, COLLECTING EQUIPMENT, FIGHTING AGAIN......
YOU TAUGHT ME THERE WAS MORE THAN THAT.

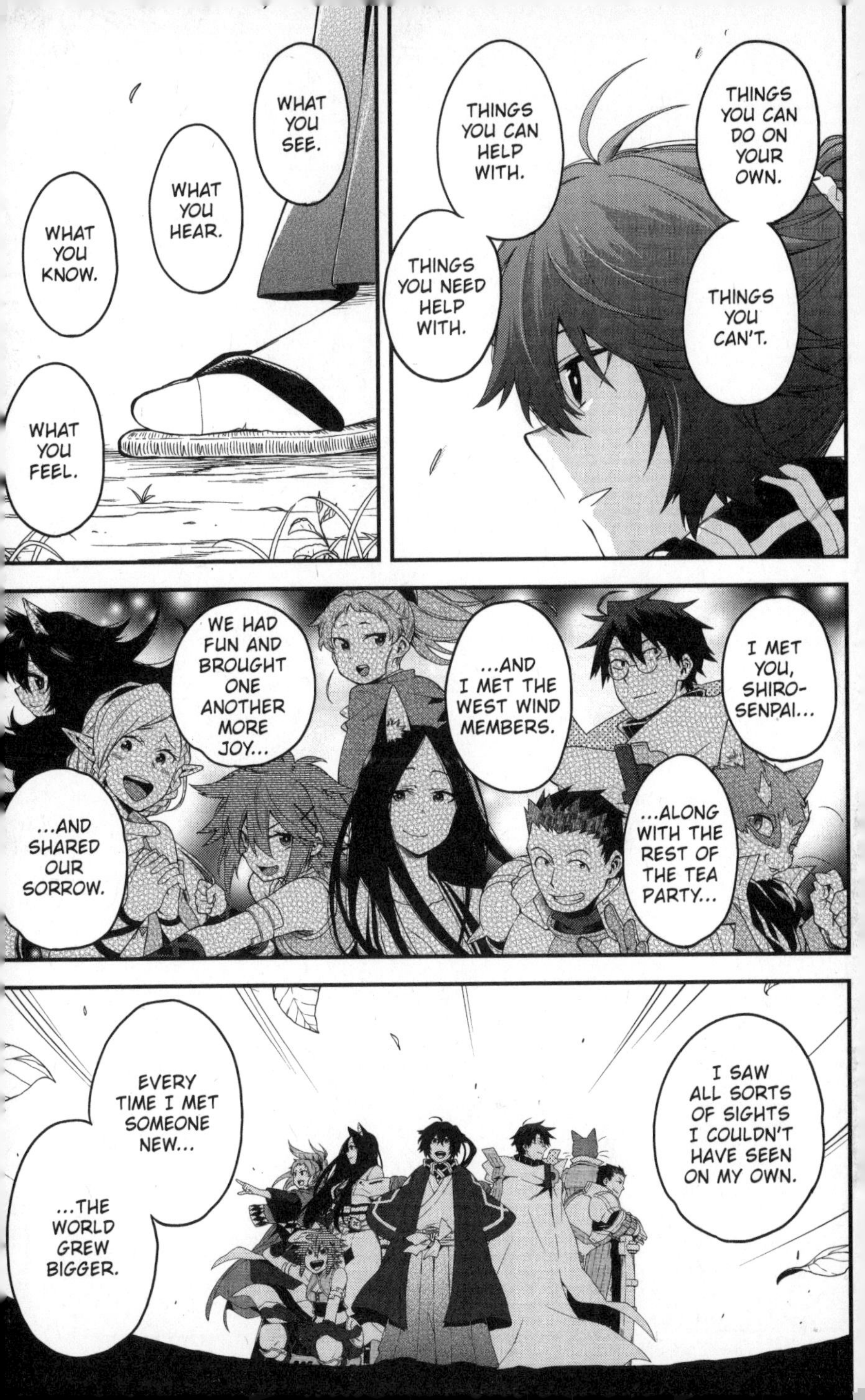
THINGS YOU CAN DO ON YOUR OWN.
THINGS YOU CAN'T.
THINGS YOU CAN HELP WITH.
THINGS YOU NEED HELP WITH.
WHAT YOU SEE.
WHAT YOU HEAR.
WHAT YOU KNOW.
WHAT YOU FEEL.
I MET YOU, SHIRO-SENPAI...
...ALONG WITH THE REST OF THE TEA PARTY...
...AND I MET THE WEST WIND MEMBERS.
WE HAD FUN AND BROUGHT ONE ANOTHER MORE JOY...
...AND SHARED OUR SORROW.
I SAW ALL SORTS OF SIGHTS I COULDN'T HAVE SEEN ON MY OWN.
EVERY TIME I MET SOMEONE NEW...
...THE WORLD GREW BIGGER.

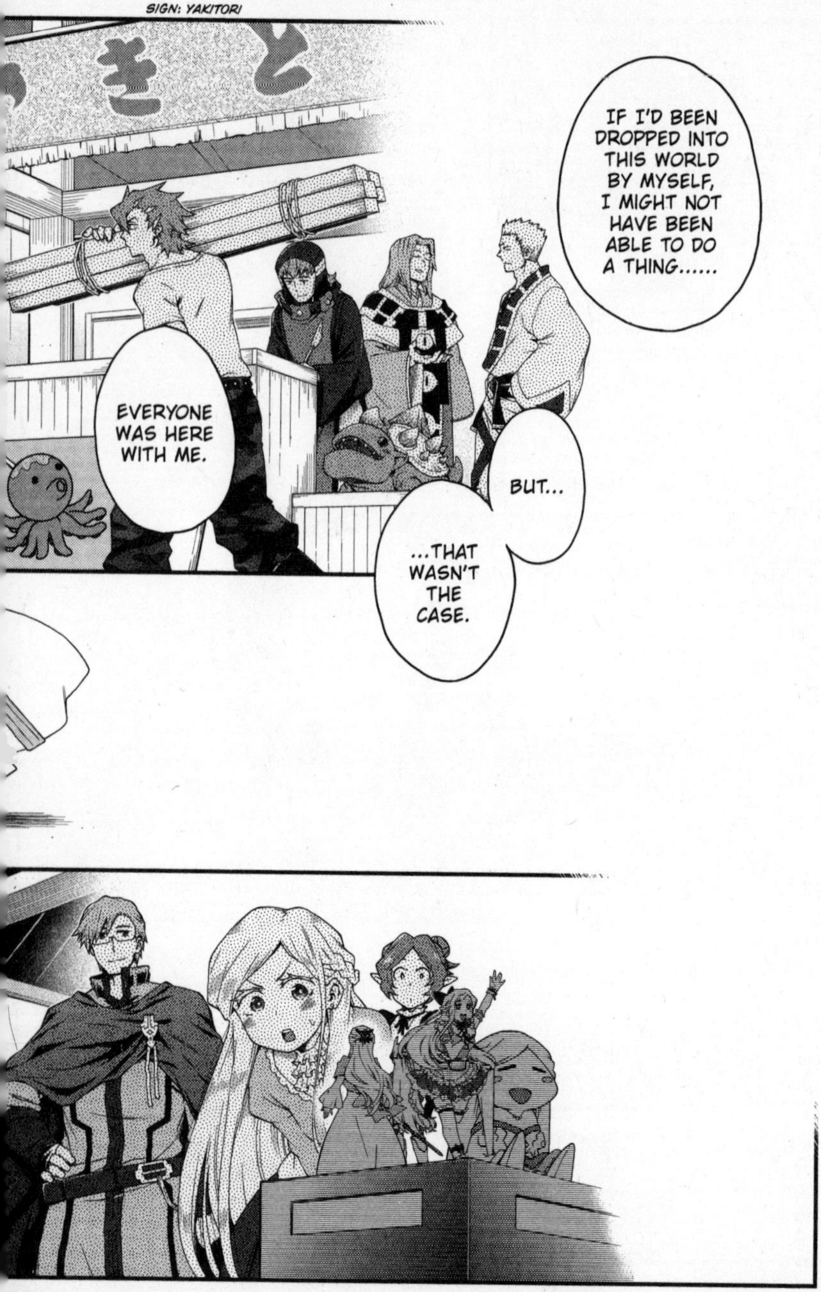
SIGN: YAKITORI
IF I'D BEEN DROPPED INTO THIS WORLD BY MYSELF, I MIGHT NOT HAVE BEEN ABLE TO DO A THING......
BUT...
...THAT WASN'T THE CASE.
EVERYONE WAS HERE WITH ME.

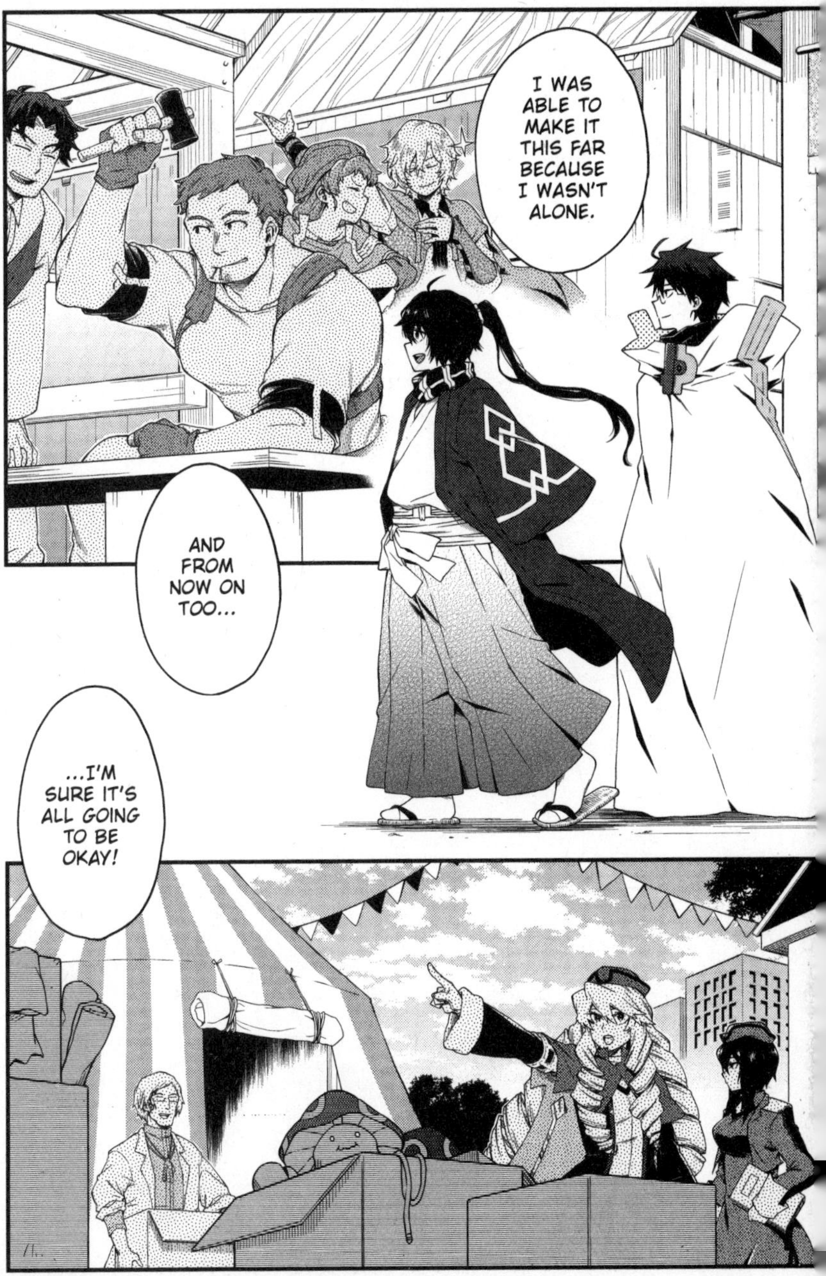
I WAS ABLE TO MAKE IT THIS FAR BECAUSE I WASN'T ALONE.
AND FROM NOW ON TOO...
...I'M SURE IT'S ALL GOING TO BE OKAY!

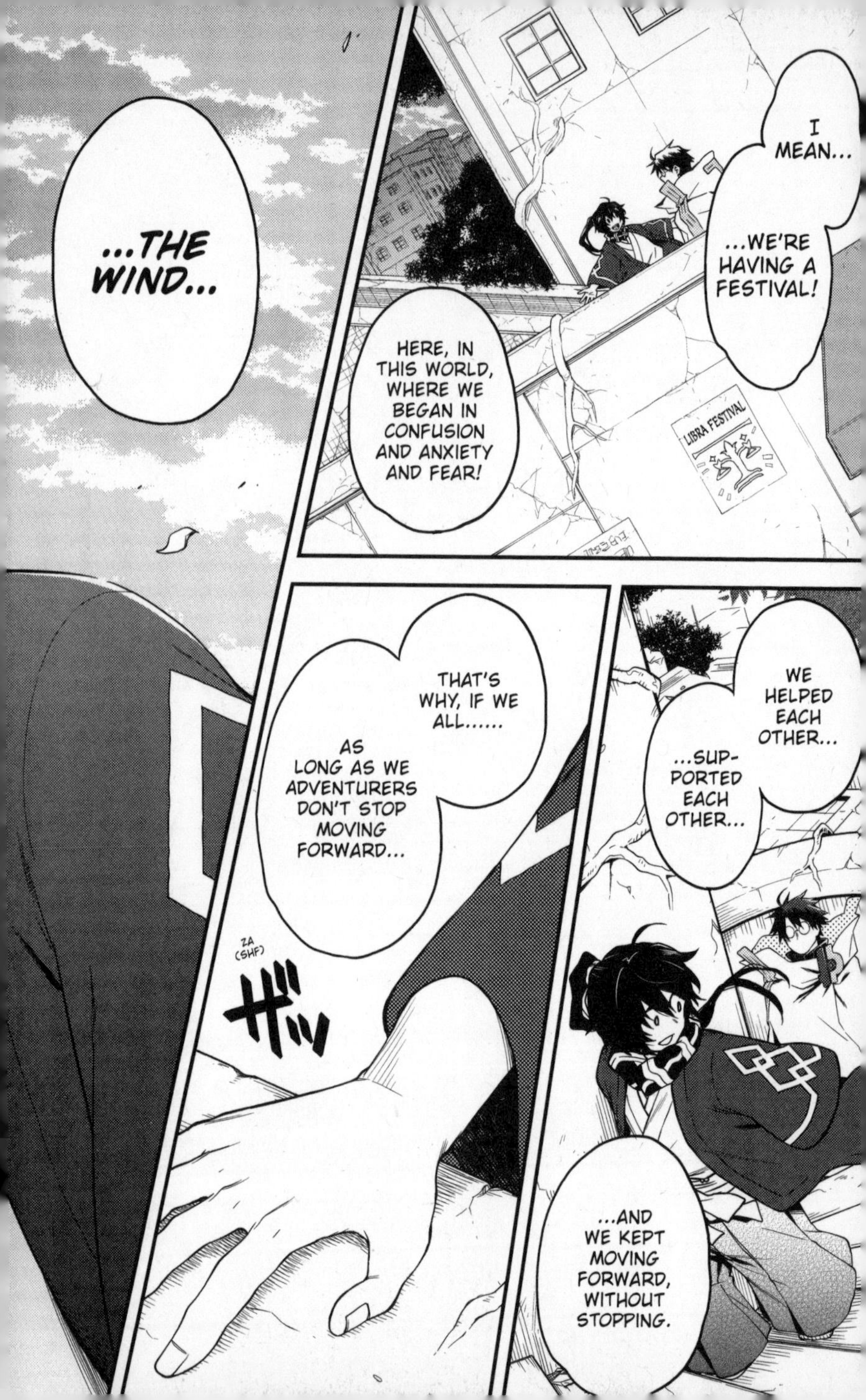
I MEAN...
...WE'RE HAVING A FESTIVAL!
HERE, IN THIS WORLD, WHERE WE BEGAN IN CONFUSION AND ANXIETY AND FEAR!
LIBRA FESTIVAL
WE HELPED EACH OTHER...
...SUP-PORTED EACH OTHER...
...AND WE KEPT MOVING FORWARD, WITHOUT STOPPING.
THAT'S WHY, IF WE ALL......
AS LONG AS WE ADVENTURERS DON'T STOP MOVING FORWARD...
ZA (SHF)
ザッ
...THE WIND...

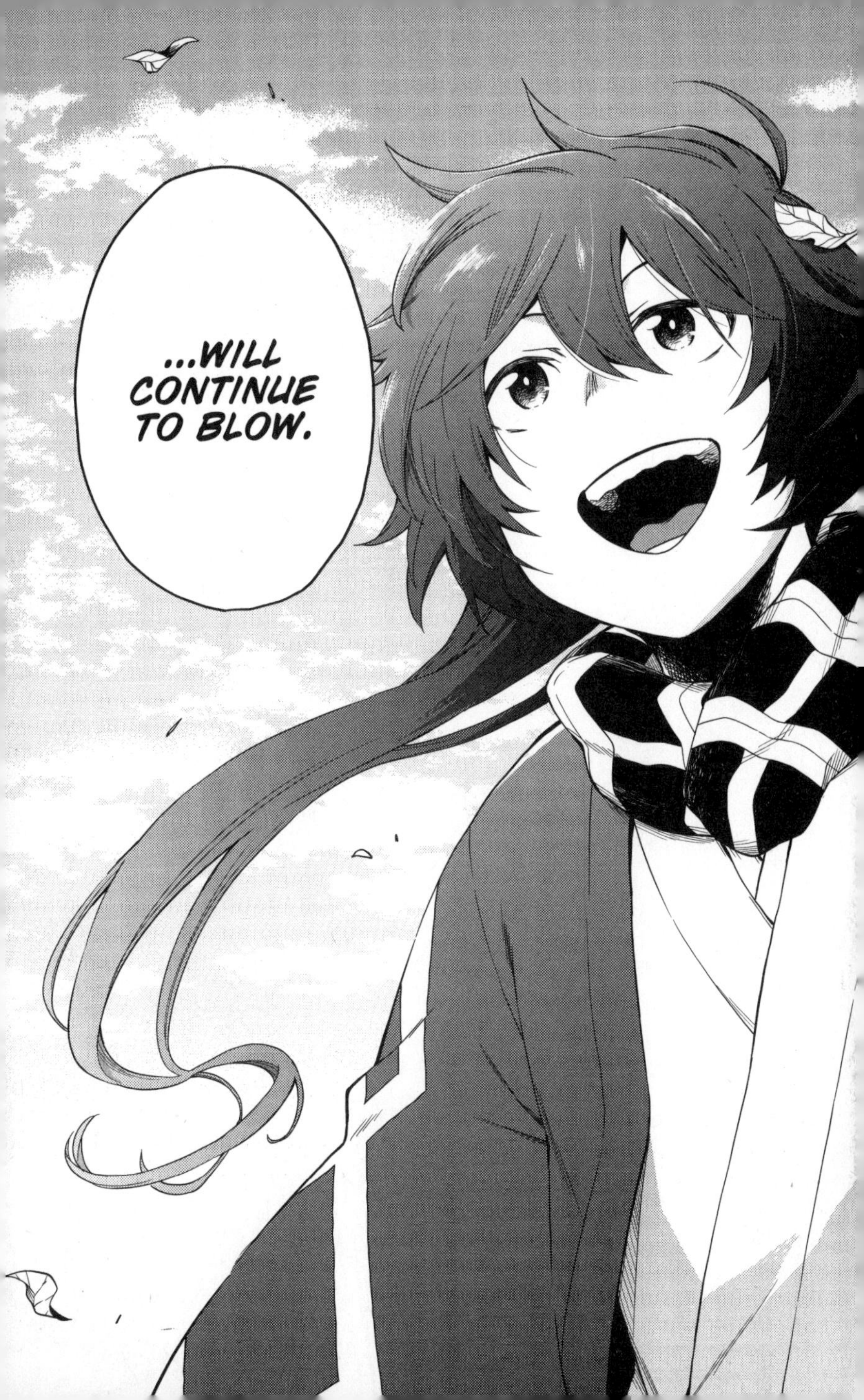
...WILL CONTINUE TO BLOW.

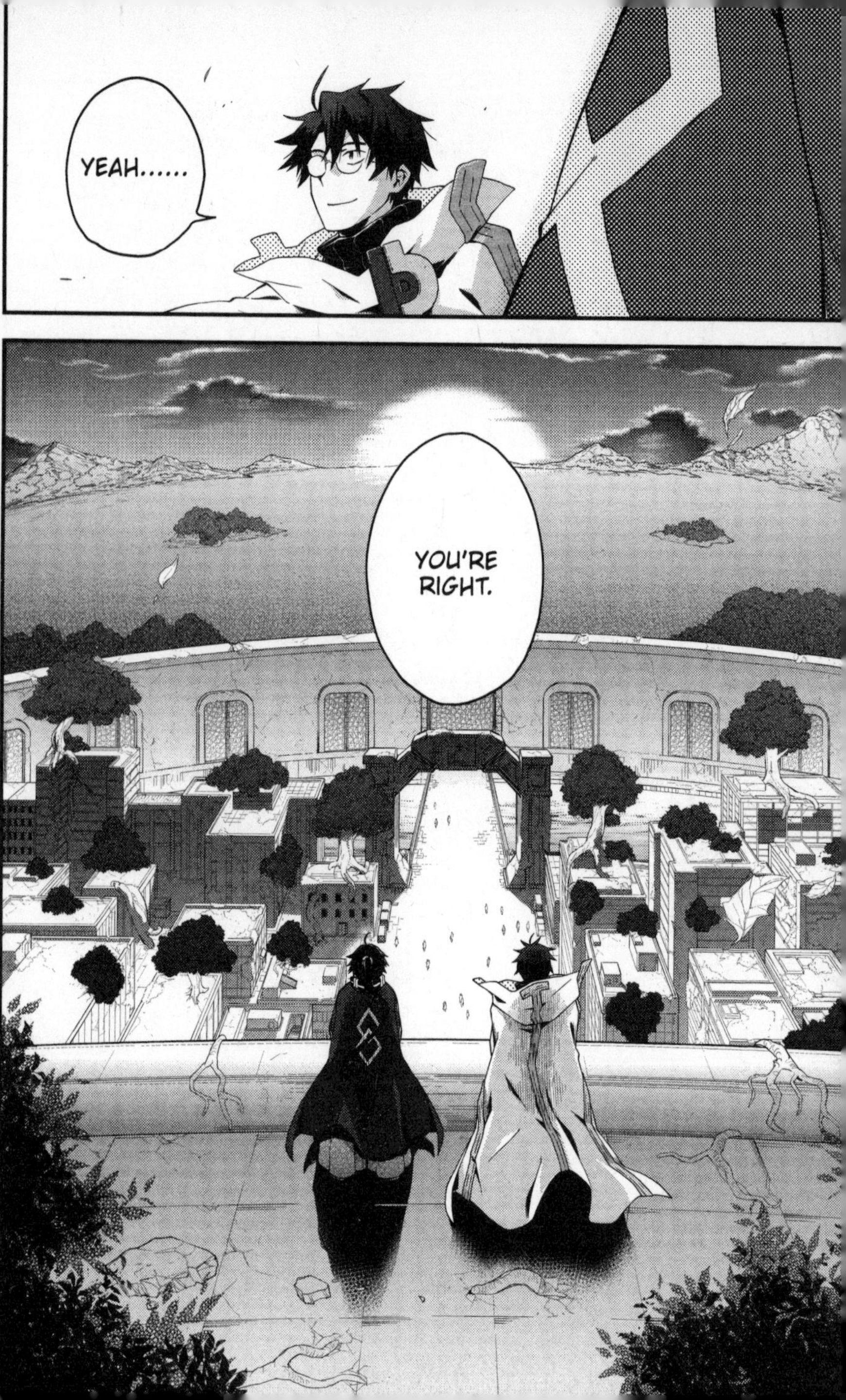
YEAH......
YOU'RE RIGHT.

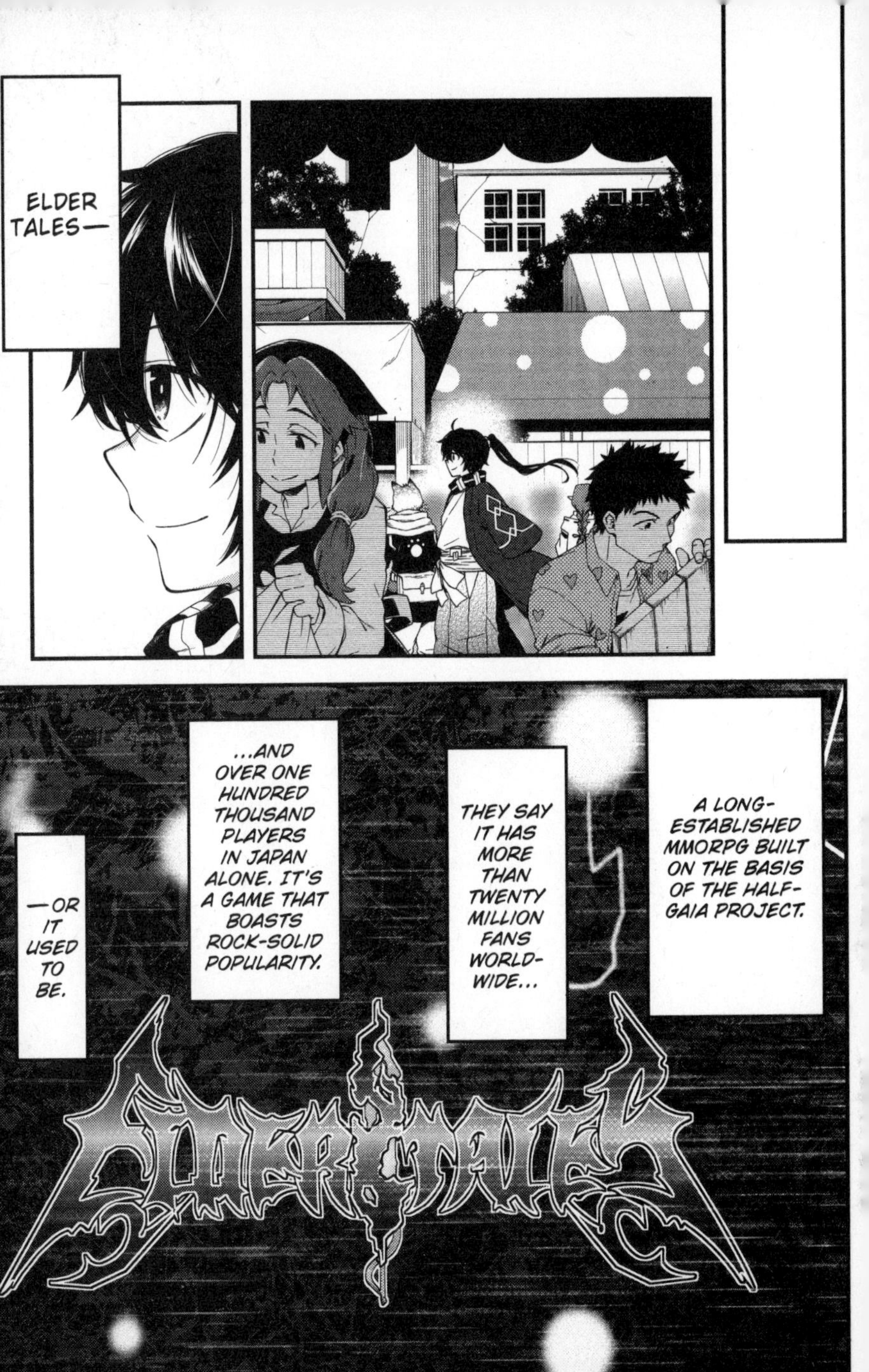
ELDER TALES—
A LONG-ESTABLISHED MMORPG BUILT ON THE BASIS OF THE HALF-GAIA PROJECT.
THEY SAY IT HAS MORE THAN TWENTY MILLION FANS WORLD-WIDE...
...AND OVER ONE HUNDRED THOUSAND PLAYERS IN JAPAN ALONE. IT'S A GAME THAT BOASTS ROCK-SOLID POPULARITY.
—OR IT USED TO BE.

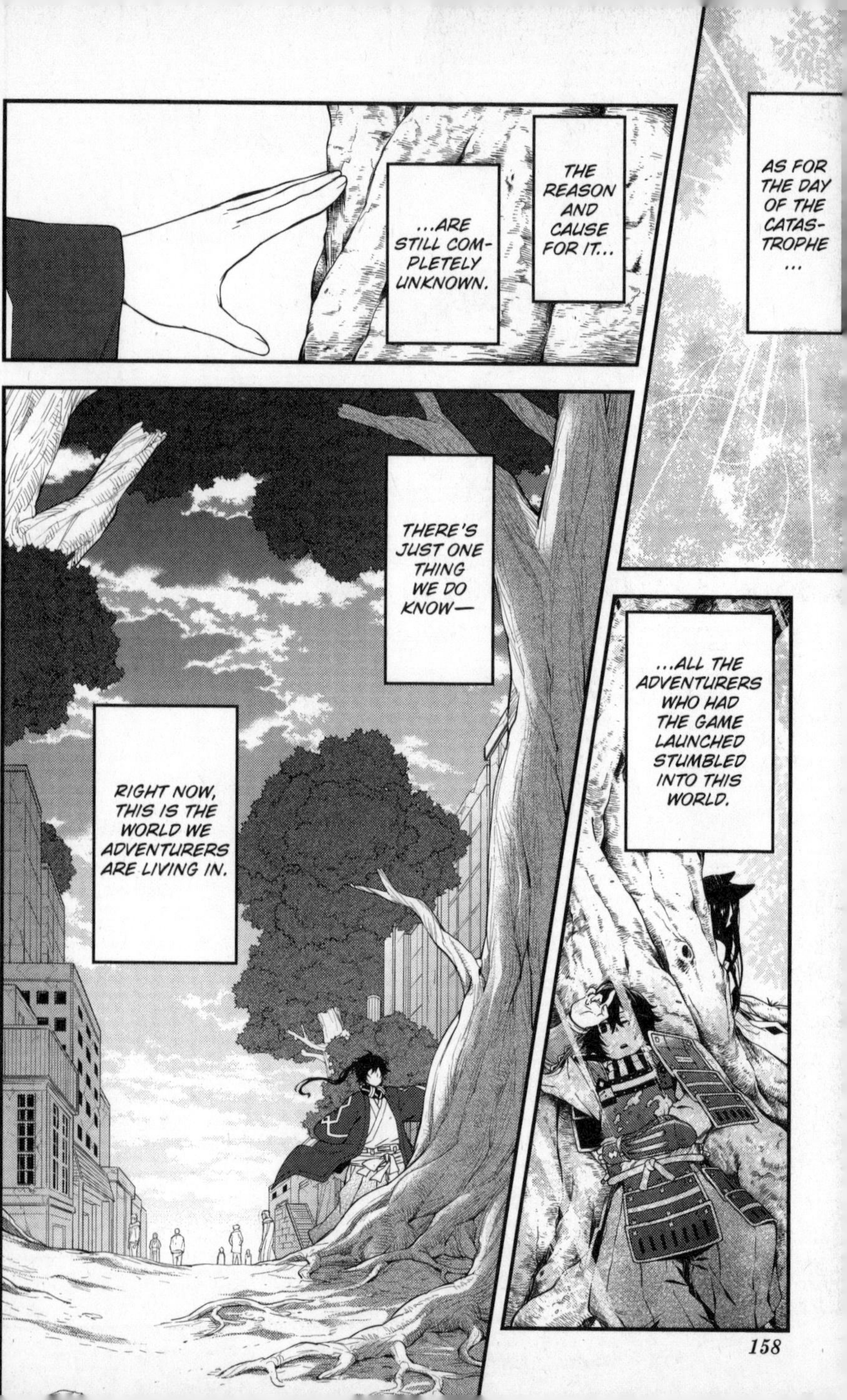
AS FOR THE DAY OF THE CATAS-TROPHE ...
...ALL THE ADVENTURERS WHO HAD THE GAME LAUNCHED STUMBLED INTO THIS WORLD.
THE REASON AND CAUSE FOR IT...
...ARE STILL COM-PLETELY UNKNOWN.
THERE'S JUST ONE THING WE DO KNOW—
RIGHT NOW, THIS IS THE WORLD WE ADVENTURERS ARE LIVING IN.

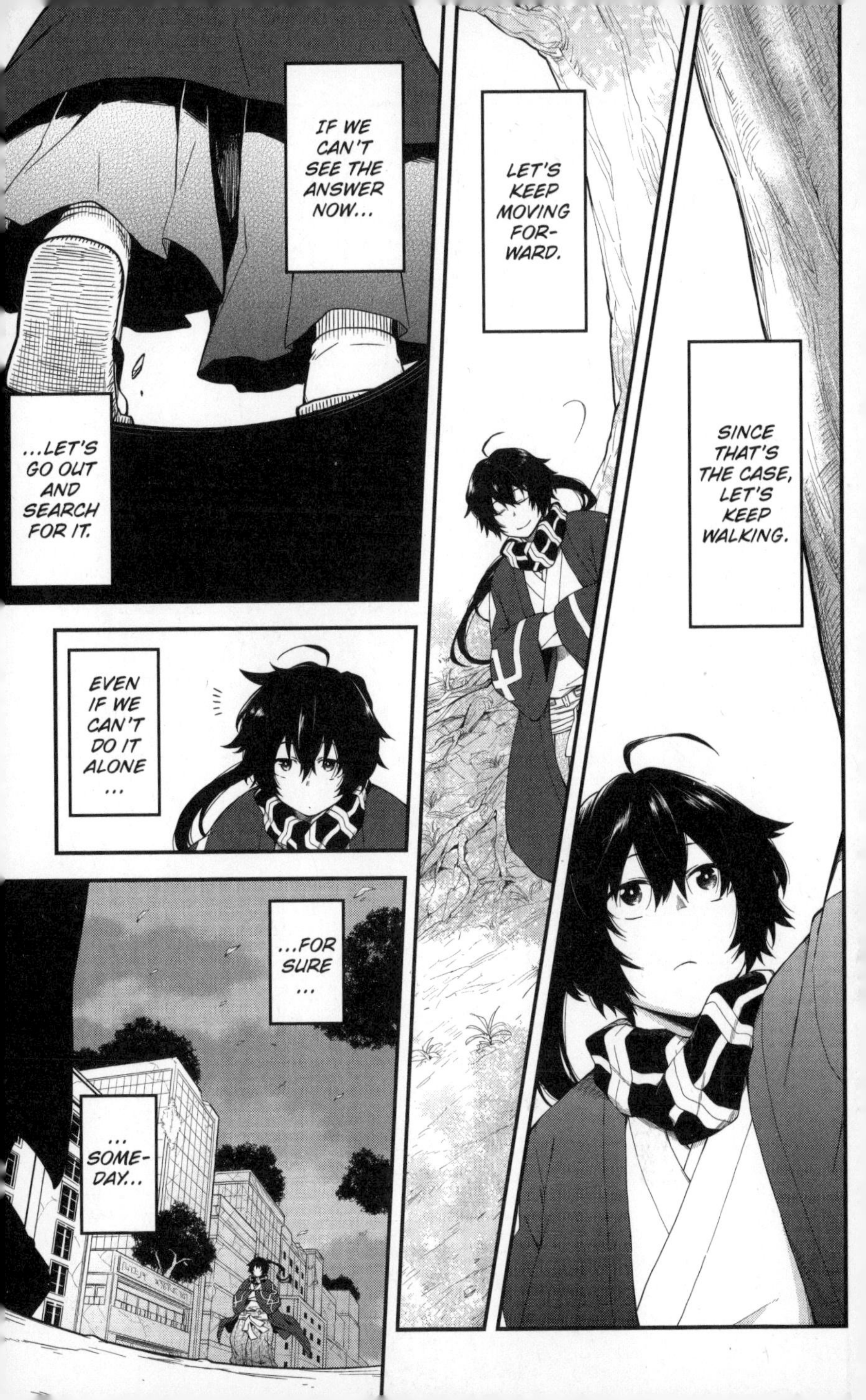
SINCE THAT'S THE CASE, LET'S KEEP WALKING.
LET'S KEEP MOVING FOR-WARD.
IF WE CAN'T SEE THE ANSWER NOW...
...LET'S GO OUT AND SEARCH FOR IT.
EVEN IF WE CAN'T DO IT ALONE...
...FOR SURE...
...SOME-DAY...

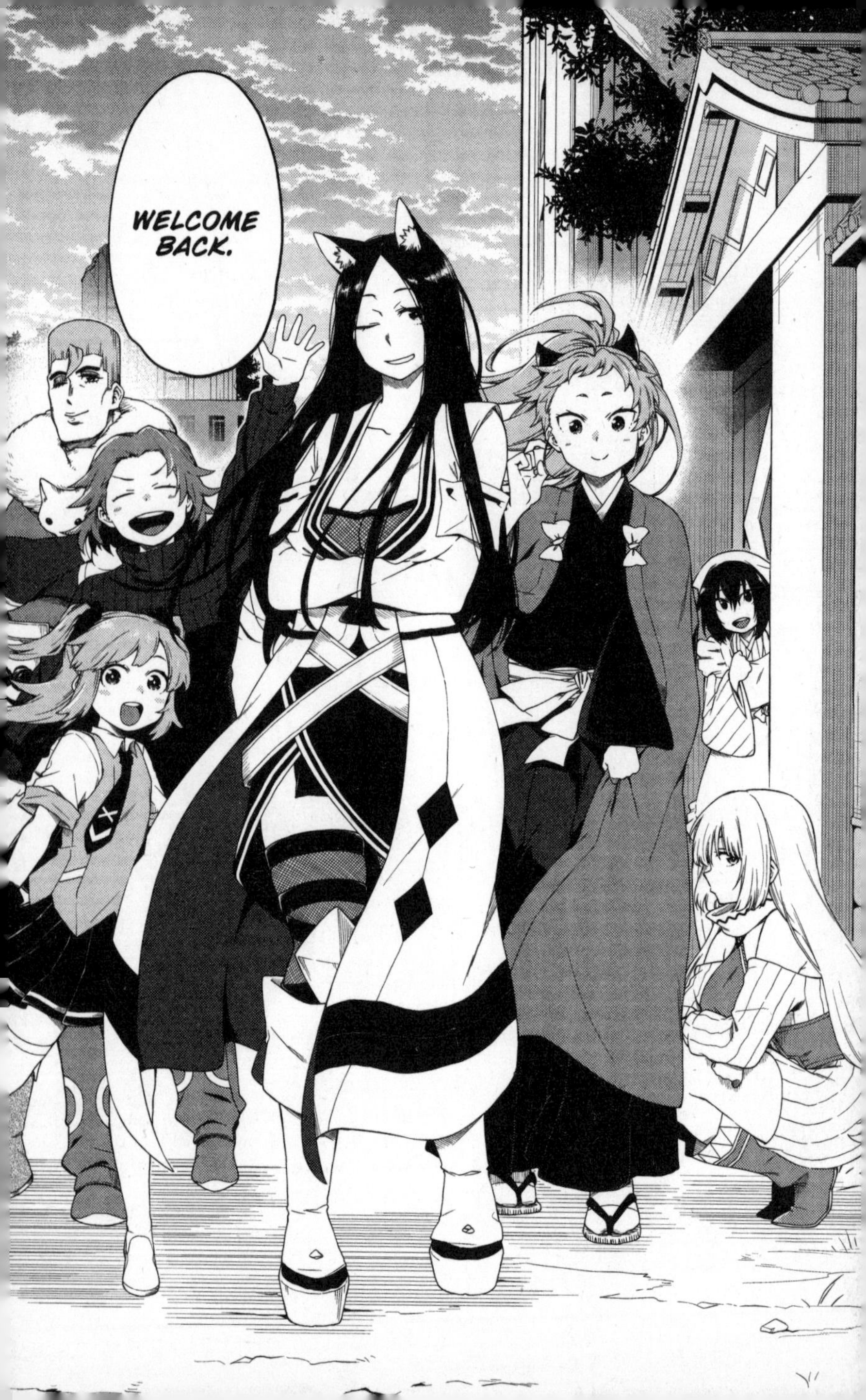
WELCOME BACK.

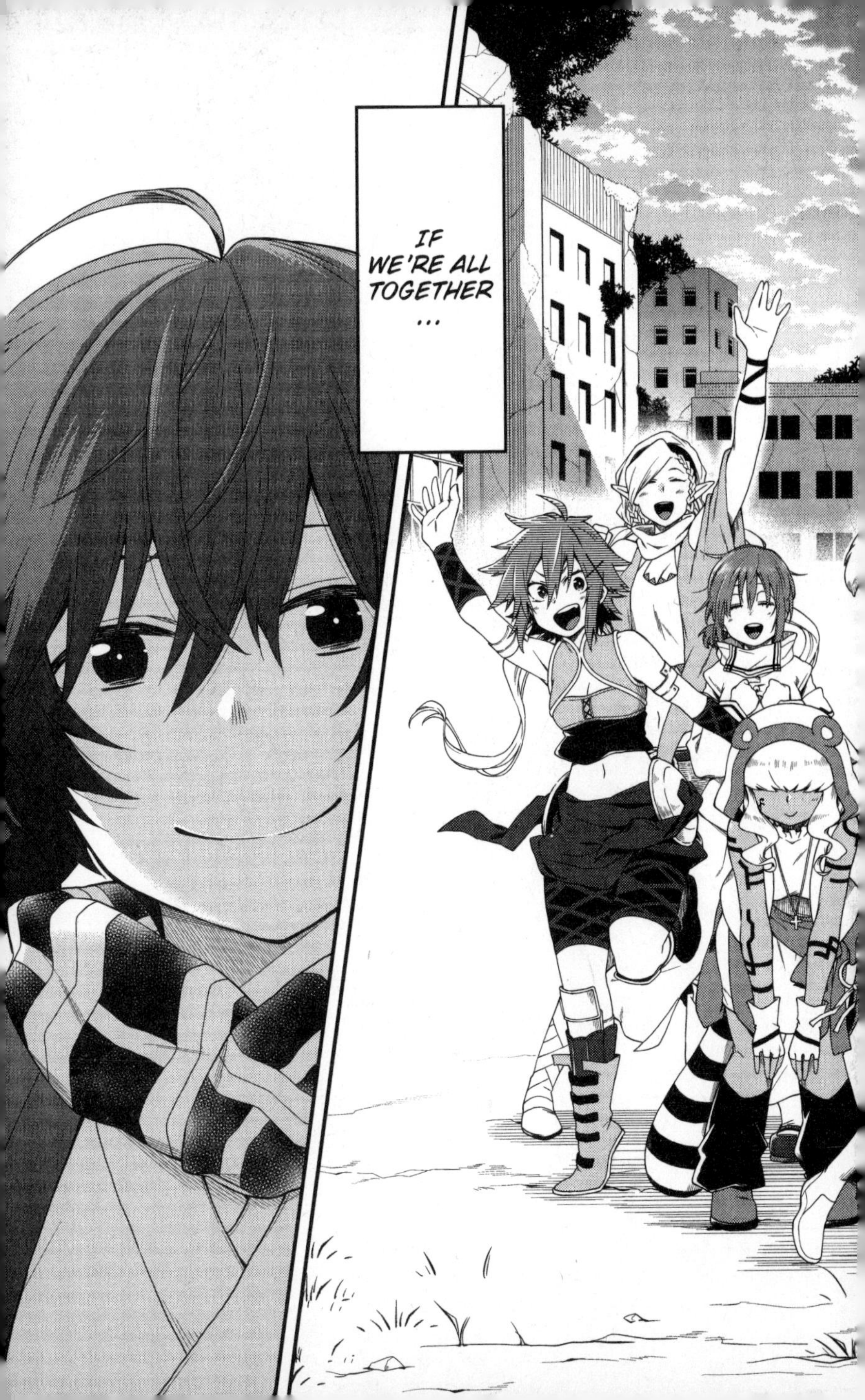
IF WE'RE ALL TOGETHER ...

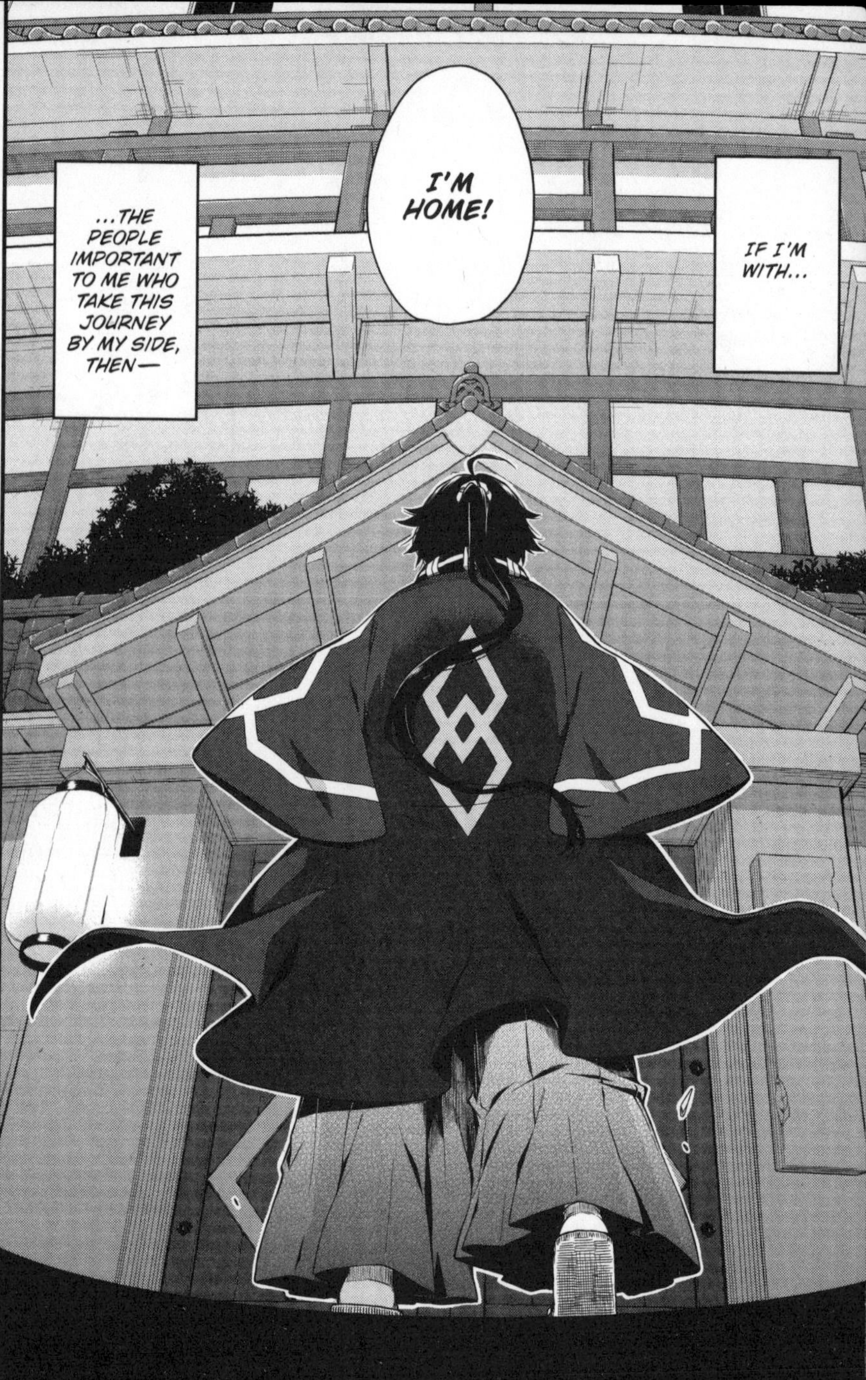
IF I'M WITH...
...THE PEOPLE IMPORTANT TO ME WHO TAKE THIS JOURNEY BY MY SIDE, THEN—
I'M HOME!

Log Horizon: The West Wind Brigade——The End

SPECIAL THANKS:
MAMARE TOUNO-SAMA
KAZUHIRO HARA-SAMA
SHOJI MASUDA-SAMA
SOUCHUU-SAMA

ATSUSHI UCHIYAMA-SAMA
YUUSUKE OZAKI-SAMA

ASSISTANTS:
SAASHI-SAN
ITSUKA-SAN

TO EVERYONE WHO WAS
INVOLVED IN PRODUCTION,
AND TO ALL THE READERS:

THANK YOU
VERY MUCH!!

LOG HORIZON:
THE WEST WIND
BRIGADE

こゆき
KOYUKI

LOG HORIZON
THE WEST WIND BRIGADE ⓫

ART: KOYUKI
ORIGINAL STORY: MAMARE TOUNO
CHARACTER DESIGN: KAZUHIRO HARA

Translation: Taylor Engel
Lettering: Brndn Blakeslee

LOG HORIZON NISHIKAZE NO RYODAN volume 11
© KOYUKI 2018
© TOUNO MAMARE, KAZUHIRO HARA 2018
First published in Japan in 2018 by KADOKAWA CORPORATION, Tokyo.
English translation rights arranged with KADOKAWA CORPORATION, Tokyo, through Tuttle-Mori Agency, Inc., Tokyo.

English translation © 2019 by Yen Press, LLC

Yen Press
1290 Avenue of the Americas
New York, NY 10104

Visit us at yenpress.com
facebook.com/yenpress
twitter.com/yenpress
yenpress.tumblr.com
instagram.com/yenpress

First Yen Press Edition: March 2019

Yen Press is an imprint of Yen Press, LLC.
The Yen Press name and logo are trademarks of Yen Press, LLC.

The publisher is not responsible for websites (or their content) that are not owned by the publisher.

Library of Congress Control Number: 2015952586

ISBNs: 978-1-9753-8401-2 (paperback)
        978-1-9753-8408-1 (ebook)

10 9 8 7 6 5 4 3 2 1

WOR

Printed in the United States of America